· THE ·
TIME
PIRATE

ALSO BY TED BELL

Nick of Time: An Adventure Through Time

Tsar

Spy

Pirate

Assassin

Hawke

• THE •
TIME
PIRATE

A NICK McIVER
TIME ADVENTURE

Ted Bell

ST. MARTIN'S GRIFFIN
NEW YORK

This one is for Byrdie, Brownie, and Benji, three kids who exemplify all that's best about the heroic children who inhabit these pages.

THE TIME PIRATE. Copyright © 2010 by Ted Bell. All rights reserved. Printed in March 2010 in the United States of America by R. R. Donnelly & Sons Company, Harrisonburg, Virginia. For information, address St. Martin's Press, 175 Fifth Avenue, New York, N.Y. 10010.

www.stmartins.com

Illustrations by Russ Kramer

Library of Congress Cataloging-in-Publication Data

Bell, Ted.
   The time pirate : a Nick McIver time adventure / Ted Bell.–1st ed.
      p. cm.
   ISBN 978-0-312-57810-7
  1. Boys–Channel Islands–Fiction.   2. World War, 1939–1945–Channel Islands–Fiction. 3. Pirates–Fiction.   4. Kidnapping–Fiction.
5. Rescues–Fiction. 6. Time travel–Fiction. 7. Jamaica–Fiction.
8. Caribbean Area–Fiction. I. Title.
   PS3602.E6455T56 2010
   813'.6–dc22

                                2009040015

First Edition: April 2010

10 9 8 7 6 5 4 3 2 1

TABLE OF CONTENTS

Prologue: ANCIENT HISTORY I

BOOK ONE: INVASION

1. PENNYWHISTLE PARK 17
2. THE WHIRL-O-DROME 24
3. SECRETS OF THE BLACK FOREST 29
4. THE CAMEL IN THE BARN 37
5. THE SPY IN THE SKY 46
6. CONTACT! 52
7. THE LONGEST SERMON EVER 61
8. CAPTAIN McIVER'S AEROPLANE 67
9. STORM CLOUDS OVER PORT ROYAL 78
10. THE BARONESS AND THE BOMBERS 91
11. PRACTICE, PRACTICE, PRACTICE 98
12. HOME ON A WING AND A PRAYER 109
13. DEATH FROM ABOVE 117
14. "WE'LL FIGHT TO THE END, WON'T WE, GUNNER?". 126
15. TREES WITH WHEELS! 132
16. ONE GOOD HAND AND ONE GOLD HOOK 141
17. BLOOD, TOIL, TEARS, AND SWEAT 147
18. CODE NAME: BLITZ 153
19. NICK EVENS THE SCORE 161
20. UP WAS AIR, DOWN WAS DEATH 174
21. THE DREADFUL KIDNAPPING OF KATE 185
22. SANCTUARY AT FORDWYCH MANOR 195
23. THE NARROWEST ESCAPE 203
24. THE KOMMANDANT AND THE SPY 211
25. 18 DEGREES NORTH, 76 DEGREES WEST 220

· TABLE OF CONTENTS ·

26. LORD HAWKE'S TROJAN HORSE 228

27. THE BRETHREN OF BLOOD 236

28. "GODSPEED, NICK," HAWKE SAID 244

29. BLOODTHIRSTY CUTTHROATS GIVE CHASE 249

30. "WELCOME TO THE BLACK CROW, GENTS" 257

31 "OFF WITH THEIR HEADS!" 265

32. NICK McIVER, TRAITOR? 276

33. "IF THEY SEE YOU, THEY'LL SHOOT YOU!" 287

BOOK TWO: INDEPENDENCE

34. A HEAVY HEART EN ROUTE TO MOUNT VERNON 297

35. THE INDIAN IN THE FOG 303

36. MARTHA WASHINGTON'S NEW BOARDER 309

37. "DON'T EVER BETRAY MY TRUST, NICHOLAS!" 317

38. "THE GENERAL IS HOME AT LAST!" 324

39. AN UNEASY MEETING WITH WASHINGTON AND LAFAYETTE 332

40. THE MARQUIS AND THE MIDNIGHT RENDEZVOUS 348

41. ALL ABOARD THE FLAGSHIP *VILLE DE PARIS* 359

42. "HOIST THE JOLLY ROGER!" 368

43. THE GREATEST PIRATE ARMADA EVER 376

44. "YOU'RE IN A PICKLE, CAPTAIN BLOOD!" 384

45. TAKING THE FIGHT TO THE ENEMY 392

46. SNAKE EYE STEPS FROM THE SHADOWS 398

47. AS BOMBS BURST OVERHEAD 408

48. ON THE LONG ROAD TO YORKTOWN 412

49. WHISTLING BRITISH CANNONBALLS 424

50. *THIS IS A HERO*, NICK THOUGHT 431

51. CORNWALLIS HAS SEEN ENOUGH 438

52. "THIS WAS THEIR FINEST HOUR!" 444

Epilogue: HOME AT LAST! 453

Illustrations by Russ Kramer

Dictators ride to and fro upon tigers, which they dare not dismount. And the tigers are getting hungry.

–WINSTON CHURCHILL

PROLOGUE
ANCIENT HISTORY

· Greybeard Island, 1880 ·

I

The godforsaken isle took its name from the thick pea-soupy fogs that persistently haunted the place. It was aptly named Greybeard Island.

Dangerous terrain and weather fueled my misery trekking across the island's rocky headland. Tired and bone cold, serious doubts about this adventure crept round the edges of the noggin: one truly nasty fall and my frozen carcass wouldn't be found till next morning.

The low-hanging sun, once a comfort, was now merely a hazy yellow wafer sliding toward the sea.

Still, I was determined to reach the old Greybeard Inn before nightfall. I am by trade a naval historian, and I'd learned that Mr. Hornby, the inn's proprietor, had a bewitching tale to tell.

***

Martyn Hornby was a rare bird, one of a small number of Royal Navy veterans of the Napoleonic Wars remaining alive, the sole living survivor of the crew of the famous H.M.S. *Merlin*, under the command of Captain Nicholas McIver.

McIver's small 48-gun English man-o'-war fought a courageous and pivotal naval battle against a massive French 74-gun frigate back in 1805. When I say *pivotal*, I do not speak lightly. I mean I believed that *Merlin*'s victory had changed the course of history.

And no other historian, to my knowledge, had ever heard tell of it!

Seventy-five years ago now, in the summer of '05, a huge French frigate, *Mystère*, was lurking off this very coast. She sailed under the infamous Captain William Blood, an Englishman and a traitor of the first order. Old Bill was a rogue who had betrayed our greatest hero, Admiral Lord Nelson, for a very large sum of capital offered by the French. Captain Blood's formidable services were now at the disposal of Napoleon and his Imperial French Navy. And it was only the purest of luck that put that villain at last in British gun sights.

Distracted by such thoughts, I slipped then, and nearly lost my footing on a sharply angled escarpment, at the bottom lip of which I spied a cliff, one that dropped some four hundred feet to the sea! Well, I clung to a vertical outcropping of glistening rock and paused trembling on the edge of the precipice. Once my heart slowed to a reasonable hammering, I pressed on.

Historians, I was rapidly learning, need an adventurous streak. Tracking down far-flung witnesses to history is neither for the faint of heart nor weak of limb. Far better were I one of those stout-hearted, broad-shouldered chappies one reads about in penny novels. The lads off felling trees in the trackless Yukon, scaling Alps, or shouting "Sail hot" from atop a wildly pitching masthead. Such were my musings when a sudden thunderclap boomed behind me and lightning strikes danced on the far horizon, revealing a fork in the road. I chose the more treacherous seaward route, for I had no choice.

There was precious little width to be had on this path, and in some spots it was little more than a shaley rock-cut ledge about ten inches or a foot wide. Far below, I heard the crash of waves on jagged rocks. Dicey, to put it mildly.

The sheer face of the vertical rock wall to my right seemed to bulge, animated, as if it wished to push my body out into space. A trick of mind? I inched along, trying to ignore the rising bile of panic and the agitated sea waiting to embrace me. Not once but thrice, I considered turning back. Only to realize I had passed the point of no return.

At last I came to a spot where could be seen, on a jutting finger of rock, a warm glow of yellow lights in the rainy gloom. The beckoning two-story house on that stony prom-ontory was aglow with promised warmth and food. My steps quickened.

I pushed inside the inn's heavy wooden door and found the old Jack Tar himself, clay-piped and pig-tailed, sitting in si-lence by the fire. I pulled up a chair and introduced myself. Had I the good fortune of speaking to Mr. Martyn Hornby? I inquired with a smile.

"Aye, I'm Hornby," he said, removing his pipe. After a long silence in which clouds of geniality seemed to float above the man's head, he spoke.

"Weather slowed you up, I reckon," he stated, and I could feel his inspection of my person.

He himself was a sturdy, handsome figure who looked to be in his late eighties. He wore faded breeches and a ragged woolen fisherman's sweater, much mended. He had a full head of snow-white hair, and his fine, leathered features were worn by years of wind and water. But, in the firelight, his twinkling blue eyes still held a sparkling clarity of youth, and I was glad of my perseverance on that final narrow ledge.

"Ye've come a long way, Mr. Tolliver."

"Indeed, sir, I have." I nodded. "As a student of history, I've a keen interest in your encounter with the French off this island, Mr. Hornby. I'd appreciate your recollections on that subject, if you'd be so kind."

"Aye," Hornby said, and then he fell silent. "I'm the last one . . . so I suppose I should tell it, if it's to be told at all. If my memory's up to it, of course." He gave a hearty shout for his barman in the next room, ordering food and ale.

The drinks soon arrived, along with a steaming meat pie for me, and we both sipped, staring into the merry blaze, each alone with his thoughts. Mine, at the moment, were solely of my poor tingling feet, more painful in the thawing than the freezing.

Suddenly, without warning, the man began to speak, eyeing me in a curious manner. "I was one of Captain McIver's powder monkeys, y'see, back in those glorious days, and–"

"Powder monkeys?" I interrupted, unfamiliar with the term.

"Boys who would ferry black powder from the holds below up to the gun crews when things got spicy. Listen. I'll tell you how it all started, Mr. Tolliver, if you want to start there at the beginning . . ."

I nodded, smiling encouragement, discreetly whipping my pen and a well-worn leather notebook from my pocket.

"We had a fair wind home to Portsmouth en route from our station in the West Indies where we'd recently captured a Portugee," Martyn Hornby began. "A spy."

"A spy."

"Aye, one much encouraged to speak his mind to avoid the

tar-pot and cat-o'-nine-tails during the crossing. We eventually learned from his lips of a wicked plot, hatched in the evil brain of Billy Blood, the turncoat captain of the French frigate."

"That would be Captain William Blood?"

"Few alive today have heard the name, sir. But Old Bill was a holy terror in his day. Gave Lord Nelson fits at every turning, he did. His plot was this: our natural enemy, the King of Spain, and the scurrilous French meant to join their naval forces and surprise Nelson en route to Trafalgar, and send the outnumbered British fleet to the bottom. It would have worked, too, had it not been for the heroism of our captain. And a few ship's passengers."

"Passengers?"

"Hawke was his name, Lord Hawke. A peer of the realm, but an adventurous sort, being descended directly from the pirate Blackhawke. Lord Hawke and a young lad named Nick McIver."

"Lord Hawke, you say?" I was scribbling furiously now.

"Long dead, now."

"And the McIver boy. Related to the captain, was he?"

"Mere coincidence they shared the exact same name, I think, though some disagreed with me."

"How did this Lord Hawke and the boy come to be aboard the *Merlin*, sir?"

"Hawke's daughter, Annabel, and his young son, Alexander, had been kidnapped and held for ransom by the French. It was Bill's way to kidnap children of the aristocracy and extort great sums for their release. Hawke had learned Blood had his children aboard the frigate *Mystère*, and Hawke was of a mind to rescue them."

"And the McIver boy?"

"There was some mystery surrounding the boy and His

Lordship's sudden presence onboard. Indeed, there were rumors as to how they appeared onboard."

"Rumors?"

"Shipboard rumors. Stuff and nonsense, if you ask me. Something about some kind of ancient time machine the McIver boy was said to possess. How he come to be aboard, in fact."

"Time machine, you say?" My confidence in the old salt's mental state was beginning to waver.

"The Tempus Machina, it was called. Supposedly invented by Leonardo da Vinci himself. Allowed a bloke to travel back and forth in time just easy as you please. A brilliant golden orb, word had it, that glowed with an otherworldly light. Contained a mechanism filled with jewels and such."

"Foolishness. Tommyrot."

"I agree most heartily. Absolute rubbish. But many of the crew swore Hawke and the boy had appeared out of thin air. Those that claimed to have witnessed it said they seemed to shimmer into place like fiery ghosts before becoming humanlike."

"So, you were actually seeking out this frigate, *Mystère*, for more than military reasons? A kidnap rescue as well?"

Hornby nodded. "We'd extracted from that blasted Portugee where Blood's ship might lie. And more. We knew he had geographical details of his scheme etched on a golden spyglass, and–"

"I'm sorry–etched on a spyglass you say?"

"Aye. And not just any glass, mind you, but one Bill stole from Admiral Lord Nelson himself the night of the mutiny! According to that damnable Portugee, the location of the intended naval ambush was so secret that Bill had scratched the longitude and latitudinal coordinates right into the metal barrel of his glass. Now, since Bonaparte himself had a hand in the planning of the thing, it was likely a cunning trap. We had to get our hands on that glass before Nelson and the whole British fleet sailed from Portsmouth ... and, by God, we did!"

"But how?"

He laughed heartily. "Therein lies the tale, don't it, Mr. Tolliver?"

2

I took a quick sip of my drink and said, "This Lord Hawke—it was he who saved the day?"

"Beg pardon, sir, but it was the boy Nick who carried the day. A scrappy one, this young Nick McIver, only one year older than myself at that time," the old fellow said, tilting his chair suddenly backward at a precipitous angle against the wall. "Nick and me became fast friends soon enough, our ages being so similar. I was ten; he was twelve, I believe, when he got his first taste of battle."

"When we laid alongside that enemy frigate after a vicious exchange of rippling broadsides, young Nick and myself secretly boarded the *Mystère* and found ourselves in the thick of things, grapeshot and all. Never saw the like of such bloody struggle in all my years before the mast."

Somewhere in the inn, a ship's bell struck. The wee hours drew nigh. A fresh blow had rushed up to haunt the eaves, and the fire had died down somewhat, lending a discernible chill to the room.

"Please continue, Mr. Hornby," I said, getting to my feet and throwing another log or two onto the embers.

"Well, it was strangely quiet when Nick McIver and me emerged from the aft companionway. The cannons on both vessels had ceased their thunder and for'ard we could see a press of sailors from both vessels gathered on her quarter-deck, with an occasional cheer in French or English rising from their midst. We heard, too, the vicious sound of two cutlasses clanging against each other. A brutal swordfight from the sound of it.

"Anyway, I looked aloft and saw the battle-torn French flag was still flapping at the top of the enemy mizzen, so I knew Old Bill had not surrendered. This despite the volume of lead and grapeshot we'd poured into him. Nick and I each took a cutlass off dead sailors, and we crept for'ard and climbed atop the pilothouse so as to look down on the quarter-deck unobserved. We inched ourselves along on our elbows until we could just peek down and see the action not ten feet below. The crews of both vessels were pressing aft, trying to get a glimpse of the fight taking place at the helm and—"

"The main fighting had stopped?"

"Aye. A great sea battle had come down to a two-man war. Captain William Blood and Lord Hawke were locked in a death struggle. What a sight! Old Bill was a spectacle, wearing what must have been magnificent finery, white silk breeches and a great flaring white satin captain's coat, but now all this flummery was torn and soiled with black powder and red blood. He had Nelson's spyglass, all right, jammed inside his wide belt. Hawke had a terrible gash down his right cheek, and his shirtfront was soaked with his own blood. Still, he had his left hand rigidly behind his back, fighting Blood in classic dueling fashion but with more fury in his eyes than I ever thought possible—another drink, sir?"

"Yes, of course! Please press on, though . . ."

Hornby called out for another round and continued.

"Hawke parried Blood's wicked blows each and all and thrust his cutlass again and again at the darting pirate. But despite Hawke's geniuslike finesse with the sword, it was immediately clear to us boys that this was the fight of his life, as Blood brutally laid on three massive resounding blows in quick succession.

"'It's finished, Hawke, surrender!' Billy cried, advancing. 'There's not a swordsman alive who can best Billy Blood! I'll cut yer bleedin' heart out and eat it for me supper!'

"'I think you shall go hungry, then, sir!' Hawke replied, slashing forward. 'No, it's the brave kidnapper of small children who's finished, Blood,' Hawke said, deflecting with his own sword a tremendous cut, which would surely have split him to the chine had he not intercepted it in the nick of time.

"Hawke, in a dancing parry and lunge, laid on a powerful blow, and a great clang of iron rang out over the decks. Billy screamed, his face flushed furious red. He charged Hawke then, like a wounded rhinoceros, bellowing at the top of his lungs.

"Hawke raised his cutlass to defend the ferocious blow, but Billy struck with huge force at Hawke's upraised blade. The sword was brutally ripped from His Lordship's hand and went clattering across the deck.

"A cold hand gripped our two young hearts as we watched Lord Hawke retreating, completely defenseless against that murderous scalawag, and stumbling backward, tripping over wounded men lying about the decks awash with blood. He crashed to the deck and Bill was upon him.

"'Lord Hawke! Up here!' Nick McIver shouted, and everyone turned to see that boy standing atop the pilothouse. He pulled the cutlass he'd borrowed from his belt and threw it down to the empty-handed Hawke. Hawke grinned as he reached up to snatch it, but Nick's toss was short and the sword fell to the deck at Hawke's feet. I saw my aristocratic new hero bend to retrieve it, but Bill was using the moment's distraction to circle in toward Hawke, his sword poised for a murderous blow.

"Hawke and his blade were coming up as Blood's blade was coming down. The flat of Billy's sword caught Hawke hard across the shoulder blades, driving him back down to the deck. His head thudded hard, and I could see he was stunned. The sword Nick had thrown flew from his hands and landed a good fifteen feet away. Nick looked at me, and I could see in his eyes what he had in mind.

"'Now!'"

"It was only about ten feet from our perch down to the quarterdeck, and Nick timed that jump perfectly. He came down squarely on the shoulders of Captain Blood, straddling his head and clamping both hands over the enraged pirate's eyes. Blinded and snorting, Bill whirled about, staggering over the bodies of the dead like some wild animal. He clawed and shook that tenacious boy clinging to him, tormenting him, but our Nick held on.

"Nick saw me then, peering down from the rooftop, and cried out, 'Down to the brig with you, Martyn Hornby! See if you can find Lord Hawke's children! His Lordship and I have this well in hand.' Nick had somehow snatched the prized spyglass from Bill's waist . . . and then I saw Nick flying through the air as Billy had finally ripped him from his shoulders and flung him like a ragdoll hard upon the deck.

"*Well in hand?* I thought, disbelieving. But I did as Nick said and slid backward down off the roof, much as it pained me to leave that grave drama and then–

"'I'll have that glass back!'" Blood roared, planting one of his gleaming Hessian boots squarely in the middle of Nick's chest. Bill poked the tip of his razor-sharp blade at him, prodding Nick's jacket. Then he slashed the boy's thin blue coat right through, and the gleaming spyglass spilled out onto the deck, rolling away as Nick tried desperately to grab for it. In a flash, Blood's hand shot out like some inhuman claw and clutched it, raising it aloft where it shone in the sun.

"'No,' Nick shouted, 'that's Nelson's glass!' He was clawing at Blood's leg, trying to rise from the deck. But Billy still had him pinned with his boot pressed painfully in the boy's stomach, and Nick could only twist frantically like a spider impaled. Then Nick reached inside his jacket for a bone-handled dagger. He plunged that blade deep into the fleshy part of Old Bill's calf. Roaring in pain, Blood didn't see Hawke approach from behind.

"'The boy said the glass belongs to Nelson,' Hawke said, the point of his cutlass in Billy's back. 'I'll thank you to return it to him. Now.'

"'Your tongue has wagged its last,' Bill said, whirling to face Lord Hawke. They eyed each other. Bill lunged first, his blade going for Hawke's exposed gut, but this time it was Hawke who spun on his heel in lightning fashion, whirling his body with his flashing cutlass outstretched. And then an awful sound, a sound one would never forget, the sound of steel on flesh and bone. The sound of steel *through* flesh and bone!

"There was an enormous howl of pain, and Billy held up a bloody stump of his right arm.

"On the deck, Blood's still-twitching hand, bloody fingers clenched round the shining golden spyglass."

I stood again and looked down at old Hornby, who was staring into the fire with the gleaming eyes of fading memories.

"Ho! Hawke had Nelson's glass?"

"Aye, we had it, for all love. The longitude and latitudinal coordinates of the ambush, scratched into the gold in code. But the Portugee spy, he'd given up that code long ago. Hawke read off the numbers plain as could be, and a marine wrote 'em down."

"And that's the end of it?"

"Not quite, sir. 'Father! Father!' came a tiny voice that pierced the silence in a way that made Hawke's heart leap up into this throat so quickly he could scarce get another word out.

"'Oh, Father, it's really you!' the two children cried, and Hawke leaped down from the binnacle, falling to his knees and embracing young Alex Hawke and his sister, Annabel, as if he'd never let them go."

A silence fell then; only a patter of rain on the roof could be heard.

"Soon enough, the barky was under way again, and she had a fine heel to her, and looking aloft I saw clouds of billowing white canvas towering above, pulling hard for England. A corps of drummers dressed with magnificent battle drums launched into a stately military tattoo that rolled across our decks. *Merlin* was a fine, weatherly ship, and I recall thinking that if this breeze held, we'd have no trouble completing our do-or-die mission. We'd reach Portsmouth in time to personally warn Nelson of the intended French and Spanish ambush."

"And you did, did you not?"

The old fellow leaned forward, as if he had a further confidence to impart, and I saw his eyes welling.

"Afterward, Lord Hawke himself came over to me, his son Alex in his arms. He bent down and looked me straight in the eye.

"'Magnificently done, young Mr. Hornby,' he said, and handed me a canvas packet, but my eyes were too blurry to know then what it was. Years later, I hung it there, on the wall beside the hearth. D'you see it?"

I rose from my chair and went to inspect the thing, glinting in the shadowy firelight. "Yes, I see it, Mr. Hornby," I said. I reached up and fingered the old leather strap, carefully, lest it crumble under my touch.

Lord Hawke's gift that day to the young powder monkey, Martyn Hornby, once a shining treasure, was now a tarnished memory of glory hung by the hearthside. It was Lord Nelson's spyglass.

"Go on, Mr. Tolliver, put it to your eye. That's history there in your hands, sir!"

I lifted the glass from the nail where it hung, and that's when it happened. The strap parted and the glass slipped from my fingers and smashed against the hearthstone. The lens popped into the air, spinning like a tossed shilling, and I reached out and snatched it.

"Sir!" I cried as I bent to retrieve the dented tube, "I'm dreadfully sorry!"

"No worries, Mr. Tolliver," he replied kindly. "It's seen far worse. Look closely, you can see Bill's inscription there by the eyepiece."

But something far more intriguing had fallen from the tube. A thin, yellow roll of parchment tied with a black ribbon.

"Mr. Hornby," I said, trying to control my emotions, "there appears to have been a message of some kind inside. Were you aware of it?"

"A message, sir?" he said, getting slowly to his feet. "Let's have a look."

I untied the ribbon with utmost care and spread the letter

upon a table. We both looked down in utter disbelief. The letter was signed and dated by Napoleon himself! Here is what it said:

> *Captain Blood,*
> *Make for Cadiz at once under a full press of sail! Once our fleets are united with Spain's, England is ours! Surprise Nelson en route to Trafalgar and all will be over. Six centuries of shame and insult will be avenged! Lay on with a will! His Majesty counts as nothing the loss of his ships provided they are lost with Glory . . .*
>
>

N.

I said in a daze, "Astounding, sir. And proof of the tale!"

"Yes. Proof enough, I should think, for the history books."

"History books I shall be rewriting upon my return to London, sir. I cannot thank you enough."

"Off to bed with you, then, young Tolliver. You've got a journey before you on the morrow."

I smiled and rose to mount the stairs, tired but exhilarated by my efforts, the inky black words of Hornby's tale already dancing on paper before my tired eyes.

BOOK ONE

INVASION

I

PENNYWHISTLE PARK

· Greybeard Island, 1940 ·

A dreamlike night, Nick McIver felt, pulling up the soaking sheepskin collar on his father's leather bomber jacket. A cold, wet wind swept mist in from the dark and restless sea as he made his way along the coast road that defined the small coastal town of Pennywhistle.

The multicolored lights at Pennywhistle Park, a tiny amusement center, were shrouded in ghostly haloes. The lights of the park's rides looked, the boy thought, the way a Christmas tree looked when you squinted your eyes, peeking at it one last time before sleepily climbing the stairs on Christmas Eve.

Strolling the empty streets, young Nicholas McIver vaguely recognized the town. His mother had a sister who lived in a village that very much resembled this one, but he'd visited only once, years earlier, and he was a bit foggy on the details.

He did recall that Pennywhistle Park was located on a rocky point sticking out into the sea. It was nearly deserted at this hour, he saw, passing under the lighted entrance. The sun was long down, and the night was growing cold. Most children were home having supper or climbing into their warm beds. Why wasn't he?

He couldn't say, really, but here he was.

The Ferris wheel, his original destination, came to a creaky stop, and a few strangely silent children climbed out of the cars and rushed into their parents' arms, all of them soon disappearing into the mist. Now, it seemed as if he had the entire park to himself. He stepped up to the ticket window. The ticket-taker, with his green eyeshade, looked an awful lot like Nick's best friend in the world, a man named Gunner. A dead-ringer, as his dad would say, down to his full white beard and gold-rimmed glasses!

"Sorry, son, park's shutting down for the night," the bearded man said when the lad approached, his money tightly clenched in his fist.

"Are all the rides closed, sir?" Nick asked, marveling at the man's voice. He even *sounded* like Gunner!

"Well, there is one ride still open, lad. The Whirl-O-Drome."

"The spinning airplanes, do you mean? That's the one I've come for, sir."

"Not just any old airplanes, son, but miniature Spitfires. Supermarines, just like the real thing our boys will be flying when the shooting war with Germany begins. Only without the working engines and machine guns, of course." The man laughed.

"Which way is the Whirl-O-Drome, sir?"

"Farthest ride out there. Follow the midway here all the way to the end of the point. See that big flashing red propeller sign spinning round out there? Bit foggy to make out, but there she is, all right. Still catch a ride, looks like, if you hurry."

"Thank you very much, sir. If I can't ride the Ferris wheel, that looks like a good one."

"Fancy yourself a pilot, do you?"

"Someday I will be one, sir. My father, you see, was a hero in the Great War. Shot down over the Ardennes, but he took more than a few German Fokkers with him. I plan to sign up with the Royal Flying Corps soon as I'm old enough. You can count on that!"

"Good lad. England will need thousands of brave boys like you before this coming war is over. I just heard over the wireless that German armies have marched into Belgium and Holland. And that Chamberlain has resigned, and Churchill is to be Prime Minister."

"I've had the pleasure of meeting the great man, sir. And if anyone can bring us safely through this war, it is Winston Churchill."

Nick McIver bade the man farewell and followed the darkened midway out to the Whirl-O-Drome. It was very windy and chilly. But he was wearing his father's old leather flying jacket and leather helmet, and both gave him a good deal of warmth.

The ride was like a big wheel set on its side, with a slowly revolving beacon light at its hub and eight tiny silver Spitfire airplanes at the end of each spoke. He noticed that all the little planes were empty. As the great wheel turned, the propellers at the nose of each plane spun rapidly in the stiff breeze off the sea.

There was a kindly old man in the ticket booth, snow-white hair and big blue eyes, like a baby. He, too, reminded the boy of someone. His grandfather. Yes, he looked *exactly* like Nick's grandfather! He smiled at Nick. This was indeed the strangest place–everyone here reminded him of someone else!

"Sir, may I have just one ride? I'm sure you're closing down for the night, and I don't want to be a bother."

"This ride never closes, Nick. I keep it open all the time. Just for young boys like you."

"But, but, sir, you called me 'Nick.' How on earth do you know my name?"

"Oh, I've seen you about, here and there. My name's Captain Orion, but you just call me Cap'n. Want to be a pilot someday, don't you, Nick? I've seen that look in a boy's eyes before, y'know."

"I'd do anything to become one, sir. My father, whose name is Angus, flew a Sopwith Camel with C Flight, Number 40 Squadron, the very same squadron as Mick Mannock, the famous ace who shot down sixty-one German planes."

"Your dad was an ace, too, before he got shot down by Baron Manfred von Richtofen over the Ardennes forest. Lost the use of one of his legs, I believe. Walks with a cane."

"That's correct, sir. The Red Baron ended my father's service to his country. But how on earth did you know about all this?"

"Why, Angus McIver is famous, too, Nick. A real hero."

"Thank you, sir. He'd be pleased. Here's my money. I'll take five rides, please."

"Your money's no good on this ride. Future knights of the air like yerself ride the Whirl-O-Drome for free. Our patriotic duty, y'see. Step inside the gate here, and I'll have you airborne before you know it."

Cap'n Orion brought the spinning ride gradually to a stop, let Nick pick the Spitfire he wanted to fly (they were all identical save the big red numbers painted on the stubby wings) and then helped him climb up inside the bare metal cockpit.

He'd chosen No. 7, his lucky number. The seat was like a small bucket with leather padding. It had a realistic-looking instrument panel, but when he reached out to touch it, he saw that the dials were all peeling and painted on wood.

"Does the joystick really work?" Nick asked, pulling back on it.

"Sure does. Pull back to bring her nose up; push forward and she'll go into a dive."

"What about these two pedals?" he asked, pushing them with his feet.

"Your rudder. She'll change course a couple of feet left or right, depending on which pedal you push, Nick. You ready for takeoff, Captain?"

"I am, sir."

"Let me go crank her up, then."

Cap'n Orion disappeared back inside the ticket booth, and sure enough, the great wheel began to revolve, round and round. The sea mist made it seem like flying through clouds, and Nick quickly made use of the stick, climbing and diving, using the foot pedals to turn side-to-side.

Orion stepped outside to watch the boy.

"Can't this thing go any faster?" Nick cried out through cupped hands as he whirled by.

The man gave him a thumbs-up and ran back inside the booth. Nick could see him through the window, turning a large wheel mounted on the wall.

Suddenly, the little Spitfire was going so fast Nick could hardly believe it. He was amazed the toy airplane didn't just fly right off the end of the long pole. Everything was a blur. He had to pull the old leather goggles down over his eyes because his eyes were tearing up so badly.

He looked around. He could no longer see the dark town or Pennywhistle Park or even Cap'n Orion inside the ticket booth. It was a little frightening, but Nick supposed he'd better get used to real speed if he was ever going to fly a real Spitfire.

Then the strangest thing of all happened. The painted-on instruments on the wooden panel began to light up one by one. He leaned forward and looked at them, tapping his finger on the rev counter. The needles were spinning behind real glass! And his altimeter was working! His altitude was six feet. His speed, however, was almost sixty miles per hour and climbing! And now there were tiny red lights flashing out on his wingtips.

He heard a strange squawking noise behind the instrument panel and reached up under it to see what it was. There was a hook under there, and on it hung an old pair of headphones, just like the real ones his dad had brought home from the war. There were small ear-holes in his leather flying helmet, and he put the headphones on over it.

"Captain McIver! Captain McIver! This is Pennywhistle Control. Do you read me? Over."

It sounded like Captain Orion, who sounded a lot like his grandfather.

"What's going on?" Nick cried, "Is everything all right? Is the ride broken? I think it's going too fast!"

"Roger, Captain, I read you loud and clear. Everything under control. You are cleared for takeoff, skipper."

"Takeoff?"

"See that flashing red button on top of the joystick?"

"Yes, sir, I do," he said, and suddenly there really *was* a flashing red button.

"Just push that button, skipper, and you'll be on your merry way. Happy flying, sir!"

Push the button? On your way? Happy flying? Being a naturally curious boy, Nick McIver had no choice but to push the red button. What happened next took his breath away.

THE WHIRL-O-DROME

· Greybeard Island, 1940 ·

The Whirl-O-Drome spun ever faster, round and round in a dizzying blur. So fast that Nick, fighting the dizziness, was sure the whole ride would just fly apart any second now, disintegrate, and fling the little planes into the air, crashing into the sea or smashing against the rocks or the rooftops of pubs across the road.

But that's not what happened.

There was suddenly a loud beeping noise inside his cockpit, and then little No. 7 began shaking hard enough to rattle his bones. He noticed his propeller was turning much faster, too, and he heard loud popping noises from the nose and then the explosive sound of a powerful gasoline engine roaring to life. Flames suddenly shot out of the exhaust manifolds, and the whole aircraft was vibrating heavily now as the great engine rumbled.

There was a screeching sound of metal on his left side, just where the airplane was bolted to a steel plate at the end of the pole. It felt as if his plane was trying to shake itself loose, separate itself from the pole!

And that is just what happened.

There was a slight popping noise and his aircraft soared, suddenly free of the pole, flung into the air, skimming out over the dark waves and gaining speed! The little seaside town spun away to a tiny point of light behind him.

"Captain, you're too low! You might catch a wave with your wingtips! Climb! Climb!" he heard Orion shouting in his headphones. Nick craned his head around to look down at Pennywhistle Park and saw Orion behind his window, staring up at him through a pair of binoculars.

Nick automatically pulled back on the joystick, and sure enough his nose came up and the little Spitfire began climbing. He saw his altimeter spinning, the needle now at one hundred feet and climbing rapidly.

"Too steep, Captain, too steep! You're going to stall out! Get your nose down until you're aimed nice and level at the horizon . . . easy, lad, steady and gentle, now . . ."

Nick eased the stick forward and the plane leveled off.

"Attaboy, now you're flying right. Where do you want to go?"

"Go?" It hadn't occurred to Nick that he could actually *go* anywhere.

"Sure. Just use your rudder pedals to turn left or right and your stick to climb or descend. All there is to it, really."

"I–I'd like to see our lighthouse on–on Greybeard Island. The place where I live. Is the island too far away?"

"Not in that plane. See the compass right in the middle of your control panel? Come left twenty degrees. Steer due north. You should see the Greybeard Light in about, oh, six minutes or so."

And so Nick flew on, the fear of flying gradually replaced by confidence in his new skill and tremendous excitement at this wondrous adventure.

Nick experimented with the rudder pedals, and it didn't

take long to determine how to bring the plane around to a heading of due north. Using the joystick, he tried to keep the nose just above the horizon line.

"How's my altitude?" Nick asked, glancing down at the sea far below.

"You're flying level at one thousand feet. That's fine. I'm about to lose visual contact with you, but you can still contact me on the radio. How is it up there, Nick?"

"It's amazing. I think I'm getting the hang of it, Captain. What do I do, if I want to, say, fly upside down? Or do a barrel roll? Or an outside loop?"

"Nick, listen, I think you just want to fly straight and level for right now, all right? Until you get the hang of it. Stay on your current heading of 060 degrees. You should see Greybeard Island and the lighthouse coming up any minute now."

"I see it flashing! It's dead ahead."

"Don't see any bogies or bandits up there, do you, Cap'n?"

"Bogies or bandits?"

"The enemy. Luftwaffe fighters or bombers. German Messerschmitt 109s or Junkers Ju-290s, most likely."

"Nope, no one up here but me, Cap'n, I'm just over the lighthouse now. I'm going to circle it a few times, see if I can wake my father and get him to come to the window to see me!"

Using his ailerons and rudder, Nick rolled his little Spitfire on its side and did three or four high-speed loops around the upper portion of the Greybeard Light, the big supermarine engine roaring and spitting fire. But everyone must have been sound asleep inside because no one ever came to the windows to see what the great noise was.

"That was fun!" Nick said, pulling out of his loop and climbing at a steep angle. "There seems to be a heavy layer of cloud about a thousand feet above me. All right if I climb up through it?"

"Sure! Just keep your eyes open for bogies once you break through the cloud tops. More German squadrons up there every night lately."

Nick hauled back on the stick, gently now, for he knew that's the way it was done. A few moments later he was inside the cloud bank, a thick fog surrounding him, and he couldn't see a thing. Then he broke through the top and entered another world.

A huge yellow moon hung off to his right, bathing the cottony top of the cloud layer in shades of soft buttery gold. And a dusting of twinkling silver stars was sprinkled across the blue-black bowl of the heavens.

"What's that?" he suddenly exclaimed.

He'd glimpsed another plane, far ahead, waggling its wings, the signal for sighting an enemy aircraft. A German fighter? A *bogie*?

He swung round to a southerly course and got right on the bandit's tail, increasing his speed and closing fast. It wasn't a Messerschmitt, Nick saw, as he closed within a hundred yards of the plane. No, no, it was an old plane, a very, very old plane. A biplane, made of paper and wood.

A Sopwith Camel, in fact, just like the one his father had flown in the Great War, with twin Vickers .303 machine guns mounted on the cowl and firing forward through the propeller disk. The Camel was lord of the skies during the Great War way back in 1916.

What on earth?

"Welcome to the boundless skies, Nick," he heard a new voice say in his headphones. This voice, too, was very familiar.

Could it be?

He banked hard left, increased his airspeed, and easily pulled abreast of the ancient warplane.

The pilot looked over at him and smiled. He was a young man, very handsome and dashing with his long white silk scarf streaming behind him in the breeze, and he reminded Nick of someone, too. A younger version of the man Nick worshipped and loved more than anyone on this earth.

"Follow me, if you can!" the voice said.

"But, where are we going?"

"To the moon and back, of course!"

Nick nosed over into a steep dive, headed right for the big golden moon hanging just above the far horizon of the world.

"I'm right behind you, Father!" Nick cried.

That fat yellow moon was so big it looked as if it might just swallow the two little airplanes right up.

And that's just what it did.

And then someone was shaking him violently, saying "Wake up! Wake up!"

· Greybeard Island, May 1940 ·

W ake up, Nicky! Wake up!" his sister, Kate, was saying, jumping up and down on his bed, excitement shining in her cornflower-blue eyes, her bright red curls bouncing about her face as if they were a bunch of springs attached to her head. She had her raggedy doll in one hand, swinging her by the hair, what little the doll had left after all these years.

Jip, Nick's big black dog, had leaped onto his bed and was lathering his master's face with sloppy kisses.

Nick, knowing sleep was now well nigh impossible, cracked one eye and used it to inspect his little sister. His room, at the very top of the lighthouse, was filled with strong sunlight. Perhaps he had overslept a bit.

"Have the Germans invaded us?" he asked sleepily.

"Not yet. But Father says it's only a matter of weeks. Or even days."

Nick McIver groaned, rolled over onto his tummy, and buried his face in his pillow. He wanted more than anything to fall back down into deep slumber, to return to his magical dream of racing his father's old Sopwith Camel to the moon. But Kate was having none of it.

"Go away, Katie. And stop bouncing, for all love," he said, his sleepy words muffled by goose down. "And you, Jipper, stop barking!"

"No! Never! Not until you get up. We have to go. And I won't stop bouncing on your bed until we do!"

"Go? Go where?"

"Out to Storm Island, silly. It's Saturday! We're sailing out there on *Petrel*, remember. For a picnic. And I get to steer the whole way. You promised, double-secret-swear promise, crosses don't count."

Nick flopped over onto his back and stared at his seven-year-old sister. She had him dead to rights. He'd promised, all right.

"Kate. You know all about promises, right?"

"Sure. You keep 'em."

"Well–right. Of course you keep them. But sometimes things happen and you have to, well, delay your promises. It's called postponing. You know what *postponing* means, don't you?"

"Sure. Lying."

"Kate. It's not really lying. It's just something you'll learn more about as you get older like me."

"Thirteen is hardly old, Nicky. I'll be twelve myself in less than five years. Unless my birthday gets *postponed*, of course."

"Well, still."

"Nicky, no. You promised and we're going. I've already packed a picnic basket and that's it. Final, final, final."

She collapsed at the foot of Nick's bed and stared at him with blazing blue eyes, daring him to break the solemn promise he'd made two days ago. But at least she'd stopped jumping up and down.

"What if I were to tell you I'd had a dream last night. And that what I dreamed was so amazing, so *real*, that I decided to try and find a way to make it come true. And you, of course, will have to help, because nobody wants dreams to come true more than Miss Katherine McIver, right?"

"Correct. But this is your dream, remember? It's my dreams I'm excited about. I don't care a fig for your silly dreams."

"Well, when you hear about mine, you will. In fact, it will become your dream, too. And you'll be excited about it, I promise."

"I'm listening. What is it?"

"It's a secret."

"Is this a trick? You know I love secrets more than anything in the whole wide world."

"I know you do. And you're going to love this one best of all. Aside from that golden orb hidden in the gun vault at Gunner's inn, it's possibly the world's best secret of all time."

"Okay. But to get out of our picnic today, you have to promise to do two things. One: Promise I don't have to carry anything heavy to the picnic, like when I helped you clean out your boat shed. Two: You have to tell me something about the secret that doesn't give it away but makes me feel better about not sailing out to Storm Island. Today. Like you promised."

"You don't have to carry anything heavier than a picnic basket."

"That's one."

"And the secret is about–well, the secret is about flying."

"Flying."

"Yep."

"Like a bird."

"More or less."

"Like Peter Pan and Tinker Bell and Wendy and Michael?"

"Sort of."

"Do I get to fly? Or just you?"

"We both fly."

"I already love this secret."

"I thought you might."

"But we still get to sail to Storm Island for a picnic."

"Next Saturday, rain or shine."

"Promise delay granted. Where are we going?"

"Those spooky woods, the ones we called the Black Forest when we were kids. Up by Lord Hawke's airstrip."

"You mean the Green Forest, don't you?"

"No, I mean the Black Forest."

"But it isn't black, Nicky. It's green! Just like every other forest on this island."

"Well. I know. But Black Forest sounds better. So just go along with me on this, all right? Besides, it's black enough when you go deep inside it, as I plan to do."

"I got lost in that place for a whole day the summer I was four! It was very, very scary. Why, if Jipper hadn't found me, I would have just died of starvation or something worse."

"Exactly. The Black Forest is not a place for the faint of heart."

"Nicky, it is a very spooky wood. I still have nightmares about being lost in there sometimes. Do we have to go through there?"

"I'm afraid so. What I'm looking for is, I believe, somewhere inside that dark wood. But, look, I'll be with you this time. And Jip, of course. Nothing spooks that dog."

"You won't leave me somewhere and run off, will you?"

"Of course not."

Kate looked her brother hard in the eye, measuring his sincerity.

"Flying, huh?" she said, sliding toward the end of his bed.

"Flying."

"And I get to fly, too?"

"Let me put it this way. If I get to fly, you will definitely get to fly, too."

Her sparkling blue eyes lit up and her wide smile returned. "Be downstairs in five minutes, Nick McIver, or I'm leaving without you!" she cried. Leaping off his completely disheveled bed, she ran from his room at the top of the lighthouse, banging Nick's door closed behind her and dancing down the curving staircase the led to the kitchen.

There was only one thing better than picnics, and that was secrets. And, as she'd learned earlier that summer, when they'd discovered the golden orb inside an old sea chest, there was no shortage of secrets on this little island.

And so they set out that morning on their new adventure. It would not be a long hike. Greybeard Island was the tiniest of the Channel Islands. Jersey and Guernsey, those were the big ones. Ministries and museums and fancy mansions with gardens and stables fit for a king. And although Nick's home islands were decidedly British, they all lay much closer to the coast of France than that of England.

Greybeard, though small, was a pretty enough place, Nick supposed, as he and his sister strolled along the leafy lane that led from the lighthouse to the coast road going to the south end of the island. The morning sunlight through the trees was beautiful, almost magical. But then he'd never really lived anywhere else.

The island roads were unpaved, and there were no motor-cars on Greybeard at all, not one, and more cows than humans. Still, as Nick had learned over the course of one amazing summer, there was plenty of excitement to be found on his little island. Oh, yes. More than enough adventure to satisfy any boy anywhere. For a lifetime.

All the excitement in the world, in fact.

Because young Nicholas McIver had now, through the most curious sequence of events, come into possession of Leonardo da Vinci's Tempus Machina.

It was a Time Machine.

A miraculous time machine, for all love! This magnificent device, a gleaming golden ball, had allowed Nick, along with his friends Gunner and Lord Hawke, to conquer time and space, using the machine to travel through time, doing good wherever he was needed. Why, he'd even helped Lord Nelson himself, in addition to rescuing his dog Jip and Lord Hawke's two little children, Alex and Annabel, from an evil pirate named Billy Blood!

Perhaps, he sometimes thought, no, *really*, the golden orb provided even a bit more excitement than he could handle. After his last adventure with the golden orb, he'd insisted Gunner lock the thing away in the great gun vault at his inn. It had a combination lock and Nick made Gunner swear never to give him that combination, no matter how much he might plead or beg.

Still, Nick had long ago decided, excitement and risk were good for any boy. Especially one who wanted more than anything to be a hero. It took adversity to mold a boy into someone worthy of being called a man. And if he was stong and bold enough, even a heroic man. That's what he thought, anyway. And that's what he was bound and determined to become.

Heroes, he knew, were molded in the face of danger. And so, instead of running from it, Nick raced after it. Or, at least, didn't turn away when he encountered it.

"A good ship is never tested in calm waters, Nicholas," as his father was fond of reminding him.

And now that the Germans were coming, the waters surrounding the Channel Islands were anything but calm. U-boats could be seen offshore at all hours of the day and night. Squadrons of German fighters, Messerschmitts they were called, roared overhead with frightening regularity.

His father, a spy for Winston Churchill himself, believed an invasion of the Channel Islands was imminent. There would be adversity aplenty then, all right, bags of the stuff.

And when the Germans, the Nazis, did come, when they invaded Nick's beloved Channel Islands, where his family had lived for generations, what then? More excitement and danger than anyone could reasonably expect, he'd wager. But he'd be ready for them, sure he would. He and Gunner and Lord Hawke and Commander Hobbes and even little Katie, who'd proved herself brave beyond measure in their last adventure through time.

They'd all be ready when the Nazis came.

Now, as he and Kate made their way along a curving path that led up toward the Black Forest, Nick was thinking about these Nazi invaders. He'd need some way to fight back, defend his island, protect his family, his home. That's why his recent dream had been so powerful, he now understood. If he and Kate could possibly find what he hoped lay somewhere in the forest, it might be a way for him to—

"Jipper!" Nick cried, "Come back here!"

The dog Jip, barking loudly, had raced ahead of the children and disappeared inside the dense and tangled wood.

"I have a bad feeling about this place, Nicky," Kate said, her brow furrowed with worry.

"Don't be silly. There's nothing in there can hurt us. Nothing but songbirds and rabbits and squirrels and such. He's probably on the scent of a rabbit."

"What about Nazis?" Kate said, looking carefully at her brother.

"What about them?"

"They could be hiding in those woods. Just waiting for someone like us to come along. Mother says she thinks she saw a parachute floating down near there last week, even though it was near dark and she wasn't sure. And remember Father and the Birdwatchers found that overturned raft washed up on Sandy Cove last week. It was off a German U-boat, Papa said."

"Kate, listen to me. When and if the Nazis do come, we'll know about it, believe me. They're not likely to be hiding in the woods, looking for children on a picnic. Now, come along, let's catch up with Jip."

"If you say so," Kate said quietly, reaching up and taking her brother's hand.

Its strength was reassuring. And besides, what was she afraid of? Nazis? She'd dealt with them before.

And won.

Kate was slipping and sliding, clinging to vines and low-hanging branches trying to make her way up the great sodden slab of slick, moss-covered granite. Nicky was already at the top, waiting for her. They'd been in the dark, deep woods for at least half an hour with no sign of Jip no matter how loudly they cried out to him.

Where could that dog have got to? Nick wondered.

"I don't like it here. There used to be a path through this wood, Nicky," his sister said with a pout as she heaved herself up to the top of the rock. She'd fallen three or four times; both her knees were skinned, She was frightfully hot, and she was not happy. "Where is it?"

"Path's grown over, I'm afraid, most of it, anyway. Looks like nobody comes through the wood this way much anymore," Nick said as they leaped down to the ground.

"Really? I wonder why, do you think?" she said, giving him a look.

"Now, Kate, be patient. I'm sure we'll find what we're looking for soon. There's a pretty little stream not far from here. Used to be full of fish. The woods are much less dense on the far side. You'll see. We should find it easily enough."

"Find *what* easily enough?"

"What we're looking for, of course. What else?"

Katie sighed deeply and looked at her brother in frustration. A sunny picnic on Storm Island had been postponed for this? Mucking about in a spooky, pitch-black forest, scratches on her arms, legs, and cheeks from the briar? No. This was not the Saturday she'd had in mind at all.

"Nick. Listen. How can I even begin to look for something if my brother won't even tell me what it is?" She plopped herself down on a fallen tree trunk and crossed her arms in front of her.

Nick sat down next to Katie, put his arm around her, and said, "Well, fair enough. I can tell you Part One of the secret now that we're here in the heart of the woods."

"About time, too."

"It's a barn."

"A barn?"

"Yes, exactly."

"You don't mean just a big old wooden building-type barn, I hope?"

"Right-oh."

"So, your big secret is a barn? I'm going home."

"Wait! Sit down. Not exactly a barn. There's a bit more to it than that."

"Like what?"

"You'll find out. See, nobody's used this particular barn for decades. I'm sure that creeper vines and ivy and such have completely covered it over. But, don't worry, we'll find it."

"It's a barn, Nicky, not a needle in a haystack! Of course we'll find it."

Nick stood up and held out his hand to Kate. She took it and slid forward off the big tree trunk, landing nimbly on her feet. Then she followed her brother, sticking close behind him now.

"So, a secret barn. Does it fly?"

"No, not really."

"But you said this secret was about flying! That's the only reason I came."

"It *is* about flying. I promise. Now come along. Listen. Hear that stream rushing just beyond those trees? We're getting very close now."

The children removed their shoes and socks and waded across the shallow stream, Nick holding Kate's hand because the rocks beneath their bare feet were very slippery. Reaching the far side, they sat down on the grassy bank and were just putting their shoes back on when suddenly they heard Jip, barking in the distance.

"Jipper!" Nick cried, pulling Kate to her feet. "Come on, let's go!"

The woods were not nearly so thick on this far side of the stream, and Nick and Kate were able to run reasonably quickly toward the sound of Jip's barking.

"See that sunny clearing beyond the trees, Katie? That's where Jipper is. Probably got a hedgehog cornered up a tree from all the commotion he's making. I'll run up ahead and see. You slow down, I don't want you tripping over tree roots again."

Nick sprinted forward and reached the clearing a good five minutes before Katie.

Across the clearing, in a small meadow filled with gently waving poppies, he saw Jip circling at the base of a large elm. He was barking at a man hanging from one of the lower branches of the ancient tree, and Nick sprinted toward him.

"Jip, down boy! Leave him alone!" Nick shouted as he ran.

He reached his dog, dropping to his knees beside him, holding him to his chest. Then he looked up at the man in the tree. It was a young German soldier. He was hanging from the harness of his parachute. Maybe fifteen feet from the ground. The chute had become entangled in the branches above. The white silk canopy of his parachute was fluttering in the breeze high above in the uppermost branches. The soldier was dead. And it looked as if he'd been dead for quite some time. Animals had gotten to him. Red squirrels and black rats. Birds, too, had taken his eyes, pecked them right out.

"Nicky!" Kate cried, halfway across the meadow, running as fast as she could. "What is it? What did Jip find?"

"Katie, stop! Stop right there! Don't come any closer. I mean it. Not one step."

She stopped, staring at her brother, who was now getting to his feet and running toward her. "What is it, Nicky?" she asked, as he put his arms around her.

"A soldier. His parachute got caught in a tree."

"A German soldier?"

"Yes."

"Is he all right? Can we get him down?"

"No. He's not all right. He's dead."

Kate's mouth dropped open.

"He's *dead*? Can I see?"

"No. You cannot see."

"Why not?"

"Because there are some things little girls should not see. And he is one of them. You will have nightmares for months if you go over there. All right?"

"But you saw him."

"And I wish I hadn't."

"What are we going to do?"

"Nothing right now. We're going to leave him in peace and go find that barn. I'll tell Father about him when we get home. He'll know what to do. Call the constabulary. The Home Guard. They'll handle it."

"Is he the one Mother saw last week?"

"He very well might be. Now, come on, let's get out of here and find that barn, all right?"

"Oh, Nicky," she said, a solitary tear running down her cheek, "it's so sad. So awfully sad."

"Yes, it is. Jipper, come boy, come now."

———

Half an hour later, they found the barn.

It was, as Nick had predicted, completely enveloped with growth from the forest—weeds, vines, creepers, ivy—it had turned it into a kind of topiary of a barn. It was standing just inside the wood, not a hundred yards from the landing strip at Hawke Field.

As Nick began to slash away at the greenery covering the wide barn doors, Kate went over to the shade of a spreading oak tree and sat beneath it, Jip cradled in her arms. She stroked his head gently and whispered to him, saying things that were meant for her dog's ears alone. Occasionally, she'd swipe the back of her hand across her eyes and wet cheeks, wiping away tears for the boy hanging in the woods.

Nick cut the last vestiges of the overgrowth away and saw that at least one of the weather-beaten doors could be opened now. He inserted his fingers into the crack and pulled. The door opened easily, creaking loudly, and the smell of decades of old wet hay and dead mice and who-knew-what-else filled his nostrils.

"Kate, it's open. You and Jip come here and we'll have a look inside."

Kate jumped to her feet, seeming much recovered, and she and Jip joined him at the barn door as Nick pulled it wide open. Light flooded in, but it was still dark in the farther reaches and the smell of the place caused Kate to pinch her nose.

"Stinky," she said.

"The air in here is over twenty years old, Kate."

"The secret is in here?" she asked, her pinched nose making her voice sound like honking.

"I certainly hope so, after all these years. Let's go inside, shall we?"

"It's dark in there, Nicky. I don't want to go in."

"Lucky for you I brought this along," her brother said, pulling a flashlight from the side pocket of his canvas jacket. The beam stabbed into the blackness, searching everywhere.

"What is it, Nicky? What are we looking for?"

Nick held the beam steady on a large object in the far corner, covered by a moldy tarpaulin. "I think that just might be what we're looking for, Kate."

"That? That's your big secret? An old tent?"

"Yes. That's it. Come help me pull the cover off, will you?"

The two children tugged at the tarp; it was much heavier than it looked. It was coming away but very slowly.

"Right, then," Nick said, "on three! One ... two ... three!"

They both yanked with all their might, and the great grey tarpaulin came away in their hands revealing ... a skeleton. At least, that's what it looked like to Katie. The wooden skeleton of a very large bird with paper-covered wings that were torn and faded.

"That's it?" she said, unimpressed. "That's your big secret?"

"Yes. Isn't it beautiful?"

"No, it isn't. I don't even know what it is."

"It's a Camel, Katie."

"A camel? Doesn't look like any camel I've ever seen. Where's the hump? And, anyway, what's this camel got to do with flying?"

"Everything," Nick said, walking toward the front of the thing. Taking in every inch of the old biplane's tattered remains. He walked to the nose and used his flashlight to inspect what he could see of the engine inside the aluminum cowling. This was the big 150 horsepower Bentley BR.1 Rotary, he knew. He reached up and rubbed cobwebs and dust off the beautiful wooden propeller and saw the wood's shiny varnished finish in the beam of his torchlight.

Behind the propeller were the twin Vickers .303 machine guns, equipped with a synchronizer gear that allowed them to fire right through the propeller. Why, Gunner could have those guns back in firing order in jig time.

"It flies?"

"Oh, yes, Katie, it flies all right."

"A flying camel."

"A flying Sopwith Camel. It was nicknamed the Camel because of that hump in front of the cockpit. This was Dad's plane. The real one he flew in the war. These little planes shot down more German fighters than any other Allied plane, you know. Including von Richtofen, the famous Red Baron himself!"

"What's it doing here, then?"

"When the war was over, Father flew it home. He told me about it when I was a kid, even younger than you. He said he'd hidden it in a barn somewhere deep in the woods. Far as I know, he hasn't come near it since."

"Was he supposed to do that? Fly his plane home?"

"I don't think so. The war was over, he was badly hurt. He was dreadfully sick, dying maybe, and he wanted to get home to Mother in a great big hurry, I think."

"He stole it?"

"Borrowed it. When he'd recovered, could walk about, and was himself again, he wrote a letter to the adjutant, telling what he'd done, apologizing, and offering to return the Camel."

"What happened?"

"He got a letter back from Fighter Command saying that after his heroic service to his country, they would be happy for him to keep it as a souvenir."

"So, what's the secret, Nicky? I mean, just an old aeroplane?"

"No. The secret is, I'm going to make it fly again."

"That pile of junk will never fly again, Nicky."

"Oh, yes, it will."

"Does Father know?"

"No, of course he doesn't. And that's the biggest part of the secret. You can never say a word about this to anyone. It's meant to be a surprise for him, you see. The biggest surprise he's ever had."

"I suppose if you fix it up a little, he'll like it well enough."

"Like it? Katie, this old aeroplane was the one thing Dad loved most of all in the world. Besides Mother, I mean. He was an ace, don't you see? A real national hero. And I'm going to make all those happy memories brand-new again."

"Can we tell Gunner at least? He's very good at keeping secrets."

Nick nodded.

Gunner, the proprietor at the Greybeard Inn, was Nick's best friend in the world. He knew he would definitely need

Gunner's help to pull this off properly. Gunner had been a naval gunnery officer aboard a battleship in the 1917 war and knew more about all manner of mechanical things than almost anyone.

"Gunner is the only one we can tell. Because, you're quite right, I'm going to need his help to rebuild this old bird. He's an expert mechanic, you know."

"You really think you and Gunner can make this pile of sticks fly again?"

"I know we can, Katie. We can and we will. By the time we're done, why, it will look brand spanking new."

"It's a good secret, Nicky, I have to admit. Having a real aeroplane to fly around in."

"Besides our golden orb, it's the very best secret ever, Kate, believe me. Besides, I've got plans for this old aeroplane. Big plans."

W hat's this all about, Nick?" Angus McIver asked his son. It was late afternoon, and they were retracing the path Nick and Kate had taken through the woods earlier that morning. It was much easier going now, since Nick had found passable sections of the old path and knew how to avoid the really dense and tangled parts of the forest.

His father, a Royal Flying Corps pilot whose leg had been badly wounded in the Great War, always walked with a stick and was having a difficult time of it. But Nick knew this was something his dad had to see.

"You'll see soon, Dad. We're almost there."

"What were you and Kate doing in the woods today, son? I thought you two were sailing *Petrel* out to Storm Island for a picnic."

"Well, we were actually going to do that. But, see, I'd seen this beautiful meadow of poppies last week, and I thought Kate might enjoy that more."

"Really? That's surprising because she told me at breakfast this morning how terribly excited she was about going sailing aboard the *Stormy Petrel*."

"Well, y–yes. But there was a freshening breeze brewing out to the west, and I was a little worried that it might get a bit too exciting out there for her. Besides, these poppies won't last forever, you know."

Poppies? His father looked back at his son with a disbelieving look, but at that point they'd reached the edge of the meadow. It was mostly in purple shadow now, as the hazy orange sun had dropped below the treeline.

"This way, Dad," Nick said, "all the way on the other side of the field."

"Nick, if you've dragged me all the way through these woods for nothing, you're going to be one very sorry young man."

"It's not nothing, Dad. It's something important. That I can promise you."

They pushed on through the broad field of swaying poppies. Nick felt his heart beating a little faster now, wondering how his father would react to the horrible sight. Suddenly, Angus came to an abrupt stop.

He saw the dead man swinging from the branch of the old elm tree.

"Merciful heavens," his father said softly. "Dead, isn't he?"

"Yes, sir."

"Poor fellow. Tough way to go."

"It's bad, Father. Animals have gotten to him. Birds, too, I guess. He's got not much face left at all."

Nick's father paid that no mind. Nick knew he'd likely seen much worse during the war. He walked over to where the corpse hung and stared up at it for a few moments in silence.

"German spy on reconnaissance duty," his father said, and turned to look at Nick. "Who have you told about this?"

"No one. And I made Kate swear to do the same."

"Good. Make sure you keep it that way. Even a hint of something like this could spread more panic across the island. We've got quite enough of that already."

"Yes, sir."

"Have you got your knife?"

"Always."

"Think you can climb up there and out onto that limb without killing yourself?"

"Yes, sir."

"All right, do it. Let's cut the poor chap down."

Nick nodded and headed for the base of the elm. By jumping up, he got hold of the lowest branch and then did a pull-up, managing to raise himself high enough to throw one leg over, straddling the branch, steady himself, and sit upright. He reached up and caught hold of the next highest branch and got to his feet very carefully.

"Easy, Nick. This isn't a race. Just go slowly."

Nick repeated the process, branch by branch until he was straddling the one where the parachute harness had become entangled. He slid out toward the first canvas strap.

"Cut this one, Dad?"

"Yes, cut all the suspension lines except the risers."

"Which are the risers?"

"The stronger straps attached through those rings to his harness. We're going to try to lower him gently. I'll tell you when I'm ready for you to toss a line down to me. I'll get him down. You understand?"

"Yes, sir."

When Nick had finished cutting all the lines, his father said, "Good lad. Now throw me that line nearest your right leg. I'll lower him with that."

Nick threw the line down. His father caught it and began

slowly lowering the corpse. Nick, meanwhile, began his own careful descent to the ground below. By the time he reached his father, the German lay face-up in the soft grass surrounding the tree.

"What now, Father?"

"Find out if he was simply a pilot who bailed out or someone intentionally landing on Greybeard Island."

"You mean, like a . . . spy?"

"Exactly."

"Couldn't he have just been blown off course in a strong blow? Ended up here by mistake?" Nick was staring at his father. He couldn't bear to look at the dead man's wretched face any longer.

"Anything's possible. Help me roll him over and let's see what he's got in that backpack."

The man was tall but not too heavy, and Nick easily rolled him over. His father was sitting in the grass beside the body, his bad leg stretched out in front of him.

"Open it up and hand me the items inside one at a time," Angus McIver told his son.

First was a thick envelope, wrapped with a rubber band. His father ripped it open and peered inside. "Came here on purpose, Nick. Have a look."

Nick looked. It was at least a thousand pounds, English notes, well used, wrapped in individual packages.

"Next?" his father said.

"A shirt, a jumper, and a pair of grey trousers," Nick said, handing each item to his dad. His father opened the shirt and looked at the label.

"Marks & Spencer, Old Bond Street, London," he said. "This chap was certainly well prepared. Probably spoke perfect English. I'll bet you ten to one he's got a pair of binoculars, a camera, and the field guide *Birds of the Channel Islands* in there as well. Some ruse or other, in case he ran into any curious strangers."

"Well, he certainly was prepared to shoot our birds at any rate, Dad," Nick said, handing a sleek black pistol to his father.

"Luger, the P.08. Nine-millimeter. Standard German sidearm. They used this same pistol in my war."

"What's this?" Angus asked, unfolding a waxed paper chart.

"It's a map of our island, Dad. And, look, here's a British passport with his picture on it."

"This is the beginning of the end, Nick, I'm sorry to say. The Germans are definitely coming, and soon. God help us all."

"I'd say they were already here, Dad," Nick replied, glancing at the corpse, feeling a chill run up the length of his spine.

"I'm afraid you're right. Has he a collapsible spade in there?"

"Yes. How did you know?"

"Standard procedure. He planned to bury his parachute and his uniform, then march off with his bird book, looking for Arctic terns or Kentish plovers, I'd imagine. A hale fellow, well met, a cheery birder delighted to have a look round your lovely island, and all that. On holiday, don't you know, ta-ta for now!"

"What are we going to do with him, Father?"

"Bury him beneath the very tree that did him in, I suppose. A fitting end, don't you think, for our unknown soldier?"

"Shouldn't we alert someone about this?"

"Oh, yes. As soon as we're back at the lighthouse, I'll ring up the constabulary, Constable Carswell, and ask him to come out to the Old Light for a private chat. We don't want a single word of this to get around the island. That might start a panic, and we certainly don't need that. And then I'll inform Lord Hawke, and we'll get the information over to Churchill as quickly as possible."

"What will you tell him?"

"That it appears the Nazis are definitely planning an invasion of the Channel Islands, Nick. We have irrefutable proof lying right here in front of us. See if you can remove his backpack, will you? We'll need that for the constable."

"But what can we do about the Germans, Father?" Nick said, struggling with straps of the knapsack. "What can I do?"

"Start with digging that one's grave," his father said, using his stick to get to his feet. "When you get tired, just hand me the shovel."

"Poor fellow," Nick said plunging the spade into the earth.

"One less Jerry to worry about, Nick. Think of it that way."

CONTACT!

I n the weeks following the burial of the German soldier, Nick spent most of his days and nights inside the hidden barn with his friend Gunner. The fall term at the Island school would be starting soon enough, and he was most anxious to complete all the repair work that needed to be done before summer ended and classes began.

The interior of the barn had changed considerably since the day Nick and Kate had first peered inside it. For one thing, it didn't smell like dead mice anymore. It smelled of glue and grease and castor oil.

Ever since he'd first laid eyes on the old Sopwith Camel, Gunner had been like a man possessed. Nick told him what he had in mind for the aeroplane, and he had never seen his old friend so excited or so happy. Clearly, for someone as mechanically minded as Gunner, this project would be a labor of love.

First, Gunner had lugged his toolbox up from his workshop at the inn. Then he had hung kerosene lanterns on all four walls, so the gloom had completely evaporated. And Gunner could work long into the night. On the second day after commencing their restoration, Gunner had shown up with a powerful searchlight he'd once removed from the deck of a sinking U-boat in the First World War. He'd mounted the light on top of a barn post and connected it to a gas generator.

"Now I can see what I'm about, lad." He'd laughed, swiveling the light so that it was aimed directly at the aircraft's massive black engine. It was completely exposed now, since they'd already removed the aluminum cowling from the nose of the plane. Today, they'd find out if they had a working engine or not. And Nick would do a series of drawings of the plane with colored pencils so they could accurately re-create the paint scheme once all the restoration was complete.

Most of the early work had been spent on the wooden framework of the fuselage. They'd ripped away all the faded and crumbling fabric covering the aeroplane. Most of it was rotten and shredding anyway. Dampness had gotten to the wood beneath the fabric, of course, and rotted out the uprights and many of the major and minor struts of the frame. It had taken two days just to replace all the trouble spots with brand-new ash, each wooden piece hand-sawn and fitted expertly by Gunner.

"Hand over that spool of piano wire, will you, Nick?"

Nick picked up the heavy spool and gave it to his friend. "Piano wire?"

"Yep. All these interior wires holding the frame together are rusted out. Piano wire, that's what they built 'em with in 1916, and that's what we'll use to replace 'em with."

"Now what?" Nick had asked, after Gunner had spent most of the afternoon replacing all the rusted wire. "What kind of fabric do we cover these bare bones with?"

"Ah, there's the trick, ain't it, lad? Only one thing good enough for our lovely Camel, Nick, and that's good old Irish linen. Expensive, I'll grant you, but worth every ha-penny. There's a right pretty little seamstress in town who's a particularly good … friend … of mine. My little Marjorie will sell me what we need at a bargain price, I'll wager."

So the days went by, and every day, bit by bit, the old aircraft was gradually restored to its former glory. When Gunner installed the new wicker chair for the pilot in the cockpit, Nick asked, "Where is the safety harness? Wouldn't the pilot fall out in a barrel roll or a loop?"

"Didn't have 'em in the Great War," Gunner replied. "The pilot tied himself in with a bit of rope over his thighs. Worked fine. Things was simpler in those days, boy. You made do, that's all."

New rubber for the wheels and the suspension bands came next. The aluminum fuel tank was removed and the whitish powder of oxidation thoroughly cleaned out. The pump was disassembled, de-gunked with alcohol, cleaned, and re-installed. New hoses everywhere. New, brightly varnished struts between the upper and lower wings were added, and all of the interior control cables to the rudder, ailerons, and surface controls were inspected and replaced.

The plywood sides of the cockpit were completely rotted out and replaced with new plywood. It looked awful, but Nick knew it would eventually be painted bright red. And now that Gunner had covered the entire frame with Irish linen, the Camel was starting to look like a real aeroplane again.

"The fabric looks kind of wrinkly, don't you think, Gunner?" Nick said carefully, not wanting to hurt Gunner's feelings.

"Aye. That's why we paint the whole thing with this stuff," he said, opening the first of many cans of a clear, foul-smelling liquid.

"What's that?"

"It's called nitrate dope. Or just dope. As it dries, it will shrink the linen till its tight as a drum. Then we'll add colors to the dope to paint the whole plane. She'll be a beauty, lad, just you wait!"

———

This morning, Gunner had the U-boat searchlight focused on the engine. This was the part Nick had been most worried about. All the spit and polish on earth didn't matter a hoot if they couldn't get that old Bentley engine Gunner had over-hauled to fire.

"Now, here's the thing, Nick—hand me that spanner, will you please—as I say, here's the thing. There's a lot to be done before we even try to get her to turn over."

Gunner was up on a wooden ladder leaning against the fuse-lage. One by one, he removed the spark plugs from the engine and handed them to Nick. They were corroded, but Gunner had Nick drop them into a pail of alcohol and said they'd be as good as new after a good soaking. Once he was finished preparing the twenty-year-old engine to start, he'd re-install them.

"Be so kind as to hand up that oil can, will you, Nick?"

Gunner took the can and carefully squirted oil into the holes where the plugs had been. It was a painfully slow pro-cess for a boy as impatient as Nick McIver.

"Smells just like the stuff Mother makes me take every day. Castor oil."

"That's because it is castor oil. Only thing these engines will burn. And they burn a lot of it."

"What are you doing now, Gunner?"

"Lubricating the cylinders, which are dry as bone after all

these years. Pistons would freeze up if we didn't do this right. Rings might be rusty, too, y'know–can't be too careful."

"Right," Nick said, trying to understand everything he could about how this flying machine worked. He never knew when he might need that information when Gunner wasn't around to help him.

"Right, that oughta do it," Gunner said, climbing down from the ladder, wiping his hands on his trousers.

"Gunner, for an old navy man, you seem to know an awful lot about aeroplanes."

"Well . . ." Gunner said, his brow furrowing as he searched for words, "I was interested in these things for a while, y'know, but my heart was always out at sea."

Nick laughed. "I know that feeling! So. We're going to fire her up now?"

"Lord, no, boy, we've got to lubricate her first!"

"How do we do that?"

"Well, first of all, we make sure the magnetos are disconnected. If they weren't, and she happened to catch, we'd be chopped to pieces."

Gunner climbed halfway up the ladder and pulled out the two twin knobs that were the magneto switches, mounted on the fuselage just outside the cockpit.

"Ready to go, lad. All you have to do is take hold of the propeller and turn it very slowly. A few times in one direction, a few times in the other, and then repeat the whole thing three or four times. Got it?"

"Aye. But what does that do?" Nick asked, grimacing. Turning the prop was surprisingly difficult. Nick supposed that was because the whole engine spun with the propeller.

"Don't you worry, boy, it gets easier."

"How?"

"Castor oil gets spread around inside. Gets the pistons moving up and down inside the cylinders. Spreads all that oil around in there. Once she's fully lubricated, we'll put some petrol in that tank and give it a shot."

"Today?" Nick asked, his heart pounding.

"Give that prop a few more spins, and we'll see how she feels."

Gunner took two jerricans of petrol and poured them into the Camel's fuel tank.

"Now you're talking, Gunner," Nick said, a flash of excitement in his bright blue eyes. He spun the prop three more times in a clockwise direction and three more times counterclockwise.

"Getting a little easier?" Gunner asked.

"A lot easier," Nick said, relieved. It was tiring work.

"All right, then," Gunner said, mounting the ladder and climbing into the cockpit, "let's say our prayers and light her up!"

Gunner settled down inside the new wicker chair. The nose-up angle at which the aircraft sat on the ground meant he could see nothing in front of him except the blue sky through the barn doors. He had to lean out over the side to see Nick.

"Give me a minute, boy," he said, putting his feet on the rudder pedals and his right hand on the control stick. He moved the stick from side to side and saw the ailerons move up and down at his command. With his left hand, he touched the throttle control and the trim lever. He tried something called the blip switch, which instantly killed the motor, and everything seemed in good working order.

"Ready, Nick? Stand to the left side where I can see you."

"Aye-aye, sir!" Nick said, repositioning himself.

"You remember the starting drill we rehearsed."

"Remember it? I can say it in my sleep."

And then a dialogue began, with Nick asking questions and Gunner answering.

"Ready to start, sir?" Nick shouted.

"Ready to start."

"Fuel on, switches off, throttle closed?"

"Fuel is on, switches are off, throttle is closed."

"Sucking in, sir," Nick said. He reached up and pulled the propeller blade down, repeating the action three times. This drew fuel into the cylinders.

"Throttle set?" Nick cried out. His excitement was building so fast he could barely contain himself.

Gunner moved the throttle lever forward half an inch and said, "Throttle set."

"Contact!" Nick cried.

Gunner reached out and flicked the two magneto switches. "Contact!"

Once again, Nick swung the propeller, pulling down with all his might but this time jumping back with alacrity immediately afterward.

The engine fired and the propeller began turning. There was an explosive sound from the big Bentley engine, a roar and a snort, and the propeller quickly gained speed until it was a blur. The sputtering, barking, roaring engine filled the barn with various noises, all of them deafening. The smell of burning castor oil was sweet perfume.

Nick, who'd tripped over a rake jumping backward, had landed on his bum on the hay-strewn dirt floor. He looked up to see Gunner leaning out over the cockpit and smiling down at him, giving him the thumbs up. Laughing, Nick jumped up and ran to the ladder. He climbed up and put his arms round his old friend and hugged him tightly.

"You're a genius, is what you are, sir! An absolute, bona fide genius! Nobody else could have done what you've done in the last two weeks, Gunner, nobody!"

"We'll let her warm up a bit. You'll need to do that every time."

The engine note rose and fell as Gunner eased the throttle forward a few times, causing masses of smoke to pour forth from the exhaust ports, and then he reached forward and turned the magneto switches off and on again in turn as a safety check. Then, a few minutes later, he hit the kill switch.

The sudden silence was startling.

"It's late, Nick, and your mum will be wondering where you are. I'd get along back to the lighthouse, I was you."

Nick looked at his watch. He was very, very late.

"I'll go. How about you? It's been a long day."

"I want to finish her up tonight. Get her painted so when you bring your dad, she'll look just like the last time he saw her."

"The sketches I drew are on top of that barrel. Have you got paint?"

"Don't use paint. I just add different pigments to the clear dope and brush it on the same way. Sides of the fuselage are olive drab, underbody is buff-colored, and the cockpit sides will be fire-engine red. Sound good?"

"Sounds beautiful."

"It'll take a couple of days for the dope and paint to dry out. What would be a good time to bring your father round?"

"Sunday morning, right after church? We always take the mule and cart, and I'll just tell him there's something I want him to see up here."

"She'll be ready, Nick. Like she just rolled off the production line. Go get yerself some sleep. We've been hard at her for over two weeks now."

"I don't think I'll sleep much tonight," Nick said, dropping down to the ground. "I'll keep hearing that roar when the motor turns over."

"That you will, lad."

"Gunner? I don't want you to take this the wrong way. But I was thinking...before Dad takes her up, do you think it might be a good idea to have Commander Hobbes go over her? Make sure she's airworthy?"

"Already spoken to him, Nick. He's coming round as soon as the paint's dry. Plans to do a complete inspection. And take her up for a shakedown flight. No worries about your dad."

Nick sighed with relief. His friend Hobbes was an aeronautical engineer and England's top weapons designer. If he said the Camel was airworthy, she was airworthy.

The boy paused a moment, brought his right hand up in a proper naval salute to his old friend. "Thank you, Gunner. Thank you for all you've done, for everything!"

"A joy and a pleasure, Cap," Gunner said, returning the salute.

Then Nick turned on his heel and ran out into the night, racing down the new-mown field under the jubilant stars.

Nick yawned, loudly. And just loudly enough so that Mrs. Harmsworth Pettigrew, her broad person and feathered hat occupying a good portion of the pew right in front of McIver family, turned completely around and gave him a decidedly frosty look.

Which caused Nick's mother to give him an even frostier look and a slight poke in the ribs with her sharp elbow. He looked at his sister, who sat primly with her white gloved hands folded in her lap. Suppressing a smile at Nick's rude behavior, she sat staring up at the rotund orator in the pulpit as if he were the most awe-inspiring man in the world, hanging on to his every soporific word.

It was all an act, of course, but then Katie was an exceptionally good actress. Why, just last summer, she'd been able to convince the captain and entire crew of an experimental Nazi U-boat that Nick's Royal Navy friend, Commander Hobbes, was her very own father, the two of them saving their lives and capturing the sub in the process!

"And stop swinging your legs back and forth," Emily McIver whispered sharply into his ear, "it's a distraction to everyone around you! Can't you ever be still for one single solitary second?"

It wasn't that Nick found church especially boring, although that was certainly part of it. No, it was that the melodic sound of Reverend Joshua Witherspoon's deep sing-song voice had a strangely powerful, sleep-inducing effect upon him. He'd seen people hypnotized by swinging pocket watches at fairs and such, and he imagined this was what hypnotism would be like. You don't want to go under, but you can't help it.

Stifling another yawn with the back of his hand, Nick looked around at the faces of the other boys in the congregation. Were they equally affected, too? Or was there something wrong with Nick? Some part of his brain that didn't function like a normal boy's when it came to churchgoing?

Church, in the main, was mostly a mystery to him. There were certainly parts he liked about it. He liked the idea of God and his angels up in heaven, the star of Bethlehem, and the flowers and candles on the altar, and, of course, singing three or four hymns every Sunday. At least when a hymn came along, you got to stand up and gaze out the open windows.

"All rise, as we now join in singing Hymn Number 322."

Sometimes, when the singing started, a stray cow would stick her head inside an opened window and have a good look round at the congregation, noisily chewing her cud. A swarm of angry bees might buzz in on a good day, wreaking havoc before some acolyte shooed them out another window.

Nick, to his everlasting shame, found himself praying for things like that: bees, stray cows appearing; sudden thunderstorms where the doors blew open with a bang and soaked everyone in the rear pews; a mouse scampering up the center aisle toward the choir. All such things rather than heavenly hosts on high, forgiveness of sins, the things he knew he was *supposed* to be praying for. He much preferred seeing the shortest acolyte standing on his tiptoes, reaching up, always unable to light the highest candle on the altar but trying every Sunday nonetheless.

Some Sundays were more difficult than others. If the sermon was about something Nick was actually interested in, say, sailing men lost at sea, or the coming war with Germany, or a great plague of locusts descended upon the land, well, he could get through that, just to see how it came out at the end. But today's sermon was about raising money for a new rectory, and Nick just knew there'd be no surprise ending this morning:

The plate would come around.

Nick picked up his hymnal just so he could sneak a look at his watch. It was almost ten o'clock. Fifteen more minutes and he'd be free! Gunner would be going over every inch of the Camel, polishing the aluminum cowling until it shone like silver, using furniture wax to make the wooden propeller and wing struts gleam. Ah, if his father only knew what he had in store for him this morning.

Gunner had told Nick the previous evening that he had a little ceremony planned for his father at the barn but would spill no more details no matter how hard Nick pressed him. All Nick knew was that this was going to be the best day of his father's life, and he loved his father more than anything. A true hero. Not just during the war but all his life, every single day.

Suddenly the congregation was singing the recessional, and then everyone was paying their respects to Father Witherspoon at the door, shaking his hand, some of them pausing to chat no matter how many people were backed up in the aisle behind them. Nick bolted for the side aisle of the church and ran for the rear door, ducking between two rather large maiden aunts who were focused on charming the unmarried minister.

There were a number of mule- and horse-drawn buggies and carts every Sunday, and Nick ran straight for the Mc-Iver's rig. He wanted to be up in the driver's seat when his family came out. Their old mule, Glory, was calmly munching grass, and Nick took the reins in his left hand and gave the old hollow-backed mule a twitch to get her attention. His father sometimes let him drive the family home, but this morning he wasn't taking any chances.

Soon enough his family emerged into the sun, made their obeisance to the hypnotic shepherd of the flock, and then wended their way toward their cart.

"You driving, Nick?" Angus McIver said, climbing up onto the front seat beside his son. Katie and his mother climbed into the rear seat, Kate telling her mother she thought today's sermon was one of Witherspoon's best.

"I loved the part about humility and unselfishness," Kate said brightly. "I think those are two of my most prominent traits, don't you agree, Mother?"

Nick flicked the reins, biting his tongue.

"May I, Dad? Drive today?"

"Of course, but you seemed in an awful hurry to get out here."

"I've a surprise for you, Father. I thought we might stop for a moment on the way home."

"Another surprise? I hope it's not like the last one. That soldier in the tree."

"Glory, get a move on!" Nick said, twitching the reins again. Then he turned, smiling toward his father.

"Oh, no. Nothing at all like that one, I promise you."

"And where might we find this great surprise?"

"You know that long meadow they sometimes use as a landing strip at Hawke Castle?"

"Yes."

"Near there."

Angus turned around to speak to his wife. "It seems Nicholas has a surprise for us this Sunday, Emily, so we won't be going directly home. Is that all right with you?"

"A surprise? Wonderful. I love surprises. Don't you, Kate?"

Nick instantly looked over his shoulder at his sister with a look that was unmistakable. One word and she was dead. And she knew it.

"I suppose so," Kate said. "Of course, there are good surprises and bad surprises. The last surprise Nick found was a very bad one. I hope this one will be a wee bit better."

Nick sighed his relief. Not great, but it would do.

Saint Peter's was across the road from the cemetery, at the south end of the little town, and Nick turned the cart around and headed south for a bit, then turned east on the little path that bordered his old swimming hole, Dutch's Pond, named for a Dutch Decoy Spaniel who'd ruled the McIver family roost for many years. From there it was only a half mile or so uphill to the turning that led directly onto Lord Hawke's landing strip.

"Nick, where *are* you taking us?" his father said a few moments later.

"Right here," Nick said, reining Glory in.

"Here?" his father said, looking at the woods to either side.

It took a few minutes for him to pick out the greenery-covered barn standing just inside the edge of the wood.

"All right, then," Nick said, "If everyone will climb out of the cart and wait here, I'll go see if everything is ready."

"Every *what* is ready?" his mother said, climbing down from the cart and looking at Kate. Kate shrugged her shoulders and smiled at her brother. She was sharing his excitement now and knew that her father would be terribly exicited by what he was about to see.

Nick had been right. He knew in his heart that waiting inside that barn was the very best secret ever.

Nick walked quickly toward the thickly vine-cloaked barn doors, his heart pounding with excitement. He rapped twice on small area of wood exposed by the door latch

"Ahoy!" he cried. "Squadron assembled and awaiting further instruction!" He and Gunner had worked out the password the night before.

"Standby, Squadron Leader!" he heard Gunner cry from inside.

Nick stood back as the two barn doors were suddenly flung outward from the inside. Nick took a quick step back, astonished to see a small brass band come marching out of the barn in tight formation. The band consisted of six of the island's oldest British Army veterans, former members of the Territorial Yeomanry.

They were playing a rousing rendition of "God Save the King," their battered brass instruments polished to a fare-thee-well, the men resplendent in their somewhat tight-fitting uniforms. Bringing up the rear, a drummer boy, beating a loud tattoo on a magnificent battle drum from the Boer War.

Nick ran back to stand by his father.

"Nick," he said, "what is all this . . . what have you been up to these last few weeks?"

"You've not seen anything yet, Papa!"

From inside the barn there suddenly came the explosive sound of the big Bentley motor catching and roaring to life. Then, to the absolute amazement of former RFC Captain Angus McIver, an old Sopwith Camel came rolling out of the barn and onto the landing strip. It was, could it possibly be, his own aircraft, looking like the day she'd been delivered to his 106th Squadron in France!

Marching alongside the gleaming Sopwith were Commander Hobbes and Lord Hawke, two old friends of the McIver family who had organized the morning's festivities. And bringing up the rear were his lordship's two children, Annabel and Alexander Hawke, ages five and six.

"Morning!" Hawke said, taking a few steps forward and embracing Nick's bewildered father, who seemed to be in a state of shock and incapable of speech.

"Ah, Angus," Commander Hobbes said, "lovely day for a Camel ride, is it not?"

"It simply cannot be," his father said, staring in disbelief at his old aeroplane, now gleaming like a newborn babe in the brilliant sunshine. And, look, there was old Gunner in the cockpit, smiling broadly at all assembled as the Camel, her engine running in loud fits and starts, rolled out onto the sun-dappled grass of the landing strip.

Gunner hit the blip and shut the big engine down—otherwise nobody could hear a bloody thing, even the tuba.

Even Nick was stunned by the Camel's appearance. Not only had Gunner painted the entire aeroplane beautiful shades of olive, buff, and tan, but he'd also added the colorful red, white, and blue British roulon insignias aft of the wings, toward the rear of the fuselage. He'd painted the bull's-eye-like roulons on the upper and lower wings of the biplane and added the distinctive markings of the Black Aces, his father's old squadron.

"It simply cannot be," McIver said, his eyes brimming. "Surely this isn't my . . . why, I–I never thought I'd lay eyes upon her again."

"Your Sopwith, Dad. The one you flew home after the war. Isn't she a beaut?"

"But . . . how? How did this happen? She must have been a heap of skin and bones after all these years in that moldy old barn."

"Gunner and I have spruced her up a bit, Gunner mostly, to be honest. Along with Commander Hobbes, of course, him being an expert aeronautical engineer and all that. He's officially certified her airworthy, Dad. You can fly her again, right now, if you'd like. Your leather flying jacket, helmet, and goggles are in a sack under the rear seat of the cart."

"Why, I–I hardly know what to say."

"Don't say anything, sir," Gunner said, climbing out of the cockpit and down the set of rolling steps Nick had wheeled up next to the cockpit. "There's a lot of blue sky up there waiting for you, Cap'n McIver. Been waiting a long time, too, I'll wager!"

Kate had fetched her father's flying gear from the cart and now handed it to him. "I helped Nicky find it, Papa!"

He kissed the top of her head, "Thank you, darling girl. It's wonderful."

"We topped off the tank, Dad," Nick said, "She's ready to fly, if you wish."

Angus McIver handed Gunner his walking stick and mounted the steps, staring down in wonder inside the cockpit.

"A new seat!" he exclaimed, laughing now. "What I wouldn't have given for that back in winter of '17!"

"And a length of strong hemp to tie you in, sir."

"Now how on earth would an old salt like you know anything about that?" McIver said.

Gunner smiled. "Pretty much a new everything, sir," he said, handing up McIver's flying gear. Angus slipped into his well-worn flight jacket, pulled on his leather helmet, and then slid his goggles up on his forehead. Then he dropped easily down into the cockpit, running his hands over everything, including the ominous-looking black Vickers machine guns, now oiled and polished to a fare-thee-well.

"If I may add my own small gift," Hobbes said, mounting the steps. He then presented Angus McIver with the Royal Flying Corps' traditional long white scarf.

"Why, thank you very much indeed, Hobbes! A most essential part of the wardrobe!" McIver said, beaming as he wound the silk scarf around his neck.

It was essential, too, Nick thought, remembering all the research he and Gunner had done on the Camel. That big rotary engine went through a lot of oil, most of it hitting the pilot. The long white scarves were used to wipe oil from the goggles. And in freezing weather, when a combat pilot was constantly craning his head around looking for enemy aircraft, it saved his neck from chafing on the leather jacket.

"Ready, Captain McIver?" Gunner said, stepping to the front of the aircraft.

"More than ready, Gunner!" Angus McIver shouted, reaching over to switch on the magnetos. He leaned out of the cockpit and gave Gunner a thumbs-up. "Give her a yank and let's have a go!"

Gunner, who was stronger than any other six men Nick

knew, reached up for the prop with his huge hands and gave her such a powerful spin that the propeller actually did a complete rotation. The Bentley caught instantly, roared out her war cry, flame and smoke spouting from her exhaust manifolds.

Angus gave everyone a brief wave, lowered his goggles, then powered up and slowly taxied out onto the long meadow. At the far end stood Castle Hawke. And beyond that, the sparkling blue sea. He let her idle for a minute or so, warming up her oil and refamiliarizing himself with his controls, checking his rudder, ailerons, and elevators.

Lord Hawke, a very distinguished man in his late thirties, tall and handsome as a West End stage star with his sharply chisled features, walked over to Nick and placed a hand on his shoulder. The band was playing again, an old Flying Corps wartime favorite called "The Dambusters," which lent a festive air to the impending takeoff.

"It's nothing short of a miracle, what you've done, Nicholas. You and Gunner. I believe this to be the happiest day of your father's life," Hawke said.

"And mine, sir. It's my gift to him. But I'm going to learn how to fly that machine."

"Are you indeed?"

"I intend to ask my father to teach me."

"Splendid idea!" Hawke said, watching the Sopwith Camel begin to roll forward. "Flying's a skill more boys should learn."

Nick looked up into Hawke's eyes and said, "Indeed, your lordship, especially with a war coming."

"England is going to need lots of young aviators in the coming months, that's for sure."

"They're coming here, and soon, aren't they, sir? The Germans, I mean. Coming to the Channel Islands?"

Hawke, along with Commander Hobbes and Nick's own

father, commanded a group of spies called the Birdwatchers. The spy network had expanded in recent months and now included many members on each of the Channel Islands. Each week they provided much-needed information on German naval and aviation activity to Churchill as he tried desperately to warn his countrymen of Hitler's intentions.

And now that the Germans were in France, only six miles away, military activity had increased dramatically.

"I'm afraid so, Nick. This Hitler may be mad, but he's no fool. He knows you can't launch an invasion against the English mainland without a toehold here in these islands. Napoleon learned that lesson the hard way."

"We'll be ready for them, won't we, sir? When the Nazis come?"

Hawke's attention was diverted by the great roar of the Camel's engine as Angus McIver began his takeoff roll.

"Watch his takeoff carefully, Nick," Hawke said, "We lost many boys who flew these things early on in France. The Camels were beastly brutes to fly until you had a few hours in them. All that weight forward, you see. Engine, pilot, fuel, ammunition. Unlike the Sopwith Pup, which came before, these you had to fly every second, hand steady on the joystick, or they'd dip their fat noses and go into a spin. But Camels were pugnacious little fighters, by God. The German Luftwaffe learned that hard lesson the hard way."

Nick had his eyes on his father as he roared off down the airstrip. There was a strong crosswind, and he was having a bit of trouble keeping her straight. And then, just when Nick thought his father about to run out of runway, the Sopwith Camel lifted her proud nose and climbed magnificently up into the blue English sky. Nick held his hand to his forehead to shield his eyes from the sun. He didn't want to miss a single thing.

The Camel kept her heading, straight for Castle Hawke's great tower, flying about a hundred feet off the ground. When it looked as if Angus was just going to crash straight into the high castle tower, he banked sharply right, then left, making a perfect loop around the massive structure before going into a slight climb.

"Hasn't forgotten much, has he, lad?" Hawke said, a broad smile on his face. "Look, he's headed back this way!"

Indeed, the Camel was headed straight toward them, very low but swiftly gaining altitude. As Nick watched in awe, his father kept climbing, climbing, right through the vertical until the Camel was completely upside down and then arching over, diving straight down toward the ground at a tremendous speed.

"An outside loop!" Commander Hobbes exclaimed. "This chap knows his business!"

Just when Nick thought the Camel would plunge straight into the ground, his father brought her nose up, leveled off, and roared just over their heads, waggling his wings.

"Now you can see why he was an ace," Hawke said. "How many Huns did he shoot down, Nick? Any idea at all?"

"He ended the war with twenty-three victories, sir, awarded both the Distinguished Flying Cross and Distinguished Service Cross, with bar. He'd have had even more had he not been badly wounded."

Hawke looked down at his young friend. The boy's eyes shone with pride for his great hero.

They both turned to watch as the Camel roared to the end of the airstrip and went into a severely steep climb, banked hard right, and raced over the treetops back toward Hawke Castle and the blue waves of the channel. Nick's heart was in his throat, thinking of all the years it had been since his father had done these aerial stunts. Was he pushing himself too far? So full of joy, that he was oblivious to danger? He suddenly wanted his dad back safely on the ground.

But the acrobatics weren't over. The Camel raced south toward the tower, did another perfect loop around it, and then came speeding toward them once more, only a hundred feet in the air.

"Is he going to land?" Nick asked.

"I don't think so," Hawke said. "He's not slowing."

"But what—"

When the Sopwith was less than a few hundred yards from the group watching from the ground, Angus McIver suddenly inverted the plane.

He was flying completely upside down now, and yet he roared just over their heads as if it were the most natural thing in the world. A few hundred yards later, he inverted again, now right side up, did a sweeping left-hand turn over the forest, and lined up for his final approach to the airstrip.

"He's bloody amazing, that's what he is!" Gunner cried, squeezing Nick's shoulder. "Fifteen years in the Royal Navy, and I never saw the like of that kind of flying, I will tell you right now."

"Good thing you remembered that length of hemp to tie him in," Nick said, struggling to deal with the mixture of emotions fighting for space inside his mind. Fear, pride, and joy, all jumbled up.

Moments later, the Camel touched down in a bumpy landing and rolled to a stop just in front of the barn. A moment later, the sputtering big Bentley was silenced.

Nick rolled the steps over to the cockpit as his father hoisted himself up and out of the aircraft and carefully made his way down the steps to the ground, where Gunner handed him his cane.

Everyone raced toward him, cheering and applauding: first his wife, Emily, embracing him with tears running down her cheeks, then little Katie, then each and every one hugging him in turn.

Nick was the last to approach him. "Dad, I was so afraid that maybe you'd–"

"What, son?"

"I–it's been so long–I didn't think you'd remember every-thing and–"

His father bent over until he was eye to eye with his young son. "Nicky, ever since that day I went down in the Ardennes forest, I've been dreaming of this very moment. In my dreams, almost every night, I was doing the things I just did. I remembered everything precisely, you see, how she felt before a stall, how much rudder to apply, how she tends to climb in a right-hand turn, or dive in a left turn because of all that engine torque. I haven't forgotten a thing because I've dreamed every moment of this day every night for over twenty years."

Nick reached up and clasped his hands around his father's neck, pulling him closer so that he could whisper into his ear. "Teach *me*, Dad. Teach me how to do all those things. Teach me how to fly the Camel. Fly her just like you did. Loops, barrel rolls, all of it!"

"Well," his father said, his eyes alight, "I don't know about that. How old are you now?"

"I'm twelve, Dad. You know that."

"Twelve, is it? Well, as luck would have it, I'd just turned twelve when my father taught me to fly in a Sopwith Cub. So I can hardly refuse, can I?"

Nick hugged his father as hard as he could and said, "I love you, Dad. When do we start?"

"First thing in the morning sound good?"

"Oh, yes, it certainly does. Yes, it sounds absolutely wonderful!"

———

And so it was that Angus McIver taught his son Nicholas how to fly an aeroplane. Feet, balletlike on the rudder pedals. A feather touch on the ailerons and elevators. The first months, Nick sat in his father's lap, both their hands wrapped around the joystick. It was terribly crowded, since the cockpit was meant for a single pilot, but they made it work.

In those first weeks, though he'd never admit it, Nick had been frightened out of his wits more than once. The Camel had a mind of its own, and if you weren't extremely careful, you'd find yourself diving out of control in the blink of an eye. Luckily, his father's hands and feet were never far from the controls, and, in an instant, he'd regain control. There were hard lessons well learned, Nick knew, because some day his father would not be there to save his life.

A few months later Nick finally heard his father say the words he'd been both dreading and longing to hear. "Well, Nicholas, I think you're ready to solo."

And solo he did, his heart in his throat, hands trembling, scarcely able to believe that anyone trusted him enough to go up all by himself. What if he forgot something? Let his mind wander even for a split second? What if—no. Such thinking was dangerous in itself. He'd been taught to fly by the best. And he would never, ever let his father down.

Everyone gathered outside the barn and watched the twelve-year-old boy roar down the runway in the twenty-five-year-old aeroplane. His mother held her breath, his father beamed with pride, and his sister jumped for joy when he lifted off the ground.

Although his father had taught him many aerobatic tricks, he thought it best, given the fact that his mother was in the audience, to simply fly straight and level toward Hawke Castle, do a simple banked turn around the tower, and then execute his best landing ever, pulling to a stop just in front of the cheering crowd.

He'd done it! He'd flown an aeroplane by himself! When no one was looking, he pinched himself just to make absolutely sure this wasn't just another dream.

Later, when he and Gunner were alone in the barn, refueling and going over every inch of the Sopwith, he turned to his friend with a question. "Gunner," he said, thoughtfully, "do you think it would be possible for you to make me some bombs?"

"Bombs, is it? What kind of bombs?"

"Small ones, I should think. About the size of a large apple, perhaps. So I could hold one easily in my hand."

"And what, exactly, do you intend to do with these bombs, lad?"

"I intend to make life miserable for those bloody German invaders, that's what I intend!"

Gunner had never seen the boy so fiercely determined in all his days. It was the kind of look he'd seen in men's eyes in wartime before. The kind of look that got brave men killed.

And it very nearly worked out just that way.

· Port Royal, Jamaica, July 14, 1781 ·

Billy Blood's lips were moving. But his long-time companion, Snake Eye, now rowing his captain ashore in the captain's jig, couldn't hear a blasted word the old terror was saying. Crews aboard almost every ship at anchor were firing their flintlock pistols and blunderbusses into the air in a night of drunken revelry.

His royal highness, Captain William Blood by name, sitting atop his throne at the stern of the dinghy, was counting the number of pirate vessels lying at anchor here at Port Royal Harbor, most likely, whispering numbers to himself as he ticked 'em off, sloops, frigates, brigs, and barkentines. And every one of them full of rum-soaked crews and flying one of the many versions of the skull and crossbones.

There were plenty of ships lying at anchor to be counted, Snake Eye saw, but not nearly half so many as he knew Old Bill had been hoping for. Why, he'd told Snake Eye that very morning he was counting on a harbor full of fighting ships laying to at Port Royal when they arrived at Jamaica. The harbor was maybe a third full, at best.

"*Combien de bateaux?*" the Frenchman Snake Eye hissed. "How many?"

"By my bloody count, only seventeen," Blood muttered, clearly displeased.

"*C'est insuffisant, mon capitaine.* Not enough. We'll need ten times that number afore we're done."

"Aye. Maybe ten times that. And more."

Snake Eye, a fearsome seven-foot-tall Algerian-French sea warrior, known far and wide for his cruelty, ferocity, and the tattooed serpents enwreathing his face and the entirety of his bald head, had hoped to see the harbor full. He'd hoped to see outlaw barkys, frigates, and brigantines, lying hull to hull. Blood had invited every living outlaw and pirate in the Caribbean to this big parley at Port Royal. But it looked like precious few had accepted his invitation.

The captain hadn't confided his plans to Snake Eye. No one aboard the *Revenge* had been told the reason for the parley. Blood kept such things to himself. But the Frenchman was content. He'd know soon enough. Old Bill was up to something. And that usually meant lead would fill the air and gold the ship's coffers.

Snake Eye happily dug his oars into the water and pulled mightily. There was a full moon tonight, and the lights along Port Royal's waterfront dives, brothels, and rum dens were all ablaze. This, after all, was the home port of the Brethren of the Coast, as all the pirate captains liked to style themselves. It was the pirates' private enclave, and a stranger entered at his peril.

Snake Eye, after a month at sea, was eager to be ashore, with a belly full of strong Jamaican rum and back in the arms of a plump wench from Cap-Haitien, a beautiful octaroon whom he'd taken a fancy to. Woman called herself Sucre, and sweet as sugar she was, too.

Perhaps by morning, Snake Eye guessed, the harbor would boast a few late arrivals. But there was a great war raging between the English and their rebellious colonists, the Americans. And Snake Eye knew many pirate captains had gone to the aid of either side in hopes of reaping great rewards.

Most had sided with the limeys, of course, believing rightly that the puny American forces under General Washington didn't stand a chance against the Royal Navy, the mightiest fleet on earth, and the deadly wrath of the well-trained British Army.

A full harbor by morning would make old Bill Blood felicitous and that in turn would have a most happy effect on his motley crew. They were a sorry lot, for the most part, half of them escaped prisoners from Bill's daring raid on the hellish penal colony at Hell's Island, and the other half thieving murderers who'd somehow evaded the law and were on the run. It was a far cry from the crew of Blood's last command, a ship's company of highly trained French officers and men who were *la crème* of Napoleon's Imperial French Navy.

Blood, who had already betrayed his native England for Napoleon's French gold, had subsequently lost command of his French frigate, the 78-gun *Mystère,* in a bizarre engagement with a much smaller warship, an English barkentine called *Merlin*. His mutinous French crew had betrayed him in the midst of battle; and a bloody English captain named McIver had taken *Mystère* as a prize off Greybeard Island in the Channel Islands.

In the midst of fierce hand-to-hand fighting on deck, Blood had lost his right hand to an English sword, too, but considered it no loss. He'd replaced it with a solid gold hook mounted on his stump, studded with rubies and diamonds. He kept that hook sharpened to a razor's edge and found in battle he much preferred a sharp hook to five measly fingers.

He looked forward to the day when he could use his hook to good effect on the very man who'd severed his hand, a rich English aristocrat named Hawke. And that devil of a boy who'd absconded with the second golden orb, the mate to Bill's cherished Tempus Machina. The boy was a wily young creature named Nicholas McIver. But Blood would deal with Hawke and the boy, too, soon enough and reclaim the second golden orb for its rightful owner, namely himself.

Once he and he alone had the world's only two time machines in his possession, he need fear no man ever again! Racing back and forth through time and space, no one could catch him, no one could *find* him! In time, the crafty pirate believed, it was his destiny to rule the world. If he could manage to lure the boy to him, the whole world was within his reach.

William Blood was a giant of a man, with flashing black eyes and a full dark beard plaited with tiny silver skulls that chimed like bells whenever he shook his head. Jutting from his mouth, a long pipe fashioned from bone, a human bone, so rumor had it. He wore a long black cape and fancy pantaloons stuffed into his highly polished Hessian boots.

Despite the loss of his French command and his good right hand, he'd at least escaped *Mystère* with his own precious Tempus Machina, that beautiful golden orb that allowed a man to roam through time itself! He had first gone to Paris to beseech the emperor to provide him with another ship to avenge his honor against the English. But Napoleon had received accounts of the action from French officers who'd witnessed Blood's lackadaisical behavior whilst in command of the *Mystère*. And so William Blood had been personally excoriated and humiliated in Paris by Napoleon himself. A French court-martial expelled him from France for eternity.

Rumor was that the enraged Emperor of France had put a price on his head as well. He'd escaped entrapment by the French Navy twice, once in Madagascar and the second time, by the skin of his teeth, in Napoli.

Now that he was wanted dead or alive by at least two countries, England and France, he'd opted for the life of a pirate and found it much more to his liking than the lot of a naval officer serving under either Nelson or, later, Napoleon. No more was Blood beholden to emperors, admirals, and sea lords with more fancy medals than guts or brains. No. He was sole lord and master of his fate, and he alone would conquer them all or die trying.

Billy had scoured the West Indies, Bahamas, and the entire Caribbean for a suitable replacement for *Mystère*. Earlier that spring, spying the huge British warship *Revenge,* lying at anchor one dark night in Nassau Town, he had planned a surprise predawn raid. He had seized the great English frigate in a brief but bloody battle. The limey sailors had been outnumbered two to one by Blood's pirate crew, and now Old Bill had a fine warship of 74 guns beneath his feet.

Snake Eye, perhaps the only man on earth Bill could trust at this point, had been made Blood's second-in-command aboard the *Revenge.* The crew had reacted in shock that such a loathsome-looking creature held their fate in his hands. But they would learn about Snake Eye in the months to come.

He was as fearless in battle as any man Bill had ever witnessed, a seaman to his very bones, and his grotesque tattooed visage struck fear deep in the heart of every man who laid eyes on him, friend and foe alike.

Snake Eye was smart enough to realize quickly that a happy crew was a highly desirable state of affairs for a man suddenly placed in charge of a huge pirate ship. Especially so cantankerous and bloodthirsty a lot as his own. Thus, he tripled their rum rations, doubled their fair share of any prizes or booty taken on the high seas, and guaranteed one week of shore leave for every month at sea.

This unheard-of generosity instantly won him the hearts and minds of every man aboard *Revenge*. And it allowed Snake Eye a more peaceful sleep of a night, with less fear of a dagger in the heart before morning.

"How many ships? How many ships?" the large red parrot perched on Old Bill's shoulder squawked. His name was Bones, and he was nigh on three hundred years old. Bones was Blood's personal winged spy, and a damn good one he was, too.

"Shut up, buzzard. I can't think straight with you screeching in me bloody ears."

"Counted twenty-two, so far, *mon capitaine*," Snake Eye allowed, trying to be agreeable by subtly enlarging the number.

"O'er that way now, and row with a will, damn yer eyes," Billy said, pointing at a black brig moored alongside the town dock. "I think that there may be the *Pearl*, Edward England's brigantine. If she's here, maybe more ships are on their way. He's got a following, you know, down in Dominique."

Snake Eye grunted agreement and took a swig of rum, shipping one oar briefly to drink and then plunging both oars into the silvery water, pulling hard for the *Pearl*, her fore and aft nightlights burning, her stern windows blazing with light.

The crew of *Revenge*, a man-o'-war of 360 tons, carrying nearly two hundred men, had spent the last month sailing all over the Caribbean posting broadsheets advertising the war council the Brethren of the Coast would be holding here in Port Royal this month.

Blood had spent many months planning this momentous event, and he wanted every man and outlaw ship he could lay his hands on. At least a hundred would be needed to accomplish what he had in mind. This paltry lot in the harbor would not do. He'd need a new plan if he was to achieve his goal, and the wheels of his mind started turning immediately as he stared at the hypnotic splashing of Snake Eye's oars.

What Billy had in mind was to make waves. To write his name in blood across the seas and into the history books. How? Why, he meant to build the greatest pirate armada of all time. He meant to claim the world's riches for himself. And, in the doing, inflict a reign of terror on all and sundry who had ever humiliated or betrayed him. There was no shortage of names on that list.

His plan was nothing less than to destroy his two sworn enemies, the French and the English, with a series of bold attacks, breathtaking in their audacity and scope. Then he'd loot their undefended coastal towns at will, confiscating what he wanted. And after that, the world was his for the taking.

"Lay alongside him," Blood told his companion as they neared the stern of the *Pearl*. The man did as he was told and shipped his oars, his gunwale bumping up against the portside hull of the infamous pirate Edward England's brig.

Bill stood in his captain's gig, a little unsteady on his pins, as he'd had a few tots of rum himself, and shouted upward, "Ahoy! Is that dog Edward England aboard?"

A crewman standing the port watch leaned over the rail. "Who wants to know?"

"Tell him it's Blood. Just made anchor. Say I'll meet him at the Black Crow in one hour."

The pirate captain drew one of his two pistols. He didn't like the man's tone. And if the man above didn't mind his manners, Blood planned to put a ball through his tiny brain.

"Captain William Blood himself, is it?"

"Aye, that's who ye've the pleasure of addressing in such disrespectful manner, you bleedin' dog."

There was new respect in the crewman's voice now. Billy Blood was notorious throughout the Caribbean and the Spanish Main as a cutthroat with uncommon devil-like powers. A ghostly figure, he was. It was even rumored he'd appeared in three or four places at the same time, shimmering in and out like some kind of banshee. He'd be spied in Barbados, and a day later someone would see him in Barcelona!

"Aye, Captain, my sincere apologies. I'll convey your invitation forthwith," the crewman said, not taking any chances, and raced up to the poop deck.

"Away," Billy said to Snake Eye. "I want to get there first. The dock by the old Black Crow is just over there. Make haste and I'll finance another jug o' poison and that jolly wench for you."

Snake Eye bent to the oars with a will, and minutes later they'd tied up the gig and were walking through the Black Crow's door. Bill smiled and drew a sharp breath. He was home. He'd taken over the top two floors of the Black Crow Inn as his temporary headquarters.

The four-story building wasn't much to look at, but it was strategically located at the center of the crescent-shaped harbor. From his top-floor veranda, he could look far out to sea for approaching vessels. And with his powerful spyglass, he could watch every move a man made aboard any ship in the Port Royal harbor.

Of course the Black Crow's saloon stank of rank sweat, stale beer, and the sour smell of spilt rum. And at this hour of the night, the intoxicated room was near pandemonium. Indeed, the riotous nature of the place Captain Blood now encountered before him reminded him of a painful scene from his youth.

There was an infamous hospital at Moorfields, just outside London Town, place called Bethlam, or "Bedlam" in the common parlance, where Bill had gone to say his farewells to his poor father when he'd first joined the Royal Navy. Bedlam was where they incarcerated those personages found guilty of incurable "moral insanity." On any Tuesday, for a penny, anyone at all could go and peer into the cells and see the "lunatics," laugh at their antics, generally of a violent or unspeakable nature. Visitors were allowed to bring long sticks with which to provoke or enrage the inmates.

Young William Blood's final farewell to his father was a famous one. Seeing a peasant repeatedly poking his own father in his one good eye with a long spindly stick, he had approached the man from behind, warned him to drop his stick, and, when he didn't, had wrapped his left arm around the man's chest and without further ado grabbed him under the chin with his right hand and ripped the beggar's head right off his shoulders. Gave it a good kick that sent it soaring over the heads of the laughing peasants.

There was a trial at the Old Bailey, a lengthy one to the

delight of the newspapers, but in the end the justices sided with the aristocratic young William Blood, a man with, according to an admiral's testimony, a brilliant future with the Royal Navy.

The two pirates stepped from the street inside the doorway of the Black Crow. At a nod from Blood, Snake Eye pushed and shoved his way through the tumultuous crowd of pirates, privateers, various scalawags, and hangers-on. When he reached the center of the room, Snake Eye leaped atop a trestle table, pulled two flintlock pistols from the bandoliers strapped across his bare chest, and fired them into the ceiling.

Chunks of plaster fell all around him, one piece sufficiently heavy to knock an already insensible pirate unconscious.

"*Mes amis*, silence, if you please," Snake Eye said. "My esteemed commander, famous throughout the world for his bravery and the size of his treasury, has summoned you here tonight because he would like a word. His name is familiar, *mais certainement! Monsieur le capitaine* William Blood!"

A drunken roar went up from the crowd at the sound of that name, for Billy was much esteemed in this part of the world. As he made his way to the table where Snake Eye stood, the crowd parted magically, and many an old crewman stepped forward to pay his respects.

A chant started with a single sailor screaming, "Blood! Blood! Blood!" and soon every voice joined in the cacophony, three hundred dastardly pirates, shouting Old Bill's name to the very rafters.

Bill leaped up onto the table, drew his sword from the scabbard, and raised it into the air, the silver skulls braided into his full beard tinkling like tiny bells.

"This be an historic night by any measure," he began, turning as he spoke so all could have a good look at him. "For when the history books of the future are scribbled down, they will tell of the greatest pirate armada ever assembled. And it will be you men here tonight, you brave and hearty souls, that history itself will be telling about. And those words will be written in blood!"

He paused to let that thought sink in.

"Are ye with me, then?" he screamed and was quickly gratified to hear another thunderous roar.

"My thanks to you all for being first of the brethren to heed the call. But this is just the beginning, lads. By the time we're ready to strike at our enemies, our number will have increased a hundredfold! And then we shall see which empire truly rules the seas! And I tell you now, it will be the empire of Blood!"

The chant of "Blood!" began again, and despite Bill's efforts to silence them, it continued unabated. He nodded at Snake Eye who raised both pistols and fired once more into the ceiling.

"Captains, I address you specifically now. I want you and your crews to sail on the morning tide. You are my messengers, and you will go forth and call all of our brethren to gather here at Port Royal a fortnight hence from this exact day. Describe to them in great detail the formation of this mighty pirate armada and its historic mission. And tell them of the endless riches in store for them that signs on!

"For no ship, city, or town will be spared our wrath as we wreak havoc and plunder on the French, the English, the Dutch coasts, and any ship under any flag foolhardy enough to place themselves in our path! Hard, bloodthirsty work there will be, and plenty, but it'll be well paid for. Double

"His name is Captain William Blood."

wages I said at the start—double wages and a bonus—and what I said, I stand by. I say again, are ye with me? Signify by sayin' Aye!"

The resounding roar was deafening. Old Bill looked closely at Snake Eye and let the Frenchman catch just a trace of the smile on his thin lips as he savored this long-awaited moment. The Caribbean pirates' battle for absolute control of the Seven Seas had finally begun.

10

· Guernsey, Channel Islands, 1940 ·

The Baroness Fleur de Villiers's blue eyes popped wide open. She stared goggle-eyed up at her dog Poppet, standing above her. The little terrier, whose shaggy coat was the same snow-white shade as her own hair, had leaped up onto her bed and now stood atop her silk duvet coverlet. The big four-poster was awfully high off the floor. Never before had Poppet attempted such a death-defying leap. The dog's big brown eyes were gazing meaningfully into her mistress's face. Was there disapproval in that soulful, questioning gaze? Fleur wondered for a moment before the truth struck her.

"Poppet! What on earth?" Fleur de Villiers said, casting a glance at the antique French clock that stood on the carved marble mantel above her bedroom fireplace. A strong shaft of sunlight pierced a crack in the dark green velvet draperies and lit up the face and the golden ormolu of her favorite clock, a gift from her late husband, Osgood. Good heavens, the sun was up—and not recently, either!

"Nine o'clock! What a frightful layabout you must think me, Poppet!" she said, gathering him into her arms and slipping from her bed. "Small wonder, then. You must be ravenous, you poor dear, Poppet. An hour past your breakfast. I must have overslept, mustn't I have? Good Lord, poor Poppet. I never oversleep, you know that."

Then she saw the book splayed on her bedcovers and remembered. She'd been up half the night, dying to finish the latest of her beloved whodunits. This one by her new favorite author, Dorothy L. Sayers, was called *Murder Must Advertise*, and it featured a charming and rather romantic figure by the name of Lord Peter Wimsey. Fleur fancied she had rather a schoolgirl crush on Lord Peter by this point and hoped that Miss Sayers planned to write many more of his dashing adventures.

She picked up the book, inserted her needlepoint bookmark between its pages, and placed the book on her bedside table. Then she slipped into her dressing gown and carried Poppet down one flight of worn wooden stairs to the warmth of the sun-filled kitchen.

Fleur de Villiers had been a voracious reader of mystery novels for most of her eighty years. She practically knew the works of Agatha Christie and Mary Roberts Rinehart by heart. And nothing was more thrilling than to discover veins of new literary gold to mine. A cracking good mystery was her heart's delight, and she found mystery lurking everywhere. And not just in the pages of the countless hundreds of books lining the sagging shelves in every room of her rambling cottage.

But at Fordwych Manor, not all the books were mysteries. There were a few of dear old Osgood's military volumes. And some scientific works, mostly in Latin. On a Chippendale desk in the large bay window of her library stood a stack of memoirs, biographies, and autobiographies. But these books were strictly for instructional purposes, not enjoyment.

Unbeknownst to anyone on the island of Guernsey, the Baroness de Villiers herself had become an aspiring author. She was writing, in fits and starts, her memoirs. The title? *The Mystery of Life.*

She knew her title wasn't quite right, not yet. Still, it was only a working title, as they called it. It was just "off" a wee bit, and she worried that it might sound too pretentious and all-knowing. She feared some readers might even mistake it for some obtuse philosophical treatise on the meaning of it all or eternity, or some such silly nonsense.

But her book *was* about the mysteries of life, wasn't it?

Yes, the big and the small, the solvable and the insoluble, she loved them all. As her dear friend Sybil Hathaway, the Dame of Sark, had once remarked of life, "The whole thing's one big mystery, and then the curtain falls, and we all have to sail out of the theater before seeing how it all comes out!"

Life was one big mystery, wasn't it?

Cook having given her her standard breakfast, a single boiled egg in a Minton cup, a pot of tea, and a solitary scone, unbuttered, Fleur returned upstairs to dress. She peered outside her opened dressing-room window to the gardens below. It was a blustery spring day, sun peeking in and out, with a scent of rain on the wind. Best take the mac, she thought; she had a good two-hour ride ahead of her.

———

Her bicycle, an ancient Raleigh with a large wicker basket mounted over the front fender, had been in service for many years. She also owned a car, of course, a venerable Rolls-Royce

Silver Ghost, circa 1920, but she seldom used the old Ghost unless the weather was prohibitive. Or if she was attending some dinner party or some gay soirée where tippling might be involved.

On those occasions, her chauffeur, who lived in apartments above the garage, would be called upon. His name was Eammon Darby. He was a funny little Irish bachelor, a smiling leprechaun of a fellow who was nearly seventy himself. Over the decades, they'd become fast friends. He was of good cheer, good at his job, and he took his responsibilities extraordinarily seriously, a trait Fleur admired in anyone in any trade.

Eammon kept the twenty-year-old Rolls looking as shiny and new as the day it had rolled off the Guernsey ferry from the mainland, Osgood having driven the vehicle down to the docks at Portsmouth from Mr. Jack Barclay's automotive emporium in Berkeley Square, London.

"Good morning, young Eammon," she said, entering the garage to retrieve her bicycle. Darby was already hard at it this morning, of course, polishing the great long silver bonnet, perched perilously atop a wobbly stepladder. The Ghost was immense, and Eammon, a former jockey who'd once rode Celsius to victory in the Grand National, was barely five feet tall in his stocking feet.

"Morning, ma'am," he said, pausing ever so briefly to lift his woolen cap.

"Anything interesting to be found on Auntie Beeb last night, Mr. Darby?"

Eammon Darby's idea of an evening's entertainment was pulling an armchair up to the old wireless after his supper, sipping his tea and Irish whiskey, and listening to the BBC all evening.

"There's talk all of our British soldiers are pulling out, ma'am, leaving the islands. Troop transports on the way, they say."

"What?" she said, putting a hand to the wall to steady herself.

"Yes, ma'am. Whitehall says our Channel Islands are of 'no strategic importance' in the coming war."

"You must be joking."

"I only wish I was. We'll be left defenseless against those Jerries, and no doubt about it. I'm worried for your safety, ma'am."

"Defenseless? I hardly think so, Mr. Darby!" the baroness said, composing herself and climbing aboard the Raleigh. She pushed off and was soon turning into the lane that led down to the coast road. It was Saturday, and today was the day she did her weekly coastal surveillance along the south shore.

She let the phrase linger on the tongue of her mind: *coastal surveillance.* Observation. Detailed maps of possible invasion sites. This is what filled her watercolor sketchbook. Not to mention U-boat sightings and the locations of various Luftwaffe bomber and fighter squadrons conducting sorties off the coast of France.

Baroness Fleur de Villiers, as it happened, had, at her rather advanced age, found herself...well, there was no other word for it...a spy.

And one not at all like those pretend, arriviste ladies auxiliary groups, up on their rooftops every night with their opera glasses, sipping champagne and looking for Heinkel bombers. No, she was the real thing all right. Spying on one's enemies, like any trade, was something to be taken very seriously.

Fleur knew there were only six miles of open water across the channel to France. And that's where the Germans were now, having bypassed the much-vaunted Maginot Line and attacked France with masses of Panzer tanks through the Ardennes forest.

They had France by the throat now, the Nazis did. The Huns held Paris, and everyone knew that England was next on Herr Hitler's shopping list. It was only a matter of time before the red, black, and white swastika flags were planted on English soil. His obvious first stop would be her own Channel Islands.

Fleur de Villiers was a charter member of a very secret espionage society called the Birdwatchers. It had been formed the summer before on the little island of Greybeard by the estimable Lord Richard Hawke and a lighthouse keeper named Angus McIver. They were a formidable group of spies now, numbering nearly one hundred, and they included cells on each of the tiny Channel Islands.

All of these Birdwatchers, in one way or another, reported directly to Winston Churchill himself. The baroness had been elected to lead the little band here on Guernsey, and in addition to her daily surveys of activity on the island, it was also her role to collect all the information gathered by the Guernsey Birdwatchers on German activities each week.

Then, every Wednesday, she would make her way to a deserted beach in the middle of the night. In her bicycle basket was the waterproof packet containing that week's intelligence, to be ferried over to Lord Hawke on Greybeard Island. A fisherman from Greybeard, a chap named Derry Moore, would anchor his fishing boat just offshore. He'd then row his dinghy to a small cove hidden from the road, and there the Baroness de Villiers, hiding in the shadows of the cove, would pass him her precious packet. It was thrilling, every bit of it.

It was then up to Lord Hawke, whose ancient family had been friends of the de Villiers for years, to somehow manage to get the entire week's intelligence reports across the channel to the mainland and ultimately to Churchill himself. And do it under the very noses of the horrid Nazis, whose U-boats were everywhere these days!

She found the whole thing all rather exciting, to be honest. After all, for a woman who loved mystery, what on earth could possibly be more full of mystery and excitement than the life of a real live spy?

She was thinking just that, peddling merrily along the coast, when she heard the roar of countless German bombers passing directly over her head. She stopped, climbed off her bicycle, and looked up the underside of the heavy bombers: the red, white, and black swastikas painted on the wings; the bomb bay doors clearly visible in the bellies of the beasts.

It struck her then, like lightning, just how vulnerable her little islands truly were. She could almost see those German bomb bay doors opening slowly, see the silvery bombs come tumbling out, raining death and destruction wherever they fell.

Perhaps Eammon was right, she thought with a shiver. After all, they had no militia. No Home Guard, to speak of.

Perhaps, after all this, they actually *were* defenseless.

· Greybeard Island ·

Had she known about it, the Baroness de Villiers would have been much cheered by events taking place at that exact moment just a few miles across the sea from where she now stood beside her bicycle.

A young saboteur was already plotting his own resistance against the inevitable Nazi invasion. Young Nicholas McIver, the would-be saboteur, was seated in the cockpit of a vintage 1914 Sopwith Camel, watching his friend Gunner prepare for his first bombing run of the morning.

Gunner was stepping off the width of Lord Hawke's grassy landing strip. He had a large wooden rain barrel in his hands. When he reached dead center of the strip, he placed it firmly on the ground. He turned the barrel so the bright red swastikas he'd painted on the staves would be visible to his pilot. He looked over at Nick, some fifty yards away, and gave him the thumbs-up signal. Nick flashed Churchill's famous *V* for *Victory* sign, and Gunner marched across the new mown grass to the Camel.

"She's dead center, lad," Gunner said. "Exactly halfway

down the length of the strip, and smack dab in the middle of it. Are you ready?"

"I was born ready, sir!" Nick said, smiling down at his friend.

"Well, don't expect much on your first few runs. It's a tricky business, this aerial bombing. I spent years behind a twelve-inch naval gun, most of them practicing. So, don't expect miracles. Going to take a great deal of trial and error before you become any good at this, y'know?"

"Aye. But we've not much time left according to the BBC last night. The assault could come at any time now."

Gunner shook his head in agreement. "We're going to be all on our own, y'know."

"What do you mean, Gunner?"

"I mean I was over to Guernsey just yesterday evening, visiting me mum. There were troop ships in the harbor, Nick. All the British soldiers are leaving."

"Leaving? I can't believe it!"

"Every last one. Apparently it's been decided in London we're not worth defending. All the British troops are sailing for home on the evening tide."

Nick regarded his friend for a long, hard moment before he said, "Well, then, nothing for it, is there? I fancy it's going to be up to us, all of us on these islands, to defend ourselves."

Gunner shook his head in agreement, but there was a mixture of sadness, fear, and anger in his crinkly blue eyes. Farmers and fishermen against battalions of crack Nazi SS units? It was likely to be a a short and very lopsided battle.

"Let's have a last look at your bomb basket, boy," he said finally, forcing a cheery smile.

Nick reached down and lifted the small wooden peach basket from his lap. It looked to be full of white cotton beanbags.

"How many bags in the basket?"

"I thought I'd start with ten. Do ten runs. See how I do. Then I'll land and we can look at the patterns around the barrel, figure out what I'm doing wrong. Then I'll go back up with ten more sacks and keep going until we get it right."

"Good thinking. We won't quit until you've dropped ten bags in a row into the heart of the barrel! Ready to start, Cap'n?"

"Ready to start, sir."

"Fuel on, switches off, throttles closed?"

"Fuel is on, switches are off, throttle is closed."

"Sucking in," Gunner said, rotating the blades three times. "Throttle set?"

"Throttle set!"

"Contact!"

"Contact! Give her a good, strong rip!"

Gunner and Nick had spent many of their previous evenings in a secret upstairs room at the Greybeard Inn. Gunner, the proprietor of the inn, called it his "Armoury" and the room was filled with all manner of weaponry—swords, firearms, small cannons, barrels and barrels of black powder. Battle flags from all nations hung out from the walls. It was one of Nick's favorite places.

While Nick sat at the center table, poring over World War I–era books on the principles of aerial bombardment, Gunner was at his workbench, filling small cotton pouches with lead shot and white flour. Sixteen ounces of shot and one cupful of flour went into each little sack before he stitched it up. This is what they'd practice with.

While Nick had been honing his flying skills night and day, Gunner had been busy making real bombs, too. Sixteen ounces was the weight of the live bombs he'd been making for Nick over these last weeks. The black one-pounders he'd designed for the young pilot were perfectly round and roughly the size of a large apple. They were filled with an oily liquid called nitroglycerine and surrounded by black gunpowder. Nitroglycerine was an extremely powerful explosive and extremely sensitive to shock. So each of Gunner's bombs was basically a pound of dynamite that would explode on contact with any solid surface.

To test his new weapon, he and Nick had climbed out of the attic window on the fourth floor of Gunner's inn, crawled to the edge of the roof, and Nick had heaved one of the very first bombs produced out onto the seaside rocks. The resulting fiery explosion sent chunks of rock a hundred feet into the air and left a vast hole on the shore where boulders had stood. The blast far exceeded Gunner's wildest expectations, and the huge smile on Nick's face made all the work worthwhile.

But this morning they wouldn't be using real bombs for their practice. They'd be using small sacks of flour.

Gunner pulled down on the propeller, and she fired up instantly. Nick then taxied out toward the barrel, made a quick right turn and firewalled the throttle selector. He was airborne moments later and flew out over Hawke Castle and the sparkling blue sea below. Making a tight left-hand turn, he slowed the aeroplane, lined up at the leading edge of the airstrip, and leveled off at two hundred feet. He adjusted his goggles and concentrated on the approaching target. The barrel was coming up fast.

He grabbed a sack from the basket, held his hand out over the side of the cockpit ... waited ... and let it fly.

Looking back down over his right shoulder, he saw a small

puff of white explode on the grass. Miles from the barrel! What? How could that be? He'd been sure he was spot on the target. But he'd overshot the barrel by at least a hundred feet. His drop had obviously been far too late. He banked hard right and went around for another approach.

This time he slowed the aeroplane considerably and dropped his altitude to one hundred fifty feet. He was well aware that he'd be vulnerable to ground fire if he flew his runs this low, but he felt he had to perfect his aim at any altitude.

Gunner watched him come roaring up the strip, saw him waggle his wings once, and saw the little white pouch hit the ground way to the left and about fifty feet shy of the barrel. He'd dropped it too soon. Nick made seven more bombing runs, and all of his drops were wide of the mark. Gunner knew he had one more flour bomb aboard.

He did a slow looping turn out over the sea and got lined up for his approach to the strip early. He kept her dead straight as he approached the barrel, flying right down on the deck at about fifty feet. Gunner saw his right arm extend out of the edge of the cockpit, saw the bag fly ... and drop right into the center of the barrel.

The boy immediately climbed, did a barrel roll just over the treetops, and circled the field for the downwind leg of his landing. He banked left, straightened out, and began his final approach.

When Nick had parked the Sopwith and walked over to Gunner, he had a sorely disappointed look on his face. He was surprised to see Commander Hobbes standing outside the barn beside his friend.

"Well done, lad, well done, indeed!" Hobbes said, clapping him on the back. "I saw that last one!"

"Only one out of ten, sir, to be honest. Quite a bit more difficult than I'd imagined. I may not be cut out for a bombardier, after all, looking at that sorry result out there."

"Practice, practice, practice, Nick. That's all it takes. Now, both of you come inside the barn. I've brought along some equipment I developed in the laboratory that I want to show you."

Hobbes, a scientific genius if ever there was one, was the Royal Navy's most famous weapons designer. He'd designed the world's first two-man submarine and a dozen other items and weapons the Royal Navy used on destroyers, battleships, and submarines every day. His recent capture, with the help of Nick's sister Kate, of the highly experimental Nazi U-boat U-33 had provided the navy with an untold treasure trove of the latest German technology, including the Crossfire propulsion system.

Inside the barn, Gunner had a lamp burning on his worktable. There were two items on the table. A long metallic tube and a rather large wooden box with brass fixtures.

"What's this?" Nick asked, picking up the metal tube. It was surprisingly light.

"Believe or not, it's lead, Nicholas," Hobbes said. "I've milled it down to one-sixteenth of an inch, but it should do the job. Without adding too much weight."

Hobbes took the tube and unrolled it out on the table. It was about four feet long and three feet wide.

"There. That should do very nicely, don't you think?" Hobbes asked, sounding very pleased with himself.

"Do what, sir?" Nick said.

"Why, protect you during your bombing raids, Nick. It's made so that it exactly conforms to the shape of the cockpit floor. And up the sides as well. We'll have to take the seat out and reattach it of course, but that will be no problem."

"How will it work?"

"It's very thin, I know, but I've invented an entirely new process. It's a thin wafer of titanium sandwiched between two lead sheets. That's made it strong enough to withstand enemy ground fire, should you encounter any. I tested it myself with a German Mauser rifle and a fifty-caliber machine gun just this morning. See those small dents? Dents, not holes, are what one looks for in a bulletproof shield."

Nick considered the thought of machine-gun rounds thumping just beneath his feet.

"Nelson the strong, Nelson the brave, Nelson the Lord of the Sea."

As usual, his little prayer bucked him up a bit.

"It's a brilliant idea, if I may say so, Commander," Gunner said. "I don't know why I didn't think of it myself."

"Too busy building bombs, I'd say," Hobbes said with a laugh. "Now. Take a look inside this case of mine."

He unsnapped two latches and opened the lid.

Nick peered in and had no idea what he was looking at. "What on earth is it, Commander?"

"A camera, Nick, a German camera, as a matter fact, since they make far and away the best lenses. It's a highly modified Leica I designed for aerial surveillance."

"You want me to take pictures from the plane? While flying? Sorry, Commander, but it's all I can manage to keep it aloft with both hands on the stick."

"No, no. When I said *modified*, I meant it. Rather a new idea I think, and I'm quite proud of it."

Hobbes lifted it out of the box and placed it on the table. It certainly didn't look like any camera Nick had ever seen. Besides, it was very complicated looking, very large, and quite heavy looking. Nick suddenly began to feel overwhelmed by the idea of flying an aeroplane in combat conditions. He loved adventure and a good challenge, but perhaps he'd gotten himself in over his head.

"With all due respect, sir, I don't think I could even lift that thing up over the sides of the cockpit, much less take a picture with it. I need my hands on the controls every second of flight."

"You don't have to, Nick! You see this section here on the bottom of the device? That's the mounting bracket. The camera mounts on the underside of the aircraft. Just beneath the cockpit."

"And how do I . . . shoot it, then?"

"See this silver button? Called a shutter release and attached to a very long wire. The wire will be fed through a hole in the bottom of the cockpit and attach to the camera. I will mount the shutter button within easy reach, right on your instrument panel. When you're over an area or object you want to shoot, say, a ship in Saint Peter Port on Guernsey, you simply press the button and take the picture. A bit ingenious, if I do say so myself."

"Pictures of the port? What else?"

"I'll explain our needs in detail later, Nick. I fully intend to take you and Gunner into my confidence. But you must swear never to breathe a word. Churchill fought within the government to keep the troops in place on the Channel Islands and lost. But that doesn't mean he's given up on you. Once the Germans have invaded, he plans to make raids on these islands, with an eye toward driving the invaders out."

"Good news to me ears, Commander," Gunner said with some emotion. "And for me poor heart as well. I thought we'd all been thrown to the wolves."

"Not so far as Prime Minister Churchill is concerned. He

knows the Germans plan to fortify the islands as part of their Atlantic Wall. Hitler's aim is to control the channel during any future Allied attack on the European mainland."

"I'm happy to help, sir. Just tell me what you'd like me to do," Nick said. He knew his work was important. This was no time for worry and queasy stomachs.

"Nick, I'm going to mount the camera on the Camel's underside now. Shouldn't take more than an hour. Would you mind suspending your practice bombing runs for the afternoon? If so, we could do a test of our photo recon system right away. Before the sun sets, at any rate. You might fly over to Guernsey, take some photos of Saint Peter Port. They've begun to evacuate schoolchildren and some parents who wish to leave with ships provided by His Majesty. Your pictures could be helpful there. I've brought a chart along to help with your navigation."

"I'm a sailor, sir. Guernsey's due west, no matter how you get there."

"Quite right, Nick," Hobbes said with a laugh.

"Who are the pictures for, Commander?"

"Prime Minister Churchill, eventually. Right now the War Office at Whitehall wishes to keep track of all events here preparatory to any attempt to retake the islands from the Germans."

"Commander," Nick said, eyeing the man carefully, "if Guernsey is evacuating children, shouldn't we be as well?"

"It's a decision each family must make for itself. But I'm going from here out to the lighthouse to discuss exactly that matter with your father."

"It's our home," Nick said, his brow furrowed. "We're patriots. He won't leave it, and neither will I."

"I certainly understand that feeling, Nick. But there are a

lot of things to consider. Every family will have to weigh the options of going or staying."

"I suppose you're right, sir," Nick said, not at all sure that he was.

"What's happening on the other islands, Commander?" Gunner asked.

"Each is different. In Jersey, the majority of islanders have chosen to stay, no matter what. That's their choice. Authorities on Alderney have recommended that all islanders evacuate, and nearly all plan to do so. The Dame of Sark has encouraged all of her 471 inhabitants to stay put on Sark, and no doubt they will bend to her iron will."

"Let's get moving, then" Gunner said. "We haven't got all day. I'll install the lead shield in the floor of the cockpit, while you get that camera mounted, Commander."

"And how can I help?" Nick asked Hobbes.

"That book on the table. *Dynamic Principles of Aerial Bombardment.* You could spend another hour with that. Based on the pattern of your first attempts, I'd recommend you pay special attention to Chapter Seventeen. It covers the principles of speed, elevation, and distance to the target. I'm especially proud of that."

"Proud?"

"Notice the name of the author on the cover?"

"RAF Flight Lieutenant B. Hobbes? That's you?"

"Lieutenant Bertram Hobbes, at your service. Book's a bit outdated now. But a bestseller in her day! Garnered some first-rate reviews from Bomber Command, I will say."

"Are you a betting man, Commander?" Gunner said, rubbing his grizzled chin.

"Indeed."

"Give the lad an hour or two with that bombing book, and

I'll wager five quid this boy will put ten straight sacks of flour right in the throat of that barrel out there by sundown tomorrow."

"Nick?" Hobbes said, smiling. "What do you think?"

"I wouldn't bet against me, sir."

"Nor would I, lad, nor would I."

12

HOME ON A WING AND A PRAYER

· Guernsey Island ·

Nick McIver's first mission as a civilian reconnaissance pilot may have commenced without a hitch. But before the day was over, he'd be a far, far more seasoned aviator. A battle-tested aviator.

As he began his bumpy roll down the grassy airstrip, keenly anticipating that great thrill when the wheels separated from the earth, he'd caught sight of the top of a familiar tree off to his right. It was the one where he and Kate had found the dead German spy just weeks ago.

The Germans were sending reconnaissance flights over the islands on an almost weekly basis now. What if he came upon one of those German planes? Would he be fired upon? Did those kinds of aircraft even have weapons? But the real question in his mind was whether or not he should try to use the twin Vickers machine guns to defend himself.

They were loaded, but Gunner had not yet trained him in their use.

If he did encounter a German aeroplane flying at low altitude, at least he could take a picture of it. And what if a U-boat should happen to surface? He could certainly dive down and get pictures of that! Surely that's the kind of thing Hobbes and Lord Hawke would be looking for. Any kind of German military activity at all.

He took off to the north, soaring out over Hawke Castle, then banked hard right, flying right along the south coast of Greybeard Island. He could see the fearsome Gravestone Rock thrusting from the sea and, not far away, his home, the Greybeard Light, standing high above the sea at the north-western tip of the island.

His first recon picture would not be for the military analysts at Whitehall in London, it would be for his mother. He intended to take a picture of their home from the air, have it framed, and present it to his mum on Mother's Day. Most of the tower was enwreathed in roses now, and it would make a splendid picture, he thought.

He circled the lighthouse a few times looking for the best altitude and angle. It was a sunny day, with puffy white clouds, and he knew the picture should be lovely. Flying about fifty feet above and beyond the lighthouse, he reached for the silver shutter release button and pressed it three times. One of them at least would be perfect, he thought.

The first part of his mission complete, he turned the plane right, coming to a heading of 270 degrees, due west. He climbed to two thousand feet, exhilarated by the mere notion of what he was doing. Aerial espionage in the service of his country. Sure, the soldiers had all gone and most of the island people would probably evacuate.

But Nick McIver planned to stay and fight.

His next stop was Saint Peter Port on the nearby island of Guernsey. The great rocky cliffs and green rolling meadows of this large neighboring island were already visible across the blue channel waters. Saint Peter Port hove into view. It was built on the slope of a hill, with tier upon tier of tall red-roofed houses clustering down to the water's edge. The houses were a mixture of French Provincial and English Georgian, with gardens high-walled against the constant winds.

On the southern side, the town was protected by a great green height on which Fort George was situated. It was the largest of the four Victorian naval forts built in the 1850s. This was a period when HM Government had been much worried about its relations with France, just six miles across the water.

Descending to one thousand feet, he made his first pass over the town's harbor. It was filled with ships of every description. Troop ships, merchantmen, even cinnamon-sailed fishing vessels, silhouetted against the irregular houses which lined the quay. The shutter release, right next to his altimeter, seemed to be working perfectly as he clicked off a dozen or so shots of the crowded harbor from different angles.

Along the quay, a massive queue of people stretched all the way back along the High Street and into the main square at the center of town. Carts and farm trucks stacked high with luggage; countless children and their parents waiting patiently in line to board the waiting vessels that would ferry them back to England.

He dropped down to a hundred feet and buzzed the crowds along the quay. Many of the children looked up and pointed at the funny-looking biplane, delighted by the sight of the old relic from another war. Surely, Nick thought, none of them had ever seen such a craft outside of their history books.

He waggled his wings as he flew over their heads, and he

saw many of the adults look up and smile at him, many of them even cheering and clapping their hands at the sight of a British warplane, even one as ancient as the Sopwith Camel, roaring just above their heads.

Nick leaned over the edge of his cockpit and smiled down at them, flashing Churchill's Victory *V* with his right hand. Then he put the Camel into a steep climb and, not without regret, turned eastward for home. He hadn't encountered any U-boats or German spy planes, not yet anyway, and he thought he'd gotten more than enough shots of the harbor to satisfy Commander Hobbes's requirements.

Did he really have to end this adventure so quickly? He took a quick look at his watch. He'd been gone only an hour. He had plenty of time to do a little exploring on his way home. He decided to go south along the Guernsey coastline, see what it looked like from the air. Who knows, he thought, maybe he'd even spy something interesting to photograph along the way?

He was content to simply fly along the coast, experimenting with his rudder and ailerons, using every second to get a better feel for flying the pugnacious little plane. But his mind was much clouded with worry. If all those children were leaving Guernsey, what about his own family? Especially his mum and his sister Kate. He had no doubt he and his father could manage living under German authority, but weren't all the women and children living on Greybeard Island at greater risk?

If, as Hobbes had mentioned, England determined to later retake the islands by force, why, that would mean all-out war then, wouldn't it? There were sure to be civilian casualties, and he was certain the Germans would show the islanders no mercy. What if they bombed the lighthouse? Or threw them all in prison? What if—

He looked down expecting to see the rocky shoreline and saw nothing but open water. By not concentrating on what he was doing, he'd veered far off course. He was now flying a heading of almost due south, far out over the Gulf of Saint Malo! Clouds had drifted in from the west, big white puffy ones that looked to have rain in them.

Ahead, he could see a green smudge on the horizon. That had to be the coast of Brittany and Normandy! There were sure to be enemy planes in the skies over France, and not reconnaissance flights either. No, there'd be Messerschmitts manned by deadly Luftwaffe pilots only too happy to blow him out of the sky.

He banked hard to his left, set a northeasterly course. He soon saw the distant cliffs of Greybeard on the horizon and set his course for home. Just fly the plane, he told himself. Feel every vibration coming from the aeroplane. Listen to every sound coming from the big Bentley engine. Learn those sounds, memorize them, so that if you ever heard a false note, you'd immediately know what the problem–

What was that? There was a boat below. Too big to be a local fishing boat, too small to be a destroyer or battleship. She was off to his starboard side and steaming along at a leisurely pace toward the coast of Brittany. An unaccompanied boat headed for France. It was unlikely to be English, Nick thought, easing the stick forward and going into a dive down through the clouds. He'd do a flyover, have a look, and if she was anything interesting, he'd snap her picture.

Not wanting to alarm the crew aboard her unnecessarily, he kept his altitude deliberately high, about five hundred feet. A few moments later he was directly above her. She was German military, all right, with cannons mounted on her bow. Along each side were racks holding great black spherical objects, perhaps fifty inches in diameter, with many protrusions. At the stern, men on both starboard and port sides were rolling these spheres down metal ramps and into the sea.

Between the ramps, snapping in the breeze, a large red flag with black stripes and a black swastika on a field of white.

She was a German minelayer. She was mining the waters off France with contact mines. He'd studied enemy mines in some detail when he'd first begun to help his father and the Birdwatchers monitor U-boat traffic in the channel. These were German electromagnetic mines, each containing almost 700 pounds of high explosives. Those protrusions were called Hertz horns, and they would detonate the mine upon contact with the hull of an enemy ship.

Nick maintained his northerly heading, thinking the situation over. He had to get a picture of this minelayer at work, no question. This could be vital military information. But he didn't like the look of those naval cannons on the bow or the swivel-mounted fifty-caliber machine guns visible on either side of the bridge. Some of the sailors had smiled up at him and even waved their caps at him on the first pass. Would they be as friendly if he made a second one? Perhaps they would. Few of the young German sailors aboard would even recognize the aircraft as being British.

And, after all, a silly-looking biplane from another era, made of sticks and cloth was hardly a threat to a heavily armored German warship.

He banked right and flew south once more, staying high and well away from the minelayer. He pressed the shutter button once or twice to ensure that it was still functioning and getting pictures of the minelayer's position relative to the coast of France. A few minutes later, he initiated a wide, sweeping turn that would bring him back on a course that would intercept the German vessel from dead ahead.

This time he would fly over her at a much lower altitude. He'd keep the index finger of his right hand on the shutter button the entire time, shooting as fast as the camera would allow. He used his long white scarf to wipe the oil from his goggles, adjusted them, and watched the boat's bow wave draw ever closer. He soon found himself looking right down the barrels of the ship's deck guns, his wheels almost skimming the wavetops!

He intended to pull his nose up just as he crossed her bow, clear her amidships smokestack, and get his pictures at a very low level.

Now! He pulled back on the stick with his left hand and began repeatedly pushing the silver button with his right. He was dimly aware of a strange thumping noise beneath his feet, when suddenly he realized they were shooting at him! Rounds were striking Commander Hobbes's leaden shield. And being deflected! If they weren't, he'd most certainly be dead by now.

He cleared the minelayer's stern, went to full throttle, commencing the steepest climb possible. Rounds from the German machine guns were whistling overhead now and all around the cockpit. He saw many holes appearing in his overhead wing, mostly on the starboard side. Then a lucky bullet struck a wing support strut and caused it to buckle, collapsing a small part of his upper starboard wing.

He had to get out of this deadly fire and soon. He eased the joystick forward going into the steepest dive he'd ever attempted, twisting and turning all the way down. When he was within a few yards of crashing into the sea, he pulled out of the dive and leveled off, flying just above the wavetops for a moment. Suddenly he started climbing again, gaining enough altitude to execute a series of barrel rolls, as he made for the safety of the towering white cumulus cloud just above him.

He was worried about that starboard wing. Fabric was beginning to tear away under the strain of his violent maneuvers. More struts could likely give way. *Take it easy*, he reminded himself, *take it easy*.

He cleared the cloud layer, leveled off, and took a quick look down over his shoulder at the German minelayer, hundreds of feet below and continuing on her course toward the coast of Brittany.

He was clearly out of range of the ship's fire now and his plane was still basically intact. If he was lucky, the wounded Camel would hold together long enough to get him back to Hawke Field in one piece. He flew on, keeping a watchful eye on the damaged wing. It seemed to be getting worse, and he reduced his airspeed to a minimum.

"Nelson the strong, Nelson the brave, Nelson the Lord of the Sea," he whispered. It was both a tribute and a prayer to his long dead hero, Admiral Lord Nelson.

What was that old expression he'd heard his father say so many times? Oh, yes. *Flying home on a wing and a prayer.*

DEATH FROM ABOVE

· Guernsey Island ·

After completing her customary surveillance tour of the harbor, Fleur de Villiers leaned her bicycle against the stone wall just up the hill from Monsieur de Lupin's French bakery shop. She quickly descended the cobblestoned street and hurried inside. She wanted to get her last bit of shopping done and then get herself home and home quickly.

Wild rumors were flying all over the island that the German invasion was imminent. Still, she'd seen no trace of any panic. The countryside was somnolent as usual. It was all business as usual in town. A stream of covered farm trucks lined the quay, filled with ripe tomatoes ready for shipment across the Channel to England.

She hadn't really wanted to go into town.

But she'd invited Lord Hawke and a small group of acquaintances, plus some literary friends, for a smallish dinner party at Fordwych Manor this evening. Cook, as she headed out the door, had informed her that she was all out of bread and caviar. Cook could bake some sourdough biscuits of course, but there wasn't a baguette on the island that could hold a candle to those baked by her old friend from Paris, Monsieur Jean-Paul de Lupin.

She found him and several other customers gathered around the old wireless, listening breathlessly to the sonorous voice of the BBC announcer. From the somber looks on their faces, the news was grim.

"Jean-Paul, *mon cher,*" she said, patting him on the back to gain his attention, "what on earth is going on?"

"*Zut alors! Les* Jerries are coming!" he said, and put his finger to his lips to silence her and turned back to the radio.

"We all know that, but when?" she persisted.

"Now!" he said, turning to her. "RAF spotter planes have reported German troopships en route to Guernsey carrying at least two battalions! *Sacre bleu!* Two battalions!"

"Whatever for?" Fleur said. "There's nobody here left to fight them. All of our own troops left us in the lurch, remember?"

"*Mais certainement, madame!* But London is saying the Germans aren't aware that the islands have been demilitarized. They think our soldiers are still here, and they are coming here spoiling for a fight!"

"Well, then, grab the sharpest breadknife in that drawer and hurry down to the beach. I'm sure you'll find someone there happy to accommodate you if you wish to fight."

"Baroness, with all due respect, this is no joking matter, I assure you."

"You're right, *monsieur,* of course. But one must maintain one's sense of humor in times of trial. Cheerfulness in the face of adversity. That's my motto. Now, give me four of your best baguettes, and I'll let you get back to your invasion."

"Take them! Take as many as you want. No charge. I'm closing the patisserie. I won't sell to these barbarians who have stolen my country, who even as we speak are bombing women and children across the water! *Non!* Never! The honor of all France is at stake."

Fleur took four baguettes from the wooden basket and put them into a paper sack. She left a fiver on the glass counter by the cash register and waved good-bye to M. de Lupin. Then she pushed through the door, stepped into the street, and turned left to walk up the slight hill to where she'd left her bicycle.

That's when the first bomb exploded.

She had the unique sensation of flying through the air and being slammed against the brick wall of the building that housed Monsieur de Lupin's bakery. She must have been unconscious for a few moments because when she came to, she had no idea where she was or how she'd come to be there. For some reason, she was covered with dust and there were a number of shattered cobblestones along with a bag of four baguettes in her lap.

Down the hill, some twenty feet away, was a huge crater in the street. The front of Monsieur de Lupin's shop no longer existed. It was just a ragged hole in the middle of a brick building. She tried to get to her feet but felt unsteady and sagged against the wall. Her face felt sticky, and when she put her hand to her face, it came away dripping with blood. She had to make it back to the shop, to see if there were any survivors she could help.

Using the bomb-scarred wall to keep herself upright, she moved slowly down the slight incline until she reached what remained of the shop. Bracing herself for what she might see, she leaned out and peered inside. There was no one in there who needed her help.

There were five or six bodies inside, some intact, many of

them simply torn apart. Great, jagged slabs of plate glass had been blown inward and caused most of the horrific carnage. She saw Monsieur de Lupin, or what was left of him, sprawled atop a marble counter strewn with loaves of freshly baked bread. For some unknowable reason, the wireless on the cupboard shelf was unharmed and she could still hear the BBC reporter talking about the impending invasion of the Channel Islands by thousands of German soldiers.

"It is no longer impending, you damn fools," she heard herself saying to the radio, possibly out loud.

She leaned back against the wall, took a deep breath, and tried to compose herself. Nothing, no bones anyway, seemed to be broken. She obviously had a sizable cut on the side of her head, just above her right ear, and it was bleeding rather heavily. She removed her white cotton jersey, rolled it up, and tied it tightly round her head. It would be good enough to get her home, she thought.

Another bomb rocked the harbor. This one struck one of the many farm trucks queued up to offload tomatoes, totally obliterating it. She was aware for the first time of the deafening roar of the masses of German Heinkel bombers in the skies above. Waves of them, and now more and more bombs began to fall, and fiery black smoke began to stream upward into the pure blue sky.

The tide was low, and the hysterical mob rushed for the only available shelter, underneath the pier. This saved hundreds of lives, but many others were not so lucky. Some of the farmers and their families took shelter under their vehicles only to be crushed when the fires started and the vans and trucks collapsed. The dying victims' blood mingled with the juice from hundreds of crates of tomatoes.

The Germans seemed to be targeting the trucks lining the quay. Why murder defenseless farmers and their families? She saw fighters strafing poor men in lifeboats. She watched one truck after another explode in flames, heard the cries of the dying and the injured until she could bear it no longer.

The Germans clearly intended to reduce her little town to a heap of rubble, and if she was to survive, she had to get out to the countryside and home.

By some miracle, her old Raleigh had survived to fight another day. Fleur gathered what strength she had left and worked her way slowly back up the hill toward the bicycle, one hand on the wall for support. The Raleigh was covered with dust but clearly usable. She bent down and pulled up her socks, which were sagging about her ankles, and climbed onto the stalwart Raleigh.

———

She walked her bicycle along the cliff walk by Fermain Bay. It was a lovely walk with a rugged path that wandered up and around the headlands. At a fork in the pathway, where a gently winding lane led eventually up the wooded hills to Fordwych Manor, she stopped her bicycle in the lane and stood quietly, watching the endless line of German soldiers in gray-green uniforms go goose-stepping by. They seemed to be coming from the airfield where Junkers aircraft were landing, unloading troops, and returning for more.

Column after column, marching in tight formation, rifles slung over their shoulders, knives and grenades stuck in their boot-tops, exuding strength and an almost demonic determination. They marched toward the little town of Saint Peter Port like some unstoppable force of nature.

Gleaming from head to toe, their buttons and boots and coal-scuttle helmets, these Nazi storm troopers seemed empowered with machinelike precision. It was unlike anything she'd ever seen in all of her eighty years. Eyes straight ahead, never wavering, blond youth at the very peak of fitness and training, they paid scant attention to the old woman with the bloodied bandage wound round her head, using her bicycle for support.

They were exactly what they looked like. A conquering army marching through enemy territory, completely unopposed.

She mounted her bicycle and headed up the lane and home, Jean-Paul's four baguettes still in her basket.

She would ring Lord Hawke immediately upon returning and tell him about everything she'd seen. There was no time now for secret meetings in dark coves with fishermen. This was war.

"Hawke, here," Lord Hawke said, picking up the receiver.

"It's me."

"Fleur," he said, "Hobbes and I are up in the castle tower. We've been looking across to Guernsey through extremely high-powered telescopic lenses. I can see Fordwych Manor still standing up on Saint George's cliff, but I also see flames and black smoke rising over Saint Peter Port. Are you quite all right, my dear woman?"

"Yes, yes, I'm fine, never mind me. But they've blown up our harbor. Not the ships at anchor, mind you, but the trucks lining the quay. I counted at least forty dead. Farmers with their families! With truckloads of tomatoes, for heaven's sake? Can you imagine the barbarity? It's ungodly!"

The conquering army

"Probably thought they were troop transports, full of our soldiers. Apparently, the Reich doesn't yet know that our military has abandoned us."

"I saw endless columns of German troops marching toward town. Shocking. I must say, they looked discouragingly effective."

"I will want to talk to you at dinner this evening about possibly evacuating, my dear Fleur."

"I'm not going anywhere. But I'm positively delighted you're still coming over to my little dinner! You and Hobbes, both?"

"Of course we're coming. Life does go on, you know, even under enemy occupation."

"But aren't the Germans looking for you? You and Hobbes are both known spies in Berlin. Your pictures are probably plastered on every wall in the Reichstag building. You should be very, very careful, my Lord Hawke. This island is literally crawling with Nazis."

"Don't worry your pretty head, my dear Baroness. Hobbes will come up with suitable disguises and false passports and identifcation. And it's the Gestapo in Berlin who want our heads—not infantry troops sent to occupy the islands. But I promise we shall be careful nonetheless. Now. Tell me everything you saw. Speak slowly so I can take notes, and I'll relay your information immediately to Whitehall. Ready?"

"Ready. It was just after two o'clock. Masses of heavy bombers over the town. Heinkel He 111s, if I'm not mistaken, the ones with those greenhouse-like cockpits. The first bomb fell into the street. A few hundred yards from the harbor. It was devastating and—? Are you still there? Can you hear me? It's Fleur calling, dear fellow, hullo?"

She stared at the receiver in disgust. The line had gone dead.

The Germans have cut the bloody telephone lines between the islands, she thought. And of course, she was right.

It was the first night of a thousand or more nights to come that Fleur de Villiers would experience a life lived under the merciless hobnailed boots of Hitler's Third Reich.

14

· Greybeard Island ·

A wing and a prayer. Nick was saying his prayers all right, no end of them. That wasn't the problem. It was his tattered right wing that he could do nothing about. Large sections of the fabric covering the upper wing had ripped away during his mad, twisting, and turning dash across the sea to Greybeard Island. Every few minutes he'd hear the loud twang of one of his support wires snapping, and the plane would veer out of control. He was amazed he still had a wing at all.

After what had seemed a nightmarish eternity, just trying to keep the Camel from going into a death spiral and nose-diving into the channel, he finally had Lord Hawke's airstrip in sight. It gave his heart a desperately needed lift, that narrow strip of green meadow that represented home and safety.

He saw Gunner emerge from the barn at the sound of his approach and sprint down the strip to the seaward edge to cheer him on, leaping up and down, waving him onward.

Cheering and waving wouldn't help much now.

He was losing a bit of altitude with every passing second. Nick didn't see how he could possibly keep her airborne long enough to clear Hawke Castle and reach land. During the flight, he'd continually lost a lot of altitude and had not been able to regain it. He was now fighting the plane for every inch, straining to keep her at least fifty feet above sea level. The Sopwith seemed determined to dive to the right, and there didn't seem to be much Nick could do about it.

And, somehow, he knew, he had to gain enough altitude to clear the tower at Hawke Castle. He had one trick left in his bag, and he'd have only one chance to use it.

As his father had taught him early on, because of the engine's tremendous torque, any hard turn to the left would cause the aircraft to climb instantly and automatically. But he had to time it perfectly. He would have to wait until the very last second, when a collision with the tower seemed all but unavoidable, to put her over hard left and hope the sudden climb was enough to get him over the top.

The tower was looming up dead ahead.

At his current altitude a crash was unavoidable. He couldn't fly around either side of the tower because cliffs rose up on either side of the airstrip and he'd crash headlong into them. He'd need at least twenty more feet of altitude to clear the top. And he'd need it at the last possible moment.

It's indescribably mentally difficult to steer an aeroplane deliberately on a collision course that will mean instant death. Every instinct in Nick was screaming at him to turn away. But he had no choice. The seconds stretched into hours as he flew on toward the tower.

He was perhaps less than twenty yards from dying when

he put the stick hard over to the left and felt the Sopwith jerk her nose up steeply into an almost vertical climb. He was flying by sheer instinct now—no one had taught him how to do this maneuver.

Sometimes you'll have to fly by the seat of your pants, son, his father had told him. He never knew what his dad meant until this very moment.

But at the very last instant, he would never know how, Nick was somehow able to get the plane's nose up and barely scrape over the top of Lord Hawke's tower.

He'd done it.

Gunner was elated, but the boy wasn't safely on the ground yet. He stood there, gesticulating wildly, as if he could somehow *will* the boy to land safely.

"That's it, that's the way to do it, lad. Now straighten her out, boy, get her level and keep yer nose in the air. A few more feet . . . come along now . . . almost home . . . almost . . ."

Nick cleared the rocky promontory by inches, hit the ground hard, bounced once or twice into the air, and then finally he was down on the airstrip at last.

Thanking whoever in heaven had been there in the cockpit with him, he found himself taxiing toward the barn, and a plainly relieved Gunner, who was running alongside him down the field gesticulating wildly, a huge grin on his pink-cheeked face.

"Now that's what I call flying, Cap!" Gunner said, as he helped Nick down from the cockpit. Nick pulled off his leather flying helmet and goggles and stared at his friend, stamping his feet, thrilled to have them back on solid ground.

"If that's flying, I might go back to sailing," Nick said as Gunner embraced him and lifted him off his feet.

Gunner put him down and walked around the nose to inspect the damaged wing. "Whatever happened to yer starboard wing, laddie? Did'ye run into something solid?"

"Something solid ran into me. Bullets. I came across a German minesweeper laying naval mines. I guess they don't like having their picture taken while they're going about their nefarious business."

Gunner continued his meticulous inspection of the damage. "Bullet holes everywhere. Yer plain lucky there ain't none in you."

"That shield Hobbes made. He saved my life."

"Did you shoot back at those blasted Jerries?"

"The only shooting I did was with the camera. You haven't yet taught me how to use those twin Vickers, remember? Or, you can bet I would have."

"That's tomorrow, soon as I get this wing repaired. Any other damage?"

"Prop felt a wee bit off on the way home. I think a bullet may have nicked it."

"Did indeed. Right here. I can patch that up easily enough."

"Gunner, flying home I saw masses of Heinkel bombers headed for Guernsey. And troop ships just off the beaches. I snapped off a few shots of the the minelayer, then I decided I'd better get home. About fifteen minutes ago, I saw smoke rising from the harbor."

"Aye, it's begun all right. Apparently they've bombed the harbor at Saint Peter Port, bloody buggers."

"So, our islands are finally at war."

"I'd say so."

"They'll be coming to Greybeard sooner or later, Gunner, German soldiers."

"No doubt."

"Are many here evacuating?"

"I saw about ten families at the ferry dock this morning, all their belongings, waiting for the weekly packet boat over to Weymouth."

"My father and mother have decided we're staying," Nick said, with some pride.

"I would have guessed as much."

"And you?"

"When I leave this island, Nick, it will be in a boat with a hole in it or a long pine box."

"Me, too. We'll stay and we'll fight, won't we, Gunner? Right to the end."

"That's the spirit, boy."

"Remember the night Churchill came to the island? After Kate and Hobbes had captured the U-boat? And he spoke after dinner at Hawke Castle?"

"Remember it? I'll never forget it."

"I saw something in Winston Churchill's eyes that night, and I've pinned all my hopes on him ever since."

"What did you see, Nick?"

"I saw victory, Gunner. Victory, no matter how long in coming, no matter how great the cost."

Gunner pulled the boy to him and enfolded him in his huge arms. "We'll get through it, lad. We'll get through it. Don't you worry."

After a moment, Gunner let him go, and Nick ducked under the fuselage. He was most eager to inspect the camera for damage. By some miracle, it appeared completely intact. He removed the metal film cartridge, confirmed that no bullets had struck the camera body or the lens, and climbed out from under his plane.

"I've got to get this film to Commander Hobbes straight-away, Gunner. Do you need my help tugging the old girl into the barn?"

"No, I can tow her in by myself. Do it all the time. I'm going to start work on this wing right away, so don't let me keep you."

But Nick was already halfway down the airstrip, headed full tilt for Hawke Castle.

H obbes was waiting at the castle entrance when Nick arrived, slightly winded. He had the film canister clutched in both hands and a broad smile on his face.

"I've brought you a wee present, Commander!" Nick said, handing it to Hobbes.

"I've just come from the tower, Nick. Saint Peter Port has been bombed. You missed that action, I hope."

"Yes, sir, I was returning from the coast of France."

"You seem to have encountered a bit of difficulty with your right wing."

"If not for your lead shield, I'd not be standing here, sir."

"His Lordship and I were still up in the tower, watching your somewhat shaky approach, when you managed to clear the tower by an inch or two, Nick. You certainly got our attention."

"Sorry if I frightened anyone. I–I really had no choice."

"Don't ever tell Lord Hawke what I'm about to reveal. This is in strictest confidence. Is that a sacred promise?"

"Of course."

"We both dove under His Lordship's desk when we saw you coming straight for the tower!"

Nick laughed and said, "Precision flying, they call that. Only a few very stupid pilots would attempt a stunt like that, with only one wing keeping them aloft."

"Quite a stunt you pulled there at the end, going into that steep climb."

"Well, you see I was determined not to ditch her, sir. No matter what. We're going to need that airplane."

"Frankly, we were both quite amazed you made it to the ground in one piece," Hobbes said, laughing and clapping the boy on the back. "Can't wait to get a look at these pictures."

"Oh, I don't think you'll be disappointed, sir."

"Lord Hawke is waiting for you in the tower study. I'll take this film down to the cellar darkroom straightaway and start developing it. See you shortly with your first recon pictures in hand."

"Can you teach me, later? How to develop my own pictures? Photo recon, I mean?"

"Of course. I could even set up a darkroom for you in the barn, if you'd like."

"Ideal, sir. Thank you."

Hobbes trotted off to a staircase at a run, and Nick headed down the long windowed corridor that led to Hawke's study at the very top of the tower. The castle was a massive, drafty old place, but it held many surprises and secrets. Like the fireman's pole in the tower, which allowed one to slide all the way down from Lord Hawke's study to the laboratory in the cellar.

Hawke looked up from his desk and smiled as the boy entered the circular, glassed-in room. The views of the Channel in all directions were spectacular, and it was Nick's favorite place on earth.

"A-ha! The boy daredevil himself! Quite an exciting landing, I dare say," Hawke cried, getting to his feet and letting his newspapers slide to the floor. Nick saw many wooden crates, filled to overflowing with Hawke's books and scientific instruments, standing around the room.

"I'm so sorry if I gave you a fright, sir. I'm afraid that landing left much to be desired."

"Nick, don't be ridiculous. I saw what condition your right wing was in. I'm amazed you even made it home alive!"

"I have to admit I'm happy to be standing here and not bobbing around somewhere in that cold channel water, sir. It looks like you're packing up to leave, sir."

"We've got to clear out of here in a hurry, I'm afraid. This castle is a secret British military installation, as you well know. Chock full of military secrets. The Royal Navy has a cutter en route to help us get everything we don't want the Germans to find off the island."

"But where will you go, sir?"

"Nick, the Prime Minister has summoned Hobbes and me to London. It seems we're to be posted to DNI for the duration."

"DNI?"

"Department of Naval Intelligence."

"What kind of work, sir?"

"As you well know, Hobbes and I, undercover, of course, have been working for Churchill for years. I imagine we'll continue. And apparently the PM is considering forming a special new Commando Unit. I'm to head the thing up. And Hobbes will remain with me, designing some new weapons systems for our squad. We'll be operating behind enemy lines, gathering intelligence, sabotage, that sort of thing."

"Congratulations, Your Lordship. Sounds like fun."

"Fun? I don't think so, Nick. The Germans have a huge head start on England in this war. It's going to be hell catching up, well nigh impossible, to be honest."

"England's in good hands now, sir. Mr. Churchill will see us through."

"I couldn't agree more. If anyone can do it, Winston can."

"When do you leave, sir?"

"A few days. As I said, a Royal Navy cutter will be arriving in the lagoon to pick up all the sensitive documents and hardware down in the laboratory. Then the entire castle will be entirely secured against intruders. Every possible entrance will be booby-trapped. You're aware of the electrified dock in the lagoon?"

"Of course."

"Never go near it. It will be fully operational as soon as we depart. Ten thousand volts. But, Nick, if you or your father ever need access to the castle, I will show you a way. A secret passage built centuries ago."

"Where is it?"

"In the lagoon. About ten feet below the surface. You have to dive down and swim through the opening in the rock. When you surface, you'll find Satan's Staircase, an ancient stone stairway leading up to the cellar. I'll show you the exact location before we leave."

"Thank you, sir. That may well come in handy."

"Now, listen, Nick. Hobbes and I are off to London tomorrow for a short meeting, returning here immediately afterward. We've been asked to provide detailed explanations of what's going on here in the Channel Islands. Hobbes and I wondered if we might convince you to come along?"

"I–I would be most honored, your lordship. If you think I might be of some help."

"I was hoping you'd say that. I took the liberty of ringing up your parents at the lighthouse and asking their permission. Both have consented, as long as I promise to bring you home safely in my seaplane. I can drop you off at Lighthouse Harbor tomorrow afternoon when we return from the mainland."

"What time are we leaving, sir?"

"First thing in the morning."

"Dark-thirty, sir?" Nick asked, smiling.

"Yes, we'll take off before sunup," Hawke said, tousling Nick's hair.

"I was wondering–where are little Alex and Annabel?"

"Already at Hawkesmoor, my family country house in Gloucestershire. And I plan for them to remain there for the duration."

Hobbes came rushing into the library with a sheaf of freshly developed prints.

"Nick, my word! These photographs are outstanding, to say the very least. The close-ups of that new German Hertz mine design are invaluable. London intelligence analysts will fall off their stools. Have a look, Your Lordship."

Hawke looked through the prints, a wide smile on his face.

"Well done, Nick, and obviously at great peril to yourself. These will be invaluable at our meeting in London."

"How did you come to spot that minelayer, Nick?" Hobbes asked.

"I got lucky, Hobbes. I drifted off course and ended up halfway to France on my way home. That's when I spotted the minelayer and those new mines."

"Who's thirsty?" Lord Hawke said, pouring a tumbler of whiskey for himself.

"I'd dearly love a cup of tea," Nick said, suddenly realizing how hungry and thirsty he was, not having eaten in hours. "And maybe a sandwich?"

"Coming right up," Hobbes said, heading for the small lift and down to the pantry.

"Nick, come over and take a peek through this telescope, would you?"

"Certainly, sir," Nick said and climbed atop a small stool so his eyes could reach the black rubber eyepieces. Hawke showed him how to adjust the focus rings.

"What do you see?" Hawke asked.

"A lovely old manor house, covered with ivy, sitting high atop Saint George's Peak."

"Yes, quite right. Hobbes and I are going over to Guernsey this evening to a small dinner party at that very house. It's called Fordwych Manor. And it's the home of an old friend of mine. Founder of the Guernsey chapter of the Birdwatchers Society. She's someone I want you to know."

"Why, sir?"

"Her name is Fleur de Villiers, code-named Flower, and she is a very important member in our little secret society. Baroness de Villiers collects all the weekly intelligence on Guernsey and passes it along to me. I in turn make sure that the information reaches the Prime Minister. But there's a problem. Once I'm gone, she'll need a contact here on Greybeard to forward the packets on to No. 10 Downing. I think you're the logical chap to take my place. My thought was, you might use the Sopwith. Fly night flights and deliver them over to Portsmouth once a week. A motorcycle courier would be standing by to speed them up to London."

"Well, of course, anything you say, sir. I want to help in any way I can."

"Excellent. I knew I could count on you."

"Sir, if I may, isn't Guernsey a bit dangerous for you and Hobbes, now that the island is crawling with German soldiers? I know that you're both wanted in Berlin for espionage."

"Oh, they'll come looking for us all right. As soon as they've set up their Guernsey headquarters and the Gestapo arrives. But tonight there shouldn't be any problems. Mass confusion over there, one assumes."

Hobbes came in with a small tray.

"Oh, there you are, Hobbes. After his tea, I thought we might take Nick down to the laboratory and show him some of those gadgets you've been working on for him all week."

"Gadgets?" Nick said, wolfing down his sandwich.

"Come along, you'll see!" Hobbes said.

The threesome descended to the cellar in the lift and stepped out into the laboratory. Nick had been there many times and was long accustomed to the amazing array of scientific equipment that filled the room.

"Over here," Hobbes said. "I've laid out everything on this table."

"What's this?" Nick said, looking at what appeared to be a wireless with a very large circular antenna.

"Two-way radio. This large unit will go in the barn, or HQ as you now call it. I'll install a much smaller receiver/transmitter in the Sopwith's cockpit this afternoon. That way you and Gunner will be able to stay in communication whilst you're aloft."

"Why that would be wonderful, Hobbes!"

"And look here, Nick, this could come in handy."

He handed Nick an item that looked like a walkie-talkie with a large loop antenna on top.

"What is it?"

"Hand-held RDF. A radio detection finder. With this instrument, you'll be able to navigate at night, in bad weather, or in fog. It will pick up the radio signal Gunner is sending from the barn and lead you straight home."

"Show him the trees?" Lord Hawke said. "My personal favorite."

"Trees?" Nick said.

"Ah, yes, the wonderful trees," Hobbes said. "I'm rather proud of them actually." He pulled a canvas dropcloth off an object about five feet tall and three feet in diameter.

"What do you think of that?" Hawke asked.

"It's a tree," Nick said, perplexed.

"True enough," Hobbes said. "But no ordinary tree, I assure you. Look here, this tree actually *rolls*."

He gave the tree a shove and it rolled right over to Nick.

Nick laughed. "A rolling tree. What on earth is this for?"

"It was your sister Kate's idea actually. She thought of the idea of rolling trees to disguise the airstrip. Gunner's agreed to make many of these. Cut trees and bushes of every size and shape, mount them on rolling platforms, covered with moss. It's a brilliant form of camouflage for our little secret airbase. When the landing strip is not in use, it will appear from the air to these nosy Germans to be simply more forest."

"From the air, they will have no idea it's our runway! And the barn is invisible from the air."

"Precisely," Hobbes said.

"Hobbes," Nick said, "I think Kate is a genius. I wonder what I would do without the two of you?"

"Well, I, uh, really have no idea! But since you have me

completely at your disposal, the question is quite rhetorical, wouldn't you agree?"

Hawke and Hobbes roared with laughter.

"Hobbes, is the seaplane fueled and ready?" Hawke said.

"Indeed."

"Then we'd best plan to take off no later than seven o'clock. You and Nick have work to do. But Baroness de Villiers is a right demon about her guests arriving at Fordwych Manor on time."

16

· Port Royal, Jamaica—August 1, 1781 ·

Captain William Blood stalked the quarterdeck of his flagship 78-gun *Revenge* like a man with a fever in his brain. His brow furrowed, his one good hand and one gold hook held stiffly behind his back, he marched to and fro behind the helm, his polished Hessian boots clomping across the freshly holystoned teak, sometimes pausing to look out across the harbor with a rare flash of grim satisfaction.

The evening sky above Port Royal was every shade of blood orange, flame, and purple as the sun sank fast beyond the far rim of the world. Blood eyed the masts and riggings of at least one hundred pirate ships, a thick forest of creaking timber etched in black against the flame. And every last one of them under his command.

It was a sight normally calculated to give a hardened buccaneer like Captain Blood great comfort, yet he wanted still more ships in his burgeoning armada. There was still scarcely a week before his fortnight-long deadline expired. But he had no doubt that word of his rapidly growing Brethren of Blood was spread like a tropical wildfire throughout the islands of the Caribbean. For pirates, and men of that like, or ilk, it was gold, second only to hot blood, that was the only real magnet or attraction on this earth.

There was a loud screech overhead. Old Bill paused and regarded the damnable birds. In the silence, as dusk fell, seven black ravens had perched on the mizzenmast boom above his head. It was surely a sign, Old Bill thought, a portent of things to come. But of what, he could not be sure. He'd seen good omens bring sorrow, and bad bring out the sun. Still, he was supremely confident of his plans to rule the seven seas. He was building a mighty fleet to overwhelming strength such as the world had never seen. But he had a bad feeling, a feeling even Jamaica rum couldn't drive from the wrinkled recesses of his brain.

He drew a pistol and fired, blasting the nearest bird into a cloud of feathers and a fine mist of blood. Oddly, the remaining six ravens held their position. Deaf, blind, or both, he decided, these winged intruders.

He decided to let the rest remain, damn them all, and went about his business. Something beyond irksome was tickling the back of his mind, and he couldn't for the life of him conjure up what to do about it.

"Where be Snake Eye?" he suddenly asked the solemn mate standing watch at the stern rail. He'd just lit the twin whale-oil lanterns hanging from the port and starboard rails. And they cast a yellow glow upon his craggy features.

"In his quarters, Captain, whittling away at his whalebone is what I'd imagine."

"Fetch him here, and quick-like."

"Aye, Cap'n," the mate said. He swallowed once, hard, and hurried below. Snake Eye was as evil a beast as ever walked this world, and he didn't much like his evening privacy being disturbed when the ship was in port.

Bill's second-in-command appeared on the quarterdeck a few minutes later, whalebone and carving knife to hand. He gave his captain the evil eye and hissed, "Yes-s-s-s-s?"

"I'll have a word with you, if the artiste ain't too busy with his bleedin' masterpiece," Blood said.

Snake Eye stuck both the bone and the knife inside the crimson sash wrapped round his bare midsection and stared hard-eyed at his master and commander. He wasn't afraid of him; he was afraid of no man. But down the centuries Blood had brought him riches beyond measure, and so he held his tongue. He had no intention of quarreling with his bread and butter.

"Seem troubled of an evening," the tattooed pirate muttered, cocking one slitted eye at the master of his fate.

"Aye. Troubled indeed. Let's repair to my cabin and have a private word. Me thoughts need airing out."

Snake Eye followed Old Bill down the dark narrow staircase that eventually led to Blood's great cabin at the stern. The great sweeping banquette under the leaded glass of the many stern windows was upholstered in blood-red velvet, as were the gilded chairs and the draperies, too.

Blood lit the many candles on the great crystal chandelier that hung above the round mahogany table at the center of the room. A rosy glow was cast over the two men. There were empty glasses, various charts and ship's manifests and such lying about on the table, and the captain simply swept them all to the floor with a swipe of his arm.

"Turn yer back," Blood ordered his companion. Snake Eye dutifully turned his back to the table and stared out the windows at the harbor and the many lanterns glowing in the rigging of ships laying at anchor. This was not the first time Blood had protected one of his many secrets, although Snake Eye had been privy to them all for aeons.

Keeping one eye on the Frenchman, Billy dropped to one knee and used his bejeweled hook to lift a small ring hidden under a loose floorboard.

The table and the round section of floor it stood on instantly and silently inverted, revealing an identical table on the other side. Only this one had a heavy cast-iron chest bolted to the middle of the table. It had only one lock, a massive one, with no visible opening for a key.

Blood pulled his key ring from his pocket, rattled it a bit deliberately so that Snake Eye could hear it, then dropped it back in his pocket. He then lifted the padlock, flipped it over, and opened a false back, hinged to the lock. He held his hook up to the flickering candlelight, saw the seven notches carved along the hook's golden tip, and inserted the hook inside a small hole in the lock. He gave his hook a quick twist, then withdrew it. The hasp of the lock popped open.

Bill removed the lock and opened the chest. Inside, on a regal red satin cushion sat one of the strangest devices ever created by mankind. It was a golden sphere, and so brilliant was its sheen under the candles that it seemed almost lit from within. The Tempus Machina. A time machine, one of only two, constructed by Leonardo da Vinci sometime in the late sixteen century. It had come into Blood's possession during a mutiny aboard the English warship H.M.S. *Merlin*.

But there was another. It was William Blood's greatest desire in this life to possess both golden orbs. Then, forever after, he need fear no man, for he could always escape through time without fear of ever being followed. Until he possessed the two, his sleep would never be untroubled.

"You can turn around," he said, thrusting the orb into the air where its brilliance lit up the enter cabin.

"Thinking of taking another time voyage, are ye then, *mon capitaine?*" Snake Eye said, eyes riveted on the magnificent machine.

"Aye. Pull up a chair and uncork that flagon of rum. We've plans to lay, you and me, and we only have a week to accomplish all I desire. The armada parley is one week from today."

"And what do you desire, *mon ami?*"

"What I desire . . . is *everything*," Blood said without hesitation.

"As always, I am your humble servant, who exists only to do your bidding."

"Look me in the eye, then, damn you! What be the name of this here vessel?"

"Revenge."

"Yes, *Revenge*. That's what I desire, you old demon. I named her so because of my heart's desire. And revenge is what I shall seek, nay, shall wreak upon my enemies. And mark you, I will soon avenge my honor on that cursed English dog, Lord Hawke. The blackguard who took me good right hand for claiming what was rightfully mine. Him and that cursed boy, too, that little hellion who even now possesses the second golden orb. What be his name?"

"McIver. Nicholas McIver," Snake Eye said, his strange features furrowed with anger. He, too, wanted revenge, following a disastrous run-in with the McIver boy aboard the English ship.

"That's him, all right. And his time has come, too."

"What do you intend?"

"Why, to lure him and his precious orb down here to Port Royal. Where I shall duly relieve him of his golden ball, and his head as well."

"You've hatched a scheme?"

"I was formulating just such ideas whilst I walked the quarterdeck. I have it now. And you and me will carry it out."

"Lure him, then? We'll need good bait for the trap."

"Aye, and it's that bait we're going to fetch!"

"Where might we be headed?"

"You may perhaps remember a pestilential English island called Greybeard, rising from the sea like a barnacle off the coast of France?"

"I do, but I'd give blood and silver to forget it. 'Tis where you lost yer hand, sire, and 'twas there we lost that beautiful crimson-colored warship, *Mystère*, and incurred the wrath of Napoleon."

For the first time all evening, Blood's thin lips curved into an evil smile. "That's ancient history, shipmate. I think this time you may enjoy our visit a bit more," Old Bill said, and, tilting his head back for a draught of rum, he laughed his strange high-pitched laugh and drained the last of the rum.

· London, June 1940 ·

Winston Churchill stood to welcome his three guests. They'd arrived at the luncheon hour, so the Prime Minister had decided to receive them in the small dining room at No. 10 Downing Street. It was, he felt, a perfect place for a quiet meeting with his dear nephew, Lord Richard Hawke, his colleague, the brilliant Commander Hobbes, and the young McIver boy, whom Churchill well remembered for his brave exploits involving an experimental Nazi U-boat a few months prior.

The room was paneled in warm golden walnut and had a small oval mahogany table that would do nicely for four people. The prime minister loved this room for many reasons, but especially the lovely bust of Sir Isaac Newton that stood in a window just above the fireplace. Whenever a newcomer came to dine, Churchill made sure he worked one of his favorite and oft-repeated jokes into the conversation.

"That bust is of Sir Isaac Newton, you know," Winston would say, "chap who discovered gravity. I've often wondered, where would we be without him! Floating around like balloons?"

He'd then take a big puff on his cigar, enjoying the polite laughter that was sure to follow.

His three guests were ushered in, and Churchill rose from his chair and moved toward the door to greet them. He took Hawke's hand first, saying, "Ah, my dashing young nephew. Welcome, sir, to my new quarters. Quite fashionable, don't you think?"

"Indeed," Hawke said, shaking his hand. "But first I must ask you, now that you're Prime Minister, may I still call you Uncle Winston?"

"My dear boy, you can call me anything you damn well please! And look, here is Commander Hobbes. Wonderful to see you again, my good fellow. We're going to need your services desperately in this war. And who is this? Why, I believe it's young Nick McIver unless I'm very much mistaken. Aren't you the lad who discovered and captured that monstrous German U-boat in the Channel Islands?"

"Well, s—sir, I suppose I played a small part in that, but the real credit must go to Commander Hobbes and my sister Kate, who—"

"There, there, Nick. No room for false modesty in this house. And never let the truth stand in the way of a good story. We're all heroes here—or we'll soon need to be, at any rate. Come sit down, and have some of this delicious potted hare. One of my favorites."

Hawke sat directly across from his uncle, and Nick and Hobbes took the chairs at either end of the table. He sat back and regarded his famous relative, finding him to be in amazingly good spirits, considering how badly the war was going.

German troops had marched into Poland on September 1, 1939. The war his uncle had so clearly foreseen had begun. On September 3, Great Britain and France had declared war on

Germany, and the then–Prime Minister Neville Chamberlain had at once named Churchill first lord of the admiralty, notifying the fleet with this simple message: "Winston is back."

In April of this year, Germany had attacked Denmark and Norway. Britain immediately sent troops to Norway, but they had quickly retreated because of a lack of air support. Chamberlain's government fell soon after, and on May 10, King George VI asked Churchill to form a new government. On that very same day, the Nazis rolled into Belgium, Luxembourg, and the Netherlands. And now France had fallen. The much-vaunted Maginot Line having simply been ignored by Hitler, who sent masive Panzer divisions through the Ardennes forest. Newsreels were full of Nazi battalions marching up the Champs-Elysée in Paris.

Never had a national leader taken over at such a desperate hour. Churchill, in a speech to Parliament, had said, "I have nothing to offer but blood, toil, tears, and sweat."

Would it be enough?

"Well, Uncle," Hawke said, taking a sip of tea, "we bring news from another front. Our beloved Channel Islands."

"I heard reports about the atrocious civilian bombing of Saint Peter Port. Barbarians. What in the world were the Nazis thinking?"

The prime minister pronounced the word "Nar-zees." Nick, deciding if it was good enough for Churchill, it was good enough for him, pronounced it that way himself from that moment on.

"I think the Luftwaffe didn't realize all our troops had been withdrawn, sir," Hobbes said, taking out his sheaf of Nick's photographs. He handed over three or four shots of the trucks lining the quay earlier that morning. Churchill began to study them intently.

"You'll see from young Nick's recon photos that–"

Churchill looked up from the pictures and said to Hobbes, "You don't mean to say that this young man took these photographs! Is it true, Nick?"

"Yes, sir. You see, I've rebuilt my father's old Sopwith, learned how to fly it, and Commander Hobbes has mounted a special camera underneath."

"And these trucks on the quay. What were they doing?"

"Waiting to unload their shipments of tomatoes, sir. I do think the German pilots believed the trucks were all carrying troops."

"Remarkable evidence of German war crimes, Nick!" Churchill said. "Let me see the rest, will you, Commander, our propaganda chaps will have a field day."

Hobbes passed the entire portfolio to the Prime Minister.

"Look at this, will you?" Winston said. "The close-ups of this minelayer! It looks like the Jerries have designed an entirely new type of naval mine! I need to get these all over to the photo intelligence section immediately." He turned to a steward standing silently behind him. "Summon my private secretary, will you? Tell him I need to see him at once."

"I'm glad I could be helpful, sir," Nick said.

"Quite extraordinary, Nick," Churchill said. "And very dangerous work. Does your father know you're doing this?"

"Yes, sir. I informed him. He's happy for me to do my part. My mum is, not . . . not fully aware of the extent of my wartime activities."

"Uncle Winston," Hawke said, "I've told young Nick here that you've summoned Hobbes and me to London for the special operations commando unit. Nick has agreed to work with Baroness de Villiers to keep the steady stream of intelligence flowing out of the islands."

"Very good of you, Nick. I know we can count on you in difficult times. I'm dreadfully sorry about the state of affairs in your islands."

"What do you mean, sir?" Nick asked.

"I tried to get the bloody government to defend your islands, gentlemen. But, as you can see, I failed miserably. But that does not mean I won't try to take them back when the opportunity presents itself. So, Nick, your continued efforts are not only deeply appreciated, but they will be vital when plans are being formulated for retaking these small islands, the oldest of the Crown Dependencies. It's the first time the Germans have occupied English soil, and if I have anything to say about it, it will be the last!"

The four continued eating in silence, all with their private thoughts about what the Prime Minister had been saying. Finally, Hobbes spoke up. "Prime Minister, I've been curious about something, and I hope you don't mind me asking a personal question?"

"Not in the slightest. Please, fire away."

"I've been wondering how you felt when King George summoned you to Buckingham Palace and told you, at this desperate hour, that the fate of our entire nation was now resting on your shoulders."

Churchill sat back and lit a fresh cigar. "A good question, Commander Hobbes, and I'll tell you how I felt. I felt as if I were walking with destiny, and that all my past life had been but preparation for this hour and this trial."

Hawke was about to speak, and then realized he was speechless. And so was everyone else at the table.

Churchill got to his feet, indicating that the luncheon was at an end.

"I'm afraid you'll have to excuse me now. It's back to business as usual, I'm afraid. But I want to leave you all with one very important thought. We face an implacable foe with resources far beyond our own. Victory is uncertain. It will be uphill all the way, I assure you. But there is one great hope. And that is America. If I can persuade President Roosevelt to join us in these desperate hours, we can, and will, win. But without the Yanks, I see very, very dark days ahead for England."

"Like the First World War Yanks who came over, sir?" Nick said.

"Yes, Nicholas, exactly so. Only this time, our situation is far more dire. We'll need not just American soldiers, sailors, and airmen, but their ships, their tanks, and their bombers as well—if we're to stand any chance at all against this Hitler."

And on that somber note, the prime minister said goodbye to them all and hurried off, with his secretary trailing feverishly in his wide wake.

Hawke stood and put a match to his own cigar.

"He'll save the world if he can," Hawke said to his two friends. "But until, and if, the Yanks come into this war, it's going to be up to ordinary Englishmen like the three of us to stand by the Prime Minister and help him in any possible way we can."

He looked at Nick, whose emotions clearly seemed about to overwhelm him.

"Captain McIver," Hawke said, looking fondly at Nick, "it's high time I got you back to your new secret airbase. And, besides, I promised your mum I'd have the squadron leader home in time for supper!"

CODE NAME: BLITZ

· Greybeard Island—July 1940 ·

Gunner arrived bright and early at the barn (now officially called Squadron HQ) only to find young Nick already hard at work. He was seated at the long worktable, going over glossy black and white photographs with a magnifying glass.

The newly repaired and repainted Sopwith Camel stood ready and waiting in the shadows. At one end of the table stood the new wireless radio set Hobbes had promised. There was also now a brand-new two-way radio, installed in the Camel's cockpit. It gave Gunner a great deal of comfort knowing he could now stay in constant contact with the boy when he was out on a mission.

"Morning, Cap," Gunner said.

"Morning," Nick replied, not looking up.

"Come outside, lad. I've got something to show you. You're going to like it."

"Just let me finish here, then I'll be glad to."

"What have ye got there, Nick?"

"A packet of reconnaissance photos, just arrived from Guernsey by fishing boat."

"Who sent them?"

"Flower. She's going to be sending them over weekly."

"Flower?"

"That's only her code name. Her real name is Fleur de Villiers."

"How come we don't have code names?"

"Do you want one?"

"No."

"Me neither. Anyway, Flower's the person over on Guernsey who has been the primary contact with Lord Hawke. They're great friends, apparently. Seems she's been spying on Guernsey for him from the very beginning of the Birdwatchers."

"She take all these photos herself?" Gunner asked, flipping through a sheaf of them.

"Some of them. She's got a lot of help. She's the ringleader of the Guernsey Society of Birdwatchers."

"So, how's she get her pictures over here?"

"It changes. Right now, a fisherman meets her in a cove every week, takes delivery, and ferries the packet over to Greybeard under cover of darkness."

"What's that picture you've got there, then?"

Nick handed Gunner the magnifying glass and said, "Take a look. That's the airfield at Guernsey. Look at all those Messerschmitts lined up on the tarmac, Gunner. Have to be fifty of them. And, look, here, see these four airmen? There are many shots of them. They're using those handcarts to ferry ammunition and bombs out to the fighter aircraft. And they're getting the ammo out of this large corrugated steel shed, right here next to the control tower."

"How did the Guernseymen get all these pictures without getting shot?"

"Concealed cameras. In a satchel or a lady's handbag. Dangerous work."

"If that big corrugated shed ain't a target for our poisonous apples, I don't know what is."

"Right. The shed and of course the fighters on the ground as well. I'd imagine they kept them fueled up, wouldn't you? In case they have to scramble? A few Messerschmitt fuel tanks blow and we could cause serious trouble."

"Aye. But look here, boy. All around the shed and all along the perimeter of the fence line. Those look like antiaircraft emplacements to me."

"They sure do."

"You got some plan to avoid getting blown out of the sky? Your old Camel ain't much of a match for a Messerschmitt or an ack-ack gun."

"Fast, aren't they, those Messerschmitts?"

"Commander Hobbes told me they had 1,200-horsepower engines and top airspeeds of over 300 knots. Four machine guns, mounted in the cowlings and the wings."

"Right, that's a problem."

"But you've got a plan, I'm sure. Always do."

"I do. I plan to take off well before sunrise, at 0400 hours. Arrive over the field at 0430. There'll be a few guards walking the fence line. But everyone else on the base will probably be asleep. I'll go for the shed first, then take out as many fighter planes as I can. I should be headed home by the time those Messerschmitt pilots even warm up their engines."

"How about the ack-ack gunners?"

"Look at this picture. Here, here, and here. Those are searchlights. The only ones I can see. I'll try to take all three of them out first. But I plan to be halfway home before the antiaircraft gunners are out of bed."

"Yer own little Blitzkrieg, sounds like."

"Blitzkrieg?"

"What the Nazis did in Poland. Means 'lightning war' in English."

"I like that word. Maybe that could be my code name. Blitz. Lightning."

"Awright, then, Cap'n Blitz, come with me. I'm going to show you something that might come in handy in this one-man war of yours."

———

They stood at the edge of the airstrip overlooking the bright blue sea. Gunner handed Nick a pair of powerful binoculars and showed him where to look.

"Brilliant!" Nick said, looking at Gunner's surprise, "absolutely brilliant!"

"So you know what it's for?"

"Of course. Practice. With my Vickers machine guns. Lovely idea, actually."

"Thank you, M'lord."

Gunner had been worried about how to get Nick comfortable with the twin machine guns mounted just forward of the cockpit. His brainstorm had come during the middle of the night and caused him to sit straight up in bed. All he needed, he figured, was a small boat, a bunch of red balloons, and a canister of helium gas. He towed the little dory out off Hawke Point behind his old fishing boat and anchored the dory. Then he climbed down into the boat and filled a dozen or so big and small balloons, letting out a couple of hundred feet of string for each one and securing them at different locations around the boat. After that, he chugged back into Hawke Lagoon and went to the barn to fetch Nick.

Nick now had a dozen fresh targets to practice his twin Vickers machine guns on.

"How'd you figure this out?" Nick asked.

"Simple. Gunners need practice. Practice takes targets. You aim to try to hit a moving target up in the air, ain't much better target to do that with than a balloon blowing in the wind, is there?"

"Brilliant."

Gunner frowned, "I ain't brilliant. I'm a gunnery officer. Two things to remember. It ain't like firing a gun at a station-ary target, both standing on solid ground. You're firing at a moving target from a moving platform traveling a hundred or so miles an hour. The balloons are just to give you a feel. Your target's not a sitting duck, either. If you're shooting at aeroplanes, they'll be moving three times as fast as you are."

Nick realized the enormity of what his friend was saying and said quietly, "Anything else?"

"Aye. You're flying at night. You acquire night vision after a while. Your pupils dilate and you take in a lot more light. Which is good. But the second you open up with those machine guns, the muzzle flashes will blind you. You won't be able to see a thing except the color red."

"Just red?"

"Right. The eye will still pick up red. That's why all instru-ments on aircraft and ships are red, y'know."

"I didn't know that."

"Still a lot to learn, boy."

"It's beginning to sound a bit more difficult."

"Nick, what you're doing is brave and worthwhile for your country. If any boy can pull it off, it's you. But it's also very dangerous. Your father has allowed this, and it ain't my place to second-guess anybody. Your mother, I doubt she knows a thing about this, and that's probably for the best. But you do something stupid, let your mind wander for one instant, you're going to wind up dead. I don't want you to forget that for a second."

"I'll be careful, Gunner. I promise you that."

Nick turned and started racing back to HQ.

"Let's go flying!" he cried.

"Boy thinks he's going to live forever," Gunner grumbled to himself. *I remember the feeling.*

As Gunner had warned him, firing the twin Vickers machine guns at swirling red balloons dancing, bobbing, and weaving some two hundred feet above the ocean was considerably more difficult than shooting ducks in a pond.

A lot more difficult. The noise, for one thing, was deafening when Nick pulled both triggers simultaneously. The side-by-side guns were belt-fed, one ammo belt to either side, and the rate of fire was amazing. Still, he'd made five or six diving passes, getting the balloons dead in his sights, and he'd yet to score a single hit. The gusting wind was causing the balloons to dip and dive and swing so wildly on their tethers, he was beginning to think hitting one was impossible.

He did a tight turn and came in for another pass.

"Blitz, this is HQ. Do you read?" He heard Gunner's voice crackle in his earphones.

"Loud and clear, HQ. Over."

"How many kills on that last pass, Blitz?" Gunner asked. He was in the barn on the radio and couldn't watch the practice session through his binoculars.

"Zero, HQ. Haven't scored a single hit yet. This is a lot harder than I thought it would be. Over."

"Are you shootin' at 'em?"

"Of course I'm shootin' at 'em. What do you think? Over."

"Stop shooting at them or you'll never hit one. Your bullets will all arrive at where the target *used* to be. Not where it *is*. Over."

"Understood. So what do I shoot at? Over."

"You shoot where you think the target is *going* to be. Over."

"And how do I know that?"

"You don't. You estimate. You guess. Based on what you've seen a target do before. How it moves and why. Where you think it's headed. You lead the target and fire where you think it will be when your rounds arrive. Watch the wind direction. See which way the balloons are moving. Up, down, sideways. And then shoot there. Where are they going to be? Shoot there before they move there."

There was a long moment of radio silence as Nick thought that one over for a few seconds. "Roger, HQ. I think I know what you mean. I'm going to climb up and circle at about a thousand feet, watch the targets' movements from above. Then I'll make a dive right through the middle of them, see how many I can take out on one pass."

"Best of British, as they say."

"Roger, HQ. Here I go!"

Gunner heard the powerful Bentley roar over the speaker and knew Nick had gone into a steep climb. He smiled to himself. Before the sun set that day, Nick would know how to fire a pair of Vickers machine guns. Not expertly, no. But at least enough to defend himself if he had to.

Gunner picked up the magnifying glass again and studied the Nazi fortifications and the Messerschmitts out on the tarmac at the aerodrome. If all went well and according to plan, the boy could deal the enemy a serious blow and escape

with his life. However, military missions, in Gunner's experience anyway, seldom went according to plan.

The bombing mission was two days away, at 0400 hours in
the morning. He had all of tomorrow to practice his gunnery.

If all did not go well, Gunner knew he would never forgive
himself.

Two days later, Nick McIver walked into the barn at 0330 hours, his leather flying helmet and goggles in one hand, a half-eaten apple in the other. His long white silk scarf was draped round his neck.

Gunner was beside the Sopwith, standing atop the step-ladder, loading the second basket of "apples" into the cockpit. Nick would have exactly twenty handmade bombs when he arrived over the Saint Peter Port aerodrome one hour from now. He looked over at Nick, saw him take a bite out of his apple, and smiled.

If he had expected the boy to look nervous, or frightened, or even excited about tonight's mission, he'd have been wrong. Nick looked like an aviator preparing to go into battle. Calm, confident, even cheerful. He seemed, to Gunner anyway, a warrior. A very young warrior, but a warrior all the same. Lord knows he'd proven himself to be one in that sea battle against Billy Blood. He had the fire in his blood, he did, that's all there was to it.

The old U-boat searchlight was trained on the Camel, and she looked splendid, Nick thought. Gunner had clearly been working on her through the night while Nick grabbed a few hours sleep before slipping quietly out of the lighthouse in the pre-dawn hours.

He'd left a note for his parents on the kitchen table, explaining that he couldn't sleep and was headed to the barn to work with Gunner on the Camel. He'd spend the night at Gunner's inn if it got too late and see them sometime tomorrow.

"She looks good," Nick said, staring at his beloved plane. "Beautiful, in fact."

"She's in apple-pie trim," Gunner replied. "Engine sweet as a nut as well."

The old seaman climbed down from the ladder and turned to face the boy.

"I guess this is it, then, isn't it?" Nick said, running his hand lovingly over the glossy red paint on the cockpit's side.

"It is, lad."

"How many bombs have I got again?"

"Twenty. Two baskets of ten, each apple carefully packed in cotton."

"Vickers guns fully reloaded?"

"As many ammo belts as she'll carry. You've got enough lead to shoot down half the Luftwaffe, should you be unlucky enough to run across them."

"Fuel? Oil?"

"Both topped off."

"Radio?"

"Working like a charm. Good old Hobbes."

"I'll do a radio check when I get out over the channel."

"Sounds good. I'll be here. Wasn't planning to go anywhere this evening until you're home safe."

"Weather looks really good," Nick said, casting a glance out the opened barn doors. "Enough cloud cover to hide the moon periodically."

"And little wind, which is good. Chance of fog rolling in, of course. I put the RDF right under your seat."

"Thanks," Nick replied, smiling as he mounted the ladder and dropped down into the cockpit. His island was named after the famous pea-soupers called greybeards. Even in good weather, these thick sea-fogs could appear out of nowhere, reducing visibility to a few yards and making sailing, and certainly flying, very dangerous. But at least he had the comfort of knowing Hobbes's Radio Direction Finder was stowed in the cockpit.

"Best of luck, then, Nicholas," Gunner said, raising his big hand up so Nick could shake it. He'd wanted to hug the boy badly but felt a good, firm handshake would benefit Nick more.

"Thanks," Nick said, eyes roving over his instrument panel.

"Wish it were me going, instead of you."

"But since you don't know how to fly, I'm probably our best bet."

"Oh, I can fly an aeroplane all right, Nick."

"You cannot. Don't be silly. You were a gunnery officer in the Royal Navy."

"Before that, I was a cadet in the Royal Flying Corps. In France with the 306th."

"What? All these years and you've never told me that? I always wondered how you knew so much about these things. What happened, Gunner?"

"A story for another time, lad, another time," Gunner said with a sad smile, and Nick let it go.

Gunner walked to the front of the plane and took hold of one of the wooden propeller's two broad, angled blades, varnished to gleaming perfection.

"Magnetos?" Gunner cried.

"Magnetos, check!" Nick replied.

Gunner hauled down on the blade and the big Bentley rotary engine caught the very first time. Now there was a good omen.

Nick gave him the thumbs-up, and Gunner stepped out of the way as the boy taxied the aeroplane out of the barn and out to the center of the airstrip. He turned right, braked, and revved his engine, listening carefully. It had never sounded better.

Sweet as a nut. He liked that.

He turned and saw his friend standing in the doorway of the barn, his hand raised, waving farewell.

Nick gave him a wave and began his takeoff roll just as the moon peeked out from behind a cloud.

"HQ, This is Blitz. I repeat, this is Blitz. How do you read me?"

"Loud and clear, Blitz," he heard Gunner reply in his headphones. "What is your location?"

"HQ, my altimeter shows me at three thousand feet. Some clouds at two thousand and below. Half a mile out from the Guernsey shore. I have the field in sight. Looks quiet."

"Searchlights?"

"Negative. Lights on in the guardhouse at the field entrance. That's it. No one visible on the ground. No lights or movement around enemy barracks or antiaircraft emplacements."

"Sleeping like wee little babies, are they? Sounds good."

"It is. I'm commencing my attack now. Blitz, over and out . . ."

"Give 'em bloody hell, lad!" was the last thing Nick heard Gunner say as he put his nose over and went into a steep dive, left hand on the stick, his right gently cradling the first apple.

Two more were resting on his lap. Three should be enough to take out his first target, the shed filled with high explosives. He hoped three would do it, at least.

He saw the ammunition shed ahead and below and coming up fast. He still had some cloud cover. Maybe no one had spotted him yet.

Pulling out of his dive, he leveled off at exactly one hundred feet, heading directly for his target. So far, he'd still seen no activity at all on the ground. The antiaircraft gun emplacements around the perimeter were all dark and silent. He scanned the perimeter for his next target, the searchlights. Too dark to make them out!

He slowed his airspeed just short of a stall as he approached the shed from the south. He lined up on the pitchline of the roof and began his bombing run. One apple into the center of the south wall, two more directly onto the roof, one to either side of the pitch if he could manage it. That was the plan.

Calculating the trajectory as he dove toward the target, he let the first apple fly. He knew as soon as he it let it go, he'd dropped it too soon. Early release! How could he have misjudged it so badly? The bomb would fall well short of the ammo shed's south wall! It did.

Concentrate!

Nick's bomb hit the ground, exploding three feet shy of the building itself. But the tremendous power of the nitroglycerine combined with black powder was enough to blow a hole in the south end wall you could drive a truck through! He was over the roof now, right hand poised, and another apple hit the angled roof and immediately exploded, tearing a huge gash in the corrugated steel roof and sending sheets of flame down into the interior of the building. A second later, he dropped his third and final bomb, just barely catching the roofline and blowing the whole front of the shed off.

He hauled back on the stick, wanting to get out of the way of what he hoped would come next. He wasn't disappointed. The blast exploded skyward and rocked his plane violently and he had to fight to keep her level.

The entire shed suddenly erupted into a second monstrous explosion that lit up the entire field. Flames and thick black smoke climbed into the air as Nick circled above, looking down with satisfaction on the tremendous destruction he had caused the enemy.

A shaft of pure white light suddenly shot into the sky, missing his plane by mere feet. Searchlight. The other two would be sweeping the skies shortly. He cursed himself for not finding and taking them out first as he'd planned. He had to avoid those criss-crossing beams and come around for another strafing run, this one right down over the row of Messerschmitts. There was cloud cover above, and he raced upward toward it, finally emerging into the clear, moonlit sky.

The fire below was intense, what was left of the shed a raging inferno that illuminated the entire aerodrome. He saw plenty of activity on the ground now. Luftwaffe pilots in flight suits racing from their barracks toward their waiting fighters. Gun crews running full-tilt toward their perimeter antiaircraft emplacements. Fire engines and equipment were roaring out of a hangar and racing toward the ammo shed, the pumpers already aiming their useless streams at the raging fire.

Too little, too late. The former ammunition shed was already a heap of twisted metal and blackened wood. Phase one of his mission had gone exactly as he'd hoped.

Emerging from a cloudbank, Nick got a good look at the

precisely aligned German fighter planes on the tarmac. The sprinting pilots were still a few hundred feet away. He put the Camel into a steep diving turn that would set him up for his final attack. He would skim down the long line of Nazi fighter planes at very low altitude, dropping his apples as fast as he could heave them over the side.

The still-rising cloud of black smoke provided fairly good cover. And the clouds above, scudding by the moon, helped now and then, giving him periodic protection from three German searchlights sweeping the skies overhead. Then, out on the edge of night, a tracer flashed through the darkness in a great arc, a star shell burst, and all hell broke loose below.

The first of the three antiaircraft guns had begun firing at him. He dove lower, until his undercarriage was practically skipping over the canopies of the fighters. The only thing that saved him from antiaircraft fire was how close he was to the formation of Messerschmitts. The ack-ack guns simply couldn't afford to target him now for fear of destroying their own aircraft.

Nick McIver had no such fear.

Heaving his bombs, he saw fire suddenly spurting from the exhaust manifolds of several German fighters as their engines exploded into life. He had them dead in his gunsights, and he pressed the trigger button on top of his joystick. The twin machine guns rattled with an enormous roar, and the muzzle flash was dazzling. He saw two or three of the enemy pilots slump forward in their cockpits, followed quickly by a great mushroom of fire and smoke climbing into the sky as some of the Messerschmitt fuel tanks started to go.

Nick was dropping apples over the side as quickly as humanly possible. He saw some pilots turn and run from the exploding fighters. He had been momentarily night-blinded by the blazing Vickers guns, just as Gunner had warned. But the fiery light on the ground more than compensated for his loss of night vision. With his right hand, he managed to grab two of the remaining apples from the first basket between his knees in one hand. Then he pulled back on the joystick and climbed through the vertical, executing an inside loop and gaining much-needed altitude.

He lined up on his target and dove down through the clouds toward the field. The enemy was shooting back now, and the return journey back across the embattled airfield looked like a thousand-mile-long death trap. But he wanted one more shot at the many fighters still intact on the ground, planes that would soon be headed for Dover to protect German bombers bound for London unless he could take them out.

Some of the Messerschmitts were beginning to pull out of the formation. They were veering left and right, speeding out onto the seriously damaged runway as he leveled off at one hundred feet, lining up for his final run. It was then that he realized throwing the bombs one or two at a time wasn't practical now. This would be his last shot at destroying as many remaining enemy aircraft as he could.

He held the stick fast between his knees, reached down and carefully lifted the bomb basket onto his lap. He'd tilt it on its side on the edge of the cockpit and let the apples fall where they may. He was flying low enough that Gunner's nitro bombs were sure to cause a lot of damage, even if a few weren't right on target. He was trying to destroy the runway, too, so not an apple would be wasted.

He sped down the line of Nazi fighters, the bombs spilling from the basket and causing a deafening staccato of jarring explosions. Each one violently rocked his little aeroplane. He tossed the empty basket over the side and hauled back on the stick, going to full throttle as he headed toward the distant perimeter at the seaward side of the Nazi airbase.

His foot, moving off the rudder pedal, brushed the second basket. He planned to drop the entire second basket on the antiaircraft emplacement on his way out. He'd have to fly over the ack-ack gun as he returned over the field for the last time, headed for the channel and home. But the antiaircraft gun beat him to the punch. He saw its long-barreled muzzle fire, and the little puffs of black smoke appeared directly in his path.

Flak.

If he caught any flak in the nose of the airplane, that full basket down by his feet, those ten remaining bombs full of nitroglycerine, well, that would mean—no time for that kind of thinking. He knew he had to get rid of the second bomb basket. Now, before he took a hit! He reached forward and grabbed the flimsy wooden fruit basket with one hand, yanked it up, and balanced it on the edge of the cockpit. He might just as well still try to take out the ack-ack gun on his way out. There was nothing to lose, not now.

He'd no time to climb over the flak layer or fly around it. He'd have to dive under it, fly just a few feet above the tarmac, heading straight into the throat of the gun emplacement. There were people on the ground shooting at him, rifle and machine gun fire, and he felt the dreaded *thunk-thunk-thunk* of rounds striking the lead shield that lined his cockpit.

He opened up with his twin Vickers and was pleased to see the deadly effect of his machine guns as German soldiers either dove for safety or fell mortally wounded or dead. The sleepy Guernsey aerodrome had come fully awake, and every German soldier on the ground had but one single objective: blow the antique British warplane out of the sky.

Time to go, Nick thought to himself, as he flew on straight toward the gun emplacement, both machine guns blazing, and managed to skim just below the first layer of flak that had been fired.

Amazing. He was still alive, and his aeroplane, though no doubt somewhat damaged, seemed very capable of getting him across the sea and home. Beyond the gun he saw the airfield's barbed-wire fence line coming up, and beyond that, waves breaking white upon the huge black rocks.

He gripped the rim of the basket tightly, waiting for the right moment. He was coming right up on the ack-ack gun now, carefully calculating his trajectory. *Now,* he thought and gave the basket a shove overboard.

A millisecond later, he saw the silhouette of a lone sentinel, a single German soldier standing atop the mound of sand-bags surrounding the big ack-ack gun. He had a machine gun, and he kept a bead right on the Camel. Nick both heard and felt the rounds whizzing by his head, ripping up his wings.

And then the basket hit and there was a huge black crater with a rising ball of fire at its center, right where the German machine gunner and the huge antiaircraft gun had been.

He was over the field, over the fence now, over the rocky coast of Guernsey. At the back of his mind were all the Messerschmitts that had survived his attack. Surely some were airborne, even now. The runways, he was glad to see, had been severely damaged, but more of the lethal fighters would surely make it into the air. He craned his head around to see, wiping oil and smoke from his goggles with his scarf, but the entire airfield was nothing but flames and black smoke climbing hundreds of feet into the air.

He flew on across the water, counting his blessings. Still

alive. Plane intact. Engine smooth, good rpms, no odd sounds. No sea fog had rolled in, thank goodness. No Messerschmitts on his tail, not yet, anyway, and—

What was that sound?

His engine had missed a beat.

Then another. It was coughing now, sputtering, still turning over and—smoke. Smoke pouring out of his engine. He grabbed his radio transmitter.

"Mayday, Mayday, this is Blitz. Do you read?"

"Loud and clear, Blitz! What is your situation?"

"Leaving Guernsey coastline, flying due east for HQ at about a hundred feet, Gunner. But I've got a problem."

"Tell me."

"Engine's smoking badly. Still turning over. Very rough, though. She's flying, but barely. Impossible to gain altitude now. Maybe I can keep her aloft, I don't know . . ."

"Any fire?"

"Uh . . . no . . . I don't . . . yes . . . yes, roger, my engine's on fire."

"Stay calm, Nick. You'll be all right. But you're going to have to ditch. Right now before the fire reaches her fuel tank or the ammunition blows. Just remember the emergency ditch drill your father taught you, you'll come out of this alive."

Nick had drilled this into his brain and now spoke each procedure aloud, the way his father had taught him when they'd practiced for just such an emergency.

Gunner, alone in the barn, his heart in his mouth, craned his head toward the wireless and listened intently to Nick's every word, the boy's voice on the speaker cracking and choked from the black smoke pouring back from his flaming engine.

"All emergency procedures complete?" Gunner said.

"Affirmative. Over."

"Good lad. Listen carefully. You've got calm seas. That's good. Get her right down over the water, quickly now, just above stall speed. Just keep her nose up and set her down as gently as ever you can, like a wee butterfly on a pond. When you stall out, she'll settle right off. Then you get out of there fast, boy, I mean you move as fast as you ever moved in your life, and you swim away from that damn sewing basket any damn way you can."

"Roger. Descending..."

"Don't forget to untie yer lap rope, lad. Slow you down gettin' out if you don't."

Nick tore at the line around his waist and whipped it away. "Thanks, I would've forgotten, too, Gunner. Lots of smoke and fire now, can barely see. I've never felt this close to... to... you know."

"All in the game. How close to the surface?"

"Twenty feet... fifteen... ten. Engine completely engulfed in flames... ammo bound to blow... I need to put her down right now, Gunner.... Over and out."

"God love you, Nicky. And Godspeed, boy."

The radio squawked once and went dead.

Gunner collapsed at the table and buried his face in his hands, unable to stop the hot tears running down his cheeks. There was nothing for it. It was in God's hands now. Nick was in grave, grave danger. Sopwith Camels didn't float. Or at least not for very long. All the weight in the Sopwith was up front, jammed into the first seven feet of the fuselage. Pilot, fuel, guns, ammunition. And, in the nose, that massive monster of an engine.

As soon as she hit the sea, her tail would come straight up, her weighty nose would plow under the water, point downward, and take her straight to the bottom.

Gunner knew this from all too personal experience.

It had been a dark night, just like this one. A young pilot returning from a cross-channel training flight to Normandy and back. He'd let his mind wander. Strong headwinds. Thunderheads about, crackling with lightning. Suddenly, he was in a death spin. He fought the controls all the way down. Then he was upside down, underwater, disoriented in a pitch-black world, not knowing which way was up.

The well-nigh impossible fact that young Royal Flying Corps cadet Archibald "Gunner" Steele had gotten out of that cockpit and survived was a blooming miracle. Few survived a ditch in a Sopwith. Hundreds did not.

It had been his last flight. A military tribunal rightly blamed the loss of the aircraft on pilot error. It was a secret he'd take to the grave. To his eternal humiliation, he'd been drummed out of the Flying Corps. After a year of drowning his sorrows at the corner pub, he'd pulled himself together. If he couldn't fly, he could certainly float. He'd joined the bleeding Navy and spent his war looking through a gunsight at the endless blue of the sea. Many a U-boat had gone to the bottom thanks to his proficiency.

But his heart had always been in the sky.

· The English Channel ·

The sea was as black as the sky. Nick couldn't even make out a line of demarcation between them. He was trying to keep the Sopwith level with the horizon. Difficult without being able to *see* the horizon. Modern fighters like the Spitfire had an instrument that told you when you were flying level. But this wasn't a modern fighter. And the last thing he wanted was to accidentally catch a wingtip in the water and go spinning arse-over-teakettle across the dark sea.

He felt, more than saw, the sea rapidly coming up to meet him. Sound of a light chop, smell of seaweed and brine. He signed off with Gunner and concentrated determinedly on setting the old girl down as gently as possible. He wanted her upright at least long enough for him to scramble out of the cockpit and swim for shore. He'd flown only a half-mile from Guernsey. Should be an easy enough swim back to shore.

He ripped his flying helmet and goggles from his head and flung them overboard. He struggled out of his fleece-lined leather jacket and heaved that over, too. Then he peered over the side of the cockpit at the water. He was close! Maybe ten feet. He let her stall, and then he set her down, like a butterfly landing on a still pond.

Things happened so quickly after that, he'd no time to reflect upon his perfect landing.

Almost instantly, behind him, he felt her tail coming up off the water and the plane rapidly pitching her nose down. There was a hiss as the nose quickly submerged, finally extinguishing the flaming engine. He knew then that with most of her weight forward, she would go down, and she would go down fast. He grabbed a deep breath, sucking as much air into his lungs as he possibly could.

Then, with no warning at all, the nose dropped sharply and the aircraft went from horizontal to vertical, tail standing straight up. The nose and cockpit were already completely submerged, and Nick knew that he was headed straight for the bottom. If he didn't act quickly, he'd be stuck in a death trap from which there'd be little hope of escape!

His first instinct was to grab the sides of the cockpit with both hands and try to lift his body straight up and out. But, even disoriented and with the water rushing past his face, he somehow knew he'd never make it out that way. His arms just weren't strong enough to fight the tremendous force of the water rushing past the fast-sinking aeroplane.

But his legs might be.

He instantly pulled his knees up to his chest and got his feet under him, boots planted on the seat of the wicker chair, crouched in position for an explosive spring outward. He hadn't a second to lose. He raised his hands above his head, holding them together, as if he was about to dive. He shoved off violently, using every ounce of power in his leg muscles.

It worked! He forcefully launched himself straight out of the cockpit. Now he was kicking desperately and clawing at the water with his hands. Every instinct told him he had a second to get completely away from the plunging aeroplane. Despite his furious efforts, he was suddenly stunned by a sharp pain in his right shoulder. He'd caught the leading edge of the upper wing as it went by him at enormous speed.

He frantically clawed at the water, trying to orient himself. Which way was up? In the cold, inky blackness, he saw a swirling stream of bubbles rising past his face, no doubt coming from the doomed plane now streaking toward the bottom.

Follow the bubbles, Nick, his brain said. Some deep part of some survival nodule in his brain was screaming. Go with the bubbles to the surface. Kick. Kick harder!

Up was air.

Down was death.

His lungs were afire and ready to burst when he finally broke through the surface, throwing his head back, taking huge gulps of air. He was amazed to be alive. Only moments ago, trapped in the plane, he'd despaired of his life, sure it was ending prematurely.

He hung in the water, composing himself, getting his breathing back to normal, and surveyeing the coastline. Behind him, a spreading pool of burning oil marked where the Camel had gone down. An easy marker for an enemy fighter or search plane. Ahead of him was a sandy white beach, some black shale, and then a hillock rising to meet the road, covered with trees. He saw no lights, no houses nearby, just an occasional automobile driving along the coast road.

He had to swim about a half-mile at most. Kicking toward shore, he began formulating a plan of what he'd do when he

Up was air. Down was death.

got there. He needed a safe place to hide and—what was that? A roaring sound, just to his right and growing louder. He saw their black silhouettes streaking toward him about twenty feet above the surface. Three Messerschmitts, probably making sure the English pilot had gone down with his plane. The pool of oil, still burning on the surface, had caught their attention, just as he'd feared.

He took a deep breath and ducked beneath the surface. He heard the planes roar overhead. He had a few seconds to surface and take another breath. He popped his head up, and saw the three Nazi fighter planes banking hard left in a tight turn. They were coming right back! Had they seen him?

He inhaled and submerged once more.

A few seconds later, the fighters were back, streaking overhead at an unbelievable speed. He held his breath as long as he could, his lungs afire. The sound of the three warplanes gradually faded, and he knew it was safe now to swim for shore.

Safe? His confidence faded quickly. Surely the Germans would send out patrol boats to the site of the downed aircraft, looking for the pilot. They were probably already headed his way, so he swam very quickly. And they might even send foot soldiers to look for him along this bit of coast, since it was where a survivor would obviously be found.

He needed to get quickly across that beach, up the hill, and through the trees. Then he'd cross the road and begin the long climb up through the thick forest on the other side. At the top of that massive peak, called Saint George's, was a possible refuge. If he could climb quickly enough, he might reach it by dawn.

About twenty feet from shore, he stopped swimming and raised his head. Something caught his eye, a brief flash of light among the black trees in the woods? He paddled silently in place, scanning the beach and the woods beyond. All seemed quiet. Still, there'd definitely been something. Some kind of light.

Now he saw it. Someone was coming toward him, moving slowly through the dark wood down toward the beach, right in his direction. It was the shadowy figure of a man, alone, he thought, with an electric torch in his hand. Still, he seemed to be speaking to someone. His tone was strange. Almost as if he was barking commands, not speaking to a companion.

Then Nick heard the furious sounds of a guard dog, as the animal began to howl. Growling viciously, the big dog was, and the man now emerged from the wood. He was shouting commands in German at the big Doberman straining at his leash. The dog was up on his rear legs, his forepaws clawing at the air. He'd caught the scent of something, Nick knew, or, more likely, someone, namely him. And his owner was a German soldier, searching this part of the coast.

"*Schatzi! Nein! Halt! Halt!*"

Nick knew enough German to know the big man was ordering the dog to stop. He drew a deep breath and submerged. If the dog had his scent, and he very well seemed to, perhaps Nick could stay under long enough for them to move on. When his lungs were bursting and he could stand it not one second longer, he rose again to the surface.

The German and the Doberman were still there. And the dog instantly renewed his howling and struggling against his leash at Nick's scent.

"*Was ist los, meine Schatzi? Was ist los?*" the Nazi soldier said, playing the light of his hand-held torch over the empty white beach. Then he raised the flashlight and began to swing the powerful white beam out over the black water, looking for whatever had gotten Schatzi's unwavering attention. For clearly, there was something, someone, out there.

Nick barely got his head underwater before the light swept over him. He'd not had time to take a deep breath and knew he could not stay submerged for long. Two minutes at most.

He raised his head for a breath and a peek.

The dog instantly howled and surged toward him, ripping the leash from the German's fist. And the huge dog then bounded toward the beach and straight for Nick. The German staggered forward, and the torch flew from his hand. He was screaming at his dog to stop, stop, but the animal had been trained to attack, and attack he would.

Could he outswim the dog? Nick had no idea how fast such animals might be in the water. But he'd certainly no intention of finding out. He submerged once more and quickly swam underwater to his left and fast as he could, too, putting distance between himself and where the Doberman had last seen him. When he exhausted his air, he rose, allowing only his eyes above the surface.

He saw the dog racing across the sand, headed for the exact point where he'd last seen Nick. The German was shouting at him, but now seemed to be pleading with him. Why? Wasn't the dog just doing his job?

The explosion was sudden and deafening and blinding. An upthrust of flame and metal. The great Doberman pinscher was no longer. Vaporized in an instant. The dog had stepped on a German landmine.

So the entire sandy beach, the one Nick had intended to scramble across just a few minutes earlier, must have been mined by the invading Nazis! Schatzi had just saved Nick Mc-Iver's life.

The soldier, shoulders slumped, stood at the edge of the

woods and stared forlornly at the blackened crater in the sand containing the scattered remains of his dog. Then he cursed loudly, turned, and returned through the trees toward the road. Was he the only one? Or were there more of these guards with their dogs patrolling the coast road? At least Nick knew why he'd been screaming at his dog to halt. He knew the beach was mined. And he would blame the unknown British pilot for the death of his Schatzi.

Nick submerged again and began to swim along the coast underwater, pausing to lift his head only when he needed to take a breath. There was a jetty jutting out into the water just around the point of land to his left. Maybe ten minutes away. He'd go ashore over those rocks. And pray that German soldier had not seen the face of the young pilot bobbing in the sea, the one who'd gotten his dog killed. That was trouble, and Nick knew he already had more than enough of that to deal with.

Nick moved carefully across the jetty toward land. Waves were breaking over the massive black rocks. They were slippery, and he could easily break an arm or a leg if he slipped in the dark. At the landward end of the jetty was the treeline. No beaches full of landmines here at least. He safely reached the jetty's end and began climbing up through the narrow band of forest to the road, his keen eyes searching the darkness, looking for any flash of light.

He soon reached the shore road and crouched amongst some heavy bushes, wanting to make sure the way was clear before he dashed across it and began his long climb to the top of Saint George's Mount.

Two minutes later, he'd taken one step into the road when

the roar of a speeding truck could be heard around a sharp bend in the road to his left. He saw the truck's headlights beginning to sweep toward him and dove back into his hiding place seconds before he'd have been seen.

It was a German half-track, full of troops bristling with machine guns. He watched it speed by, praying it was on routine patrol and would just continue along the road into Saint Peter Port. But less than half a mile down the road to his right, the armored half-track braked to a screeching halt. He saw the silhouettted soldier who'd lost his dog on the beach rush up to the cab and leap onto the running board. He was shouting and pointing down at the spot on the beach where Schatzi had tripped a mine.

Nick knew he had to cross the road *now* or risk being seen as the soldiers came out of the truck. He dropped to his belly and snaked across the rough macadam road as fast as he could, watching the storm troopers and barking guard dogs come piling out of the truck and begin fanning out through the woods leading to the beach. At this distance, on his belly in the dark, he thought he'd be hard to spot.

A powerful spotlight on top of the truck was suddenly illuminated. It swept in great stark white arcs back and forth along the treeline. Now the light was headed this way. They were looking for him, all right. They knew the pilot, whoever he was, had not gone down with his ship. The dog caught his scent.

He scrambled from the road and dove into the brush, heart pounding. After catching his breath, he chanced a peek down the road at the Germans. None of them were coming back this way along the road, thank goodness. They were all searching the woods along the sandy beach. The only thing in his favor was that he'd swum to the jetty. No tracks in the sand. But he couldn't kid himself. Sooner or later they'd come searching this side of the road, up this very hillside, and he wanted to be as far away from those nosy Dobermans and their handlers as possible.

The grade was by turns steep and slight and would then flatten out for a bit as he passed through a meadow before entering another forest. He was tired, he suddenly realized, but the dogs and the adrenaline pumping through his veins kept him moving ever upward. Suddenly he came upon an opening and a narrow granite cliff that jutted out over the forest with a clear view to the sea beyond. He carefully stepped out along its edge. One misstep and he'd plummet a thousand feet to his death. His heart leaped to his throat when he looked below.

The Germans had crossed the road. All of them. He could see their torchlights flashing through the trees below. They were fanned out, coming up Saint George's Mount through the woods, dogs howling, beams of light streaking upward, flashing everywhere through the black trunks and stark limbs of trees. The dogs had obviously caught his scent. He had a good head start on them, thank heavens. But now he would have to run the rest of the way to the top of Saint George's Mount. And he was exhausted.

He took another breath. He'd have to will himself to summon energy he knew he didn't have. He'd have to find a place inside himself he wasn't even sure existed.

If he didn't, he knew with absolute certainty that his life would end by his being torn apart by vicious dogs. Not a good way to go. And even at the top, he was not sure he'd find safety.

The Germans had of course seen his engine catch fire and watched the old Sopwith Camel go down in flames. That's why that first guard was searching the beach with his dog. Near where Nicky had ditched his beloved Sopwith. The Germans wouldn't be happy until they had found the downed pilot who had destroyed so much of their aerodrome and fighter squadrons. He'd done them enormous harm. And it wouldn't matter much if he was caught dead or alive.

· Greybeard Island ·

Kate McIver burst into her brother's room first thing that morning, swinging her favorite doll by its thinning red hair. Fresh salty air wafted through the opened windows; the little whitewashed room near the top of the lighthouse was filled with brilliant sunshine. All of Nicky's wooden battleships and destroyers were scattered around the floor, just where he'd left them when one of his endless sea battles had ended.

The big black dog, Jip, was sound asleep at the foot of Nick's bed, nestled in a pool of warm sunlight. But no Nicky.

She eyed his bed carefully. The pillow was scrunched up, yes. But the bedcovers had not been touched. It was fairly obvious to her—and she was no great scientific detective like Lord Hawke or Commander Hobbes—but it was apparent that Nick had not slept in his bed last night. Which meant he hadn't come home at all. The whole night! Which meant he was in big, big trouble.

A little half-smile formed on her face. *Should she tell?*

Kate didn't necessarily like to *cause* trouble. But she was always happy to see it come along, especially if her older brother was the one in trouble and not she herself. Staying out all night was definitely going to cause a major hurricane, and she turned on a heel and left the room, practically skipping down the long spiral staircase that led to the kitchen.

Something was cooking down there, and the fragrance of a fresh-baked strawberry pie filled the staircase. Her favorite thing in all the world was a strawberry pie, made by her mother, with berries fresh from the lighthouse strawberry patch. It was funny. A few months ago, her mother had said they might find Nazis hiding in the strawberry patch. Now they were dangling from trees!

She arrived in the kitchen with mischief on her mind.

Her parents were seated at the banquette in the bay window that overlooked the gardens and blue sea beyond. Mum was having her shredded wheat, blueberries, and Prince of Wales tea, and Father his steaming Irish oatmeal. Both had their noses buried deep in the newspapers, reading about the creepy old Nazis and the invasion and bombing of their islands.

She slid into her seat at the table, thinking she had a little bomb of her own to drop this sunny morning.

"Morning, Father," she said, cheerfully. "Good morning, Mummy."

"Morning, dear," they both said, not looking up from their newspapers. She waited as long as ever she could, and then she spoke.

"Nick not down for breakfast yet?" she asked, the very picture of innocence.

Both nodded their heads no.

"Hmm," she said, "that's interesting."

No comment.

"Are you done with that first section, darling?" her mother asked her father.

"Here you are, darling," he said, handing the paper across the table to her. They called each other that word so much, she'd begun to think of them as "The Darlings." "Things aren't looking good on Guernsey, as you'll see."

"Awful. Just awful, isn't it, darling?" her mum said, folding the paper. "Abandoned to our fate, I suppose. We'll just have to make the best of it."

Kate put her fist to her mouth and made a small cough to gain everyone's attention. "Am I the only one here who thinks it's just a wee bit strange that Nicky has not come down for breakfast?"

"Hmm," her father said, not glancing up. From her mum, silence.

"No one is the least bit upset?" Kate said, incredulous.

"I suppose you are, dear," her mother murmured, turning the page. "You certainly seem to be upset."

"Well, I think both of you should march right upstairs to his room and have a look at his bed."

"Really?" her father asked, lighting his pipe, "Why on earth should we do that, Katie dear? We're in the middle of breakfast."

Her mother looked at her carefully. "Feeling all right, are you, sweetheart? You seem a bit out of sorts this morning."

"It's not me who's out of sorts, I'll tell you that much. It's Nicky."

"Really? And why is that?"

"Because if you go up to his room, you will see, as I did, that he didn't come home at all last night. His bed's not even been touched."

"Didn't come home, yes, quite right," Angus McIver said, turning another page of the *Island Gazette*.

"That would account for his bed not having been slept in, wouldn't it, dear?" Emily McIver said to her daughter.

Kate sat back against the cushion and crossed her arms across her chest, her lips pursed in frustration. "And no one cares," she said, color rising in her cheeks. "He stays out all night, and it's perfectly all right. Not even in the slightest bit of hot water. I come home from school fifteen minutes late and get into no end of trouble."

"He left us a note," her mother said, smiling at her, "saying that he couldn't sleep, would be working in the barn quite late with Gunner, and would spend the night with him at Greybeard Inn."

"Oh. He left a note?" Each word was like the barest wisp of air seeping out of her balloon.

"You don't think your brother would stay out all night without letting his parents know, do you, Kate? Your brother's a very fine, responsible young man, in case you hadn't noticed."

"No, I didn't think he'd do anything so terrible. I was just so . . . so terribly worried about him. That he'd been . . . kidnapped or something."

"Kidnapped? Whoever would kidnap Nick?"

"I don't know. Bad people. Like pirates or Nazis."

"The Nazis don't seem to think Greybeard is worth bothering with," her father said, "so far, anyway."

"Kate," her mother said, smiling at her, "do you smell something in the oven?"

Good. Change of subject.

"I do, I do! The most wonderful smell ever."

"It's a strawberry pie."

"My most, most favorite. Is it for me? Please say yes!"

"No, Katie dear, of course it's for your dear brother. He and Gunner have been slaving away over that airplane for weeks now. And I thought they deserved a special treat, don't you?"

"I–I suppose so," Kate said, trying to muster up some believable amount of enthusiasm for the notion. This morning was not going according to plan.

"Good. Well, it's ready to come out of the oven, and your father and I thought it would be fun for you personally to deliver it to them at the barn. It's a lovely day for a stroll through the woods, isn't it?"

"Yes, Mother," Kate said, as her mum rose from the table, put on her silly stuffed mittens, and removed the steaming pie from the oven.

"Here, I'll put it in this basket and cover it with this linen napkin to keep it nice and warm. But you'd best hurry up, or it will be cold by the time you get there."

Kate slid off the seat and took the wicker basket. This morning, which had started off so splendidly, was definitely not turning out at all as she'd imagined it.

She marched over to the door, opened it, and paused a moment looking back at her parents. "I've been doing my part in the war, too, you know."

Her father looked up from his paper. "Have you indeed, little Katie? And what, pray, have you been up to?"

"I've been going into those scary woods is what. I've been laying flowers on the grave of that poor boy who died in the tree."

"How lovely, dear," her mother said.

"Well, German or no, he was only a boy. Has a mum and dad at home somewhere grieving for him, hasn't he?"

"It's a lovely thought, Kate. Here, take these fresh-cut roses and lay them on his grave on your way through those frightful woods to the barn. Is that a good idea?"

"Yes, mother," Kate said, and then she was down the lane, feeling like a popped balloon.

Now she'd have to go through the woods, she thought, muttering to herself. She hadn't been fibbing; she really had been placing nosegays or sprays of lily on the mound of earth in the meadow where the poor dead boy lay. She hadn't been going through the awful woods, of course; she'd been taking the lane up to Hawke Field and then walking past the barn to his grave. But she'd promised her mum this time, and she was in no mood this morning to break any promises.

She would go through the woods no matter what lay in wait for her. And any beastie, ghost, or goblin who got in her way would be very sorry.

And so she entered the black forest.

Goodness. Woods were scary places no matter what her fearless brother Nicky said. Crowded, dark, uncontrolled places where nature, with long slithering fingers, crept up on a little girl. Trees, their branches intertwined above her head, weaving themselves in frightful patterns to form a vault over her like a great green church. Making a place where light had to struggle to be seen. The ground beneath her feet was choked with brambles and moss, and it was all she could do to maintain her balance, clutching the heavy basket for dear life in one hand.

Carrying on, she began to calm herself. She'd been in far worse spots than this one, she reminded herself. Like the time when she and Hobbes had been rammed by a U-boat on a foggy night in the middle of the channel. And then their lovely boat *Thor* was sinking, and they were captured by Nazis and taken aboard a giant German submarine that was terribly smelly inside.

She'd been afraid then, but she'd dared not let anyone see it. And in the end, she and her wonderful Hobbesie had triumphed over the Germans, hadn't they? Captured the experimental U-boat and got a medal from Winston Churchill himself. And now he was Prime Minister!

Grimly determined, she marched onward. She knew she would soon reach the river that separated the two sections of the wood. Once across that narrow river, her heart stopped fluttering, the white birch trees were sparse, and the golden light on the forest floor made everything seem friendly, bright, and free of any monsters lurking behind her.

Soon she was in the little meadow where the river burbled along, a stream weaving this way and that through the lilacs and tall grass. Once she'd crossed that river, her troubles were over. She'd place Mum's roses on the poor soldier's grave and then head for the barn to give Nicky his oh so well deserved pie. He'd promised to take her up for another ride in the beautiful plane, and maybe today he would! It was wondrous up there in the clouds. Much better than she'd ever imagined, sitting on her brother's lap as they soared like birds.

As she approached the river, she saw a very strange sight indeed. There appeared to be two men, one large, one tall and muscular, perched on a large boulder side by side, fishing in the river. In all her life, she'd never seen anyone fish this river! Why, few people even knew the stream existed, because everybody knew except her brother that these woods had been haunted by faeries and gremlins long before she was even born.

She thought about circling far upstream, but the river was

much wider there, and there were no broad rocks in mid-stream to make crossing a simple matter of being carefully surefooted on the mossy stones.

She approached the men from the rear, quietly, because she knew from past experience that fishermen everywhere hated any kind of noise or unexpected disturbance that might spook their prey. They were both wearing black mackin-toshes with hoods, even though it wasn't raining, which she found strange.

When she got within a few feet of the two fishermen, both sitting quite still, she paused and said, "Any luck? What are you gentlemen fishing for today?"

There was a frightfully long pause, and she thought per-haps they were deaf mutes. Then the tall, slight one slowly turned his horrible face toward her.

It was Snake Eye. She screamed. Even with the hood throwing heavy shadow across his visage, she recognized the hideous tattooed snakes that curled around the French pi-rate's eyes, over his mouth, rising up inside his nostrils when he smiled his evil grin.

"*Bonjour, mademoiselle,*" the human monster hissed. "*Un grand plaisir* to see you again. You ask what we are fishing for? I'll let me shipmate answer that one, if you please. *Mon Capit-aine?*"

The other man abruptly turned to face her, and she heard the horrible tinkling of the many small silver skulls woven into his beard as his great head swiveled on his shoulders. She recognized him at once. A face she'd hoped and prayed never to lay eyes on again. Her trembling heart almost came to a complete stop.

Billy Blood.

"Fishing for the female of the species, we are today, and

you seem to be our first catch of the day, lassie," Blood said, in his awful musical voice. "We was hoping you might swim along this stream."

She screamed again and turned to run.

"And this be our hook!" He laughed. She saw it then, lunging for her, the gleaming golden claw that had replaced the hand Lord Hawke had sliced off with his sword.

And then his great golden hook was hard round her ankle as she tried to run, and she was jerked off her feet and into the arms of the most evil pirate ever to stalk the earth.

"We're taking a wee time trip, lassie," Blood said, staring into her terrified eyes.

"My brother will get you for this," she said, staring back, kicking as hard as she could, trying to catch his jaw.

"I only hope he does. Come for you, that is. This is me plan, you see. He's the big fish and you're the little bait. Now behave like bait, and shut your little mouth whilst my comrade Snake Eye and I set our trap."

Blood pulled a roll of foolscap from under his cloak and a pen to write with.

"What trap?" she cried.

"Tell him where you lie, lassie. Back in time. You're going to leave him a little love note on this here paper. Giving him your exact location in Port Royal, Jamaica. He'll be using his time machine to rescue you, and that's what we're counting on. What's in the basket, dear?"

"None of your beeswax!"

"He asked you what was in the basket," Snake Eye said, putting his face close to hers. "Don't make him ask again, or–"

"A strawberry pie. For my brother and Gunner."

"Gunner!" Snake Eye hissed. "He's the dog almost blew me hand off with that blunderbuss aboard the *Merlin*!"

"Here be what we do, now," Blood said. "We put this note from you under the dish cloth with the pie. Leave it just outside the barn where that cursed boy will be sure to find it."

Blood reached inside his cloak again and withdrew the gleaming golden ball called the Tempus Machina. He smiled at Katie and said, "You've never been on a time trip, have you, wee lass? You're going back in time over two hundred years. I think you will find it quite adventuresome."

As Kate picked up the pen and began to write the words (thank goodness she was good at spelling) Blood told her to say, writing with trembling hand, she found she couldn't stop the tears that were flowing down her cheeks. She loved Nicky very much, he was her best friend on this whole earth, and the very last thing she wanted to do was help these two evil creatures get Nick in their clutches.

Still, she knew her only hope of rescue was her brother, Nick. Only Nicky and the bad captain, of all the people in the world, had time machines. So only her dear brother could travel to the past and find her. So she did what Captain Blood told her to do.

22

· Guernsey ·

Nick knew he was in serious trouble. Exhausted by the long swim in cold water and racing uphill through the dense forest, he felt as if he might collapse to the ground at any moment. One trip over an exposed root or a fallen tree and he'd never find the strength to make it to his feet again.

Hot on his heels were at least a dozen of Hitler's Nazi storm troopers and their vicious Dobermans. He could hear the fierce snarls of the beasts getting ever closer. He was running now by sheer willpower and adrenaline. But there was not enough left of either to keep him on his feet for much longer.

But he knew that if he stopped, he would die a horrible death, ripped to shreds by vicious dogs. And so he staggered forward, using his arms for help by grabbing low-hanging tree limbs and hauling himself up that way. His left arm was a help. His right screamed with pain when he used it. His legs felt like rubber, and he could no longer count on them. He had to pause, even if only for a few precious seconds, to catch his breath. He stopped and leaned against a large oak, sucking down huge lungfuls of air. And still the howling dogs came.

But he heard something else now, in that brief moment that the blood wasn't pounding so noisily in his ears. And for the first time he felt a glimmer of hope. He heard the sound of rapidly moving water. There was a river, sizable by the sound of it, maybe less than a hundred yards ahead of him. That river might mean salvation, and he sprinted up toward the sound of running water with the newfound energy of hope.

He came upon the grassy bank seconds later. It was a wide river, too wide to swim across in his condition and not get caught. But there was a small wooden bridge arching over the river, and the sight of it caused something to stir deep in his memory.

What was it? A scene from one of his most favorite books, *Robin Hood.* That was it! Robin and Little John are on foot, running headlong through the forest, trying to escape from King John's men mounted on horseback. Robin spies a small pond surrounded by tall reeds and coaxes Little John into the water. He uses his knife to cut two lengths of reed, and the two men submerge, breathing through the reeds as King John's henchmen race past the pond and on into the heart of Sherwood Forest.

There were large clumps of reeds sprouting from the water along the banks on both sides of the river. Nick slid down the slippery bank on his bottom and crawled under the bridge. The dogs still had his scent, and they were quickly gaining ground. Nick whipped out his pocketknife, grabbed a thick green reed, and sliced off a three-foot section. He could hear the loud shouting of the Nazi SS troopers, urging the dogs onward, as he slid down the muddy bank and into the water, one end of the reed already in his mouth.

The trick may be an old one, but it worked well enough. It was surprisingly easy to breathe through the tube. He was only a foot or so underwater, in the middle of the thick stand of reeds, so he could hear the wild yips and howls of the Dobermans as they raced toward the bridge. Suddenly the dogs stopped, just shy of the bridge, and he could hear the soldiers urging them on. Obviously, they'd lost his scent. He heard a loud, angry voice shouting in German. So where was he, this English pilot who had caused such destruction? Have we lost him?

From below the surface, he saw at least a dozen powerful electric torchlights scanning the roiling river. He heard more voices rising in mounting frustration. And then a dog and a soldier came under the bridge, barely two feet from where Nick was hiding. The beam of light flashed on the reeds directly above him, as the Doberman poked his nose in among the reeds, even pushing Nick's own reed aside. Then, mercifully, the dog retreated, and the German aimed his beam at the reeds on the far side of the river.

"*Nicht hier!*" the lone soldier called up to his superior officer, and soon man and dog disappeared.

After an unbearably long period, in which the dogs were searching frantically for their prey in the nearby woods, he heard a shouted command from an officer. He dared to raise his head a fraction, only his eyes above the surface.

Immediately, he heard the yelping, frustrated dogs race across the wooden bridge and into the woods on the steep hillside above. Right behind them, the clomping of dozens of heavy boots on the run. Had he done it? Had he really fooled them?

He was mightily tempted to surface and climb out of this frigid water. Cold was seeping into his bones. But they were clever, these Nazis were, he'd learned that as a junior Bird-watcher, and he would not be surprised if they hadn't left a lone officer at the bridge armed with a machine gun. Just in case they'd somehow missed the fleeing pilot who had done such horrible damage at the aerodrome.

So he stayed down, hidden in the reeds, until he felt as if the soldier above would surely have run out of patience at his lonely post in the chill night air. By now, surely he would have rushed up to join his comrades still in full pursuit, wouldn't he? Nick dared not take the chance. His teeth were chattering now, but he stayed put.

It felt like hours, but it was probably only half an hour or so. He heard the man grunt and saw the glowing coal of a cigarette flicked from above land in the river. Then the last German was gone. Nick's whole body was shaking violently as he heaved himself up onto the bank and collapsed, lying on his back, staring at the underside of the bridge. He was glad to spit the now mushy end of the reed out of his mouth and take gulps of cool air. He was cold and wet, muddy and exhausted, but he was still alive. He lay there on the muddy bank, considering all of his options, one by one. By the time he'd gotten to the third, he'd fallen fast asleep.

———

He awoke with the rising sun glinting off the river, sharp daggers of light in his sleepy eyes. He sat up, rubbing his face vigorously, remembering how he'd come to be under this little wooden bridge. His clothes had dried a bit during the night, but he felt a shiver as he scrambled up the bank to look around. No dogs. No Nazis.

He was pretty sure they'd given up on the search sometime during the night. The dogs had lost his scent, and the soldiers must have been at least as tired as he was. The evening had turned much colder while he slept. The SS men were probably even now snoring peacefully in their warm barracks.

He stood up, climbed the banks, took off his sodden jacket, and spread it across some bushes in the warm sun. He took stock of himself. Apart from his painful right shoulder, where a section of the Camel had caught him on her way to the bottom, he seemed in reasonably good shape. And just the fact that he'd managed to outsmart those bloodthirsty dogs filled him with enough confidence to face whatever came next.

Surely some German soldiers might well still be out there looking for him. But he doubted they would still be searching these woods, the dogs having been unable to find him.

Rejuvenated by this newfound optimism, he put on his still-damp jacket and headed across the old wooden bridge. He would make his way to the hilltop, in hopes that he might find sanctuary there.

He had seen Fordwych Manor, which stood atop Saint George's cliff overlooking the Gulf of Saint Malo, from the air. The day when he'd made his first aerial surveillance flight over Guernsey. He knew it belonged to one of Lord Hawke's oldest friends, an elderly Baroness named Fleur de Villiers, one of the original founders of the Birdwatchers secret society along with Lord Hawke.

He had never met the Baroness, but as he made his way slowly up the narrow lane that led to her home, he was fairly sure she would recognize his family name when he presented himself. The McIver clan had enjoyed a brief moment of celebrity when his sister, Kate, and Commander Hobbes had captured an experimental Nazi U-boat. They'd then managed to keep the submarine penned up inside Hawke Lagoon until Winston Churchill and a team of Royal Navy engineers had flown in from London and inspected her from stem to stern. Kate McIver, only seven years old, had been the talk of every pub and shop on both Guernsey and Greybeard islands for weeks. She was actually–though no one in her family would ever dare tell her so–famous.

The imposing manor house stood at the very summit of the cliff, surrounded by acres of green parkland. It was rather grand, even by Guernsey standards, but Nick would not describe it as a castle or a fort, though it had many of the features of both. There was a great, high stone wall surrounding the place, with massive iron gates. And there were tall turrets with battlements atop them and a great tower, covered in ivy, that looked as if it might once have been home to a massive cannon pointed seaward.

The lane had eventually turned to gravel, and Nick marched up to the iron-gated entrance. It was open, not much but enough for him to slip through. At the entrance to the house, a little man was busily washing an amazingly large automobile, singing "The Rose of Tralee" in a lovely Irish tenor.

Almost as big as a locomotive, the auto appeared to be made completely of sterling silver or some kind of highly polished metal. Why, the bonnet alone was nearly the length of Nick's small sailing sloop, *Stormy Petrel*.

"Good morning, sir!" Nick shouted as he approached, not wanting to startle the man. He stood up, turned round, and smiled at the approaching boy.

"And top of the mornin' to you, sir," the little fellow replied, in an Irish voice so beautiful and light it was almost like singing. He had to be at least seventy, yet his bright blue eyes, red cheeks, and white smile made him seem almost elf-like.

"I am Nicholas McIver, sir," Nick said, extending his hand.

"Are you indeed, Mr. McIver? And I am Eammon Darby, formerly of Galway Bay. And where are ye from, young Mr. McIver. You dinna look like a Guernseyman."

"Greybeard Island, sir, and I'm trying to get back there as quickly as possible so I can—"

"McIver from Greybeard, eh? Surely not related to that little girl who—"

"She's my sister."

"Sister, is she? Must be a right scrappy little colleen, then?"

"Scrappy doesn't even begin to describe her, sir."

"Want to get home, do you? I could drive you over," Eammon said, patting the gleaming bonnet of his car and laughing, as if it was the best joke ever.

Nick said, "I've never seen an automobile like that. What is it?"

"She's called the Silver Ghost, sir. Made by the Rolls-Royce company back in the year 1922. I'm taking her into town this morning for her weekly exercise. Otherwise her muscles get stiff. Say, Nick, yer lookin' a bit grey about the gills, lad."

"I—I'm afraid I require assistance, Mr. Darby."

Darby stepped back and appraised him from head to toe. "You do look like you've been through a bit of heavy sledding, lad. A rough patch. Are ye all right? Yer right arm hurting you, is it, now?"

"I did injure my right shoulder, but that's about it. I'm mostly cold. Cold and very, very hungry, Mr. Darby."

"What have ye been about then, to bring yourself to such a state."

"Hiding from Germans, sir."

"I see. On the run, are you? Well, we can help with that. So you could use some food, I imagine?"

"Ever so grateful."

"Well, yer in luck. Food, now that's something we can provide here at Fordwych Manor. We've a fine kitchen garden and a right good cook, though temperamental at times she is. Bronwyn makes a good stew. Not a fine Irish stew, mind you— she's Welsh. But her lamb stew will make yer heart sing!"

"I wonder, sir. Is the Baroness herself at home?"

"She is indeed. See that blue and white flag flying atop the battlements? That means she's in residence."

"I wonder if I might have a word with her, sir?"

"Does she know you, laddie?"

"No, sir. But I believe she would know my father. And, of course, my famous sister."

"Well, nothing to it, then. She's in her library, paying the monthly bills. She hates spending money, she does, and I'll wager she'll be happy for the distraction. Just follow me, I'll take care of you, young McIver, never you worry. Come along now, we'll get you some nice hot tea and cakes for starters!"

Nick and Eammon found the Baroness at a small French desk in a bay window that overlooked the sea. There were floor-to-ceiling books on every wall. Nick, deliriously happy to have a mug of warm tea in his hands, was starting to feel much better. The white-haired woman with the startling blue eyes looked up from her desk as Darby and the disheveled boy entered the room.

"Beg pardon for the intrusion, ma'am," Mr. Darby said, "but may I please introduce young Nicholas McIver, madame? I'm afraid he requires some assistance."

"McIver, did you say? You're not related to—"

"She's my sister, ma'am."

"Kate's brother! Great fun having such a famous sibling, I imagine. Well, then, what's all this about assistance? What kind of assistance?"

"Any kind would do, ma'am," Nick said.

"Come closer and let me get a look at you, Mr. McIver," she said, waving him toward her with a pale white hand. "Mind you don't get any of your mud on my rug."

Nick did as he was instructed. The sun was strong through

the windows. And he was very conscious of his soggy, ragged appearance.

The Baroness peered into his eyes, looked him up and down, and said, "You're Angus McIver's boy all right."

"Yes, I am," a startled Nick said.

"You're the living spit of him, boy. I'd recognize those blue eyes and that pugnacious chin anywhere." She stood up and offered her hand across the desk. "I know all about you, Nick McIver. Lord Hawke, my good friend of many years, is a great admirer of yours."

"Well, I—I'm, I mean to say, I don't–"

"Always accept a compliment. It's bad manners not to. Now, Eammon, weren't you planning to take the Ghost out for some much-needed exercise? Stetch her legs a bit?"

"Indeed, I was just about to leave when the lad appeared on our doorstep."

"Well, hop to it. I'm sure young Nicholas and I will have a great deal to talk about."

Mr. Darby did a little bow and pulled the doors closed behind him.

"You look awful, my child," she said. "Come over here and sit by the fire. I'll bring you some nice warm blankets and a bowl of stew. Back in a flash," she said and winked at him merrily.

"Thank you, ma'am."

Nick must have fallen fast asleep by the fire because it truly did seem like the work of a moment before she reappeared with a tray and some soft woolen blankets.

When he was settled and determinedly eating his lamb stew as slowly as humanly possible, she pulled up a velvet slipper chair, leaned forward, and said, "Someone bombed the aerodrome last night, Nick. The Germans are in a frightful uproar about it, I daresay. They're going house to house in Saint Peter Port, turning everything upside down."

"Looking for the pilot," Nick said, staring into his bowl, thinking of all the trouble he'd caused his fellow islanders.

"Yes, they are. This pilot was, if I heard correctly on the telephone, flying an old World War I aeroplane when he executed a daring nighttime raid. You wouldn't know anything about that, now, would you, Nick?"

"Yes, ma'am."

"First-hand knowledge?"

"Yes, ma'am."

"You were the pilot?" she said in some amazement.

"Yes, ma'am."

"Well, it was brilliant. Really quite marvelous. Apparently you destroyed half their fighter squadon's Messerschmitts and blew up their entire ammunition dump. I've never heard of such a thing attempted by a . . . mere child. How old are you, Nick?"

"Twelve years old, ma'am."

She shook her head in wonder. "Where is your aeroplane, now, Nick?"

"On the bottom of the sea, I'm afraid."

"You had to ditch her?"

"I did. She was on fire."

"What happened?"

"As I was leaving the field there was a lot of flak and heavy machine-gun fire. I think it was the flak finally got her. A hunk of shrapnel must have hit her fuel line. The engine caught fire, and there was no chance to make it home."

"You're lucky just to be alive, child, ditching a burning aeroplane out there in the dark."

"Yes, ma'am."

"Now, what can I do for you? What do you need?"

"I'd like to go home to Greybeard Island, ma'am. Tell my parents and Gunner that I'm still alive. Then I'd like to go see our family doctor in town, Dr. Symonds. My shoulder hurts pretty badly."

"I'll get you home, Nick. I've got an old launch I could ferry you across in. Barely seaworthy, but Eammon keeps the steam engine running somehow. Meanwhile, I'll have a look at that shoulder. No blood, so a bad bruise, I imagine. A poultice should do the trick."

"I'd certainly appreciate that, ma'am. Can we call the lighthouse and tell my parents I'm all right?"

"I wish we could, but the Germans have cut the inter-island lines. Now, listen carefully, Nick. I'll have Bronwyn take you upstairs, where you can have a nice hot bath and a good rest. I've a nephew about your size, and she can find you some clean clothes. As soon as it's dark, I'll take you down to where my boat *Toot* is docked. No moon tonight, and I've been watching the German patrol boats day and night from atop my tower. I know their exact schedule. Silly Germans, you might think they'd understand that random patrols would be more effective! We can slip through tonight. Sound good?"

"Thanks ever so much, ma'am, I don't–"

At that moment Eammon burst through the double doors, his face white as a ghost. "Germans coming, ma'am! A lot of them. They're headed this way, up our lane!"

"What?"

"I was on my way down when I saw them winding up through the woods below. A big Mercedes staff car with two officers in the back, and following that, a half-track full of soldiers!"

"Did they see you?" the Baroness asked.

"I don't think so. I put the Ghost in reverse and backed all the way back up the hill. Tricky, that."

"How long have we got?"

"Ten minutes, ma'am. Maybe less. They were going pretty fast for that curvy little lane."

"Do they know what you look like, Nick?" she asked.

"There was one soldier on the beach with a dog. He may have seen me swim ashore. And then when I climbed along the jetties he might have gotten a look at me. I can't say for sure."

"We have to hide you," she said, her mind obviously racing. "But where? The cellar?"

Eammon said, "They'll search every inch of it, ma'am. But we could put him in the garage attic. It's a wee space and very hard to reach without a very shaky ladder."

"They always search attics and cellars," the Baroness said, looking hard at Nick, as if staring at him might give her an idea. She jumped to her feet, "I've got it!"

"Where to, ma'am?" Darby said.

"The chapel, of course."

"Wherever could he hide in the chapel?"

"In the priest-hole, naturally!"

Eammon nodded, and being a good Irish Catholic, he knew all about priest-holes. He just didn't happen to know there was one at Fordwych Manor. And he'd been in service here over thirty years!

"The priest-hole?" Nick asked, having never heard of such a thing.

"Hasn't been used for aeons, mind you. It's not quite the Ritz. Quick, follow me. Nick, bring your blankets. It's very cold in there, and you might have to hide for quite some time.

Depending on the persistence of these wretched Huns in searching my house."

As they reached the main hall, they heard the two German vehicles roaring up the drive.

"Eammon! Go to the front door and stall them there as long as you can. I'll take care of the boy."

"What shall I say, ma'am?"

"Heavens, Eammon, I don't know. There's a black livery jacket hanging in the hall coat closet. Fling that on and pretend you're a butler. A butler who's very hard of hearing and a bit off his nut, you understand? Not altogether there. Now, go!"

Fleur de Villiers and Nick raced down a long hallway full of large portraits and suits of armor. At the end was a stone arch and beyond that, an arched door.

The chapel was much larger than Nick would have imagined one family needed. It had beautiful stained-glass windows, and the altar beneath the crucifix was massive and lacquered with gold. And two great golden candelabras stood atop it, a burst of fresh lilies set in a vase between them.

The baroness had her arm around Nick and hurried him up the aisle to the altar.

"I don't see a place to hide in here," Nick said, his eyes darting everywhere.

"Behind the altar," she whispered.

"Behind that?" Nick asked, wondering how on earth a boy and an elderly lady could possibly move such a huge object even an inch. "How could we ever–"

"It's hinged to the wall. And it's on wheels. When Catholicism was forbidden, the penalty for priests was beheading. All these old houses have priest-holes. Now, help me. We'll both work from this end . . . you push and I'll pull it out from the wall."

Nick started pushing with all his might, but he was hampered by his bad shoulder. The altar didn't move an inch.

"Nick, I know that bruised shoulder must hurt terribly. But now you have to ignore the pain. You must push and push with everything that's in you. Or else..."

Nick took a deep breath and said, "On three, then. One... two... three!"

He pushed and the pain almost brought him to his knees.

But the heavy altar had swung away from the ancient wall, and there gaped his salvation: a simple hole in a stone wall about four feet thick. The hole was round, about three feet in diameter, roughly a foot off the floor.

"Dive in. I think I hear them coming! There are candles and matches in there. Don't worry about the light. No one can see anything once the altar's back in place."

Nick dove through the hole, then turned and looked back at the Baroness. "Can you possibly close it by yourself?"

She smiled and said, "Do you think this is the first time in my life I've had to do something all by myself? Besides, there's this rope connected to the back of the altar. Here, take this end and start pulling for all you're worth, Mr. Nicholas McIver."

Nick sat on the cold stone floor and braced himself, putting his feet against the wall on either side of the hole. Then he pulled as hard as he could, and with the Baroness pushing, the altar swung back in place a second after Nick heard loud German voices echoing down the long hallway.

It was pitch black inside the priest-hole. His fingers skittered across the floor until he felt a large taper and a box of matches. He lit the candle and held it up. He was in a small arched room with brick walls. Along the back wall stood a wooden cot. He crawled over to it and saw that it had a straw-filled mattress and even a pillow. And, from under the pillow, he pulled out a very old Bible.

He lay down upon the bed, blew out his candle, put his weary head back on the pillow, the Bible resting on his chest, and fell into the deepest sleep of his life.

"D elicious tea, Baroness de Villiers," Kommandant Wilhelm von Mannstein said, setting down his cup and plucking another cucumber sandwich from the silver platter. He was very young for a general, tall, blond, and quite handsome, were she to be honest. Although he was wholly unaware of it, she was surreptiously searching his face, ticking off clues to his character. Vanity. Susceptible to flattery. Prone to alcohol abuse. Intelligent but not wildly keen. Cruel.

"Danke schön, danke vielmals, Kommandant," she said in reply.

"You're quite welcome. And please tell me, how is it that you speak such lovely German?"

The Baroness sat back in her chair by the fire, looking carefully at the young officer over the rim of her teacup.

"I was born in Bavaria. In Berchtesgaden, in a lovely home overlooking the Königssee, Kommandant. My mother was German, a von Steuben, and my father, Auguste, was a French diplomat. So I grew up speaking both languages."

"No English blood? That's surprising on this island."

"Well, I would have moved back to my beautiful Bavaria

years ago had I not promised my late husband I would look after this lovely old fortress until I died."

"So your heart still lies in Germany."

"Yes, sad to say it, but it's still true. The fatherland calls to me. Even after all these years."

"Your beautiful home is filled with so many exquisite things, Baroness de Villiers. Art, antiques, crystal. I am sure you are worried about the presence of my soldiers in your home. Let me assure you that although they are conducting a thorough search for this missing British airman, I have instructed them that nothing under this roof is to be harmed or left out of place and the harshest punishment will be meted out to any soldier who ignores my command."

"That's very kind of you, *mein General*," she said, smiling at him with her sparkling eyes.

Was she flirting with him? A man half her age? How appalling! But perhaps necessary.

At that moment, a sergeant appeared in the doorway, saluted, and told the general the house and ground search was complete and the missing airman had not been found.

The general nodded and dismissed him with a wave of the hand. Then he stood up and offered his hand, shaking hers warmly. "Frankly, I never expected to find this English pilot in your house, Baroness, but I have so much enjoyed our little visit."

"And I as well," Fleur said, smiling.

"You know, something occurs to me. Perhaps it will offend you, but with some knowledge of your background and your feelings toward the Fatherland, perhaps not."

"What are you suggesting, Kommandant von Mannstein?"

"Baroness, you and I could be very helpful to each other

during this occupation, I think. It would be good to have someone I could trust who knew the island and the islanders."

"To do what?"

"Give me information I could not get otherwise. I am sure there will be minor civil rebellions at some point. The citizenry will grow to resent our presence here over time. There will be more attacks like the one on the aerodrome last night. Saboteurs will plot against us. It would be extremely helpful to have someone of your standing in the community–"

"An informant."

"Precisely."

"Perhaps I would be willing to consider it. But I would need certain guarantees. I would need to get about freely and unchallenged. You have set up so many checkpoints and–"

The general strode over to her desk and said, "May I borrow pen and paper?"

"The center drawer."

He spent a few minutes writing something on a stiff white card, and then handed it to the Baroness.

"What is it?" she asked, seeing his huge signature scrawled beneath a long paragraph.

"An official *Reisepass,* Baroness, what you would call in French a *passe-partout*. Just show this to any one of my men who stops you or bothers you in any way. I assure you, my signature at the bottom will guarantee you free passage anywhere you want to go. With no difficulties, I promise you."

"I would be betraying friends of many years," she said, reading the document. "It would be very difficult for me. I pride myself on my honor and loyalty."

"Yes, but where does your loyalty lie? Now, your home country is at war with England. And in wartimes, one must do what one can for one's country. The Fatherland needs you, my lovely lady."

She turned and looked away from him, not turning back when she spoke.

"I accept your offer, Kommandant von Mannstein. I will provide you with whatever I can."

"A wise decision. And you have my undying gratitude, on behalf of *der Führer*." He clicked the heels of his highly polished boots together and raised his stiff right arm, saying, "*Heil* Hitler!"

"*Heil* Hitler," Fleur said softly. "Will I see you again soon?"

"I could come to Fordwych Manor once a week for your delightful tea. And there you could share any news I might find useful."

"Yes, let us say every Tuesday at four o'clock. I shall be expecting you."

"*Auf Wiedersehen*, Baroness de Villiers."

"*Auf Wiedersehen*, Kommandant von Mannstein."

And he was gone from the library and striding in his lovely boots toward the front entrance, where all his officers and soldiers were waiting in the two vehicles.

As soon as she saw the last of the Germans drive out of the courtyard, Fleur pulled the tasseled cord that would summon Eammon, wherever he was. A few moments later, he appeared at the library door.

"Shall we fetch the boy, ma'am? That priest-hole was a stroke of genius, if I may say so. I held my breath while they searched the chapel, but all they did was crawl around the floor looking under the pews."

"Thank you, Eammon. Now, listen. The boy and I will be

using *Toot* to steam over to Greybeard. It's up and running, I assume?"

"When were you thinking of going?"

"Now."

"Now? But what about all the checkpoints? And the Nazi patrol boats are out in force this morning, looking for our young Nick."

"It was dark last night. I'm sure no one got a good look at his face. And besides, I have this," she said, handing him the stiff white card.

"What's it say, ma'am?"

"It says, my dear Eammon, that I am free to go anywhere I want, any time I want, without question. And that anyone who tries to stop me shall answer to Kommandant von Mannstein."

"But . . . how?"

"I shall explain it all in great detail later, Eammon. Now come along. We're going to the chapel to get that brave boy out of his cell."

———

Half an hour later, they were watching Eammon wave goodbye as they steamed away from the dock. Nick stood beside Fleur de Villiers inside the tiny wheelhouse as they made for Greybeard Island, six miles away.

"So, now you're a double agent, then?" Nick said, looking at her in wonder.

"I am, indeed. Isn't it exciting? I adore our beloved Birdwatchers Society, of course, but now that I'm doubled, I feel like a real spy!"

"But however will you do it?"

"Simple. Once a week at tea, I will share with the general some bits of information. Misleading information, of course."

"You mean, like—disinformation?"

"What a clever boy you are! I like that word. I'll think I'll start using it. Yes I would give the Germans disinformation. In the meanwhile, I will ply the general with schnapps and brandy to loosen his tongue. Ask him seemingly innocent questions about German operations in the islands. Find out whatever I can. You see? For the Birdwatchers to pass along to Churchill."

"I think it's brilliant," Nick said, looking at a large boat fast approaching on their starboard bow.

"Nick, what's wrong? You look terribly worried. Like some giant black cloud has appeared."

"My friend Gunner. He was on the radio with me when I went down. He knew I was on fire. I'm sure he probably thinks I've bought it."

"Well, you'll be back on your lovely island in twenty minutes. He'll be delighted to see you, won't he, risen from a watery grave."

Nick smiled. He'd come to greatly admire this wonderful woman, so brave, so full of life and energy.

"Nick?" Fleur said, a note of worry in her tone.

"Yes?"

"That boat approaching us. He seems to be on a collision course. And he's going awfully fast. There's a pair of binoculars in that drawer. Take a quick peek at him, will you?"

Nick raised the old binocs to his eyes.

"It's a German patrol boat, ma'am. I think we should stop."

Nick had seen twin .50-caliber machine guns on the bridge decks and a large-bore deck gun mounted on her bow.

The Baroness, with surprising equanimity, throttled back gently, and *Toot*'s bow dropped a bit as the little boat settled into idle speed, just enough to keep forward momentum.

"Should I go below, ma'am? Perhaps hide in the forward anchor locker?"

"No, no. They've already seen you through their high-powered glasses. Why don't you take the wheel, and I'll go aft and see what the dickens they want."

The big Nazi boat carved a sweeping turn right across *Toot*'s bow, came roaring up from astern, cut her engines, and stopped right along her starboard side. Nick pulled his throttle back to neutral. A German crewman heaved a line at Baroness de Villiers, which she caught deftly and tied off on a stern cleat. Nick caught a fleeting glimpse of the crewman's respect for this quite elderly lady who so obviously had her sea legs.

The German captain, in all his naval finery, descended from the bridge deck to the rail and looked down at the charming little steamboat, a boy at the wheel and an elderly woman working the deck.

"A steamboat, is she?" he asked in English. "Haven't seen one in years."

"Yes. I bought her on Lake Windemere decades ago."

"She looks to be in good condition—tell me, what does this English name on her stern mean? *Toot*?"

"If you wish to have tea whilst aboard, you can bleed off a little hot water using this engine valve here. When you do, like this, it makes a little 'toot.'"

"How amusing. Who are you and where are you going, dear lady?"

"I am the Baroness de Villiers from Guernsey, and this is my young nephew, Simon. We are going to Greybeard Island for a picnic."

"Ah. *Das ist gut.* A picnic. You picked a lovely day for it, Baroness. Would you be so kind as to pass your identification

papers to my lieutenant? We are looking for an English saboteur. A young man by our information. Perhaps your nephew
should step out into the sun?"

"Don't be ridiculous, Captain. He's a boy, barely twelve
years old."

"Still, I should like to get a good look at him. The man we
are searching for is small of stature. Kindly ask him to step
out to the stern. We can't be too careful, you know. No one is
above suspicion."

"Captain, we have no papers. Why should we need them?
We are out for a simple cruise. I will give your lieutenant a
document which should explain everything to your satisfaction."

"*Gut*. Bring the boy out, please, and hand us your document."

Nick stepped out into the sun as the Baroness handed
across the card from von Mannstein. She watched as he took
it from its envelope and read the contents. His face was a
broad smile as he looked up at the Baroness.

He shouted across: "You are obviously a friend of our beloved Kommandant, General von Mannstein, I see."

He handed the card back to the lieutenant who quickly
leaned across the water and returned it to Fleur de Villiers.

"*Ja, ja*," Fleur said, "a new friend but a very good one."

"Then we shall bother you no further. Please accept our
apologies for this delay and proceed on your course and enjoy your picnic on Greybeard Island. We are in fact looking
for a young German officer who disappeared on that island
some time ago. If you see or hear anything, I'm sure Kommandant von Mannstein would appreciate hearing about it.
The missing boy was his son. *Guten tag*, Your Ladyship, and
may I wish you bon voyage."

He saluted her and ducked back inside the wheelhouse.

Fleur took the line off the stern cleat and easily heaved it back to the seaman waiting for it. Moments later, the patrol boat roared away at very high speed, with sirens blaring, racing toward a Guernsey fisherman, poor fellow. He'd likely not be shown the same treatment as had been shown the Baroness de Villiers.

Nick thought of telling Baroness de Villiers about the German soldier he and his father had buried in the forest. On second thought, he decided not to. In wartime, it paid not to have too much dangerous information.

· Greybeard Island ·

Gunner, wake up! It's me! Nick!"

But Gunner wouldn't wake up, wouldn't even move a muscle or crack an eye. Nick surveyed the scene. He'd passed out in his favorite chair before the great stone hearth at the Greybeard Inn, his boots still up on the hearthstone. Beside the chair was an empty bottle of Irish whiskey, lying on its side. Gunner was snoring loudly and shaking his head back and forth, as if he was having some very bad dream. He'd probably started drinking when he lost Nick on the radio. Their last communication with each other had not been filled with hope.

Nick was, above all, most anxious to get to the lighthouse and see his parents, but since they had no idea he'd been in any danger, and Gunner did, he was at least compelled to let Gunner know he'd survived the crash at sea. Gunner, the propietor of the old inn, was probably sick with worry about whether Nick was dead or alive. No, make that "definitely sick."

Nick had never seen his friend like this. Oh, he'd have his occasional "wee dram" of rum or the like, or a lager of an evening, but an entire bottle of whiskey? Never. Nick had tried shaking him, pinching his nose, and screaming into his ears. Nothing, it seemed, would rouse his old friend from his stupor.

"Don't go anywhere," he yelled into Gunner's left ear, "I'll be right back."

Nick went into the kitchen, or galley as Gunner called it, and made a large pot of coffee, as black and hot as he could get it. Then he searched the many cabinets for a large kettle. He grabbed the biggest one he could find. It was cast iron and weighed a ton, and he felt a sharp stab of pain in his sore right shoulder as he lifted it. The poultice had helped, though, and he was on the mend. He placed the kettle in the deep sink and turned on the tap. Cold. The colder the better for his purposes.

This was not something he wanted to do, he thought, watching the water fill the kettle. But he really could think of no alternative. Then he grimaced as he thought how heavy the kettle would be when full. When the water reached the brim, he turned off the tap.

Somehow, grimacing, he lifted the kettle out of the sink. But he immediately set it on the floor. He would have to drag the thing into the lounge bar, where Gunner was waiting for his big surprise.

Nick lost about a quart of water, dragging and sloshing the kettle all the way from the galley to the lounge with his left arm only. It seemed to take an hour, but finally he was in position behind Gunner's chair. But he had one more chore.

He returned to the galley and poured a large mug full of steaming hot coffee. Back in the lounge, he placed the mug and a steaming pot of coffee on a table near Gunner's chair.

He wanted to get this hot coffee down Gunner's gullet as quickly as possible. He needed his friend's attention, and he needed him to make some sense.

"Gunner," he shouted, "please wake up!"

No effect.

He knew he would have only one shot at lifting this heavy kettle above Gunner's head, and lord knows what it would do to his shoulder. But there was nothing else for it.

He squatted behind the pot, right hand on the handle, left hand under the bottom, and rose up, using his leg muscles to get him upright and his upward momentum to get the kettle high enough. And then he tilted the kettle over Gunner's head so that most of the cold water splashed full into his face and the rest drenched his chest and stomach.

Gunner sat straight up, sputtering, and shouted, "Who's there?" not even seeming to notice that he was now drenched in cold water and soaked to the very skin.

Nick stepped around to the side of the chair, where Gunner could see him, now holding a mug of hot coffee.

"Who're you?" Gunner mumbled.

"Why, Nicholas McIver, of course. At your service, sir. Just returned from the briny deep."

"Nick?" he blurted out, rubbing the water from his already bleary eyes. "Nick McIver, as I live and breathe?"

"In the flesh."

"God above, I ain't dreamin'! It is you!" he said, reaching his arms out for his young friend. "You're alive, for all love! Come! Come here," he said. "Come and let me hold you a moment before I realize 'tis just a dream after all."

Nick bent down and embraced his sopping companion, patting him warmly on the shoulder. When Gunner released him, still in shock, Nick put the mug into his trembling hands and said, "Drink. All of it. Now."

Gunner tilted back his head and quaffed the entire mug in one draught. Nick instantly refilled it from the pot, and said, "One more. I need you awake."

Gunner downed the steaming coffee and said, "Enough! I'm awake and most anxious to hear your tale of survival. How on earth did you get out of the sinking Camel?"

"Got my legs under me on the seat and shot straight out. She was going down fast, Gunner, clipped my shoulder. Lucky to be standing here, I think."

"Praise God, Nick, praise God."

"I will when I get the chance. Now, Gunner, I must hurry to the lighthouse to see my mother and father. I will tell you all of my adventures later."

A dark cloud passed over Gunner's face.

"What is it?" Nick asked, heart in his throat.

"There was a German search party here a few hours ago. They're looking for a young German officer who parachuted onto the island a while ago. A spy, probably. He has not used his field radio or made any contact with Nazi HQ located in town hall on Guernsey. They believe he may have been killed by an islander, and they're looking into it. They went house to house all over the island rounding up various people to take back to Guernsey for questioning. And–"

"And what, Gunner? Tell me please."

"I'm afraid your parents were part of that group."

Nick looked stricken. "Did they take Katie?"

"No. I don't think she was home at the time of the search."

"We've got to help them!" he cried.

"How? Storm the prison? Nick, I think they'll be all right.

They don't know anything about this bloody German spy, and I imagine they'll be released soon enough."

Nick didn't answer, thinking about the young soldier they'd buried beneath the oak tree. But Gunner was right. They were made of sterner stuff, both his parents. He'd no doubt they'd be home tomorrow or the next day. So far, except for the brutal bombing of the port, the Germans seemed to be treating the islanders in a fairly civil way. He decided the dead soldier was something Gunner, like Fleur de Villiers, was better off not knowing about and so kept quiet, thinking about his poor parents. There had to be a way to help them. He'd think of something.

"Gunner, I saw a basket on your kitchen table. It looked exactly like one my mum has. What's in it?"

"A strawberry pie from the smell of it. I think Katie must have brought it up to the barn for us and left it there last evening."

"Have you seen her?"

"No, but I'm sure she's somewhere, in a flowery glen, knitting bluebells into haloes or something."

"I want to have a slice of that pie right now," Nick said, suddenly famished.

"Think I'll join you. But first, in all the excitement, I'm afraid I just remembered something. She left a note for you under the linen. It just says 'Nick,' but it's Kate's handwriting all right."

"Let's have a look," Nick said and headed for the kitchen, Gunner right behind him. Nick lifted the linen cloth and saw the rolled-up piece of paper with only his name showing. He said, "It's too dark in here to read. Let's go out by the window."

Gunner collapsed into his favorite chair. Nick sat at the desk, unrolled the paper, and began to read.

"What's it say?" Gunner asked, looking at Nick. The boy had gone white as a sheet and put his head in his hands.

"Nick, c'mon, lad, it can't be as bad as all that."

"Yes, it can," the boy said, his eyes brimming with tears.

"Well, what is it, for all love?"

"The Nazis have got my parents. And, now, Billy Blood's got Katie."

"What? God help us, that blackguard Blood is back? Took that little angel? Why?"

"He wants my golden ball. Only now it's in exchange for my sister's life. He says he'll slit her throat if I don't appear within the next forty-eight hours."

"Where? Where does he have her? We'll go and fetch her right from under his wretched nose, by heaven!"

Nick had a magnifying glass out, studying Kate's scribblings, mostly numbers. "Have you your maritime charts nearby?"

"Right in the drawer in front of you."

Nick wiped his eyes and pulled out a sheaf of navigational charts, placing them on the desk before him.

"Obviously Blood forced her to write this ransom note. She's put down the longitude and latitude coordinates, the time and place where she's held captive. And the hour of the deadline."

"Where's he taken her?"

Nick got up, handed Gunner Kate's note, and said, "Read the coordinates out loud, Gunner, and I'll locate that devil on the chart."

As Gunner slowly read the numbers out, Nick flipped through the maritime charts until he found the right one. "The Caribbean, well, that's a start," he said, running his finger over the chart until it stopped on 18 degrees north latitude, 76 degrees 50 minutes west longitude, the precise location Gunner had just given him.

Gunner bent over Nick's shoulder to get a look and said, "Jamaica."

"Aye, Jamaica all right. The town of Port Royal. A piratical haven, if ever there was one."

"He's taken her back in time, too, hasn't he, lad?"

"Yes."

"What date does he want to meet?"

"First October, 1781. Before the sun sets."

"We should retrieve the golden orb from its hidey-hole in the Armoury and make preparations for the time trip," Gunner said. "A wee girl, brave as she is, held captive in a den of murderin' pirates? She shouldn't remain there a minute longer than she has to."

"Yes. Listen, Gunner, I've an idea. Just the beginning of one, but it holds promise. There is only one possible way to effect Katie's rescue, but I'm going to need Commander Hobbes's help. He and Lord Hawke are preparing to shut down the castle and to leave for England soon, so we've got to be quick about it. May I use your telephone? I want to call the commander and tell him we're on our way to the castle with a favor to ask."

"What's yer plan, boy?"

"Don't ask. There's no time. Please go up the Armoury and fetch us the orb!"

Gunner returned to the Greybeard Inn's lounge, polishing Nick's golden orb with a soft cloth. This miraculous machine, built by Leonardo da Vinci and bequeathed to Nick by his beloved ancestor, Captain McIver of the Royal Navy, gleamed like the sun itself, casting sharp shafts of golden beams on the walls and ceiling.

"Beautiful thing," Gunner said, "sends a right chill up my spine every time I look at it."

The boy said, "If this works the way I intend, we'll have Kate home before sundown. Even if my parents are lucky and are released early, Kate will be home before they even know she was kidnapped!"

"Lad! Do you think we can manage all that?"

"Of course we can." Nick laughed. "We've got a time machine, remember? Time is on our side. Once we've got her safely away from Blood's lair, we just return here, to the inn on this very morning!"

"Your parents will never even know?"

"Isn't that a good thing, Gunner? To save them all the worry? They've got more than enough to worry about at the moment, haven't they?"

"Aye. If we succeed."

"*If* we succeed, Gunner? Of course we will succeed. We must. And that's part of my plan," Nick said. "Now, come along, we must get to Hawke Castle at once and explain the situation to his lordship and Commander Hobbes. They are critical to a successful rescue mission."

And out the door they went, both of them knowing there was dire trouble ahead, no matter what the plan was. Billy Blood was a wily, vicious, and cruel man. And extricating Kate from his clutches would be no spring stroll in the garden. But Nick, Gunner, and Hawke had crossed swords with Captain William Blood before, and they had won.

Nick believed in his heart of hearts that he and Gunner just might be able to do it again. What was a battle for, if not for winning?

A sudden storm was threatening and Hawke Castle looked dark and foreboding. It stood atop the cliff, thrusting toward a lowering sky of black clouds sparking with lightning. Nick and Gunner were silent as they climbed the hill that led to Lord Hawke's hulking Gothic residence. Both of them were thinking the same thing. This would be their one and only chance to save little Katie.

As they approached the forbidding iron gates at the entrance, they saw the towering clouds begin to spit rain. Inside the castle, two of the most brilliant men in all England were waiting. Without their help, all would be lost.

Nick saw brand-new signs mounted all along the iron fence, frightening things, warning KEEP OUT! and that the surrounding barbed-wire fence was electrified to ten thousand volts. The signs were, Nick noticed, printed in both English and German. Each one depicted a large red jagged bolt of electricity piercing a skull and crossbones. It was certainly enough to scare anyone away.

"I think His Lordship's trying to say, 'Pop in for tea any time,'" Gunner grumbled. He had never been comfortable here. Too many old tales of ghosts and spirits for his liking.

"He has to protect the castle during the occupation. Lord Hawke is joining Churchill's war cabinet. Part of a new counterespionage unit. He and Hobbes may be away for the balance of the war," Nick said. "This is, after all, a secret British military installation."

"So how do we get in, Master Nick?"

"Easy." Nick bent to push a nearly invisible black button on the back side of the bottom of a gatepost.

"Yes?" came a deep voice over a hidden speaker.

"Hobbes, it's Nick and Gunner."

"Ah, good. I'll buzz you in straightaway."

Minutes later, they entered the great hall. Every single piece of furniture had been covered with dust-cloths, as had all the art and sculpture. It seemed to Nick like a castle filled with silent ghosts. There were a few uncovered chairs before the massive fire roaring in the hearth, and Lord Hawke was sitting in one of them, one leg hooked over the arm of his chair, enjoying his tea.

He stood to greet them. "Nicholas! Gunner! What joy to see you both. We're shoving off for the mainland tomorrow, you know, closing the old pile down for the duration. I've already sent little Alex and Annabel to Hawkesmoor in the Gloucestershire countryside. Pull up a chair and sit down, won't you both? Hobbes and I are just having tea."

"Welcome," Hobbes said, pouring tea for them and offering a tray of cakes.

Hobbes cleared his throat and said, "Nick, I must tell you I am at an absolute loss for words to describe my reaction to your mischief over on Guernsey in the wee hours last evening. His Lordship and I saw the fiery effects of your daring raid on the aerodrome last night. I must say you wreaked havoc on those bloody Jerries. Surely you took some antiaircraft fire? But you obviously managed to get the Camel home safe?"

"Afraid not," Nick said, looking down at his feet. "She lies in about thirty feet of water."

Lord Hawke looked at Nick. "Bad luck. But look at it this way. She was built in 1917 to fight the Germans, and fight them she did. And now, thanks to you and Gunner, she lived to fight them another day. Went out in a blaze of glory, too, I daresay. Well done!"

"I don't know about glory, but she was certainly blazing," Nick said, a hint of a smile forming around his eyes. The truth was he had actually enjoyed the air raid and his narrow escape from the Germans. He'd always hoped that someday he might get the chance to become a true hero and come to the aid of his country. His one regret was that the beautiful aeroplane was lost . . . and, with it, his opportunities of future air attacks on the Nazis.

Hobbes seemed to have been reading his mind. "You know, she may be salvageable."

"What?" Nick said. "How on earth?"

"Relatively simple matter. A diver goes down and attaches numerous canvas bladders with air hoses. Wait for a dark night, position a boat with an air pump above her. Inflate the bladders and she'll pop right to the surface and you tow her home."

"Excellent idea," Hawke said, "and the time may well come when we do that, but right now I have the feeling there are more pressing problems."

Hawke leaned forward and looked at Nick and Gunner. "Nick, when you rang, you said you had two urgent matters to discuss. Let's get right to it. We haven't much time. A Royal Navy submarine is picking the commander and me up inside Hawke Lagoon at dawn."

Nick drew a deep breath and let it all out. "Two things, sir. The Nazis have imprisoned my parents, sir. Took them to the Guernsey prison, where they are being interrogated."

"Interrogated about what?"

"About a missing German parachutist on Greybeard Island."

"Surely they don't know anything about that?"

Nick looked at Gunner, now wishing he'd told the truth. "They do, I'm afraid. My father does, at any rate. I found the German soldier myself, hanging in a tree from his chute. He was already dead and we buried him."

"I can help there, Nicholas," Hawke said. "Fleur de Villiers has the new Nazi Kommandant wrapped around her little finger. One word from her, and your parents will be treated with kid gloves, I assure you."

"Thank you, sir," Nick said, much relieved. He was surprised he hadn't thought of contacting her himself. Then he remembered that the Germans had cut all the undersea telephone cables. No doubt Lord Hawke had other ways of communicating with her, of course.

"And the other matter, Nick?" Hobbes said.

Nick turned and looked directly at him. His eyes blazing with anger and resolve. "Billy Blood has kidnapped my sister, Kate."

"Good Lord," Hobbes said, his teacup rattling, hot tea sloshing over the rim. Hawke got to his feet, visibly shaken. Billy Blood has Kate! You do have a lot on your plate, Nick. Any idea where he's taken her?"

"There was a ransom note, written in Kate's hand. She's been taken to Port Royal, Jamaica."

"What year?" Hawke asked.

"In the year 1781."

"No doubt what ransom he's after," Hobbes said, a worried frown on his face.

"Of course, Hobbes. He wants possession of the second Tempus Machina," Hawke murmured, gazing into the fire thoughtfully. "He won't rest until he gets it."

Nick said, "He threatens to hang Katie by her heels and slit her throat if I don't arrive with the golden orb in hand within forty-eight hours."

"You can't let him have it, Nick," Hawke said with great conviction. "You simply cannot do it. It would make that devil powerful beyond imagination. With possession of both time machines, he would be unreachable."

"I know that, sir, and that's why I don't intend to give it to him."

"You have a plan, Nick?" Hobbes asked. "A *ruse de guerre*?"

"What's that?" Gunner asked."

"A trick of war," Hawke translated. "Like the Trojan horse. Please proceed, Nick. We obviously need some kind of scheme, and we need it now."

"This may sound a bit cockeyed, but..."

"Don't be shy, lad, spit it out."

Nick clasped his hands behind his back and began pacing back and forth before the fire. "Well, Hobbes, I was thinking, perhaps it might be possible to create another Tempus Machina. Not a working one, of course. But an exact replica of my own, to the last detail. Down in your laboratory. It has to be absolutely identical to the real thing, inside and out."

"You exchange the fake one for your sister's freedom."

"Yes. And by the time Old Bill realizes he's been tricked, I hope we'll be long gone. I've thought long and hard about this. I think it's our only chance."

"I think it's brilliant," Hawke said. "And with a little luck, it might actually work."

"Can you make one, Commander?" Nick said, hope gleaming in his eyes, "A perfect simulation of Da Vinci's time engine?"

Hobbes smiled and said, "I can make anything in that laboratory, Nick. Anything in the world."

"Needless to say, it won't need to be a working model," Hawke said. "The minute Blood tries to actually use it, he'll know it's a fake."

"It doesn't have to actually work, sir. It just needs to buy me and Gunner enough time alone with my sister so we might escape using the real machine."

"Would you like Hobbes and me to accompany you, Nick? We'd be happy to help in any way we can."

"Thank you, sir. I knew you would offer. But I think that Gunner and I, in some kind of disguise, stand a better chance alone."

"If you don't return, there's no way on earth we can ever find you again, Nick," Hawke said, "ever."

"I know that, sir. But I believe in my heart we can succeed."

"Well then," Hobbes said, getting to his feet, "we've got a lot of work ahead of us down in the lab. You've brought the real machine?"

Nick stuck his right hand inside his shirt and withdrew the orb from the hidden leather pouch that hung beneath his arm. Hobbes took it and examined it carefully.

"We'll need real gold, of course. Do we have any gold bars left in the vault, Your Lordship? Any bullion at all?"

"Afraid not. It all went out with the last shipment. It sits safely in the Bank of England vault now."

"That's a problem, then," Hobbes said, rubbing his chin. "Difficult to simulate real gold to a man like Blood who deals in the stuff every day. He just might test it before he agrees to the exchange."

"Test it?" Gunner asked, "How would he do that?"

"Quite simply," Hobbes replied. "He'll splash it with a glass stopper which has been filled with nitric acid. If it's pure gold, twenty-four-karat, it will remain untouched and unchanged; if not, the solution will become blue from the formation of nitrate copper. False gold, you see, always contains copper."

"So, we can't do it," Nick said, crestfallen.

"Not without real gold, I'm afraid. No."

"Hold on!" Hawke said, "There's still solid gold flatware and cutlery in the drawers in the pantry. Place settings won't be packed up and shipped over until this afternoon," Hawke said, smiling. "Please feel free to melt down as many forks and spoons as you need, old fellow."

Hobbes leaped to his feet. "Excellent! Come along, Nick, we'll go grab as many golden knives and spoons as we can. Melt them down, and we're off to the races!"

Nick had opened the Tempus Machina and held up both halves for Hobbes to see. "What about the interior, sir? That will be the most difficult. All these jewels and intricate etchings."

"Yes, yes, but I think I can manage. We'll need real jewels, too, I'm afraid," Hobbes said, examining it closely.

The machine had an emerald button to initiate time travel and a brilliant ruby to stop any motion, backward or forward. And small diamonds representing various constellations, and secret Greek and Egyptian symbols.

"Hobbes," Hawke said, "you know the silver jewelry box atop the dresser in my dressing room? Inside is an old neck-lace my grandmother gave to me just before she died. It's a lovely thing, all emeralds and rubies and diamonds. You're welcome to use it in any way you see fit."

"Marvelous. Thank you," Hobbes said, much relieved.

Hawke laid a hand on Nick's shoulder. "And, Nick, don't worry. I'll get a message to the Baroness de Villiers about your parents immediately. They'll be quite safe while you're gone, I assure you."

"With all due respect, sir, how will you reach her? The Germans have cut all the undersea lines between the islands."

Hawke smiled. "Some of us have undersea telephonic lines the Germans are not aware of, lad."

Nick, who felt as it he'd been holding his breath all day, expelled a great sigh of relief. There was now a chance, albeit a very slim one, that everything might turn out all right after all.

Of course, it could all go dreadfully wrong, as well.

· Port Royal, Jamaica—July 14, 1781 ·

N ow, Cecily," Katie said, "I am telling you, you have absolutely nothing to be afraid of. As soon as my brother Nicky finds that letter I left for him in the pie basket, he will certainly come and rescue us. Besides, you have to realize that I have been in far more frightening situations than this silly one. Why, I was once kidnapped by real Nazis and held captive aboard a giant U-boat! But, in the end, my friend Hobbesie and I outsmarted them, captured the U-boat in Hawke Lagoon, and here I am." She paused a moment and added, "Kidnapped again."

Kate was lying on the thin mattress of the cot in her small white-washed room on the third floor of the Black Crow Inn. She was having a very serious conversation with a raggedy red-headed doll named Cecily about their impending rescue from the despicable pirates who'd stolen her away from her dear home and family.

Because of the white walls and the big tall window overlooking the Port Royal harbor, the room was filled with sunshine all day. She had a splendid view. It seemed that every ship in the world had come to Port Royal. The harbor was full to overflowing with ships of every description, but, she'd noticed, they all had something in common.

Every ship, be it large or small, was flying the skull and crossbones flag at their mastheads. Pirate ships! So many, in fact, there were at least twenty or so anchored well outside the narrow entrance to the harbor.

The streets were filled night and day with throngs of rowdy pirates, most of them drunk as far as she could tell. Coarse language, rum bottles smashed in the cobbled streets, fights breaking out every few minutes. It was great fun sitting in her chair by the window and gazing down at the pandemonium in the streets and out in the harbor, aboard the great vessels themselves. The sound of steel on steel would bring her running to the window—that meant a sword fight!

So far, no one had hurt or even threatened to hurt her or Cecily. She was locked inside her room, of course, and never let out, but a kindly old black man named Lucius, from the inn's kitchen, tapped on her door thrice a day. With a key from the great ring of them hanging from his belt, he unlocked her door and came in with a tray of food and a glass of wine. She kept asking for water, but Lucius was a bit addled and never remembered.

"You got lemons, you make lemonade," he'd said this morning when she'd complained.

"A lemonade would be lovely!"

"We ain't got lemons, miss. Or potable water. We got wine."

She hated the taste of the wine, and it made her hiccough, but she was ever so thirsty and so she drank every last drop. It made her feel a bit odd for a while, but the feeling soon passed if she lay down and slept. She hated to think what her mum would say if she knew her precious daughter was drinking three glasses of wine a day. Of course, the only one who could tell on her was Cecily, and she wasn't much for conversation.

Kate awoke that very morning to the sound of loud shouts and violent arguing in the room right next to hers. Blood and his crew often stomped up three flights of stairs to that room. The plastered walls were not very thick, and she heard the booming voice of Captain Blood and then the voices of other pirate captains raised in disagreement or shouting their approval. What on earth could all the fuss be about?

She'd taken her wineglass and put it to the wall so she could hear more clearly. It was a trick Nicky had told her about in a Sherlock Holmes mystery story. It actually worked, she discovered. The room next door sounded full of men, shuffling their boots and cursing. It must be a much larger room than her own. Some kind of meeting room like Gunner's Armoury.

And Captain Blood must have been standing pretty close to the wall that separated them because she could hear him through the glass the most clearly. She knew eavesdropping was impolite, but she and her brother were officially spies, indirectly working for the British government, so she supposed it was all right. More than that, it was her professional duty. She knew any scrap of information she could pick up would be invaluable to Nicky when he showed up to rescue her.

She heard Blood say, "You captains, you hearty souls, you all know why we're here. We've assembled the largest pirate armada the world has ever seen! Nigh on a hundred or more vessels! We come from every point of the compass. But we all have only one thing in our minds. What may that be, now, captains?"

"Rule the seas! Rule the seas!" the men cried out in unison, and in her mind she could see Billy standing there, waiting for them to stop.

Finally, he said, "Right ye are and, by God, we *will* rule the whole world and own all the riches of the Seven Seas afore we're done!"

There was another deafening cheer, and then Blood continued, "And, afore we're done, the world will shiver in terror at the mere mention of our name. Snake Eye here and I been thinking on a good name for our pirate fleet. I even had a flag sewn up. Snake Eye, give 'em a look. The Brethren of Blood! That's who we are and forever more shall be!"

At this point, Kate didn't need the wineglass. There was a great stomping of heavy boots, fists pounding on the table, and howls of approval and shouts of "Brethren of Blood! Brethren of Blood!"

"Quiet down, now, the lot of you, whilst I move on to the important part of this meeting. We all decided our first foray. We unanimously agreed we would strike the coast of France. But one of our brave number, a Frenchman who survived one of Nelson's swords by a whisker, brings vital information to our midst. So give him your attention. Captain Guy de Vincennes, take the floor!"

"*Merci beaucoup et bonjour, mon capitaine et mes amis!* I've just come from Saint George's on the isle of Grenada where I witnessed a mighty battle for control of that island from a cell in King George's prison at Fort Frederick.

"A huge fleet, flying the colors of the French Navy, and under command of a certain Admiral de Grasse took that island. And, I hear, the isle of Tobago before that. And de Grasse looted them both of enormous treasure, too. He's loaded to the gunwales with it, I'll tell you! I escaped when the French set fire to the fort. Flames were licking at my

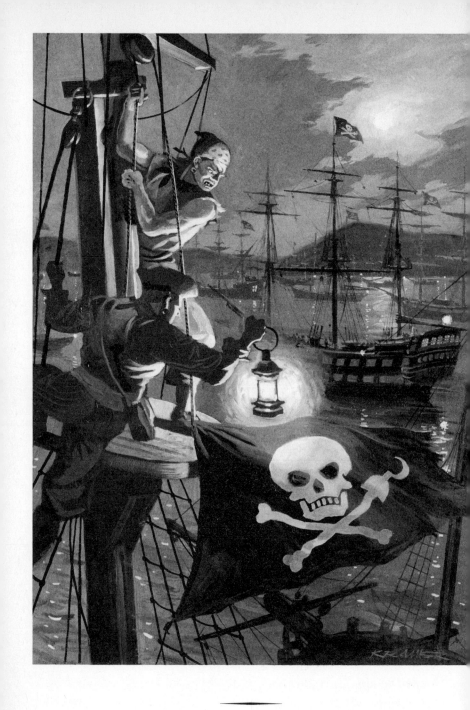

"Rule the seas! Rule the seas!"

heels, by my oath. A fellow French officer saw my plight and released me from my cell and certain death."

"How many men has he under his command, this here Admiral de Grasse and his fleet?" Blood asked.

"The fleet carries five thousand French troops en route to America. They say it's to help the Revolutionaries defeat Cornwallis and the British at Yorktown in Virginia."

"That fleet must be loaded down with so much booty, I'd be surprised if they could make headway!" someone shouted.

"Aye, but they'll use the Gulf Stream and sail up through the passage between the Florida Keys and Cuba. The stream itself will give 'em seven knots."

Kate heard Blood raise his voice above the hubbub. "Silence, you scoundrels! I have a proposal to lay before ye. I say we surprise this Admiral de Grasse en route to Virginia and relieve him of all that ill-gotten booty! What say you? All in favor, signify by saying 'Aye.'"

Kate had to step back from the wall, the chorus of "Ayes" was so thunderous. When they quieted down, she put the wineglass back to the wall.

"When does he sail for the American colonies?" Blood asked.

"Three weeks hence. The French fleet now lies at Saint George's while de Grasse makes repairs and re-provisions."

"Slide that chart across the table, will ye, and be quiet whilst I study it."

The room went dead quiet for a few minutes, and then she heard Blood's voice rising again. "Roll up that chart and put it under lock and key in this here table. We sail in a fortnight. And regroup ten leagues off the nor'east tip of Nassau Town. Admiral de Grasse will have the distinction of being the first to feel the might and steel of the Brethren of Blood!"

There was a mighty roar, and then Blood screamed, "And now let us repair to a day of rum and wenches! Tomorrow we begin to plan this ambush in earnest."

She heard the door creak open and the sound of heavy boots as the laughing and shouting pirate captains strumbled down the hall toward the narrow staircase. One of them, probably Blood himself, pounded on her door hard enough to splinter it. Then he roared with laughter at the notion of scaring the little girl to death, and stomped away.

The one staircase to the left led to the ground floor. There were two staircases, she'd noticed. The one for guests on the harbor side, and the one at the rear for the staff and Lucius.

"Cecily, now you listen to me," she said, picking up her doll and seating herself at the small wooden desk beneath the window. "This is a very serious business. Do you realize what has just happened? I, the only true British spy on this island, am now privy to the most secret plans of that awful Captain Blood. Now we know why he has this huge armada. Why, when Nick learns of all this, there's no telling what he might do with such important spy information. Now, you take your nap while I write down all the details of Blood's plan before I forget them."

She opened the drawer of the desk beneath the window and took out several sheets of writing paper. There was a quill and inkpot on the desktop. She dipped the quill in ink and wrote BRETHREN OF BLOOD at the top of the page.

This, Kate thought as she wrote, was surely the pinnacle of her entire career as a spy. She had secret information that could affect the lives of hundreds. All of it, every word, in exquisite detail. Now, all she had to do was get it on paper and turn it over to her brother, Nick, for his consideration. She had no doubt he'd come up with a brilliant plan to thwart Blood's ambush of Admiral de Grasse and his fleet en route to Virginia to help the American rebels.

At school she'd learned a bit about George Washington and these American colonialists and their disloyal rebellion against the crown. But something about their stalwart bravery, farmers and cobblers standing up to the world's greatest power, gave them a tiny piece of her heart.

She'd seen a portrait of the American general in one of Nick's many history books. A big man in a splendid uniform, he looked quite formidable astride his white steed.

Her brother, Nicky, was clever, maybe not quite so clever as she was, but when it came to taking action against evil men like Billy Blood, there was not a braver boy in all of England. Or, maybe, all the world!

Nicky, where are you? she thought, staring out the window at the forest of swaying masts and wind-whipped black flags in the harbor, thinking of the foggy night she'd first seen Blood and Snake Eye, for the very first time, sitting there in the flickering shadows by the fire at the Greybeard Inn.

The two pirates had scared her then, and though she would scarcely ever confess this dreadful secret to Cecily, they'd scared her in the forest and they scared her now.

Don't you fret, Cecily, Nick's coming.

She could feel it in her bones.

"GODSPEED, NICK," HAWKE SAID

· Greybeard Island—July 14, 1940 ·

Three hours after he'd disappeared down into the laboratory, Hobbes reappeared in the lift and stepped into Lord Hawke's circular study atop the castle tower. He carried two round objects, each draped in black velvet. Smiling, he placed the objects on Lord Hawke's desk. Every candle in the chandeliers above had been lit, and the room was ablaze with light in anticipation of this moment.

"Have you done it, Hobbes, made its match?" Nick cried, leaping to his feet. "A perfect match?" Hobbes saw that Nick was now wearing the clothes of a ragged eighteenth-century cabin boy. Gunner was attired as a typical scalawag from the Spanish Main, with a bandanna tied round his head, a black patch over one eye and a golden hoop dangling from one ear.

The last time Nick had traveled back in time, he'd been wearing his normal clothes. It had caused much astonishment and consternation aboard the English warship they'd gone back in history to save. At Lord Hawke's suggestion, they'd been raiding His Lordship's costume wardrobe, which, long ago, had been used for the many fancy dress balls held in those days at Hawke Castle.

"A perfect match, you say? Only you three can be the judge of that," Hobbes said, now placing his hands atop the treasures. "Come have a look!"

Hawke, Nick, and Gunner gathered round the desk, staring at the black-draped balls.

"Confound it, Hobbes," His Lordship said. "Enough drama. Show us what you've done!"

Hobbes, with a dramatic flourish, whisked away the velvet covers. Two golden orbs sat upon the desk, gleaming like the sun itself.

"Someone please point out the original," Hobbes said, puffed up a bit with pride.

Hawke picked up his large ivory-handled magnifying glass and leaned in to inspect one, then the other.

"Impossible to tell," he said, handing the glass to Gunner. "Have a go, Gunner."

After a close inspection, he, too, deemed it impossible to choose. "Identical," he declared, handing the glass to Nick.

The boy took his time, peering at the gleaming golden balls through the glass from every possible angle. "Circumference looks the same," he said. "Engraving is perfect."

"Exactly the same," Hobbes said.

"And the weight?" Nick asked. "The weight will be very important."

"Not a gram's difference between them."

"You've done it, Hobbes!" Nick said, smiling up at his friend. "Can we have a peek inside?"

"But of course. You open one and I'll open the other."

The machines opened along the equator by twisting the top and bottom halves in counterclockwise directions. Once opened, Hobbes and Nick placed the machines side by side on the table. His three companions leaned over the desk and examined each machine in turn.

Hobbes said, "I had a bit of trouble cutting the stones to fit exactly, but as I've often said, it's a poor craftsman who blames his tools."

"They look perfect," Nick said, admiring his friend's handiwork.

"The glass, M'lord?" Hobbes said, offering the magnifying glass to Lord Hawke.

"I don't need it. By heaven, you've done it, Hobbes. Not a man on earth could distinguish any difference between the two. Not even an expert jeweler at Van Cleef in Paris. Well done, old fellow, well done indeed!"

Nick turned to Hobbes and flung his arms around him, hugging him. "I can never thank you enough, Hobbes," Nick said. "If Gunner and I have any chance of success in saving my sister and holding on to the Tempus Machina, it will only be through your magnificent efforts."

Hawke opened a drawer in his desk and removed a beautifully ebony box inlaid with ivory. "Nick, Gunner, I want you to take these with you. To be used in case of an emergency. You're going into a pirates' den, and I think it unwise for you to enter such a place unarmed."

Inside the felt-lined case were a pair of matching pistols, small silver automatics with ivory grips. Hawke handed one to Nick and one to Gunner. "A Walther PPK. It fires a small .25-caliber round, so it's no good at any distance. But for close-in work, it will come in handy. These leather holsters should be worn in the small of your back, under your shirts. The magazine holds nine rounds. If you must use them, use them wisely."

"Nick," Hobbes said, "I took the liberty of working up an

identical leather orb pouch to the one you conceal under your arm. My thought is you should entrust the real machine to Gunner and carry the replica in your own pouch. And do not, under any circumstances, hand over the duplicate machine until you've seen Kate alive, unharmed, and in your presence. Do you understand? He releases her into your hands before you hand him the orb."

"Won't he wonder how we intend to get home without it?" Nick asked.

"An astute question. But I would stake my life on his euphoria driving him to distraction. The miracle of finally possessing the twin orbs will send him into such paroxysms of ecstasy, he will scarcely care what happens to you. But if he tries to trick you in any way, shape, or form, tries to take the three of you against your will, you must use the guns, Nick; you must escape his sight and use the real machine to return home."

"I will remember that, sir," Nick said. "Thank you."

"Well, lad," Gunner said, trying on a smile, "I think we should let His Lordship and the commander finish closing up the castle and go back and get yer little sister, Kate."

"Yes," Nick said, "here's Kate's note, Gunner. Will you enter the exact time and geographical location into the machine?"

"I will indeed. I became quite handy with this blasted thing on our last adventure, you'll remember."

Gunner spread the ransom note out on Lord Hawke's desk and began to enter the time destination into the Tempus half of the orb, and the geographical location into the Locus half. Not until the two halves were rejoined would Gunner and Nick find themselves in Port Royal in the year 1781.

"Godspeed, Nick," Lord Hawke said, laying a hand on the boy's shoulder. "You, too, Gunner. The Commander and I wish you every success. If anyone can do this, and come home safely, it's the two of you. And when you have returned, remember, I'll be counting on you to keep an eye on those damnable Nazis for me."

"We will, sir," Nick said. "Are you ready, Gunner?"

"Aye," he said, holding out his half of the golden ball.

"We're off, then," Nick said with a brave smile. He held his half out to Gunner, and the two halves began to glow and pull strongly toward each other, time and space rejoined.

There was the familiar tinkling of a thousand tiny bells as each atom of the two time-traveler's beings turned into countless tiny fireflies, which began to wink out one by one until Nick and Gunner were no longer standing in Lord Hawke's study.

In the wink of an eye, they'd returned to the year 1781, to a Jamaican town called Port Royal, a place where a man watched his every move and called no man his friend.

· Port Royal, Jamaica—1781 ·

Nick and Gunner found themselves in a foul-smelling back alley, perhaps a block from Port Royal's harbor, judging by the sound of creaking rigging and snapping canvas nearby. A light rain was falling and the breeze off the sea was freshening. Nick had arrived seconds ahead of Gunner and so heard the soft tinkling bells and witnessed the millions of tiny fireflies swarming together to form Gunner's physical being. Nick held his breath until Gunner was standing there fully in the flesh, praying that no passerby would chance to stumble upon the alley and the scene now taking place.

But as luck would have it, they were alone. No one had chanced to see them arrive, an event which surely would have caused a lot of unwanted attention.

"Bit o' luck," Gunner said, looking down the alley toward the deserted street.

"Yes, but–" Nick felt something nibbling at his boot and looked down.

Rats. Hundreds of them, it looked like. A swirling sea of

horrible slick-skinned rodents, writhing and squirming, more like snakes or worms than any four-footed animals.

"Maybe we should get out of here," Nick said, kicking away at the rats trying to climb up inside his trouser legs.

"I was just thinking that exact thing myself. Funny, ain't it, two blokes arriving at the same conclusions at the same time?"

There was a cobbled street at the open end of the alley, angling downward toward the harbor. A flickering gas streetlamp cast a pool of hazy yellow light on the glistening cobblestones. There seemed to be no one about, and Nick ran through the swarming creatures, most eager to escape the alley. Gunner was behind him, walking gingerly, trying to avoid the slimy things. He'd lived with rats on shipboard most of his life and had special fear of the loathsome creatures.

"Harbor's to the right, lad!" Gunner called ahead to Nick, who was nearing the street.

"How do you know for sure?"

"I can smell it. Hear it."

Gunner saw Nick go flying around the corner into the street and then, in the mere blink of an eye, he came hurtling back, flying through the air now and landing on his backside with a hard thud.

Gunner was about to call out to him when he saw an unruly gang of five or six men arrive, all staring at the boy lying in the street. Obviously Nick had run headlong into the lot of them and been solidly knocked backward for his troubles.

Gunner meant to race forward out of the shadows into the street and help Nick to his feet, but some instinct told him to remain hidden for a moment or two more.

Nick got to his feet and brushed off the back of his trou-

sers, smiling all the while at the five drunken ruffians looming over him.

"Excuse me, gentlemen," Nick began, "I wasn't watching
where I–"

"Silence!" the largest of the pirates shouted at Nick, lunging toward him, slurring the word. "I've a mind to run you
through for that, you scurvy little pup." The huge pirate drew
his sword and pointed the sharp tip dangerously close to
Nick's chest, flicking the buttons on his shirt.

"It was only an accident," Nick said, not backing down.
"Where I come from, sir, when a gentleman apologizes, no
matter where the fault lies, the offended gentleman accepts
his apologies."

For a moment the gang was shocked into silence at the audacity of this mere cabin boy.

"Where he comes from? Is 'at what he said?" a fat little
matey said. His friends roared with laughter.

"Are ye sayin' I ain't no gentleman?" the big man said. He
took another step toward the boy, raising his sword. He looked
back at his men, a cruel smile on his lips. "What say ye? Run
'im through? Or relieve him of his insolent head?"

"Off with his head!" the other four cried in rum-soaked
unison. "Off with it now."

"Aye. I agree," he said, drawing his sword back to deliver a
blow that would surely sever Nick's head. Gunner saw Nick's
hand reaching behind him for his gun, but it was too late.

Just at the moment the blade began its swift descent, there
came the sound of a sharp explosion in the dark alley and a
flash of flame. The pirate's sword clattered to the street, the
echo of steel clanging on stone reverberating the length of
it. The drunken buccaneer stayed on his feet for a moment,

swaying, and then he fell face-first to the ground like a stone, blood pouring from a wound in his left temple.

Gunner stepped out into the light, his small automatic pistol trained on the remaining members of the rowdy crew, now staring in stunned silence at their fallen leader.

"Who's for more of this?" Gunner said, taking aim at the street lamp atop the post. He fired the gun again, exploding the glass.

"Apologize to the boy," he said to the nearest of them, putting the muzzle of the gun to the blackguard's head.

"What do you–"

"I'll kill you where you stand, sir, unless you do my bidding."

"Beg pardon," the bewildered pirate muttered to Nick, as the pool of blood flowing from the dead man's head spread around his boots.

"Good enough," Gunner said. "Now all of you be on your way, and quick about it. You can come back for that one later, if you think he's worth burying. But trouble me and this boy again, and I swear I'll blow all yer sodden brains out, too."

The pirates stared at Gunner for a moment, looking at the small silver weapon still smoking in his hand, and then bolted up the hill and disappeared over the top of it. Gunner stuck his gun back into its holster.

"Thank you," Nick said, stepping over the corpse and smiling at his friend. "I think he really meant to do it."

"Oh, he was intending to do it, lad, no doubt. The Brethren of Blood these Caribee pirates call themselves. And every last one of them would rather kill you than look at you."

"This isn't going to be easy, is it, Gunner?" Nick asked.

"No, lad, it ain't going to be the slightest bit easy."

"The story will spread. Think they'll come looking for us?"

"They might. If those four drunkards could find anyone to believe them."

"You just saved my life."

"I did."

"I'd like to repay the debt."

"I've little doubt you'll get the chance before this night is over."

They walked down the hill to where the street dead-ended at the harbor. Both of them stopped dead in their tracks at the sight before them.

"Good Lord," Gunner said, staring openmouthed at the sheer number of ships filling the harbor.

"All flying the Jolly Roger," Nick said, a bit of awe in his voice. "Every last one."

"It's a bloody pirate armada," Gunner said. "Never in me life seen the likes of it!"

"How many ships do you imagine?"

"A hundred at the very least."

"Blood's behind this. I'd bet me last guinea on it."

Nick had noticed a lone woman standing on the corner of Harbour Road. She was under a street lamp and had smiled politely at him as he and Gunner passed. She was fancifully dressed, as if for some kind of gala, with great hoops of gold dangling from her ears. She wore a skirt of scarlet that touched the ground and a frilly white blouse that scarcely covered her gently heaving bosom.

"Excuse me, madam," Nick said, walking toward her, "we're new to this town and could use some help."

"Help is my stock in trade, lad." She laughed, her dark eyes flashing. She was even prettier when she laughed, Nick thought. "How about your handsome friend there, does he need help as well?"

"Yes," Nick replied, motioning for Gunner to join him. "We both need help, to be honest."

"Well then, you've come to right spot, laddie. I'm the most helpful girl on the island."

"Evening," Gunner said to her, tipping his three-cornered hat.

"And you the same, sir." She smiled at him. "The boy here says you could use some help."

"Indeed we could."

"Exactly what kind of help might you gents be interested in?"

"Directions," Nick said.

"Directions?" she said with a puzzled look. "What kind of directions?"

"We're looking for a tavern, ma'am. Called the Black Crow."

"The Black Crow, is it? she said, laughing. "Well, I can direct you there, to be sure. I work there some nights as a barmaid. Tonight's me night off."

"What's your name?" Nick asked, extending his hand to her. "I'm Nick and this is my friend Gunner."

"Sabrina's my name. Lovely to make your acquaintance, Nick. I had a boy, y'know, looked remarkably like you, he did. Same smile. His name was Henry. Died at age nine at the hands of drunken pirates nigh on five years now. Did it for a laugh, they did. A lark."

"I'm sorry," Nick said.

"The Black Crow lies in that direction, about four blocks. You see that footbridge over the canal? Right beyond that, you'll see it. But I wouldn't recommend that place."

"Why not?" Nick asked.

"Because it's the most dangerous tavern in the most dangerous town on the most dangerous island in the Caribbean, that's why."

"Why?"

"Because a bloke named Billy Blood owns this town now. And there's nary a more dangerous man to cross that walks this earth. You've had your warning. Give 'im wide berth and leave him be."

"Is that his fleet in the harbor?" Nick asked.

"Blood's armada, it is. Did you ever–?"

"We better be off!" Gunner interrupted. He was looking back up the street they'd just descended. Where the hill crested, a mob of angry men with torches and swords raised were marching toward them. A lot of angry men.

"What do they want?" Sabrina asked, warily looking at the mob, quickly moving Nick and Gunner out of the lamplight.

"Our lives," Nick said. "We killed one of them. In self-defense, of course."

"Quick. Come with me. I know a place you can hide. Fast as you can to the footbridge! Now!"

Sabrina lifted her skirts and raced along Harbour Road in the direction of the Black Crow. Nick and Gunner were right behind her. They could hear the swelling cries of the mob descending the hill.

Sabrina cried over her shoulder, "When you get to the bridge, leap into the canal. It's shallow, don't worry. We can hide under the bridge. But we must reach it before they turn the corner!"

Nick, who could run very quickly, raced ahead. A moment later he was vaulting over the railing of the footbridge, landing on his feet in the black water below. His heart was pounding. He knew Sabrina could make it in time, but what about Gunner?

A second later he saw Sabrina flinging herself over the rail. Gunner was right behind her, and the three of them quickly waded through the filthy, waist-high water, stopping under the old wooden bridge.

"Did they see you, Gunner?" Nick whispered, breathing hard.

"I took a quick look back as I reached the bridge," Gunner said quietly. "I saw the light of their torches reach the harbor, but not one had rounded the corner when I jumped."

"Quiet," Sabrina said. "Here they come!"

Nick and Gunner both pulled their pistols from behind their backs.

The bloodthirsty cutthroats couldn't be more than fifty yards behind them. They were in a frenzy now, bellowing curses that echoed off the walls beside the canal. Then they were on the bridge proper, just three feet above Nick's head, and a stampede of wild horses couldn't have been louder than the sound of pirates' boots on that wooden bridge.

Nick tried to figure their number, but it took so long for all of them to cross the bridge, he gave up at fifty or so. As the last of them crossed and the loud shouting grew more distant, Sabrina put a finger to her lips, telling them to remain quiet. Sure enough, a few minutes later, a group of rowdy stragglers crossed the bridge, trying to catch up with the main body.

Then, silence.

But taking no chances, they stayed where they were, silent and unmoving, as the foul sludge of debris and garbage from the old town flowed past them and out into the harbor proper.

After ten more minutes Gunner said, "Any chance of getting out of this bleeding cesspool?"

Sabrina laughed and started wading away from the harbor. "Follow me. Only a short way."

"Where's the Black Crow, Sabrina?" Nick asked, just be-hind her.

"Right here," she said. "It's this very building on your left. To your right is the warehouse where Blood is storing black powder and ammunition for the coming war."

"War? Who's he fighting?"

She laughed. "The whole bloody world, as far as I can make out. I hear things, you know. Keep my ears open."

Nick looked up at the four-story tavern rising up beside the canal. It was built of crumbling old brick, oil lamps were burning in most of the windows.

"I think my sister is somewhere inside that building," Nick said.

"What?" Sabrina said. "You must be joking. What's her name? I'd know her if she works there, believe you me."

"Her name is Kate. She's only seven years old."

"A child! What's she doing in a place like that?"

"Blood kidnapped her. He's holding her for ransom. That's why we're here. To rescue her."

"You'll have a hard time rescuing anybody now, I'm afraid, with half the pirates in Port Royal screaming for your head."

"We've dealt with Old Bill before, Gunner and I have. We're not afraid of him."

"If you ain't afraid of Billy Blood, maybe you've got rocks in your head, Nick."

"I *know* Nick's got a few loose rocks in his head," Gunner said. "But so far, it hasn't been much of a problem."

"Here we are," Sabrina said. "There's a set of steps that lead up to the rear of the Crow. There's the back entrance right there. Nobody uses it but the barmaids and Lucius."

"Who's Lucius?"

"Kitchen man at the Crow. A Barbadian. As fine a fellow as there is around here. But a little addled in his old age."

They climbed the slippery steps up from the putrid black canal and stood for a moment at the rear entrance of the Black Crow. Sabrina put a hand on Nick's shoulder. "Listen to me, Nick. Your sister may well be held captive here, and she may not. If she isn't, don't fret. I know where to find her."

"Where?" Nick asked.

"There's an old English fort out at the entrance to the harbor. Blood's taken it over and installed a garrison of men and countless cannons. He'll defend Port Royal and his fleet, should anyone be foolish enough to attack. It's called Fort Blood now, naturally enough. The dungeons, I hear it said, are full. That's where Bill imprisons his enemies or anyone who looks at him sideways or crosses him. I think that's where you'll find your Kate, sorry to say."

"Blood's ransom letter told me to come to the Black Crow by sundown if I wanted to see her alive. My guess is she's imprisoned here."

"If she is, Lucius will know about it. We'll find him in the kitchen."

As they entered the rear of the tavern, Gunner leaned over and whispered to Nick, "Keep yer gun handy, Master Nick. In yer hand with yer hand in yer jacket pocket. We don't know what we're up against inside this den of thieving scoundrels."

"Good idea," Nick said, pulling his gun from the holster at his back and sliding his gun inside his pocket.

"This way," Sabrina said, leading them through the door and through some kind of storeroom, or larder, where the smell of overripe meat and rotting vegetables attacked Nick's nostrils.

"Customers don't come for the food, I guess," Nick whispered to Sabrina.

She laughed. "Grog and ale and strumpets, that's what they come for. This door leads directly to the kitchen. We'll find out soon enough about your sister."

Nick's heart was beating fast, ratcheting up, as they pushed through the door. Kate was nearby. He could feel it in his bones. There was an elderly black man pouring red wine into a glass on a small wooden tray. There was also a plate of something Nick couldn't identify and wouldn't eat even if he was starving.

"Evening, Lucius," Sabrina said.

"Why, Miss Sabrina! Dis is your free night. What you doin' here at de Crow?"

"Lucius, these are my two new friends, Nick and Gunner. They've come looking for Nick's little sister."

"Little thing? Bright red hair and big blue eyes?"

"That sounds like Katie!" Nick exclaimed, hope suddenly lighting up his face.

"That's her. Katie. Lordy, what a little angel. This is her supper I been fixin' right here. On my way upstairs to her with it."

"She's here, Gunner! She's here!" Nick cried.

"Don't let us interrupt your work, Lucius," Gunner said. "We'll just follow you upstairs, if you don't mind."

Sabrina moved to the door, taking her leave, and said, "I'm very happy you've found her. But the faster you can get that child away from here, the better. This time of night, Old Bill's probably right in the next room with a bellyful of rum in 'im. Glad I could be of some help to you gentlemen."

Nick moved to her and took her hand. "I owe you a huge debt of gratitude, Miss. And someday I'll come back and re-pay it. I promise."

"We owe you our lives, too, ma'am, and we thank you kindly for everything you've done," Gunner added.

"What floor is she on?" Nick asked Lucius after Sabrina left.

"Child on de third floor—you jes follow me."

Gunner and Nick followed the old fellow's slow progress up three flights of wooden steps. Halfway down the hallway, he paused outside a door and pulled a big brass ring of keys out of his pocket. He knocked first, inserted the key, and opened the door.

Kate was sitting at a desk, chin resting in the palms of her hands, staring out the window at the evening stars and the light mist of rain.

"Miz Kate, you got some visitors," Lucius said.

She turned around and saw her brother, Nick, and Gunner standing just behind Lucius, smiling at her. Without saying a word, she leaped from the chair, ran to Nick, and wrapped her arms around him.

"I told Cecily you were coming, but she didn't believe me!" Kate said.

"Who's Cecily?" Gunner asked, looking around for another captive in the tiny room.

"You know Cecily!" Kate said, holding up the doll.

Nick nodded to Gunner, who turned to Lucius and said, "If you don't mind putting down the tray, we'd like a little time alone with the child."

"Nossuh. Fine with me. I got fish to fry."

Gunner followed him to the door and waited until Lucius had disappeared down the staircase. Then he pulled the Tempus Machina from inside his jacket and separated the two halves.

"Kate," Nick said, "we don't have much time. Blood's just downstairs, and we've got to get out of here. He might show up at any second. When Gunner has finished entering our destination, we all place our hands on the ball, understand?"

"I know how it works, Nicky. I came here with Blood and Snake Eye, remember?"

"Right, let's be off, then."

"Nicky, I have to show you something first."

"There's no time, Katie. We have to go *now*, while we still have a chance."

"This is very important. You'll understand when you see it. It's in the next room."

"Oh, all right, but make it quick. Gunner, could you stow the orb until we're ready to go?"

He nodded, screwed the two halves back together, and slipped it back into his hidden pouch.

The adjacent door was locked. Gunner forced it easily, slipping his knife blade between the lock and the doorjamb. The large room was bare save a large wooden desk in the center. Nick asked Gunner to remain at the door, a lookout.

"It's in that drawer, Nick. Open it. You'll see," Katie said.

Finding the drawer also locked, Nick used his knife to trip the lock and pop it open. Inside the drawer were charts and documents.

"What is this?" Nick asked.

"Only Captain Blood's plans to use his armada to take over the world, that's what."

Nick looked at Gunner, his eyes alight.

"You were right to show me these charts, Kate," her brother said, ruffling her hair, as he quickly scanned Blood's secret papers.

"I know," Kate said. "I find I'm usually right at least most of the time."

Nick instantly rolled the lot of them up tightly, stuffed them down the front of his trousers, and buttoned his jacket. He closed the drawer carefully so that it would look undisturbed, then looked at Gunner standing guard. "Clear?"

Gunner stuck his head out the door for a fraction of a second. He jerked it back inside and turned to Nick. "Sounds coming from the front staircase. Sounds like someone coming up maybe. Just reaching the second floor now, I'd guess. No time to use the orb, Nick."

Kate's hand flew to her mouth. "Oh, what will we do, Nicky?"

"We'll go down the back steps and hide under the bridge!" Nick cried. "Gunner, take Kate in your arms and fly down those back steps. I'll be right behind you!"

But as Gunner and Kate turned the corner into the rear stairwell, Gunner saw a sight that froze his very blood: Captain Blood starting up the steps. Right behind him, five or six of Blood's crew.

Nick saw Gunner turn and shout, "Blood! We'll have to try the front steps!"

They raced toward the front steps. They were halfway down the hallway when Snake Eye appeared at the far end, grinning evilly. Then Nick heard Blood's eerie voice behind him.

"Why, if it ain't the McIver boy and his mate Gunner. What, yer early, right are ye? Lucius told me the child had visitors, but I didn't expect you two till the morrow. Welcome to the Black Crow, gents."

"I want my sister," Nick said, trying to control his temper.

"And I want yer golden orb, boy. That's how kidnapping works. Have ye brung it?"

"Yes, I've brought it all right. And I'll exchange it for her freedom, but only on one condition."

Blood laughed. "You're in no position to make conditions, little swabbie. But tell me, what is it you want?"

"You must first swear to use the orb to return the three of us safely home to Greybeard Island."

"But that was me plan all along. Port Royal's no place for the likes of you."

"Swear it."

"I do so solemnly swear. Now, let's all go below. The boy and I will make the formal exchange and celebrate with a tot of rum afore I takes you three home."

Nick nodded yes, his mind racing, desperate for a way to get Kate away from Blood, a man in whom he had no trust at all.

"Snake Eye, you take the girl until we've made the swap."

The tattooed Frenchman went to Gunner and took Kate from his arms. She had her eyes squeezed shut, and she wasn't about to open them.

Snake Eye, Kate in his arms, led the way, and they all descended the staircase, Billy Blood bringing up the rear. When they entered the pub on the ground floor, Nick took a deep breath to calm himself. The gun in the small of his back was little comfort now; things were spinning rapidly beyond his control.

The room below was filled to overflowing with drunken pirates. All stone silent and staring daggers at the three visitors. And coming through the door were the four angry mates of the man Gunner had recently shot, a mob of angry pirates hard on their heels.

"OFF WITH THEIR HEADS!"

Blood banged his golden hook on the bar and shouted at the barmaids, "Rum, rum for all these scoundrels I call mateys! We're going to have a proper farewell soiree for our three new friends here before we send them off!"

"Huzzah!" everyone cried in unison, lifting their sloshing mugs in a salute to their infamous leader.

"This boy here claims to have brought the old Blood a gift. A gift of gold, ain't that so, boy?" he said, squeezing Nick's shoulder painfully with his one good hand.

"It is so."

"Well, let's have it then! Complete our transaction."

"You'll have it. But not until my sister is released and returned to Gunner's arms."

"You don't trust me, lad?" He grinned and the crowd roared with delight.

"No."

"Smarter than you look, ain't you? All right. Snake Eye, return the little angel to her guardian."

Safe in Gunner's arms once more, Kate hugged him around the neck and whispered into his ear, "Don't worry, Gunner. I'm not afraid. Nicky will get us out of this. I just know he will."

"Of course he will," Gunner whispered back, but he didn't believe a word of it. They still had their guns, but they were useless against an enemy this size.

"Now!" Blood cried out. "'Tis time for the completion of our bargain, Nicholas McIver. I lost my right hand the last time I held the object of my desire. I don't see that happening tonight. Hand it over!"

Nick reached inside his jacket and pulled the gleaming golden ball out of its pouch. Blood's face lit up at the sight of it. "Put her there on the bar where I can admire it whilst my comrades join me in a toast to my new possession."

Nick placed it carefully right in front of Blood, who began stroking it lovingly with his left hand. Then Blood raised his mug and turned to regard his men. "Join me in a salute, boys?"

"Aye!" they shouted back.

"Three cheers for the Brethren that rules the seas!"

"Huzzah! Huzzah! Huzzah!" they all cried.

"Now, now, my little friend," Blood said, slipping the orb into the side pocket of his crimson velvet captain's coat. "I've arranged a very special send-off for you and your friends. A parade of sorts. There's a mule and a cart waitin' outside that door, ready to take you on a tour of the harbor, all the way out to Fort Blood, where you'll depart from. I understand the streets are lined with citizens and mates of mine who want a glimpse of you three before yer departure. I hope that suits you?"

"Just take us home," Nick said, staring into Blood's eyes, his own eyes hard as stone. If nothing else, he'd not give Blood the satisfaction of seeing his worry and fear.

"Home, he says! Why, that's exactly where you're headed. Come along, let's get on with the celebration."

The throng of pirates parted to make way for Captain

Blood, followed by Nick and Gunner, who held Kate in his powerful arms. As Blood pushed through the heavy wooden door, Nick was stunned at the sight that greeted him.

Both sides of the harbor road were lined with the mostly unsavory citizens of Port Royal. In some places they were standing five or six people deep. Many were holding flaming torches aloft, casting an orange glow upon the whole scene. He saw young boys sitting on rooftops and in the limbs of trees. There were women, too, many of them dressed similarly to Sabrina, smiling and laughing.

Sabrina stood among them, her eyes filled with sorrow.

Gunner, too, was dumbfounded by what he saw. As he lifted Katie high up and put her in the mule-drawn cart full of straw, he could think of only one thing. This was the way a crowd looked and acted prior to witnessing an execution. He climbed up into the wooden cart, sat down, and took Katie into his arms. Nick, who stumbled once climbing up, was heaved roughly by two men up into the cart.

Blood, mounted atop a huge black stallion, sat smiling at his three captives as the cart started to roll forward.

"Where are you taking us?" Nick screamed at the grinning man.

"Why, to Fort Blood, of course."

"Fort Blood? Why there?"

"Because that's where you'll be makin' yer departure, lad." And then he threw his head back and laughed, the silver skulls braided into his beard sounding like tiny sleigh bells. He kept his mount just a few feet behind the cart so that he could keep an eye on them and make sure they didn't try to escape.

It was not a pleasant ride for the occupants of the wooden cart.

All along the route to the fort, the inhabitants of Port Royal hurled insults and worse at them. There was a wicked tone to their taunts and shouted curses, Nick thought, as though they were screaming for blood.

At one point Gunner was hit in the back of the head by a rotten tomato. Nick, furious, stood up and cleaned the mess off his friend as best he could with the sleeve of his jacket.

More rotten fruit and vegetables were thrown at the occupants of the cart. Nick remained on his feet, batting some of it away or just taking it, darting around Gunner and Kate so he, Nick, would be hit and not them.

As the cart neared the towering stone walls of the fortress and finally rattled across the wooden drawbridge into a cobblestone courtyard, Nick bent and whispered urgently into Gunner's ear. He deliberately spoke softly enough so that his sister would not hear what he said.

"Nod your head if you think they're going to kill us," he whispered.

Gunner nodded his head violently.

"Me, too. Our only chance is to use our guns and try to shoot our way out."

"Too many of 'em."

"I know. But it's still our only chance."

"Maybe not."

"What? What are you thinking?"

"If you can somehow stand real close to me, stay between me and Blood, maybe I can slip the machine out and enter time and destination."

"But if he even glimpses a second ball, we're as good as dead—he'll draw his pistols and shoot us where we stand."

"It's only a chance, Nick. I think we–"

But at that moment the cart lurched to a halt. Blood rode his horse right up the rear of it and unlatched the flimsy wooden door.

"All out," he said. "Quick-like."

Nick jumped to the ground and held up his arms for his sister. Gunner handed her down gently and Nick noticed she was silently weeping.

She knows what's coming, Nick thought, and the knowledge was a knife piercing his heart.

"I want to walk," she said. "Please hold my hand, Nicky. Gunner, you hold the other one."

Their pirate guards had their guns out now, and they prodded Nick and Gunner in the back, directing them toward the fort's entrance, two heavy wooden doors, with iron bands.

As the crowd ahead parted to let them through, Nick caught a glimpse of a strange wooden contraption the French had invented. He'd seen a picture of such a device in one of his history books. It was a guillotine, like that used during the Terror in France.

It was a simple machine. A tall, upright frame, from which a heavy razor-sharp blade was suspended. The victim put his head on the block; the executioner raised the blade all the way to the top with a rope and then released it. The blade fell swiftly and stopped with a thud. A basket stood ready to catch the decapitated heads.

"You didn't invent it, you know, Nick," Gunner said as they got closer to the guillotine.

"What's that?"

"Being afraid."

"Close your eyes, Katie," Nick said.

"Why?"

"I've told you before that there are things best not seen by little girls. Now, close them."

"Do you know what I wish, Nicky?" Katie said, squeezing her brother's hand. "Right now?"

"What, Katie?"

"I wish I had a pair of invisible wings and we could all hold hands and fly away."

Nick tried to keep the despair from his voice. "I wish so, too, Katie. I wish so, too."

As they approached the guillotine, Nick found himself whispering his old prayer for courage in desperate times. And these were as desperate as even he'd faced.

Nelson the strong, Nelson the brave, Nelson the Lord of the Sea.

Gunner looked over at Nick, and the boy saw there was not even a trace of fear in his eyes. "This is it, then, Master Nick. Quick and painless, so I've read. I'll go first."

"No. I'll go first. You stay with Katie and cover her eyes. Ask someone for a blindfold for her. It's the very least they can do."

"A blindfold for the child, you scurrilous dogs!" Gunner shouted at the top of his lungs.

"No," Katie said, her voice barely above a whisper, "I want to see."

Nick allowed himself a small smile. If he was going to die, he could not imagine braver companions to face his executioner with.

But when they reached the terrible beheading machine with the waiting basket, the crowd behind kept pushing them forward. And, they kept walking! Went right past the guillotine and up the stone steps to the fort's entrance. Blood was leading the way now, and there were countless pirates, buccaneers, and as many citizens as could fit in the courtyard, all screaming for the prisoners' heads.

They passed through many rooms and halls and finally reached a set of steps leading down into the gloom. Nick lost count of how many levels they went down.

"Where are you taking us?" Nick suddenly asked Blood. "You swore to take us home with the machine."

"Never trust a pirate's word, lad. Never." Blood laughed.

"I asked you a question. Where are we going?"

"To the dungeon. To a very special place called the oubliette. The crowd out there wants yer heads to roll, of course; they love to see heads roll and blood spill. But I've decided the blade is far too quick for the likes of you. All the trouble you've caused me deserves special treatment. A long, slow end is what yer facing, boy, you and yer sister and yer friend. Won't be a pretty way to go, I'm a'feared. But you've earned every minute of it."

Finally they reached the bottom. There were no cells there, just a wide round room of moldy brick, lit by guttering torches mounted on the ancient walls. In the very center of the room was a hole about five feet in diameter. It looked like a deep well.

About twenty of Blood's crew filed into the room and lined the wall, all with their pistols drawn and aimed at the victims. Nick knew now that the guns given him by Lord Hawke were utterly useless.

They'd been condemned to death in the most cruel way imaginable. The oubliette. Nick had read about them in his history books, too. *Oubliette* came from the French word meaning "forget." They threw you into a deep hole ... and forgot about you. Eventually, insane with hunger and thirst, you died of starvation. Men cast into the pit were known to kill one another and eat human flesh, starvation driving them to cannibalism.

And forgotten for all eternity. It was not the way Nick Mc-Iver had intended to die.

Blood and Snake Eye walked to the center of the room and stood on either side of the yawning black hole, evil grins on their faces.

"Who wants to go first?" Old Bill asked, drawing his sword. Nick saw instantly what Blood was thinking. It was like walking the plank. On shipboard, if the victim showed the least hesitation to leap to his death in open seas, he was prodded along to his death by the tip of a sword.

Gunner looked solemnly at Nick. "I'll go first, lad. I can catch Katie. Break her fall. Then I'll catch you."

Nick nodded, knowing that Gunner, who was immensely strong, just might be able to do as he promised. And then Gunner walked forward, glaring at the smirking Captain Blood. It was all he could do not to disarm the old monster and shove him into his own hole. But that would just get them all shot.

"I'll see you in hell someday," Gunner said to Old Bill, pausing at the edge.

"You'll certainly precede me." Blood smiled. "Do you wish to jump or be persuaded? Either is fine by me."

Gunner said nothing, just stepped off the edge and disappeared. Nick heard no cry of pain from the depths below. He didn't know if that was a good thing or a very bad thing.

"Next?" Blood asked, with a little bow.

"My sister," Nick said, walking with a trembling Katie in his arms, constantly whispering encouragements to be brave in her ear. "Almost over now, don't worry. You won't get hurt. Gunner and I always take care of you, don't we? And we will now and forever."

When they stood at the edge, he said, "It's all right, Katie, I promise. Gunner's down there. He'll catch you. Then I'll be right behind you. We'll all be together again. Are you ready?"

"Yes. I'm not scared, Nicky. I've got you."

Nick hugged her to him, then put his hands around her waist and held her out over the opening. He looked down into the well and thought he could make out Gunner standing at the bottom with his arms outstretched.

"Gunner?" Nick shouted down into the hole, "Ready?"

"Aye" came the hollow reply from below.

Nick McIver dropped his little sister into the oubliette.

There was no cry of pain, which surely meant Gunner had caught Katie safely.

Nick turned to face his mortal enemy. "You will regret this someday, Captain Blood. You have my word on it. However long it may be, whatever it may take. I am going to make you sorry you ever saw my face."

"I'm already sorry, you mewling little pup," Blood spat and viciously cracked Nick across the shoulders with the flat of his blade. Nick pitched headfirst into the hole. He could hear the echoes of Blood's laughter all the way down.

He landed in Gunner's powerful arms, hard, for it was a long drop.

"You all right, lad?" he heard Gunner say in the semi-darkness, as he lowered him gently to the ground.

"Yes. Where is Katie?"

"Right here beside me where she belongs."

"Oh, Nicky," she sobbed. "Look at all the bones. Are we all going to die in this horrible place?"

It was indeed horrible. The skeletons of countless victims lay scattered across the dirt floor, and Nick could see many sitting where they'd died, backs to the wall. Fresher victims, their flesh torn from their bones as if they'd been attacked by wild dogs, lay nearby, and the smell of rot and worse was well-nigh insufferable.

"Katie," Nick said, "didn't I promise you I'd take care of you? Have I ever lied to you?

"No. B—but this place is so terrible. How are we ever to get out?"

"Would you like to go home, dear Kate?" Nick asked, kneeling and pulling her toward him in the gloom.

"Home? Oh, yes, Nicky! More than anything in this whole wide world!"

"How about you, Gunner?"

"Home sounds such a lovely word."

"No time like the present then, as I always say, wouldn't you agree?"

"Aye, let's abandon this monster and his foul prison, Nicholas."

"Indeed. Mr. Gunner, sir, would you please hand me that small round object you have carefully concealed on your person?"

Gunner reached into his secret pouch and brought Nick's authentic time machine out of its hiding place.

"Would you like to set our course for home, Master Nick?"

"Indeed I would, sir!"

Nick carefully took the Tempus Machina in both hands and turned each half counterclockwise. The moment he separated the two, the faces of each half began to glow brightly, illuminating the jeweled dials. He entered the exact time he wanted to return to, time to be home for supper on July 15,

1940. And then, from memory, he entered the exact latitude and longitude coordinates for the Greybeard Inn on Greybeard Island.

He could already feel the steady pull of the two halves toward each other, but he had one more thing to do before he closed the machine.

"Blood?" he called upward, "can you hear me?"

He saw Blood's face appear far above, peering over the edge of the oubliette, a torch lighting his face.

"What's that bloody light down there?" Blood cried.

"What might you think it is, Captain?" Nick called up.

"What is it, I say, tell me now!"

"Why, it's my Tempus Machina, Captain. The one I gave you is lovely, but a poor substitute for the real thing. We'll bid you farewell now."

Nick rejoined the two halves, as Kate and Gunner placed their hands over his on the gleaming orb.

A second later, a red-faced Captain Blood was howling in an absolute rage of anger and frustration. He'd just seen his three prisoners disappear. Right before his disbelieving eyes.

That boy, that damnable boy, had tricked him again.

· Greybeard Island—July 1940 ·

Nick nearly wept for joy at the look on Katie's face. She stood stock-still for a second, looked around, and suddenly realized where she was. Home. And then all three of them burst into peals of laughter. The three time travelers had arrived back on the lovely green island in the summer of 1940. They found themselves standing just outside the front door of the Greybeard Inn. It was a beautiful midsummer afternoon, few clouds, and the golden light striking the lighthouse in the far distance.

His sister, Kate, still remembering her captivity, was actually pinching herself to see if this miracle was possibly true.

It was. She'd escaped the horrible nightmare. Blood had meant them to starve to death in that terrible hole filled with skeletons and horrible rats. But now she was home! She leaped up and flung her arms around her brother's neck, kissing him on both cheeks.

"Oh, Nicky," Kate said, "do you know the very last thing Mother said to me? 'Make sure you and your brother are home in time for supper.' And, look, the sun's still up! We *will* be home in time."

Nick put her down and looked at Gunner. "When did you realize Blood had made such a very stupid mistake?"

"I thought for sure we'd lose our heads. But then, in the bowels of the dungeon, I saw you make that tiny smile, looking longingly at that black hole. That oubliette. Then I knew we'd got the best of him."

"He's going to be very angry."

"We've not seen the last of him, I'll grant you that."

"He's not half so clever as he thinks he is. Which works decidedly in our favor. But now he's got a powerful armada, the Brethren of Blood, to back him up."

Gunner said, "Why don't you and Kate come inside for a wee moment? I'll serve up some hot tea and cakes. Of course, if you want to go straightaway to check up on your parents, I'm understanding of that. And have you told your sister about yer recent misfortune?"

"What misfortune?" Kate said.

"The Camel," Nick said. "I had to ditch her."

"Ditch her? What kind of ditch?"

"He means she went into the drink," Gunner said. "All the way to the bottom."

"Oh, Nicky. That beautiful old aeroplane is gone?"

"'Fraid so."

"Have you told Father?"

"No. I haven't seen him since it happened."

"When did it happen?"

"Right before Gunner and I came to Port Royal to bring you home."

"Do you think Father will be terribly angry?"

"I don't think so. Sad perhaps but not angry. I'm sad, too, Kate. I loved that flying machine. And I had a lot of big plans for it, too. But accidents happen."

"I been thinking on it, Nick," Gunner said. "My theory is, it ain't the worst thing in the world that could have happened, the old girl going down. Seeing as how you escaped, of course."

"What do you mean, Gunner?"

"I mean those Nazis have a bone in their teeth. They'd have found that aeroplane in the barn sooner or later. And then they'd have come looking for who owned it. People around here are scared. Somebody would have spilled the beans. And then where would we be? You and me and your dad?"

"Prison."

"Or worse, most likely. In one night you took out almost an entire squadron of Messerschmitts. And most of their ammunition. Enough to earn the lot of us the unfriendly attentions of a firing squad, I'd wager."

Nick nodded. Gunner was right. One good air raid was all he was ever meant to get out of the Camel. And by all that's holy, it had been a jolly good one!

He smiled and pulled the stolen roll of Blood's charts from inside his trousers and handed them to Gunner.

"I think Kate and I should hurry right home now, Gunner. But first thing in the morning, we should all gather up in the Armoury and have a look at all the charts. And hear what Katie has to say about Blood's armada and his intentions. Knowing his plans, it might be nice to make them go seriously awry."

Gunner looked at Kate. "Kate, God love you, please tell us you remember at least some of what Blood said."

"All of it."

"All of it?"

"Of course, silly. I made sure I wouldn't forget."

Kate reached into the deep pocket of her ragged sweater and pulled out what appeared to be sheets of writing paper, folded into the smallest square possible. For the first time,

Nick noticed what a bedraggled little ragamuffin he now had for a sister. Well, hardly her fault. She'd been dragged halfway round the world into another century and spent her time in the company of filthy pirates.

"I wrote down everything I could. I couldn't spell a lot of the words, and I missed some, but it's mostly all there. What I heard with my glass to the wall."

Nick hurriedly unfolded the pages and scanned the words, his eyes racing down each page. "She's got it all, Gunner, Blood's immediate naval plans of battle for his armada. An attack on some French admiral named de Grasse."

Nick refolded the paper and stuffed it into his pocket. He'd go over the charts carefully with Gunner in the morning. At this moment, he had no urge at all to take on the greatest pirate armada in all history. But something told him Blood's plans held some future importance for him. It was only a hunch, but he'd learned to trust those feelings.

Kate and Nick walked hand in hand along the Coast Road in the fading light. The road finally ended at a rocky path that led up to the lighthouse. The sun had set, leaving a bright orange band on the blue horizon. Nick had been quiet for most of the walk. He was carefully considering the words he might use to tell Kate what had befallen their parents. In the end, with the lighthouse clearly in sight on the cliff top, he chose to be completely straightforward.

"Kate, I'm afraid I've some more troublesome news. I've not had the chance to tell you, but I think you should know before we get home."

She gripped his hand more tightly. "Know what, Nicky? We're home, aren't we? What could be better news than that?"

"It's about Mum and Dad."

"What about them?"

"I'm afraid the Nazis have taken them away."

"Taken them?" She looked up at him. "Taken them where?"

"Not far away. Just over to Guernsey."

"Why on earth would they do a thing like that?"

"An investigation. They took many of our neighbors, too. They're looking for that German soldier we found in the tree. They think someone on the island has murdered him and is covering it up."

"But it's not true!"

"Of course it's not. It's just that I wanted you to know they might not be home when we get there, that's all. If they're not, I don't want you to worry. I've got a new friend over on Guernsey who can help us. We'll get Gunner to run us over in his motorboat and visit her in the morning. She'll have them home in jig time."

"Oh, Nicky!" Kate cried. She turned and ran up the steep path to their front door, calling out for her parents. She flung the door open and burst inside, Nick right on her heels, a minute behind. Strangely, Nick thought, all the lights were off in the house. A single candle was flickering on the kitchen table. Nick saw his mother seated at the table, holding Kate to her in a tight embrace. They both seemed to be crying.

"Mother, you're home!" Nick said, going to her.

"Yes, Nicky, I'm home." Something was wrong with her voice. And her face. Her right cheek was badly bruised, he could see in the candle's light, and her left eye was black and blue and swollen shut.

"Mother, tell me what happened," Nick said, sitting down at the table across from her and reaching for her hand.

"A Nazi soldier," she said, looking up at her son and trying for a brave smile. "When we were all being processed at Gestapo headquarters. He—he made some very vulgar remarks to me, said he had to search me and—and he—he touched me in a terribly improper fashion. When I raked his cheek with my fingernails, he threw me against the wall and hit me in the face. I must look horrible, mustn't I? I haven't had the courage to look in a mirror."

"Those filthy Nazis!" Nick said, his face flushed with anger. "I'll get them, don't worry, Mother. I'll make them sorry for what they did, every last one."

"It's all right, darling. I'm not badly hurt. But they are vicious brutes, and we shall all have to be very, very careful around them until this dreadful occupation is over. Luckily, we have someone on our side. A wonderful woman named Fleur de Villiers. She came to the hospital, to visit your father and—"

"Father's in hospital?"

"He'll be all right, Nick, it's nothing serious," Emily McIver said. "When he saw that horrible soldier attacking me, he broke out of line and pulled the man off me. He did a lot more damage to the German's face than the German did to mine, you'll be glad to know."

"But why is he in—?"

"He's in hospital because the guards hurt him badly, ripping him off the beast who'd been abusing me, beating him mercilessly. No broken bones, but he's horribly bruised. But he'll be out soon, possibly tomorrow. This friend of your father's is named Baroness de Villiers, pulled some strings with the German High Command. Your father had been arrested. After release from the hospital, he was headed straight to prison. But Baroness de Villiers took care of that easily enough. A few quiet words with the Kommandant and your father was a free man."

"How did you get home, Mummy?" Kate asked.

"The Baroness was kind enough to bring me home in her little steam yacht this afternoon, after I saw your father."

Nick stood up. "I want to go to the hospital and see Father. Right now."

"Nick, no. He's quite all right. They've given him some pain medication and muscle relaxants, and he needs his sleep. Anyway, I want you to stay as far away from these Germans as you can. Promise me that, both of you."

"I *hate* Nazis," Kate said.

"All right, Mother, I won't go near them," Nick said, thinking of just how close he'd come to the Nazis lately. The patrols on the beach and in the woods the night he'd ditched the Camel. Nick hated lying and keeping secrets. And so he always felt a twinge of guilt when it came to his parents' lack of knowledge about his adventurous exploits. Especially about the existence of the Tempus Machina. But it couldn't be helped.

Only five people on the island knew of the machine. Kate, Gunner, Lord Hawke, Hobbes, and himself. Hawke had sworn them all to secrecy about the miraculous machine and its powers. And Nick, knowing first hand the dangers associated with knowledge of the golden orb, would never break that vow.

But he was determined, if nothing else, to help his country through this dark period of war in any way he could. That's what he had learned from Admiral Lord Nelson. Duty. Duty to country first. Everything else was secondary.

And he knew for certain that his mother would recoil at the danger he sometimes placed himself in. Why, she'd never again let him out of her sight if she knew even *half* the things he'd been up to lately. Until the age of about nine, when he'd learned to sail the little sloop, *Stormy Petrel*, that his father had built for him, he'd been tied to his mother's apron strings. But there were no strings now, not a one.

Not since he'd discovered what a grand adventure life could be if you jumped in headfirst without fear and were prepared to take your knocks. Nick had two great heroes in his life: Winston Churchill and Admiral Lord Nelson. Thanks to the machine, he'd been able to help Lord Nelson in the year 1805. Nelson had personally pinned a medal for heroism on Nick's chest.

But shiny medals did not a hero make.

Only a lifetime of bravery in the face of danger, and a willingness to sacrifice all in the pursuit of one's sacred duty to country, would ever give him a chance of becoming a true hero.

Before a quiet candlelit supper, just the three of them sharing a shepherd's pie his mum had made, they all joined hands and said a prayer. They prayed for Father, of course, and they prayed for their tiny island's survival and ultimate victory over her invading enemies. And, finally, they prayed for dear old England, whose very future this night was far from certain.

"To bed with you children," his mum said after supper. "I'll clean up the kitchen. It will give me something to do. School will be starting soon, and I don't think either of you has even begun your summer reading assignments. Katherine, you haven't cracked a book since June, have you?"

"Only *Black Beauty*."

"Doesn't count. And you, Nick?"

"I've been a bit busy, Mother."

"I don't care about old aeroplanes. I care about the education of the mind. And Nick, if you want to keep up your marks in history this term, I suggest you pull that big blue book down off your shelf. It's not mere decoration, you know; it's meant to be read. Without the lessons of history, we'd all be savages. What are you studying this coming term?"

"Eighteenth-Century English history."

"Should be enough excitement there to keep your eyes open. Off now, to bed with the both of you! With any luck, your father will be home tomorrow. I'm going to get up early and fill the house with roses."

"Yes, Mother," Nick said.

Nick thought there were still plenty of savages around in the Twentieth Century, but he kept that thought to himself as he climbed the stairs to his small bedroom at the top of the tower. He loved the study of history and actually looked forward to cracking the big blue book.

Mounting the winding steps, however, he realized he was desperately tired. Still, he would climb into his bed and delve into the stories of heroes and villains for as long as he could keep his eyes open.

———

An hour later, Nick McIver was still wide awake. He had opened that great door-stopper of a schoolbook, Fitz Hughes's *A History of England*, to a random chapter. It was the tale of George Washington's siege against General Lord Cornwallis's British Army troops at Yorktown, Virginia. Not quite random, he'd corrected himself. It was the date at the top of the page that had caught his eye. The year 1781, to be exact. Why, Nick had just returned from a brief but exciting holiday in the Caribbean in that very same year. That was why he had stopped at this particular page. And now he began reading the chapter feverishly.

The British, harried and pursued by Americans under the

command of General Lafayette, were well fortified on open ground, good fields of fire in all directions and their backs to the sea. There were 7,200 British soldiers inside the fortifications. On August 19, General Washington with 3,000 soldiers under his command, and his ally the French commander Comte de Rochambeau, with 4,000 troops, began their steady march to Yorktown for a showdown with the British and Cornwallis. Lafayette, with his 4,000 troops, was eagerly awaiting the arrival of Continental Army reinforcements.

Despite his excitement over the story of the Battle of Yorktown, Nick felt his sleepy eyes longing to close. Then he read the following passage:

General George Washington hoped to trap Cornwallis at Yorktown and defeat him. A victory now would mean the end of conflict and independence for America. Lafayette, already in place, was blocking Cornwallis' escape by land. Meanwhile, a French fleet, under the command of Admiral de Grasse, was scheduled to arrive at Chesapeake Bay to prevent Cornwallis from escaping by sea. Cornwallis desperately called for help but none came. The British were surrounded, low on ammunition, and quickly running out of food. On October 19th, 1781, General Cornwallis surrendered. The Battle of Yorktown brought an end to the Revolutionary War. The Americans were victorious. But Washington's victory was made possible only by the timely arrival of the French fleet under Admiral de Grasse.

Nick's eyes opened wide. If Billy Blood's great pirate armada succeeded in ambushing de Grasse's fleet en route from the Caribbean to Yorktown, Virginia, the outcome was certain.

The Americans would lose the Revolutionary War. There would be no America.

Somehow Nick seemed to feel, he had to warn Washington of Blood's lurking armada, lying in wait for de Grasse off the coast of Nassau.

He yawned and turned out his light. He was going to need all the rest he could get if he was going to set out for Virginia in the year 1781.

As Nick drifted toward slumber that night, Churchill's dire warning kept repeating and reverberating in his mind. "If the American's don't come to England's aid, we cannot defeat the Nazis."

Realization struck like lightning.

In order for there to be an America to come to England's aid in 1940, it meant there had to be an America! The Americans had to win at Yorktown. Of course!

And it meant that Nicholas McIver, a boy who loved England above all else, would have to do all in his power to help ensure his own country's most humiliating defeat.

There was a name for what he was about to do.

"Treason," he whispered in the dark.

And with that terrible word dying on his lips, the boy rolled over and slept fitfully until dawn.

General George Washington!" Gunner exclaimed. "But he's the bloody enemy!"

Gunner and Nick were upstairs in the Armoury at the Greybeard Inn. They had Kate's notes and all the charts stolen from inside Blood's desk in Port Royal spread out upon the round table. De Grasse, with twenty-eight warships and five thousand French troops, would most surely sail southwest once he'd reached Jamaica, set a course between Mexico and Cuba, and then veer northwest through the straits of Florida. The seven-mile-an-hour northerly current of the Gulf Stream would help his heavily laden ships make good time.

But lying in wait for him, just off the northeast coast of Nassau Town, would be Captain William Blood's pirate armada, numbering some one hundred ships! The gravely outnumbered French fleet would be lambs to the slaughter. Burned after the treasure had been offloaded, sunk without a trace.

Nick looked at Gunner, thinking about how to reply to the outrage at his plan. "Washington may have been England's enemy then," Nick replied, tracing de Grasse's route north on the chart with his finger, "but his America is England's only hope now."

"Which means?"

"I heard it from Prime Minister Churchill himself, Gunner. Unless America comes into this war on England's side, we've no chance at all of defeating Hitler and the Nazis."

"He told you that, did he?" Gunner said, expelling a blue cloud of pipe smoke into the air.

"He did indeed, sir."

"And there will only *be* an America if they win their Revolution against our Crown."

"Correct."

"We couldn't have beat the Germans without the Yanks' help in the First World War, I'll grant you that," Gunner said, musing upon the situation.

"And we can't do it in this one, either, Gunner, believe me! That's all there is to it. Unless I act, and now, England will be defeated. Hitler will crush us beneath his hobnail boots."

"You propose to warn General Washington about Blood's armada?"

"It's the hardest decision I've ever had to make, Gunner. I'm sacrificing everything I believe in, except duty, of course."

"And you think it's your duty to warn our enemy. Give them information which will ensure our own country's defeat?"

"I do."

"It's treason, Nick. Plain and simple."

"I know."

"You'll hang for it, lad, if yer caught, and die a traitor."

"I know."

"You don't care."

"I do not."

"I was afraid you'd say that."

"Sometimes the ends justify the means. Will you help me, Gunner?"

"Of course I'll help ye, boy, God save me. When have I not? What's yer plan?"

"According to Kate's notes, Blood sails for New Providence Island on this date logged here. It will take him approximately one week, by my calculations, to reach Nassau Town's harbor."

"And just how do you plan to stop an entire armada of those murderous dogs?"

"I'll need help, that's for sure. First, I must use the orb, travel to Virginia, arriving near Washington's home, Mount Vernon, in early September 1781. Just as de Grasse sails from Saint Domingue. The Americans have our troops under siege at Yorktown. But there's a lot of fighting going on in the countryside still, skirmishes between our Redcoats and Lafayette's Continentals, trying to rally the Virginia militia. And Indians, too, tribes fighting for both sides. I'll need some kind of believable disguise. I was thinking of a regimental drummer boy."

"Drummer boy, eh? On whose side?"

"Ours. If the Redcoats see me, I've no problems."

"What about the Continentals? If they see you, they'll shoot you."

"I'll take my chances."

"I've a book up there on the shelf. *Military Uniforms of the British Empire*. We could use that for yer outfit. And I'm pretty handy with a needle and thread; y' know."

"That was my thinking, Gunner."

"What else?"

"Well, here's my thought, sir, and if you've got a better one, please don't be shy."

"Spit it out."

"I know from my history book that General Washington

makes a stop at his home, Mount Vernon, en route to York-town, to see his wife, Martha. His first visit home in six years."

"I'm listnin'."

"I want to arrive at Mount Vernon first. I want to be there when Washington arrives home. It's the only sure way I can guarantee our paths will cross."

"You know from yer books the exact date on which he arrives?"

"I do. September 9, 1781. Having ridden sixty miles from Baltimore in a single day."

"And, for the orb, we can get the longitude and latitude coordinates for that part of Virginia from a modern chart."

"We can, sir. The general's great white house sits high on a hilltop overlooking the Potomac River. Not far from Williams-burg, Virginia. And Yorktown."

Gunner tipped his chair back and interlaced his fingers behind his snow-white head. His little gold spectacles were so low on his nose, Nick thought they might drop off. "There's one little matter we need to discuss, boy, afore I help you."

"Anything."

"You'll remember when we first used the golden orb to go back in time and help your ancestor Captain McIver defeat Billy Blood in 1805?"

"I'll never forget it. Admiral Lord Nelson made sure of that."

"And do you remember a solemn oath we all swore to, at Lord Hawke's insistence? Before we used the machine? A sworn promise to, as he called it, 'protect the flow of history'?"

"To not intercede in major historical events in a way that might have dangerous unintended consequences in the future. Yes, I remember."

"You're aiming to break that vow."

"Gunner, I appreciate what you're saying. But in order to save our country in the future, I've decided I've no choice but to betray her in the past. It's been a frightful decision to make, and it may yet have disastrous consequences. But I'm afraid I shall have to betray England and Lord Hawke, as well. I have no other choice."

"You'll brook no argument, I can see it, then. You are bound for America, no matter what good sense I offer."

"As Admiral Lord Nelson said, 'If a man consults whether he is to fight, when he has the power in his own hands, it is certain that his opinion is against fighting.'"

"Nelson said that?"

"Of course those are Nelson's words, Gunner. He's the only one who sees me through these treacherous times. Duty first, last, and always."

"You've thought it all through, seems like."

"As well as I'm able. I love reading history, but I am no scholar. Meanwhile, my own dear father is still held in hospital by the Nazis for attacking a soldier beating my mother. I have vowed to do everything in my power to help Mr. Churchill defeat this evil madman Hitler. I will lie, betray, cheat, and steal, Gunner, anything, if I have the remotest chance to help save England."

"Despite everything I've said, you'll risk life and limb to betray your own country?"

"It's simply my duty. As I see it, anyway."

Gunner looked deep into Nick's eyes, sighed, and looked away. It was hopeless. "I'll retrieve the orb from the gun safe. Meantimes, you can start entering yer calculations. Then I'll start sewing you a fine drummer boy's uniform, copy it from the book down to the last button, I will."

"Thank you, Gunner."

"Ain't nothing any friend wouldn't do for another. But I'm thinking, despite my objections, I should be going with you, lad."

"Why?"

"Why? Well, a boy all on his own in uncivilized territory with a war going on. All that blood and thunder. Indians, too, as I recall. Boy like that could use a former military man like meself handy with weaponry, like that blunderbuss Old Thunder up there on the wall."

Nick glanced up at the gun. Gunner could kill a gnat at one hundred paces with that antique. "Gunner, from what I've read, aside from their disloyalty to King George, these Americans are quite civilized. Most of them, anyway."

"Civility only goes so far in wartime, Nick. You'll be wearing a red coat, sure enough, if I can scrape up some broadcloth the proper shade of scarlet. And that is as good a target as any other for those country farmer American sharpshooters, I'd reckon."

"Yet you, too, would betray king and country for this cause, Gunner?"

"For you, yes, I would, boy. I guess I've always loved you like a son, had I ever been lucky enough so as to have one of my own."

His friend turned away and went to his gun safe, hidden behind a hinged false bookcase in the Armoury. A moment later, he was back. "Here's your magnificent Tempus Machina, lad," Gunner said, his eyes shining with tears. "Only because yer so bound and determined to go to war, in God's holy name. But, Good Lord, I do hate to see you go alone."

Nick smiled and put his hand on Gunner's shoulder. "I think I might be better off all by myself, with all respect, Gunner. I'll need to be able to move with the situation pretty quickly, I think, if I'm to get within spitting distance of General Washington."

"You'll be wearing a red coat, not a blue one. You get within spitting distance of the general, he might just shoot you himself."

"I don't think so."

"Why not?"

"I have a plan."

"You always do. I pray it's a good one, Nick."

"I've been praying so all night."

"Then, Godspeed, Nicholas McIver. Go do yer duty. As you see it, at any rate."

"Thank you, Gunner. I will."

BOOK TWO

INDEPENDENCE

· Colony of Virginia—September 1781 ·

Nick McIver arrived in the American colony of Virginia on a chilly, rainy afternoon in mid-September. He was alone, in a deep, dense wood, with heavy undergrowth carpeting the forest floor. The leaves of the trees towering above were dripping on his head, and he realized he'd have to find somewhere dry and warm to sleep tonight. The scarlet coat Gunner had made for him looked authentic enough but provided little in the way of protection from the elements.

He had deliberately chosen this heavily forested spot because it was only some ten miles from his destination, General Washington's home at Mount Vernon. It was uninhabited woodland for miles in any direction, so he'd been fairly certain his arrival would not have any witnesses save the creatures of the forest. He had pored over Mr. Fitz Hughes's chronicles of the weeks leading up to the Battle of Yorktown and had seen no reference to any major battles or even minor skirmishes being fought in this neck of the Virginia woods.

Nick sat down at the base of a huge tree, the leaves so thick above that the ground was relatively dry. He wanted to collect himself and get his bearings before setting off. From his haversack, he withdrew his hand-drawn map of Virginia and his compass. Since he knew his exact destination and location, it was fairly obvious in which direction he had to travel—due east. Because the wood here was thick, he wouldn't be able to move quickly, but he was determined to cover some ground now and, if he was lucky, find shelter for the night before sundown.

He stood, brushed the seat of his britches off, and moved around the trunk of the tree. He heard the arrow's whistle first, then its *thunk* as it sank deeply into the tree's bark perhaps six inches from his head, still vibrating at the impact, some grey feathers from its fletchings spinning to the ground.

"Get bloody down!" a voice behind him cried. He felt himself being yanked to the ground and dragged by the feet behind the tree. He craned his head around and saw a young English cavalry soldier, his red coat much soiled and his long blond hair matted with blood from a wound on his forehead.

The soldier had a musket primed to fire, and he got to his knees, moved out beyond the tree trunk, aimed, fired, and ducked behind the tree. Reloading, he barely looked at Nick, speaking out of the side of his mouth and saying, "What's your name, drummer boy?"

"Nicholas McIver, sir. I never ever saw you. Where did you come from?"

"See that branch above your head?"

"You were up in this tree?"

"General idea when you're trying to ambush someone, isn't it? It was working, too, until you came along."

"An Indian, is he?"

"Of course, an Indian boy. These rebels aren't keen on

bows and arrows. This fellow's a Creek scout, one of three who ambushed me earlier."

"Where are the other two?"

"Dead. They shot my horse out from under me. I managed to shoot one, put a knife in the other. But Chief Powatan over there has been playing hidey seek with me all afternoon. Excuse me a moment, will you? I have to deal with this savage."

He stood up, moved to his right, braced his musket against the trunk, and waited. A moment later, Nick felt and heard the broad blade of another arrow bury itself deep in the tree.

He heard the musket boom, followed immediately by a howl of pain from the woods beyond the clearing.

"Got him at last, I did," the soldier said, collapsing beside Nick. "Now, who the devil are you, Nick McIver, and what are you doing stumbling around these woods all alone?"

"I got separated from my regiment in a skirmish with the Yanks, sir. Near Mount Vernon on the Potomac."

"Which regiment?"

"Second Light Infantry, 82nd Regiment, under the command of Major Thomas Armstrong," Nick said, glad he'd memorized most of the British units at Yorktown noted in the big blue book. And their commanding officers.

"You couldn't make it back to our lines?"

"I was in the process of doing so, sir, but I was captured by the Americans and taken to Fredricksburg. I escaped three days ago."

"Escaped without your drum?"

"I was relieved of it, sir. A Yank officer's trophy now."

"Well," the soldier said, getting to his feet, "I'd best be on my way, steal the first sturdy horse I see. We'll rout these dogs at Yorktown, you'll see."

"Are you headed for Yorktown?"

"No, I'm a courier, Scots Guards. I'm carrying a dispatch from General O'Hara, second-in-command under General Cornwallis. I'm bound for New York, and I'm a bit behind schedule, so I'll bid you good luck and safe passage, Nicholas McIver."

"And you as well, sir. I've been looking for a back road to Mount Vernon in hopes of finding my unit. Any idea where one might lie?"

"Yes. Head due east through this wood for two miles. You'll come to it. Not much traveled. Mind yourself, though. General Washington's home is near there, and it's well guarded by his Home Guard. Not to mention forests full of Creeks and Cherokees on the Yanks' payroll. Are you armed?"

"No, sir."

"Here, take this," he said, pulling an odd-looking flintlock pistol from beneath his coat.

Nick noticed it was double-barreled, side by side, with twin hammers and triggers. "Quite extraordinary looking. What is it?"

"A Light Dragoon flintlock, twin barrels. My father is the finest gunsmith in Ayershire. He made this gun especially for me when he learned my regiment was bound for the colonies. Two shots are better than one, being his theory. Can't argue that."

"I cannot possibly take it."

"Of course you can. I've a pair of them, the other's in my satchel. And I've got my musket. You're obliged to thank a gentleman who offers you a gift, Nicholas. Here's a pouch of cartridges, powder, and balls."

"Sir, I hardly know what to say."

"Thank you will suffice."

"Well, I thank you, then, with all my heart. What's your name, sir?"

"Lieutenant Robert Burns, same as the poet's, Scotland's favorite son, though no relation to the bard, I'm sorry to say."

"I bid you farewell, then, Lieutenant Burns," Nick said, "I've enjoyed your company. And I will never forget your generosity."

"Nicholas, before we part, a question?"

"Certainly."

"Just before you arrived at my hiding place, did you see some kind of strange, dazzling light at the base of that yonder tree? It was very odd indeed."

"A sharp ray of sunlight, sir, streaking down through a break in the clouds."

"Ah, that explains it. Well, I'm off, then. Godspeed and God save the King, His Royal Majesty King George III."

"Godspeed. May He bless you and keep you, sir."

Nick watched the young Scotsman until he could no longer see him, heard him whistling a cheery tune as he went off through the woods in search of a horse to steal.

A sudden wave of sadness swept over Nick as he turned and made his way east through the wood in search of a road. He had very much liked the handsome young Scot and hoped no harm came to him. And yet, that was precisely why he was in these colonies, to bring harm to Lieutenant Burns and thousands of young English soldiers just like him.

He was a traitor, he knew, but a traitor with a keen and relentless conscience. Right and wrong were as plain to Nick as black and white.

And he well knew now, that whether he succeeded or

failed in his mission to alter the outcome of this great war, his conscience would never again rest easy. With a heavy heart, he set out to do what must be done and soon found himself on the winding, deeply rutted dirt road that led to Mount Vernon.

THE INDIAN IN THE FOG

A rushing river flowed to Nick's left, some distance below the road. The sharp embankment on his left extended down to the banks, and through the trees Nick could occasionally catch glimpses of white water and rocky rapids. This was surely not the Potomac River, which he knew from his studies meandered wide and placid.

Due to the rain, which seemed to be steadily increasing, the road was sodden and muddy. His progress was slow and the sun would soon be down. He had little hope of finding shelter, even an old barn, for the thick green woods to his right were clearly uninhabited.

Uninhabited, that is, except for Indians most likely. And if they were indeed up there in the heavy wood to his right, they would surely see him long before he saw them.

"Nelson the brave, Nelson the bold, Nelson the Lord of the Sea," he whispered, an all-too-familiar prayer recently.

He was shivering with the cold but took some small comfort from the pistol he'd stuck in his waistband. Still, he knew that with each step he took, an arrow to the heart was a very real possibility. He didn't want to die on this road. Although his beating heart was torn apart by the moral dilemma Gunner had presented, an arrow in it now would be of no use to anybody. And so he slogged on as the rain continued to pour down, turning the road into a soupy brown stream, one which sucked at his boots and made every step he took an effort.

But each step closer to Mount Vernon brought more determination. In his mind, he saw his hero Winston Churchill, heard his frightening warnings about England's certain fate without the Americans. As terrible as what he was about to do might be, he had to hold fast to one thought: duty. The greater good of his country, that much was clear. And that thought kept him strong, kept him trudging the terrible road even as darkness fell and the booming thunderstorms bellowed loudly above.

He squinted, trying to see the road ahead. In this downpour, little was visible.

He held his hand up in front of his face. Why, he could barely see it for the drenching rain. Thunder rumbled heavily overhead, and nearby lightning strikes lit up the ancient trees on either side. He kept his eyes on his boots, trying to stay within the borders of the road. Should he stray and slip off the edge of the embankment, it was one long, treacherous fall to the raging river.

Just as he entered a long bend in the road following the snaking river, a sharp bolt of lightning struck, frying the very air he breathed. A huge oak, on a hillside just ahead, had been split in half all the way to the ground. The great tree, rent asunder, sent smoke curling aloft.

In that brief and terrible flash, Nick had seen something else, too. A figure had leaped from the ruined tree down to the road a second before the bolt had struck. Having jumped six feet and somehow landed without falling, that shadowy figure was now walking steadily toward him through the blinding rain. Without the lightning's instant of brilliant illumination, Nick would not even have seen this stranger until he collided with him.

Something in him caused his hand to embrace the curve of the pistol's stock, his finger to cock the hammer and then find its way inside the trigger guard and curl around that lethal crescent. He squinted his eyes, using his hand to shield them from the rain, trying to see who was coming toward him.

As the stranger approached through a dense grey curtain of rain, Nick saw long dark hair falling about the shoulders. A woman? He relaxed for a moment, his finger slipping off the trigger.

"Devilish weather, is it not, ma'am?" Nick said.

No answer. This rather tall and large woman was closer now, no more than six feet separating them as Nick plodded forward, his boots making loud sucking sounds in the muck.

"Sorry, I said, it's devilish—"

And then with a most horrible howl, the figure lunged toward him. No woman at all but a long-haired Indian brave, his terrifying face slathered with war paint, his eyes blazing through the rain, his powerful right arm raised above his head, a tomahawk clenched in his hand, the razor-sharp blade descending directly toward Nick's startled face.

Nick leaped backward at the last second, and the blade whispered by his ear. He'd been struck a glancing blow, high on his left arm, but one that caused a red pain, momentarily blinding him. He staggered and stumbled, back-pedaling toward the embankment. Raising his pistol with his right hand, he knew he'd get just one chance at this Indian brave, now gleefully raising his tomahawk for a second blow to finish the job.

The wild-looking man, whose face was painted with fierce stripes of yellow and red, approached him slowly, enjoying the moment. He was grinning evilly as he closed in for the kill. But the brave's eyes widened in fear as Nick aimed the pistol, still backing away as quickly as the treacherous surface would allow. Now. He pulled the hammer back, squeezed the trigger, and fired.

But he'd missed! As the ball left the muzzle, it went mere inches above the attacking warrior's head. Nick, in the act of firing, found himself falling backward into space, plunging over the edge of the embankment. He bounced a few times, rolling and sliding rapidly down the steep slope toward the river, finally slamming painfully against the trunk of a tree. He looked up and saw his sure-footed attacker making his way quickly down the slippery, rocky ground. He was almost out of the woods now, about fifty yards away.

Nick having discharged his weapon and missed, the Indian brave knew he had the advantage now. But he didn't want to give his victim time to reload. The warrior advanced carefully along the muddy bank, sure-footed and smiling.

Nick scrambled to his feet and faced the wild-looking man, his pistol hanging loosely at his side. He braced his left foot against a root of the tree, stabilizing himself in the muck as the savage drew closer. Seeing the boy not running for his life, he grinned once more and raised his tomahawk, which Nick now saw was decorated with beads and feathers matted with dried blood. Even as Nick raised the pistol and took dead aim, the Indian crept closer, that same evil look in his eyes that Nick had seen up on the road. He enjoyed both the hunt and the kill.

The tomahawk started downward.

Nick pulled the trigger and fired his second barrel. At such

But he'd missed!

close range, gunsmoke obscured his attacker. Had Nick missed again? If so, the tomahawk would soon split his—no! The smoke cleared a bit and he saw the wounded Indian stagger, then topple headfirst into the raging river. Nick watched his attacker being swept downstream. When the brave disappeared around a bend in the river, Nick looked down at the pistol in his hand, remembering the young British courier who'd given it to him for protection. When had it turned so cold? he wondered, breathing heavily and shaking badly.

Had he just killed a man? He'd never know, and it was just as well he didn't.

Darkness had fallen in the woods.

Nick looked up through the tall trees to the road above. He hadn't the strength to climb up nor the will to walk one step farther in the cold rain. He opened the haversack slung on his back, wrapped the pistol with the oiled cloth and stuck it in his waistband. He spread his thin waterproof cloth on flat ground beside the tree trunk, and lay down, wrapping up as best he could. Gunner had packed a surprise at the bottom of his sack. Food! He ate hungrily, first the flatbread and then the dried meat. It didn't taste like any meat he'd ever eaten, but he wolfed it down, saving only a small portion.

It was as delicious a meal as ever he'd had. His belly filled somewhat, mercifully he slept, oblivious to the tumultuous skies above.

· Mount Vernon ·

Sometime after dawn next morning, Nick awoke to a beautifully clear day, the skies high above a bright pink and blue; the rising sun sent rose-gold shafts of light streaking through the trees to the forest floor. It was not nearly so cold, and he bestilled himself for a time, eating what little remained of his food. He found his brain turning over the events of the prior day: the kindly courier, the deadly warrior, and the lessons to be learned from both encounters. As the hot sun rose higher, the rain-soaked trunks of the old trees began to smoke with steam, making it seem as if the woods were about to burst into flame.

Time to get moving.

When he stood, though, he felt feverish, lightheaded, and weak. He touched his hand to his forehead, which felt very warm. He was shivering, too, his teeth chattering in his mouth. During the night, he'd bound up the fresh wound to his left arm, using a strip of cloth ripped from his shirt, but the bandage was blood-soaked and useless now. His right shoulder had at least ceased to bother him, thanks to the ministrations of the Baroness de Villiers.

He gathered up his few scant belongings. There included his bone-handled knife, tricornered hat, the waterproof tube Gunner had made for Blood's charts, the pistol that had saved his life, plus powder, cartridges, and ammunition. He rolled up his poor waterproof and placed it into his haversack along with his other possessions. Slinging the haversack over his shoulder and whistling a cheery tune, he began his climb upward to the road.

Two hours later he caught a glimpse of a great mansion in the near distance. It stood atop a high bluff overlooking the Potomac River. A wide green lawn swept down to the banks of the river. The house itself was gleaming white, with a steep red roof capped by a lovely glass-windowed cupola. He could see there were many outbuildings—he counted at least ten, truly the estate of a most wealthy gentleman.

George Washington's home, Mount Vernon.

Now that he had his destination in sight, his spirits lifted considerably, and he started forward on the final leg of his journey.

He hadn't gone more than half a mile when two blue-coated Continental soldiers stepped from behind trees on either side of the muddy road and leveled their muskets at him.

"Who goes there?" one of them said.

"A defector, sir, a friend of America."

"Pulaski," the other soldier said, challenging him.

"Poland," Nick replied, remembering the password and the proper response Washington had ordered. Thank goodness for old Fitz's history book. Without it, he might have been shot.

"Defecting, are you, boy?"

"I am indeed."

"What is your rank and unit?"

"Drummer, sir. Second Light Infantry, 82nd Regiment, under the command of Major Thomas Armstrong," Nick said.

"You've come from Yorktown, then."

"Aye, I have done."

"Are you armed?"

"Yes, sir. A pistol and a knife. In my sack."

"Open the sack and throw down the weapons."

Nick did so and the two soldiers approached from either side.

"You're wounded. Badly it would seem. How did that happen?" the older of the two Americans said.

"Tomahawk. I was attacked by an Indian."

"And the Indian?"

"Dead or wounded, sir."

"You must be pretty handy with this pistol, I'd reckon, for a mere drummer boy."

The older soldier looked hard at Nick and said, "The way you're shaking, I might take you for a liar. Saying you're a drummer don't make you a drummer. Neither does saying you're a defector."

"He knows the password, Sam," the younger one said, "Let's at least let him speak before we shoot him."

"I am both a drummer and a defector, sir, and have never been a liar. And I possess knowledge of the fortifications at Yorktown and the plans of General Cornwallis that I wish to provide to General Washington."

Both men laughed. The young soldier picked up Nick's knife and gun. "Strange-looking weapon," he said.

"My father is the finest gunsmith in Ayershire, sir. He made it for me when he learned my regiment was sailing for the colonies. He said, 'Two shots are better than one,' and he proved to be right."

"Meaning what?"

"I got the Indian with the second shot."

Both soldiers laughed again. "What's your name, drummer boy?"

"Nicholas McIver, sir."

"Well, get a move on. We'll escort you up to the mansion and have someone stitch up that arm afore you bleed to death. Then we'll figure out what to do with you."

"I'm most grateful to you, then."

"You first," the young soldier said. "We'll be right behind you with our muskets on the chance you may change your mind about defecting."

"Or in the more likely case that you're some clever young British spy, sent by General Cornwallis," the older soldier said. "It wouldn't be the first time. We don't look kindly upon spies here at Mount Vernon, boy. We generally shoot them."

"I'm sure the information I'll give General Washington will prove the truth of my statements."

"He thinks he's going to meet General Washington!" the older man said, and the two soldiers burst out laughing once more.

The guards took Nick, not to the main house of course, but to a small outbuilding connected to the mansion by a covered walkway.

"What's this?" Nick asked the guards as they approached the door.

"The kitchen house. We don't have a proper surgery here, so we leave any stitching needs to be done to Mum Bitt."

"Mum Bitt?" Nick said as the guard pulled the door open for him.

"Mum's the General and Mrs. Washington's cook. Nobody in Virginia can stitch up a stuffed turkey better'n Mum. Hey,

Mum, we got a young gobbler here needs your ministrations of needle and thread!"

A large black woman turned from the great kettle she was stirring and looked at Nick. There was a lot of hubbub in the busy two-roomed kitchen, much chattering and laughter from all the Negro slave women working at various tasks. No one paid much attention to the arrival of two guards and someone with a bloody wound. It must have been something that happened all the time.

"What's wrong wid dat po' chile?" Mum Bitt said.

Nick smiled at her and held up his bloody left arm.

"Lawsy me, chile, you 'bout to bleed to death," Mum said, going over to him, "look at you, shakin' like a leaf on a tree! You got the fever?"

"Yes, ma'am, I believe I do."

"Sit y'self right down here at the table and let me take a look at that arm. You two soldier boys get your noses out of my pots and on back to your posts now before Miz Washington comes in here and finds you malingerin' in my kitchen stead of standin' sentry out there where you belong."

"Yes'm," the young guard said and headed for the door. "He gives you any trouble, Mum, just holler."

"He ain't gone give me no trouble. Look at him. This poor boy's burnin' up with the fever and bleedin' like a stuck pig. Now, git, both of you."

After the door banged shut behind the two sentries, the cook bustled over to a chest and retrieved a black leather case from one of the drawers. Nick, who was in a slight state of shock, noticed for the first time that the kitchen was chock full of people preparing all kinds of food. Game, fowl, a roast pig, cakes and pies of every description.

"What's your name, sweet honey chile?"

"Nicholas McIver, ma'am. It's a pleasure to meet you," he said, extending his hand and shaking hers.

He'd seen many African men and women working in the wheat fields on his approach to Mount Vernon. But Mum Bitt was the first African woman Nick had ever met. He knew from his history books that there'd once been thousands of African slaves working as personal servants in England. But the practice had been banned in 1772.

Nick felt it was cruel and morally wrong for one man to own another. He knew America, too, would one day abolish the abhorrent practice of chattel slavery. But it would be a century in coming. And it would come at a cost that would tear the young country apart, brother fighting brother, countless dead on countless battlefields, their blood soaking half a continent.

Mum Bitt carefully pulled the blanket from around Nick's shoulders and then removed his scarlet British Army jacket and bloody shirt.

"You know whose house this is, boy?"

"Yes, ma'am. General Washington's."

"That's correct, and the General, why, he doesn't look too kindly on English soldiers in this house. You're lucky he ain't arrived home yet."

"The General is coming here?"

"He certainly is! That's why the whole house is so full of joy. It's been nigh on six years since we laid an eye upon that blessed soul. Greatest man who ever lived. But he don't like your King George much, nor any man in your scarlet-coated army."

"I'm not a Loyalist nor an English soldier, ma'am. I'm a deserter. I left my regiment to defect to the American army."

"You did, huh. Ain't that something. Look at your arm, chile!

Looks like somebody hacked a big chunk out of you. What happened?"

"An Indian got me with his tomahawk, that's all."

"Indian got you, huh? You get him back?"

"Yes, ma'am."

"Good."

"Ouch!"

Now, honey-chile, you best be still and bite down on this old musket ball. Use your back teeth. I won't lie to you–this is going to hurt like the devil hisself."

"Yes, ma'am . . ."

Nick flinched and bit down on the lead ball when the needle first pierced his skin. He squeezed his eyes shut and tried not to make a sound as she stitched him up with catgut.

"Go on and cry if you want. I know it hurts. Can't hep it. It'll be over in a minute and you–"

Suddenly the entire kitchen staff went silent as a beautifully dressed woman in blue silk with a blue bonnet atop her white curls swept into the kitchen. She was not tall, perhaps five feet, with a gently rounded figure, and she had beautiful porcelain skin, plump rosy cheeks, and a twinkle in her wide-set brown eyes. She seemed almost doll-like as she dashed about the kitchen, flitting from one station to another, lifting lids off kettles and sniffing pies and pastries fresh from the oven. Then she plucked a bright red tomato from a basket, took a delicate bite, and pronounced it perfectly ripe.

"Whatever on earth happened to this poor child?" she asked, catching sight of Nick. She came over to the table where he sat grimacing in pain and gently placed a comforting hand on his cheek.

"Indian got him, Miz Washington. With a tomahawk, ain't that so, Nicholas?"

"Yes, ma'am, most definitely a tomahawk."

Mrs. Washington bent from the waist to inspect Nick's nearly sutured wound and said, "Mercy, this poor child looks like death itself, Mum Bitt. Bring him to me upstairs when you've finished stitching him up, and I'll put a poultice on that wound."

Nick smiled at the word. Another poultice.

He ought to be in bed, Miz Washington. You felt his face. He's burnin' up with the fever."

"Just bring him to me. I'll take care of him. How is the great welcome feast coming along? Will we be ready for the General's arrival tomorrow? He's riding all the way from Baltimore, and I imagine he'll be famished."

"Feast don't look like much yet, Miz Washington, but when Mum Bitt gets through with it, the general is going to think he's gone to heaven itself."

Martha Washington put her tiny hands on her hips and said, "Mount Vernon *is* his heaven, Mum Bitt. His heaven and earth. And, good Lord, won't we all be thrilled to see him home again at last! After all these years!"

Everyone in the kitchen shouted, somewhat in unison, "Praise the Lord, Praise the Lord!"

The General is certainly a beloved figure around this house, Nick thought. It was a good sign. Maybe he would listen.

When Nick awoke next morning he had no idea where he was. He felt like Mr. Washington Irving's Rip Van Winkle, the man who'd been asleep for twenty years. Beyond the window beside his bed, he saw the great lawn sloping down to the wide blue river flowing past it. It all started to come back. That was the Potomac. This was General George Washington's home, Mount Vernon. And the lovely little lady sitting sweetly at his bedside was the general's wife, Martha, who, he had learned, was always called Patsy by her husband.

She'd been sitting right there when he'd fallen asleep, after carefully spooning hot tea into his mouth because his hands were trembling so badly with the fever. Had she remained there all this time?

"Good afternoon, Master McIver," she said, smiling and patting his hand. "Nice to have you among the living once more."

"Afternoon?" Nick said, sitting up in bed and turning toward the window. "But, madam, the sun is rising."

"It is setting, Nicholas. You've been asleep for more than twenty-four hours."

Nick rubbed both eyes with his knuckles and yawned deeply. "That can't be! I never sleep for–"

Mrs. Washington put a cool hand on Nick's forehead. "You had a terrible fever, Nicholas. But it broke around midday. I think you're going to be fine now. You must be terribly thirsty. And hungry, too."

"Oh, but I am, ma'am, indeed, a good bit of both."

"I'll have something brought up from the kitchen house. I think you should remain right here in this bed until at least tomorrow. Get some rest. The General will be here in the morning, the good Lord willing," she added, excitement shining in her eyes. "A courier informed me he's getting close to home at last!"

"Will it be possible for me to meet him?"

"I should certainly think so. You're a guest in his house, after all."

"Oh, that would be wonderful. He's one of my great heroes, ma'am, even though I'm, well, you know, English."

"He's been through a terrible trial in this war. I was with him and General de Lafayette at Valley Forge three years ago. Mercy, I don't know how any of us survived that coldest and grimmest of winters. Many of our poor troops had no blankets or tents, little food, and many didn't even have shoes! But the General *has* survived this long war, and I've no doubt he'll see us to victory over our tyrannical oppressors."

"Yes, ma'am, I, too, am quite sure he will. In fact, I'm quite certain of it."

Nick smiled briefly–he couldn't help himself.

She eyed him very carefully. "Nicholas, I understand you came to us from Yorktown."

"I did, ma'am."

"In service to His Royal Majesty, King George, judging by

the bright scarlet color of your coat when you arrived with the sentries. What regiment?"

"Drummer, Mrs. Washington. Second Light Infantry, 82nd Regiment, under the command of Major Thomas Armstrong now serving at Yorktown."

"A drummer boy. You're not going to beat a poor patriot senseless with drumsticks, are you, Nicholas?"

She favored him with a smile and Nick returned it. "Never, ma'am. I couldn't be more grateful to you for taking me in and . . . providing such powerfully good care for me."

"We Americans aren't quite the savages your king and countrymen perceive us to be. We pride ourselves on our kindness and hospitality to strangers. Now, what, pray, is a young English drummer boy doing walking miles through cold rain from Yorktown to Mount Vernon, of all places? Over a hundred miles! Have you been sent by Lord Cornwallis to spy upon us, Nick? Stranger things have happened in this war. The General trusts no one. Not since Benedict Arnold. "You've heard of him? That despicable traitor?"

"Yes, ma'am. No, ma'am. I'm no spy. I've only come to help. Help General Washington, I mean."

"Help? Help him how?"

"It's rather a complicated story, I'm afraid, and—long."

"Lucy?" Mrs. Washington called out, and a strikingly pretty young African girl in a long white smock appeared in the doorway. "Yes'm, Miz Washington?" she replied.

"Please go out to the kitchen house, will you, and tell Mum Bitt that our young English patient has finally awakened from the dead and is positively ravenous. Perhaps some vegetable broth or chicken soup? And some nice hot tea for us both?"

"Yes'm. I'll be back quick as I can," Lucy said, and in the blink of an eye, she'd disappeared.

"Thank you, Lucy," she called out, and then, turning to Nick, she pulled her chair closer to his bedside and smiled at him.

"I wonder, Nicholas. How do such men as Arnold live with themselves? Traitors. Liars. How do they ever stand before God?"

"I—I'm sure I don't know, ma'am. I'm sorry."

"Well. No matter, child. You've got your whole life ahead of you to consider such ponderous questions."

"Yes. I suppose I do."

"Now, Nicholas, I do so love a good story. Pray, tell me yours," she said.

Nick paused a moment, taking a deep breath before he launched into his tale. He often worried about how easily fabricating falsehoods came to him now; and, to be honest, he was not at all proud of this newfound ability to do so. He had to keep reminding himself that he was, in fact, a spy. On the Nazis, and now on his own countrymen.

And spying meant lying. There was just no getting around that.

One thought consoled him as he looked into Mrs. Washington's kindly brown eyes. He was here to help her husband win what was widely thought to be an unwinnable war. If he didn't intercede on behalf of the colonists, the American war for independence from the Crown was lost.

He looked General Washington's wife in the eye and began his tale.

"I come from a small island in the English Channel called Greybeard Island, ma'am. I lived there with my mum and dad. He was the lighthouse keeper, and the Greybeard Light itself was our home. There being no schoolhouse on the island, I was home-schooled by Mum. She was a great lover of history, literature, and heroes, and taught me to share her feeling of kinship with the past. Then, soon after the current war broke out, my mum died of the scarlet fever."

"I'm terribly sorry, Nicholas. My sympathies."

"Thank you kindly, ma'am. She was a fine person, a wonderful mother, and I loved her very much. Father, as well, was lost without her. We barely spoke for six months. One day, when the mourning time was over, he told me we would be sailing soon for London. He'd decided that we'd both join the British Army. He was a crack shot and would enlist as an infantryman. Because of my age, I was to be a drummer. Because of my beliefs, I didn't want to go to war against the colonists, but as my father was determined, I had little choice. And so we did."

"You believed in our glorious cause?"

"I did and do, as do many of my countrymen, though they remain silent. History, as I learned, is filled to overflowing with tyrants but not nearly so many as those yearning to be free. My mother and I would never admit this to Father, of course, but the more we followed the events of this war in the news journals from London, the more we came to admire brave men like General Washington, who would risk everything in the cause of freedom and democracy. Such thoughts were treasonous on our part, of course, but it was our little secret."

"So, you and your father sailed for America together?"

"We did. He made sure I was always attached to his regiment. Because of his battlefield skills and bravery, he was quickly promoted to lieutenant major, and he kept me at his side as much as he was able. As Father was second to Major Armstrong, our commander at Yorktown directly under Lord Cornwallis, I spent much time in their august company.

Keeping my eyes and ears open, I was able to gather a lot of valuable information, as you might guess."

"Military secrets?"

"Yes, ma'am," Nick said, reaching beneath his bed for the leather tube he'd hidden there. "There are charts and documents here that are vital to the General's success. That's why I walked from Yorktown to Mount Vernon. In hopes of getting all I knew into the General's hands."

"Did you tell your father you were deserting? Stealing military secrets and defecting to the Colonists' cause?"

"I wasn't able. He was killed, ma'am, in a mortar attack on the fort two weeks ago today."

"I'm so terribly sorry, Nicholas, for your grievous losses. You're all alone in the world now, aren't you, child?"

"Yes, ma'am. But I'll see my mum in heaven someday. And Father died a hero, defending his most cherished beliefs. When my time comes, I only hope it will be in the same fashion as my father."

"You're a very brave young man, Nicholas McIver."

"I thank you for that compliment, ma'am. But I don't think I've earned it yet. Words count for naught."

At that moment Lucy suddenly appeared with a silver tray, and the room was filled with wonderful aromas. Nick had never been so hungry in his life.

"Thank you, Lucy," Mrs. Washington said, as she put the tray on the table beside Nick's bed.

"Yes, thank you so much," Nick added, smiling at the pretty Lucy as she silently withdrew.

Mrs. Washington stood, sipping her tea and watching Nick devour the steaming vegetable broth.

"I've a great deal left to do before my dear husband's arrival, Nicholas, so I shall leave you in peace and go about my preparations."

"Thank you for all you've done, ma'am."

She nodded, crossed the room to the door, paused, and looked back at him. "Nicholas?"

"Yes, ma'am?"

"I've a special place in my heart for children that have been sorely tested by the almighty. It's good to have a child under this old roof again. I had four children of my own. I lost three of them when they were very young. Only my son, Jacky, survived. He's a grown man now and married. It's a terrible, terrible thing when a mother loses a child, her children, you must understand that."

"I'm sorry for what you've suffered, Mrs. Washington."

"I trust you, Nicholas McIver. You seem a good boy, with a keen mind and a brave spirit. I shall introduce you to my husband tomorrow when I find it suits him. Tell him what you will, share your secrets. But I shall tell you one thing, and you should think well upon it."

"Yes, ma'am."

"Don't ever betray my trust."

She closed the door before he could reply, and he was left alone with his thoughts.

Next morning Nick was up bright and early, his whole being tingling with excitement. Beyond his upstairs window, the sun shone benevolently in a cloudless sky, scattering gold coins on the river. He was surprised to find his white breeches, stockings, and tunic all cleaned, neatly pressed, and folded on the chair beside his bed. His scarlet British Army coat had somehow disappeared, which was probably all to the good. Redcoats, be they human or uniform, weren't exactly welcome in the great General Washington's home. And, Nick knew, the famous man was returning to Mount Vernon this very day.

He removed his linen nightshirt (borrowed by Lucy along with other clothes from the Washingtons' now-grown son, Jacky) and dressed quickly. The house seemed full of noise and excitement. Perhaps the General had already arrived. There was certainly a great hubbub below stairs. The merry sound of laughter and excited chatter rising up the staircase from the ground floor was contagious—he heard Lucy's distinctive high-pitched laughter just outside his door.

He cracked his door and saw her racing up the main staircase. Reaching the landing, she went immediately to a window on the far side of the house. She flung open the sash, leaned dangerously far out, and shouted down to the crowd of house servants and field hands below, "He's coming! General is on his way!"

A great hurrah came from unseen crowd gathered below, and Nick saw countless straw field hats hurled up into the air, watched them rise and fall hypnotically in the blue beyond the window.

"The General has arrived?" he asked Lucy, beginning to feel the thrill of the approaching moment himself.

She turned and smiled at him, her dark eyes flashing with excitement. "Not just yet. But, he'll be here shortly, I reckon. He sent a courier ahead to tell Miz Washington how nearby he was. Why, Miz Washington's so juned up this mawnin', lady can't hardly contain herself! I'm going upstairs to watch it all, if'n you want to come with me."

"I surely do, Lucy. Can we see everything from up there?"

"It's my secret lookout. Ain't a real secret, but I call it mine just because. You can see the whole world from up there. Follow me and don't make any noise."

Lucy raced up the stairway on tiptoe to the topmost floor of the house. It was more like an attic with dormer windows. They arrived in a large room with bare wooden floors and four doors, two on either side of the room, guest rooms most likely. But what caught Nick's attention was the sturdy white wooden ladder in the center of the room, bathed in light streaming down from above.

He followed Lucy up the ladder. As he'd guessed, it led up to the beautiful eight-windowed cupola on the rooftop. He'd seen it when he first approached the grand white house from a distance.

"Only room enough up there for two of us," she said,

quickly climbing the ladder. "Hurry up, you don't want to be missin' this!"

Nick hauled himself up and joined Lucy inside the small light-filled cupola. There were no seats as such, just wide crisscrossed beams where you could perch. The weather was brilliant, and the views, which were in every direction, were breathtaking. Small wonder. Mount Vernon sat atop one of the highest hills in Virginia, and this windowed cupola sat atop the highest part of the mansion. To the east, beyond the wide Potomac River, endless forests stretched to the horizon.

On the inland, western side of the house, where Washington would be arriving, Nick saw a green oval of grass that stood in the center of the mansion's circular drive. Beyond were kitchen gardens, ornate flower gardens with serpentine walkways, fruit orchards of every description. In the distance, a broad, lengthy expanse of rich, fertile green, with deep borders of woods to either side, stretched out to the main thoroughfare.

The West Gate, as it was called, was the main entrance to Mount Vernon. It was set in freshly painted white fencing, and it was where Washington would first appear. Just inside the fence, to the right side of the drive, stood a small fife and drum corps made up of household servants wearing the elegant Washington livery. They were already playing a welcoming melody. Nick could hear the song only faintly, but it sounded stirring.

"What is that tune they're playing, Lucy?"

"'The Rose of Tralee.' One of the General's favorites. Look! There he is now. Yes! Do you see him?"

Nick strained his eyes to see, but there was no mistaking the figure leading the long line of dirty, threadbare troops marching in a slow and solemn step, regulated by drum and fife. Horses, mule-drawn fieldpieces, and ammunition wagons followed each brigade.

In the forefront rode General George Washington, a giant of a man. He sat astride an iron-grey stallion, ramrod straight in the saddle. He reined in his mount and turned to speak briefly with some of the officers riding beside him. Then he saluted them, rode through his gate, accompanied by only a few other officers, raced up the tree-lined road to where his family waited.

Beyond the gate, the troops continued on, and it seemed to Nick as if the line must be at least two miles long. At the rear were the general officers, mounted on noble steeds, with endless wagons of baggage in their wake.

As Washington drew closer on the long drive, he spurred his horse on to a full gallop. Nick found himself staring open-mouthed at the historic figure approaching his home. His uniform was simple but splendid, his jacket dark blue faced with gold, gleaming epaulets on his shoulders. He rode with the easy grace of a natural rider, his muscular legs extended on long leathers, his toes pointed down in the stirrups. He was as powerful and captivating in person as he'd been in Nick's history books.

"What's his horse's name, Lucy?"

"Why, that's Blueskin. Ain't afraid of nothin'. One of his most favorite war horses, been riding him since war broke out— Look! Mrs. Washington is running out to greet him. Couldn't stand to wait there in the doorway another minute, I reckon. Lawsie, how she been missing that old man of hers."

At the sight of his dear wife, dressed in a long, blue satin gown, gathering her skirts and running out to meet him, the General quickly reined in Blueskin, dismounted, and handed the reins to another officer. Two liveried grooms approached and led the horses away to the stable.

"Come all the way from Baltimore, haven't you, old man?" Martha cried, opening her arms to her husband. "Sixty miles in one day! You must have been in a terrible hurry! I wonder why."

Overcome with joy at the sight of his wife, Washington raced into Martha's open arms, lifted her easily off the ground, and whirled her about, much to the delight of everyone who'd turned out to witness the great man's arrival. He finally set her down, kissed her lips and both cheeks, and turned to the distinguished young officer who'd accompanied him. He offered his hand, but Martha Washington stepped forward and embraced the elegant young man like a long-lost son.

Then the two new arrivals, with a beaming Mrs. Washington betwixt them, holding both their hands, approached the mansion and the thunderous applause and huzzahs of the hundreds of farmers, field hands, house servants, and neighboring friends who had gathered to welcome the General home for this brief visit en route to Yorktown.

"Who is that young officer?" Nick asked Lucy. "His son?"

"No, his son Jacky is hugging his papa right now. That other gentleman is a Frenchman fighting alongside the general. Miz Washington calls him the Marquis de Lafayette, and she says he's one of the greatest friends America has."

Lafayette, of course, Nick thought. It was his men who now kept Cornwallis and the English troops at bay in Yorktown. The long line of soldiers still marching along the thoroughfare in the distance had to be regiments of Continentals plus the five thousand French under command of French General Rochambeau, if he remembered his history correctly.

The Battle of Yorktown was about to commence in earnest. Nick could feel it coming in his bones.

"Lucy," Nick said, smiling at her pretty brown face, "would you do me a small favor?"

"Course I will. You're Miz Washington's special guest. Told me so her own self jes this mawnin'."

"Thank you. If you could slip out the east side of the house and go around to the kitchen house, I'd appreciate you asking Mum Bitt to make me a small plate of food? Anything will do."

"You're not attending the great banquet? I'm sure Miz Washington's expecting you."

"She won't miss me in all that excitement. Anyway, I think it's better if I stay in my room for now. If she asks after me, just tell her I wasn't feeling too well and you brought some soup up to my room."

"That's what you want, I'll bring it up to you. But I think you're not thinking right. This is mos' likely to be the grandest gala we ever had in this house!"

"You can tell me all about it this evening, Lucy."

"Don't you worry yourself about that none. I got a secret place in the back of the pantry closet where I can see and hear everything that goes on in the dining room."

Nick laughed. "Lucy, if I didn't know better, I'd swear you were a natural born spy."

"A supernatural spy is more like it. A spirit. Mum Bitt calls me the Ghost of Mount Vernon. She swears on the Bible she's seen me disappear right before her eyes. I pops up in the kitchen or in the kitchen garden or the stables or anywhere else on this whole plantation, like to scare people half to death."

"You don't look like a ghost, Lucy. So, how do you do it?"

"There's hidden underground tunnels and secret passages all over this place. And another thing. An Indian taught me how to walk."

"An Indian?"

"My mammy is a full-blooded Cherokee."

A tapping at Nick's door brought him fully awake. He'd fallen asleep reading one of the American history books from General Washington's study that Mrs. Washington had thoughtfully stacked by his bed. The door cracked open a few inches, and he saw Mrs. Washington's smiling face peek inside. She was holding a candle, and the light flickering on her face was lovely. She was still dressed in the gown she'd worn to the gala.

"Nicholas?"

"Yes, ma'am?"

"Am I disturbing you?"

"No, ma'am."

"How are you feeling? Better?"

"Particularly better, thank you."

"I missed you at the grand banquet."

"I'm most sorry to have missed it."

She came into his room and sat beside his bed. Taking his hand, she said, "I've told the General all about you. He's most anxious to meet you. And so, may I add, is the general's closest friend, the Marquis de Lafayette."

"It would be a great honor. I've just been reading about the general's exploits in the French and Indian wars. He's the bravest of men, ma'am, the kind of hero I'd like to be one day."

"He loves these colonies and their cause like no other man.

He has a boundless vision for America's future. He can see clear from the Potomac all the way to the Ohio Valley and to the great Pacific Ocean beyond. That's what he is fighting for. A great, wide-open country where men and women can live and prosper in peace and freedom."

"I predict history will place General Washington amongst the greatest of men who have ever lived, ma'am. In fact, I'm sure of it."

"He's in his study, now, Nicholas. Going over final battle plans for the siege at Yorktown with the Marquis. He asked me to find out if you were feeling well enough to come downstairs, that he and Lafayette might make your acquaintance. They are both, in fact, most curious about this information you claim to possess."

"Oh, yes. That would be wonderful. I would count it as the greatest honor of my life to meet His Excellency."

"Well, then, Master Nicholas McIver, I shall leave you in peace while you go about your business. But don't tarry. Very, very few guests at Mount Vernon are ever invited into his private study. He is expecting you. And he doesn't suffer tardiness well."

"Two minutes and not a second more, ma'am."

"Good boy. I shall tell him to expect you at once."

Nick descended the stairs slowly, one at a time, the leather tube containing the charts he and Katie had stolen clutched in his right hand. He could feel the Tempus Machina concealed in the leather sling beneath his left arm. His heart was thudding in his chest, and he had to will his hands to stop shaking.

He hadn't felt this nervous since he and Gunner had stood outside Admiral Lord Nelson's office at Saint James's Palace, waiting to be announced. Why? What was there to be afraid of tonight of all nights! He tried to analyze this troublesome emotion and quickly recognized it as fear of General George Washington's reaction to the inconceivable notion of time travel.

He didn't fear disclosing the secret of Captain Blood's planned ambush of the French fleet. No, the charts and documents he carried provided ample proof of that. Nick knew all of Washington's hopes for victory at Yorktown depended on the timely arrival of Admiral de Grasse and his fleet. It was de Grasse who would blockade the entrance to the Chesapeake Bay and repel any attempt by the Royal Navy to rescue Cornwallis by sea.

Admiral de Grasse's large fleet would destroy any hope the

British command or Cornwallis had of escaping Washington's siege. The trap would be secure. The noose would tighten further around Lord Cornwallis. A great American victory was so close at hand. But only de Grasse and his ships could seal Cornwallis's fate.

Washington would immediately seize upon the importance of the naval intelligence Nick possessed. Which was all well and good, he thought, as he slowly approached the door to the General's study.

But what about the General's reaction to the golden orb he carried?

Yes, that was it, all right. That was the single-most troublesome thing about this entire endeavor. He'd been worried about this moment for weeks. Washington was an eminently sensible man. Would the General think him absolutely mad? Nick would have to convincingly describe the miraculous wonders of the Tempus Machina. It was entirely possible the man might erupt in furor at such an outrageous proposition.

Nick himself had scoffed at the very notion of time travel when Lord Hawke and Commander Hobbes had first explained the workings of the machine to him at Hawke Castle. He had thought they were both quite mad at the time and was angry at their attempt to convince him that the impossible was, in fact, possible.

But he'd learned, as his sister Katie frequently reminded him, that *nothing is impossible.*

Why should he expect less skepticism from the great General? In a few moments, he might well find himself thrown out of Mount Vernon on his ear! With good reason! And who would be blamed for allowing this rapscallion of a boy, mad as a hatter, inside the General's beloved home? Inside his sanctuary?

Martha Washington, of course. "Don't ever betray me," she'd said. Was he even now about to do that very thing?

"Nelson the strong, Nelson the brave, Nelson the Lord of the Sea." Whispering his silent prayer for courage, he raised his hand to rap upon General Washington's study door.

Could he do this?

Yes. He could and he would. He had no choice.

Nick took a deep breath and knocked smartly on George Washington's mahogany door. "May I enter, sir?"

"Come in, come in!" a deep voice boomed from inside.

Nick turned the handle and stepped inside the inner sanctum of the greatest man alive.

It was not a large room by any means. But it was full of many things that gave clues to the man who spent his private time here: old surveying instruments, a globe, telescope, and compass on the large desk, the famous revolving circular chair. On one wall hung the skeleton of a fish, fierce-looking, with long jaws full of razor-sharp teeth. Souvenirs brought from Barbados, Nick knew, where, at age nineteen, he'd gone with his ailing half-brother Lawrence, dying of consumption.

In the hearth, a fire was blazing against the late evening chill. General Washington and the Marquis de Lafayette sat in two leather armchairs on either side of the hearth. But it was Washington's presence that completely dominated the room. He was an imposing figure, well over six feet. His large bones, hands, feet, and thighs gave Nick the impression of great physical strength. His face, storm-beaten and tanned as leather from years of the soldier's life, bore traces of smallpox scars. Beneath his powdered wig, his large, penetrating eyes were grey-blue set very wide apart, and gave an unexpected hint of humor.

Washington, in his dress blue uniform coat, immediately got to his feet as Nick entered. He turned toward the boy with a smile, extending his hand. Nick shook it briefly, not wanting the General to notice his trembling. The man was a towering presence in this small room, his giant shadow flickering up the wall and stretching across the ceiling. Across the whole Earth, Nick thought.

Nick, who like his mother was very good at reading faces, saw a great deal in the man's eyes. After five long years of the harshest circumstances, he saw patience, the ability to bounce back again and again from bitter disappointments and shattered hopes. But in the main, he saw too many defeats and too few victories. And, in the General's warm smile, hope.

"It is a great honor to meet you, sir," Nick managed to say without stammering. "I am Nicholas McIver, sir."

Washington laughed. "Oh, I know very well who you are, Nicholas. My dear Patsy can't seem to stop talking about you. You seem to have both charmed her and won her heart in the short time you've been under my roof. A good-looking fellow like you, hale and hearty—I should have cause to worry were you not so very young."

Nick felt his cheeks burning, and it was all he could do not to turn away and flee the room.

Laughing at his friend's joke and Nick's reaction, the elegant young French General in a pristine white uniform rose and bowed in Nick's direction. "General de Lafayette at your service, Monsieur McIver."

Slightly built, with a long pointed nose, narrow egg-shaped head, and a receding line of reddish hair, the Marquis was anything but handsome. But the eyes sparkled brightly with intelligence and courage.

Nick said, "A great honor to meet you as well, sir."

Washington pulled up a small side chair for Nick and everyone sat down. Nick, his hands trembling slightly, placed the leather tube across his knees.

Washington turned his smile on Lafayette. "Nicholas Mc-Iver, it seems, has forsaken king and country for our glorious cause, General. He was a drummer, Second Light Infantry, and an aide to Armstrong and Cornwallis. I understand he has some news of the enemy to share with us. I suggest we dispense with pleasantries and see what the boy has to say. Anyone who's spent time under Lord Cornwallis's tent shall have my full attention. I caution you, Nicholas. Should I determine you to be merely an agent provocateur, you shall find yourself in prison when the sun arises. The floor is yours, sir."

"Yes, sir, as you wish, I hope you—" Nick paused, swallowing hard, not quite sure how he should go about this.

"Please begin," Washington said. "Time is of the essence, and the Marquis and I are all ears. What have you there across your knees?"

"Charts, sir, describing an ambush at sea. I believe you are most anxiously awaiting the arrival of an Admiral de Grasse and his fleet at Chesapeake Bay? Sailing up from Cap-François on the island of Saint Domingue?"

Washington, so shocked and startled that a mere boy might be in possession of one of his most closely guarded secrets, was momentarily unable to speak. He looked at the Marquis, who appeared equally shaken.

"Confound it, lad! How on earth did you come by that?" Washington finally said, his eyebrows rising in astonishment. "A topic of utmost secrecy, vital information known only by three people in my entire army. And two of them are sitting in this room."

"Three, plus one twelve-year-old boy, it would seem," the Marquis said, leaning back in his chair, an amazed expression on his face. "Astonishing! I simply cannot believe my own ears! Where, pray tell, did you come by this knowledge, Nick?"

"Lord Cornwallis has many spies in the West Indies, sir. News arrives by fast frigate at his headquarters constantly. I managed to borrow some charts from his tent the night I made my decision to escape from Yorktown and join the Continentals. I have the charts here for your inspection."

"You stole these documents from under his nose? Has he no sentries?" Washington asked.

"Yes, sir. But they are friends of mine, long accustomed to seeing me come and go at all hours, retrieving and delivering messages for the Earl and his officers. I hid the documents in this tube and shoved it down my trouser leg, sir, stuck it well inside my boot. It was quite invisible in the dark."

"If what he says is true, Cornwallis knows all," Lafayette said darkly. "A tragedy of the worst order."

Washington frowned and said, "And what does Lord Cornwallis intend to do with this knowledge? Has he summoned the Royal Navy at New York to intercept de Grasse's fleet? I have reports British Admiral Graves is sailing south from New York."

"Lord Cornwallis has done nothing about de Grasse, sir. He knows he *need* do nothing to stop de Grasse. It's pirates who are the source of the French Admiral's trouble, not the British Royal Navy."

"Pirates, you say? Trouble? What kind of trouble, Nicholas McIver?" George Washington said, leaning forward toward Nicholas with the most startlingly intense look Nick had ever seen.

"An ambush, sir. A trap not yet sprung."

"What kind of ambush?" Washington asked.

"Perhaps you have heard of a notorious English pirate captain named William Blood, sir?"

"I have not."

"I have heard tell of him, and nothing favorable," Lafayette said. "I had a brief encounter with his 74-gun *Revenge* off the coast of Spain once. He ran away before we could sink him. The Brethren of the Coast they call themselves. 'Heathen of the Coast' would suit them better, by my lights."

"This newly formed lot under Blood's command call themselves Brethren of Blood, sir," Nick said.

"First, tell me all you know," Washington said, his voice low and deadly serious. "And then show me the evidence."

Nick looked first at Washington and then at Lafayette. He found himself gathering confidence as he spoke. "Blood has, in these last months, assembled a formidable pirate armada at Port Royal, Jamaica. Perhaps numbering one hundred ships and—"

"Beg pardon," Washington said. "Did you say *one hundred* ships?"

"Aye, sir, one hundred. Blood's fleet will lie in wait for de Grasse."

"A hellish plot," the American General said, staring forlornly at Lafayette. "Please continue, Nicholas."

"Well, sir, you see, Captain Blood has spies everywhere, so he is well aware of Admiral de Grasse's intentions to sail north to the Chesapeake Bay off Yorktown. Blood cares nothing for this war and has no stake in the outcome. But he knows the French fleet carries much gold and plunder from their recent victories at Saint Lucia and Tobago."

"And five thousand French marines we sorely need at Yorktown," Lafayette said grimly.

The two men looked at each other. Both knew that unless de Grasse and his fleet arrived unimpeded off Yorktown, preventing Cornwallis from escaping by sea, all was lost.

George Washington stood, looking down at Nick's leather tube. "The charts, if you please. Now would be a good time."

"Of course, sir," Nick said, and handed him the tube.

The General cleared a space on his wide desk and then removed the tightly rolled charts from the tube. He spread them out, weighting down the four corners with three small bronze cannonballs and the replica of an American field cannon. Lafayette and Nicholas joined him at the desk. On top of the stack, the details of Blood's plot, sketched upon a map of the Caribbean.

Washington and the Marquis huddled together, perusing the map in minute detail. Strategic notes and heavily red-inked course lines made Blood's intentions crystal clear. The notes included an assessment of the size of de Grasse's fleet, now moored in the harbor at Cap-François on the isle of Saint Domingue, and the French fleet's intended route toward the Florida straits, where they would catch the great current of the Gulf Stream flowing north.

Blood had inked in a great black Maltese cross, marking the location where his pirate armada, masses of warships armed to the teeth, would lie in wait to the northeast off Nassau Town.

Washington and the Marquis immediately engaged in an intense discussion of this startling situation. They paused only to ask Nick whose handwriting it was that appeared in the notations marking the Caribbean chart.

Nick said, "That would be in Captain William Blood's own hand, sir. I've some personal letters from him, so I know it by sight. As you'll see in the other charts and documents, some of which are dated just last month at Port Royal"–Nick saw the crestfallen look on General Washington's face and quickly added—"Sir, perhaps it's not too late! Perhaps we can still warn Admiral de Grasse of the ambush!"

Washington looked stricken, all of the color suddenly drained from his face. What he had feared most, right from the very start of this action, was now plainly unfolding. His heart had long been set on a plan of enormous complexity. Everything had to come together at once. Timing was critical. Now, without the French fleet's arrival, Cornwallis would slip away from him, escape by sea, rescued by the British Royal Navy fleet, even now en route from New York.

"No, no, no, lad! It's far too late," Washington said. "According to my most recent information, Admiral de Grasse has already sailed, and this pirate armada now stands off Nassau, waiting to pounce and destroy our only hope of victory. These pirates have sealed our fate. Short of a miracle, our cause is doomed."

The General rose to his full height and slammed his fist on the desk, a mighty blow. "What in God's holy name can we do now?" he bellowed to the heavens. "What on this good green earth am I to do?"

"General," the Marquis said, "if we could quickly organize a team of mounted couriers, racing south at full gallop day and night, with a relay of fresh horses along the way, we could get word to General Nathaniel Hathaway, now garrisoned on Florida's Atlantic coastline at Saint Augustine. With luck, Hathaway might dispatch a swift frigate southward and intercept the French in the Florida straits prior to the ambush."

"A good plan, sir, but still too late, I fear. Even the fastest riders could not now reach Hathaway in time. No. We must think! All hangs in the balance now! Our very fate! We must find a way to salvage this desperate situation ... or, by heaven, I tell you, we will lose this battle at Yorktown. And the war along with it. Has this all been for naught? Our great cause? All this sacrifice of blood and treasure? All for naught?"

The General stared down at the chart, his mind racing furiously and—there came a knock at the door.

"Who is it?" Washington cried, frustration evident in his voice, angry at the intrusion.

From beyond the door, Martha's sweet voice. "It's your Patsy, General. May I come in?"

Washington strode to the door and pulled it open. His beloved wife stood smiling up him. Angry as he was, he managed a warm smile for her.

"I'm so sorry to bother you, dear husband," she said, but Brigadier General Mason and two of his officers have just arrived in much haste from Yorktown. They say they have a matter of utmost urgency to discuss with you. A battle raging at Redoubt No. 10, heavy casualties on our side, and they wish permission to withdraw."

"Yes, yes, yes, tell them I shall come at once." Washington said, and then turned and stared at Lafayette. "My dear young friend," he said, "so very much is now at stake . . . I cannot deal with the future now, only the present. We have seen much hardship and effusion of blood these last years. We cannot now allow this, this despicable pirate, to intercede in events at this critical hour. I know it is most certainly too late to warn de Grasse. I am giving you an impossible task. But I implore you to put your agile mind to this. I shall return as quickly as possible, but I could be a good half hour or more. We must find a way to warn de Grasse. We simply must."

Washington turned and followed his wife through the doorway, pulling the door shut softly behind him.

"The General is a very great man," Nick said, almost to himself.

"Indeed he is," Lafayette replied. "Possessed of a perfect harmony, which reigns between his physical and moral qualities . . . brave without temerity, laborious without ambition, generous without prodigality, noble without pride, virtuous without severity . . . the greatest and best of men— Nicholas McIver. Now, what have we here?"

The Marquis de Lafayette snatched Blood's chart from atop the pile and collapsed back into his deep leather chair, a pained look on his face, despair in his eyes, reading and re-reading the dates and notations. The facts left no room for dispute. Their hope, their only hope for victory, was that de Grasse's fleet would arrive at Chesapeake Bay in time. Without that event, all would be lost.

Nick quickly sat down opposite him, his eyes blazing with excitement. He'd been handed a great gift. This was his one chance. Mrs. Washington's interruption had been a godsend. There was not much time to make Lafayette believe the un-believable before Washington returned, but he struggled to compose himself before plowing ahead.

"Sir? If I may?" Nick said, and Lafayette peered at him over the top of the chart with furrowed brow. Then he slowly low-ered the chart so that it lay across his lap, and he gave the boy his full attention.

"All is lost," Lafayette whispered to himself. "All is lost."

Nick took another deep breath and said, "There may be a way, sir."

"A way? A way? There cannot possibly be a way. *C'est im-possible.* The General is correct. It's too late, boy. Would that you had arrived a week ago, even days earlier, perhaps then there might have been some way. The mounted couriers, the fast frigate south. But now . . . it's simply too late."

"With all due respect, sir, I must tell you that it is not at all too late."

"With all due respect, Monsieur McIver, I assure you that, without a miracle, it is indeed too late."

"I happen to have a miracle, sir," Nick said simply.

"You what?"

Reaching inside his shirt, Nick withdrew the golden orb, gleaming in the candlelight, and held it up for Lafayette to see.

"What in heaven's name is that?"

"An object from the sixteenth century, sir. Leonardo da Vinci's Tempus Machina. It came into my possession some time ago."

"*Tempus Machina*? Time Machine?"

"It is, indeed sir."

"Please, spare me your foolishness, boy. What does the bauble do? Is this some kind of ruse? A joke in these desperate hours? Because if you–"

"I use this machine to travel backward or forward in time. Arrive at a precise location anywhere on this planet at any time I wish. Past, present, future."

"*Non! Ridicule! Impossible!*"

"All is possible. This very instrument is how I came to be here at Mount Vernon tonight. To warn General Washington of Blood's perfidy."

"Impossible, I say. Do not push me to anger!"

"I understand your natural reaction. Mine was the same. Please permit me to show you how the orb actually works, sir," Nick said, beginning to twist the two halves in opposite directions.

Despite himself, the Marquis leaned forward in amazement

as Nick separated the two golden hemispheres, for a radiant heavenly light suddenly filled the entire room.

"Mon Dieu!" Lafayette said, staring wide-eyed in wonder.

Nick tried to keep the excitement out of his voice as he described the machine's inner workings. "This left half, sir, is called Locus; the other is Tempus. When I'm ready to depart for my next destination, I will insert the exact longitude and latitude for the harbor at Saint Domingue into the Locus hemisphere. Next, I will enter the time I want to arrive, let's say, the evening before Admiral de Grasse's departure. I rejoin the two halves, and in the blink of an eye, I arrive in Cap-François on the eve of departure."

"You actually believe what you are saying!"

"I don't believe, sir, I know."

The Marquis cocked an eyebrow and said, "And, young McIver, when you 'arrive', as you put it, in Saint Domingue, what are your further intentions?"

"Simple. I will locate the admiral's flagship, the *Ville de Paris*, and warn de Grasse of Blood's armada lying in ambush off Nassau town."

"And ... when you ... arrive ... are you a spirit? A ghost? Some invisible being?"

"Not at all, sir. I will be flesh and blood, just as you see me now."

The Marquis, shaking his head in disbelief, got to his feet and poured a dollop of brandy from a heavy crystal decanter into a silver goblet, downing it at a draught. "This is absolutely absurd," the Frenchman said, but he seemed a little less certain of himself. "Travel through time? It's preposterous in the extreme. By my word, I've never heard such drivel." He poured himself another brandy.

"Believe me, sir, I understand your disbelief. Originally, I felt that way, too. But it is not at all absurd, it is in fact quite true."

The Marquis, still shaking his head, sat back in his chair. *"Mais non, mais non, mais non. C'est impossible."*

"Impossible or not, General, I fully intend this very night a time voyage to Saint Domingue to warn Admiral de Grasse of Blood's armada. It is our only hope."

"So, what do you do? How will you do it?"

"I will make my departure from Mount Vernon, fully hidden from view, in a remote place out there on the estate. I invite you to personally witness this event. You'll find it fascinating . . . and convincing. And if you should change your mind at the last moment, you may accompany me to the past by simply laying your hand upon the orb itself. We will leave and arrive together."

"One disappears from one place and time and reappears in another? Is this what you are saying?"

"Exactly so."

"And you return to this place and time in precisely the same way?"

"We do."

The Marquis rubbed his chin, knowing full well this predicament had reduced him to clutching at absurd straws of illusion. What had General Washington said? "We must find a way, we simply must!"

Lafayette drained his glass and said, "Well, I suppose I've nothing to lose by going along on your fool's errand. Watch you make a silly fool of yourself."

"You've nothing to lose at all, sir, and a historic victory to win. The world will never know what is done here this night. But the results of our voyage will never be forgotten."

"Tell me, then. At what hour do you propose to conduct this incredible scientific experiment?"

"Precisely at midnight."

The Marquis de Lafayette rubbed his weary red eyes, clearly turning Nick's astounding offer over in his mind. He drained his glass and said, "I still don't believe you, of course, but I do have one question."

"Anything, sir."

"Do you speak French?"

"No, sir, I do not."

"Then how do you plan to converse with Admiral de Grasse?"

"A very good point. I suppose I shall be in need of a translator, sir."

"I suppose you shall indeed," Lafayette said with a smile. "Very well, I shall be there at the stroke of twelve. Where shall we meet?"

Nick laughed with delight and said, "Turn left round the circle as you leave the main entrance of the house. Go halfway round the drive and take the first turning, a white gate leading to a stone path passing through a number of rose gardens. There is an octagonal garden house just beyond the far hedge. I will be waiting there at midnight tonight. I would be most grateful to have your company on this voyage, sir. Delighted, in fact."

"The stroke of midnight it is, *monsieur*. Now, pray close up that bizarre oddity before our great friend returns and has us both thrown bodily into the nearest asylum."

Nick stared fixedly at the gleaming golden orb as he joined the two halves together, extinguishing the glow in an instant. "Until midnight, sir," Nick said, stowing the globe beneath his left arm and rising to leave before Washington returned.

The Marquis looked up. "Upon further reflection, I warn you, I may come to my senses before the clock strikes twelve."

"I hope not, sir. The Tempus Machina is, I assure you, General Washington's one and only chance to avoid certain defeat at Yorktown."

"You sound almost as if you foretell the future."

"Because I do, sir. Or rather, I remember the future."

The Lafayette looked at the boy as if the child was mad but said nothing and just shook his head as Nick quickly left Washington's study and raced upstairs to his room. There was a lot of thinking to be done before midnight.

Pale blue moonbeams streamed through the eight windows of the octagonal garden house. Nick, who carried Gunner's Royal Navy pocket watch, flicked it open. Normally, he'd have worn his father's standard issue Royal Flying Corps wristwatch from the Great War. But, at the last moment, he'd realized the watch would be out of place, a cause for much consternation in the year 1781.

Nick knew there was a word for such an inappropriate object and had looked it up in the dictionary before his voyage. An *anachronism*, a thing or style that belongs to a different time in history. Gunner's pocket watch had softly chimed twelve midnight a little while earlier. Nick saw it was now exactly quarter past the hour.

He heard a rustling sound outside and quickly looked up. Seeing nothing, he imagined it to have been a squirrel or some other small creature of the night.

Still no sign of the Marquis de Lafayette.

Because of the many windows, he had views in all directions. He knew there were many sentries about the Mount Vernon grounds, but he'd not seen one yet. Since arriving fifteen minutes earlier, he'd been keeping an eye on the mansion's circular drive and the garden path. Nick decided to give Lafayette five more minutes. Then, with or without him, he was going to Saint Domingue in search of the *Ville de Paris* and Admiral de Grasse.

He had no doubt Lafayette would be of great value on the voyage, but Nick had already determined his course of action. He'd been carefully studying the charts up in his room all evening. He knew the possibility of slipping by Old Bill and his massive pirate armada was slim to nil.

But, he saw, suppose the French fleet did not do what Blood expected, suppose they—he heard footsteps now and saw Layfayette in his splendid white uniform hurrying along the path toward the garden house. His heart lifted. With General Washington's most trusted and brilliant military strategist at his side, the vital task ahead stood a far better chance of success.

"You thought I was not coming, eh, Monsieur Nick?" Layfayette grinned as the boy swung the wooden door inward to admit him.

"I really did not know, sir. I certainly hoped to see you."

"*Excusez-moi, mon ami,*" Lafayette said, stepping inside. "I am unpardonably late, young Nicholas. But, you see, General Washington, after much anguished conversation, has only just now bade me good night and retired to his bedchamber. I could not leave him before then. He would have thought it passing strange."

"You did not tell him about the orb?"

"Of course not. The last thing he needs now is to perceive his most trusted military adviser as a madman."

"Thank you for coming."

"*Mon plaisir,*" Lafayette said, bowing from the waist. Nick thought the Frenchman and the famous American General had perhaps had a few more nips at the brandy decanter before Washington retired. Lafayette seemed in a rather jovial mood. It was optimism, Nick knew, the vital trait of all great leaders, the belief that any obstacle can be overcome.

Nick had set the golden orb upon a rough wooden table among trowels, flower pots, spades, and various garden implements. He now picked up the orb and cradled it in his two hands. Even now, in the pale blue light, it was radiant.

"Sir, have you come to say farewell, or will you be traveling with me?"

"Nicholas, I am normally the most circumspect of men, and trusting of but few," Lafayette said, smiling at him, "but, tonight, upon serious reflection, I find myself in full agreement with your earlier statement. I have far more to gain than to lose this night by placing my trust in you and your lovely bauble."

"An honor, sir, to have your confidence," Nick said, much relieved, "but I must swear you to absolute secrecy about the existence of this orb. I've taken a grave chance letting anyone into my confidence. In fact, I am about to break a solemn oath. But I have no choice."

"Allons-nous!" Lafayette whispered. "Let's go!"

Nick twisted the two halves of the orb apart. Instantly, the octagonal garden structure's interior was filled with luminous golden light.

The Marquis, with a loud intake of breath, stepped forward and closely inspected the exquisite inner facets of Leonardo's masterpiece. One hemisphere was inscribed Tempus, the other Locus. It was quite the most miraculous piece of intricate clockwork jewelry he'd ever seen. And so exquisite as to defy description.

Nick cast a worried eye toward the mansion. A luminous

glow in one of the garden houses at this hour would be a beacon to the stealthy sentries circling outside in the darkness. But there was nothing for it. He just had to pray that luck was with him this one more time.

Lafayette saw that numerous sparkling jewels were embedded within the face of each half of the strange machine. And on the Locus hemisphere, delicate scrolled writing, in Latin, surrounded a wondrously detailed engraving of the sun and its surrounding planets. Lafayette, a scholar as well as military genius, studied this diagram of the solar system closely and looked up at Nick.

"Two questions. This Latin inscription—it's written backward. Why?"

"Leonardo's 'mirror-writing,' sir. All of his journals are written this way, so that one can only read them by holding them up to a mirror."

"Ah, yes, I seem to remember that now. It is certainly encouraging as to the provenance of the machine. But another question, Nicholas."

"I will try to answer."

"There are nine planets in this illustrated system. When Leonardo da Vinci died in 1519, there were only five known planets in addition to earth. In March of this very year 1781, another planet was discovered by the astronomer Herschel. That makes seven. How then do you account for the other two?"

"At some point in the future, two more will be discovered. I have to believe Leonardo traveled to some future date and recorded exactly what he saw through more powerful telescopes," Nick answered. "Nine planets."

This answer obviously pleased the young Marquis. "If this improbable magical intrigue of yours should succeed, I shall count you a genius among men. If it fails, I shall find work for you among the great stage actors of our age, for clearly you are the one or the other."

"I'm no actor, sir. And it's Leonardo's genius, sir, not mine. I simply came into possession of his fabulous instrument thanks to one of my beloved ancestors."

"How, may I ask?"

"Rather a long story, sir."

"Another time, perhaps. But, pray, tell me how does it work, this Tempus Machina?"

"Our precise destination, a hillside overlooking the harbor on the island of Saint Domingue, is being entered into Locus now. Notice that I am using the exact latitude and longitudinal coordinates for Cap-François harbor, according to this chart. 18°45'N latitude, 64°42'W. Our time of arrival will be early on the evening before Admiral de Grasse sails. The next day on the morning tide. Shall we arrive at, say, five o'clock in the afternoon? It will still be light."

"*Parfait*! Are we ready to depart? What must I do?" Lafayette's eyes were now alight with excitement. He *wanted* to believe.

"As soon as I have finished entering the time and rejoined the two halves, the machine will begin to vibrate. It will glow far more brightly, like the sun, causing you to shut your eyes. You will hear the pleasing sound of countless tinkling bells. At that precise moment, place your hand over mine on the orb."

"And then?"

"Your body will suddenly be filled with the most delightfully warm and tingling sensations. For a mere instant. And then we shall find ourselves, hopefully, standing above Cap-François harbor and not swimming in it."

Nick shuddered at the memory of the cold channel waters the night he'd crashed the Sopwith Camel. The tropical waters of Saint Domingue would be warmer, still he hoped for Lafayette's sake that they'd arrive on dry land.

The Marquis laughed aloud and Nick said, "Are you ready, sir?"

"I am beyond ready, Nicholas McIver! Let us away!"

Nick joined the two halves together twisting them tightly. A blinding light apperared, and a moment later, the Marquis de Lafayette placed his hand over Nick's.

A lone sentry, now patrolling the gardens near the mansion, stopped short, having witnessed an amazing sight. One of the garden houses seemed to be suddenly filled with brilliantly incandescent light, as if countless thousands of tiny fireflies were filling the interior. When he gathered his senses and ran to inspect it, yanking open the door, he saw nothing. No, he heard only the faint echo of tinkling bells. The little shed was as cold inside as an ice house! And there was a slight acrid smell, as if something had just been burning but was now extinguished.

———

"Mon dieu, c'est magnifique, Nicholas!" were the first words out of the Marquis de Lafayette's mouth when he found himself on the isle of Saint Domingue, standing on a hillside clearing with a sweeping view of the harbor spread out below. Behind them lay a thick green jungle ablaze with tropical flowers of every color and description. The sun was lowering in the west, but they had a good two hours of daylight left. Lafayette and Nick stood side by side, gazing down at the marvelous sight of twenty-eight French warships still riding at anchor in Cap-François harbor. In the middle of the fleet, the largest

naval vessel in the world, Admiral de Grasse's flagship, the *Ville de Paris.*

Nick's luck had held. Placing the orb into his pouch, he heaved a sigh of relief at the sight of the French fleet lying at anchor. There had always been the chance that de Grasse would have a last-minute change of plans, perhaps even sailing a day early on the evening tide.

"*C'est incroyable,*" Lafayette exclaimed, laughing with sheer joy. "It is most incredible, most unbelievable, this little machine, Nicholas! A small miracle!"

Nick smiled. "The machine itself is small, sir, but I think the miracle is as great as anything on this earth."

"You are right, of course, my dear boy genius."

Nick laughed as the joyful French General began dancing about, plucking at his clothes, pinching himself as if he wished to make sure he was all there. He even leaped high into the air, landing hard on both feet, stamping his boots to make sure he was really on solid ground. He plucked a brilliant violet flower from a branch above his head, buried his nose within the blossom, and breathed deeply. Then, to Nick's consternation, he popped the blossom, into his mouth and ate it!

"Ah," he said, delighted, "delicious!"

But when he looked up, the tip of his nose was covered with yellow pollen and he sneezed violently and repeatedly, which only made Nick laugh harder at his antics.

"I think we should go find our Admiral now," the Marquis said sternly, using his handkerchief to remove the pollen from his face, then rising to his full height in an effort to regain his dignity.

Nick was about to apologize for his behavior, but the Marquis held his forefinger to his lips and said, "*Non, non, il n'est pas nécessaire.*"

He marched off into the jungle in the direction of the harbor below, and Nick followed at a discreet distance, allowing the embarrassed Marquis a few moments to compose himself.

It took no more than half an hour to descend the hillside and reach the town. Along the waterfront, all was a beehive of activity, as French sailors hurried to and fro with final stores and provisions to be rowed out to the warships waiting at anchor.

The general, in his brilliant uniform, and the boy, in his simple white breeches and white linen shirt, caused quite a stir as they strolled the waterfront in search of de Grasse's flagship. All eyes were on Lafayette. Clearly, Nick thought, here was a man who commanded great respect in his native France.

"Do you know the *Ville de Paris* by sight, sir?" Nick asked as they dodged a donkey cart laden with 24-pound cannonballs.

"But of course, she is the largest warship in the world. A triple-decked first rater of some one hundred guns, I saw her anchored in the midst of the fleet. Look, you can see the Admiral's pennant fluttering from her maintop."

It did not take long to find transportation. Another hundred yards along the quay, and they came upon a young French naval officer who stopped dead in his tracks at the sight of the famous General de Lafayette. Clearly this was the last man the young officer expected to see strolling the quay at Saint Domingue.

"*Mon Général!*" he exclaimed, clicking his heels together and saluting smartly.

"*Mais oui*, Lieutenant. Perhaps you might be of assistance?"

"*Mais certainement*, sir. How may I help you?"

"My aide and I find ourselves in need of transport to the

Ville de Paris. I wish a word with Admiral de Grasse. Perhaps you could arrange a captain's gig to ferry us out to the Admiral's flagship?"

"It would be my honor, sir. Please allow me to introduce myself. I am Lieutenant Pierre de Valois. That is my personal gig you see out there at the dock's end. I have the honor to serve aboard the *Ville de Paris*, and I am just returning to my vessel. Please, sir, follow me."

"*Merci beaucoup*, Lieutenant de Valois," Lafayette said, and he and Nick followed the man toward a pristine gig moored at the far end of the dock.

The handsome young lieutenant kept looking over his shoulder at the marquis as they walked. "The Admiral is not aware of your presence on the island, *mon Général*. Have you just arrived? We did not see any vessels enter the harbor today."

"No, I've been here for some time, Lieutenant. Looking after some personal affairs. My family owns a banana plantation here."

"*Très bien, monsieur.*"

The marquis leaned to whisper in Nick's ear. "Good for shipboard gossip. You've no idea how quickly that banana plantation fairy tale will spread on the good ship *Ville de Paris.*"

Nick smiled. "I was wondering how you planned to deal with that problem, sir. A good one."

They reached the end of the dock and boarded the small gig bobbing in the choppy waters of the harbor. The sun was sinking lower in the colorful tropical sky, and many of the fleet had begun to light their lanterns, fore and aft, and many hung high in the rigging. Nick thought it was all very beautiful but was determined to stay focused on his mission

Four sailors with oars sat amidships in the gig, Lieutenant

de Valois was at the stern, while Nick and Lafayette sat on a thwart seat at the bow.

As soon as they pushed off and were under way, the Marquis de Lafayette put a hand on Nick's shoulder. "Nick, I must warn you now that our Admiral de Grasse may not greet us with open arms. He may, in fact, have us thrown into the brig. I have many enemies among the officers of La Royale."

"La Royale?"

"It is what we affectionately call our navy. Our headquarters are in the rue Royale in Paris."

"Why are you not welcome, sir? I can't imagine it."

"I did not leave my native France under the best of circumstances. I begged the King for permission to go to America and fight for the glorious cause. But he denied me. Kings and emperors are not fond of these new notions of freedom and democracy, as you might guess. As my sovereign, our beloved monarch, Louis XVI, is so fond of saying, 'I am a Royalist by trade.'"

"I don't understand."

"He's got a job like everyone else. It just so happens that his job is king, and he wishes to keep it."

Nick smiled. "So how did you come to America? Without the King's permission, I mean."

"I vanished. To England on business. Then I let it be known in France that I was ill and would be abed for some time. I returned in disguise to France, where I purchased a vessel for the crossing to America. Preparations were just about complete when I learned the king had put a price on my head. So I fled to Spain, finished my business, and sailed for America. And here I am."

Moments later, the *Ville de Paris* hove into view. She was,

Nick saw, a magnificent ship of the line. Three decks towering above the water, bristling with more than one hundred cannons of every size and description. It was dusk, and the massive warship was ablaze with lights from stem to stern. He was much relieved at the sight and firepower of her, knowing full well it would be needed off Nassau. And, he thought, Yorktown.

The oarsmen pulled silently alongside a gangway on the starboard side. There was a floating dock at the foot of it, and two armed sentries snapped to attention at the sight of the brilliantly attired French General seated in the bow. Another fellow, the officer of the day, also saluted Lafayette smartly.

The pure white national ensign of France was snapping in the breeze at the stern, and both Lafayette and the young Lieutenant stood, turned to face the flag, and then saluted it. Then Valois turned and saluted the young officer of the day.

"His Excellency, Monsieur le Marquis de Lafayette and his aide request permission to come aboard, sir!"

Lafayette was a man of great renown in France, and the officer on the floating dock was somewhat taken aback at this announcement. But he managed a sharp salute and said, "Permission granted, sir!"

Nick's heart was pounding wildly in his chest as he climbed the steep gangway. He knew that in a very short while, he and his new friend, Lafayette, would either be behind bars deep in the brig of this great vessel or in Admiral de Grasse's after cabin, where this night the very future of America would be decided.

Nick and Lafayette were escorted aft along the main deck of the great ship, while Lieutenant Valois hurried ahead to de Grasse's cabin to announce the presence of Lafayette onboard. There was frenzied activity everywhere, from the ordinary seamen of the afterguard on the quarterdeck to the gun crews of the fifteen men it took to ready each of the thirty massive 36-pounders for action. There were, too, sailors on winches, lowering the final stores into great yawning hatches, to the men working high above in the rigging, shouting instructions to one another as they worked their way along the crosstrees, tending the furled sails.

Not a few heads snapped around at the sight of the famous Marquis making his way aft to the admiral's cabin. Many saluted; some even cheered and clapped their hands. It was clear to Nick that Lafayette had enjoyed much fame in France before escaping to America and that word of his successes under Washington had spread throughout the French Imperial Navy.

"It's a hero's welcome, sir," Nick whispered to Lafayette.

"I've sailed with many of these men. I've enjoyed cordial relations with most of them, that's all. Don't be fooled by a smiling crew. Admiral de Grasse is very close to the king. If he shares the monarch's current displeasure with me, this will be a most unpleasant encounter."

"I think the charts might well keep us out of the brig, sir. We have, after all, come to his rescue."

"Let us hope you are right."

The two new arrivals followed their naval escorts down a dark, narrow staircase, lit only by the flickering oil lamps mounted on either side. A private companionway led to the single cabin at the stern. A few moments later they were standing outside Admiral de Grasse's door.

One of the two escorts rapped discreetly, and the door was swung open by one of the admiral's Imperial Marine orderlies. Beyond lay the richly furnished quarters of the Comte de Grasse. He was deep in conversation with Lieutenant Valois. Upon seeing Lafayette, he rose from his desk and, much to Nick's relief, turned to the young Marquis with a broad smile.

De Grasse was a giant of a man, taller even than Washington, Nick saw, heavyset and extremely handsome. The smile still on his face, he addressed the Marquis. "Nothing in my long life has given me such pleasure as the joyous news that you were aboard the *Ville de Paris*, Monsieur le Marquis."

Lafayette bowed deeply and whispered to Nick, "No brig for us tonight, lad."

Lafayette replied, "Your successes and valor at sea have long brought your name to my ears, Admiral. I am honored to meet you, sir. This young fellow is my aide-de-camp, Master Nicholas McIver."

"A great honor, Admiral," Nick said.

"Come sit, won't you?" De Grasse said, pulling out a chair for Lafayette. There were eight chairs at the round table set with fine linen, crystal, and silver. It was set, Nick knew, for the ship's officers who traditionally dined with their commanding officer most evenings. At least, that was the British Royal Navy way.

With a wave of the Admiral's hand, two orderlies quickly cleared the table. Lafayette took his seat, pointing at the one to his right for Nick, and then de Grasse sat in his oversized straight-backed chair. Valois took the chair next to the Admiral.

"Rum?" de Grasse asked, as a steward approached and filled his silver beaker.

"Thank you, no," the Marquis said, "perhaps just some hot tea for Nicholas and me?"

The steward nodded and said, "*Tout de suite*, Your Excellency."

"So, General Lafayette, to what happy fortune do I owe this great honor? I understand you have been on the island attending to some personal affairs?"

"*Mais oui.* My family maintains a banana plantation in the mountains above Cap-François. When word reached me that your flotilla had arrived in the harbor, I determined immediately to have a word with you. The timing is most propitious, sir."

"Whatever do you mean, sir?"

"I am desperate to return to Washington's side at Yorktown, where our own French troops and the Americans have Lord Cornwallis under siege. I know that you are aware of this, as I have been made privy to your correspondence with General Washington and General de Rochambeau."

"I know you've become indispensable to the great American. I am surprised you are not at his side even now."

"Ah, yes. Unfortunately, sir, the swift frigate meant to return me posthaste to Virginia was lost, with all hands save one, in a storm off the coast of Saint Domingue. My aide here was the sole survivor. Young McIver somehow managed to swim ashore. He is just arrived here in Cap-François with urgent communications from General Washington. Unless I am very much mistaken, you intend to sail for America? The Chesapeake Bay?"

"I do, indeed. On the morrow, in fact. I have twenty-eight ships of the line and four frigates, manned by fifteen thousand sailors. We raise anchor at dawn to catch the morning tide. We bring siege guns, powder, and 2.5 million livres, generously donated by the women of Havana, sympathetic to our cause. In addition, we carry two thousand troops, which shall be entirely at General Washington's disposal."

"General Washington is deeply appreciative of your every effort and most anxiously awaiting your arrival. And my own arrival as well, I might add, as he pointed out in a dispatch that arrived with my young aide."

"I understand Washington's anxiety. It has become a race against time, as you well know, sir. It is my intent to arrive off Virginia prior to Admiral Graves and the British Navy; Graves will soon sail down from New York to the Chesapeake. Only my timely arrival at that location first can prevent Cornwallis from escaping. If I am successful, and the wind and the heavens cooperate, I shall arrive in the Chesapeake Bay three weeks hence."

"Have you space for two additional passengers? We eat little and drink less."

"I would be honored to have you aboard, Your Excellency. Nothing should give me greater pleasure than time spent in the company of the great hero of our Franco-American war against King George's regulars!"

The tea arrived on a silver salver and was served with much ceremony. When the steward had retreated, Lafayette said, "Admiral, I wonder if we might speak in private for a few moments. I have some rather urgent news to deliver."

"Of course," he said, and, turning to Valois, "Lieutenant, will you excuse us? See that the sentries admit no one." Valois saluted and was gone in an instant.

Admiral de Grass sipped his rum, leaned forward, and said, "Urgent news?"

"Indeed," Lafayette replied. "My young aide here was enlisted by Washington as one of a number of spies we have operating inside Lord Cornwallis's fortifications on the York River. As he was formerly a Continental drummer boy, he was dressed as a British drummer. Under cover of darkness, and with his very life at stake, he managed to slip in and out of Cornwallis's headquarters with some vitally important information. This is intelligence of the gravest importance. And it concerns you, Admiral de Grasse."

"Me? How, in heaven's name?"

"Nicholas, please show the admiral the purloined charts."

"Yes, sir," Nick replied, and pulling the leather tube from inside one leg of his trousers, he began removing Blood's charts and secret orders, handing them to Lafayette. The Marquis held the tightly rolled documents a moment, making sure he had the Admiral's undivided attention.

Lafayette began quietly. "Admiral, thanks to young Nicholas here, we have evidence of a plot to ambush your fleet en route to the Colony of Virginia."

"An ambush?"

"Indeed, sir."

"It's that blasted Englishman, isn't it? Baron Rodney. Ever since Admiral George Romney was appointed British Commander-in-Chief of the Leeward Islands, he's been dogging my every move! What is the arrogant scoundrel up to now? By heaven, I'll make him wish he'd ambushed someone else!"

This emotional outburst seemed to have taken the Admiral's breath away, and he sat back, regaining his composure.

"With respect, it is not Romney and the British Royal Navy that lies in wait, sir."

"Who, then?"

"Pirates."

"Pirates? This mighty fleet has no fear of pirates, sir. I've a massive number of warships under sail, as you see. We carry five thousand marines. I'll make short shrift of these rogues, have no doubt of that!"

"Under normal circumstances, I should have no doubts, Admiral. But these are not normal circumstances. Captain William Blood, of whom you may have heard, has assembled the greatest pirate armada the world has ever seen. I fear, even at your strength, you will be greatly outnumbered, sir."

"It is frequently not the number of ships in a battle that spell the difference but a certain stiffness of spine, a keenness of eye, and the well-seasoned brain inside a commander's skull. I've heard tell of this notorious Blood and his exploits. I've no fear of him, I assure you."

"I wholly concur, sir. But in this case, the numbers will come into play. How many warships in your flotilla, Admiral?"

"As I say, I boast twenty-eight ships of the line, sir," he said proudly. "And four supporting frigates. Why, my flagship alone, the *Ville de Paris*, carries one hundred eighteen cannon and a crew of nine hundred forty."

"An insufficient force to go against Blood, I fear."

"What? Insufficient you say? How many ships has he, this pirate?"

"At least one hundred, and growing daily, sir."

"One hundred! You cannot possibly be serious!"

"I'm afraid I am, sir. Young Nick here was an eyewitness to the assembly of the pirate armada at Port Royal."

"You were at Port Royal as well?" the Admiral said to Nick, mystified. "You certainly seem to pop up everywhere, lad. How much does the Marquis pay you? Perhaps you fancy a life at sea."

Lafayette smiled. "He was there, Admiral, and saw the Armada. I will vouchsafe the truth of his account."

The admiral looked dumbstruck.

"Good heavens, outnumbered four to one, we'd be decimated," he finally managed. "All is lost, I fear."

"Not necessarily."

"But surely we've no chance against such numbers. If we but knew when or, more importantly, where this villain intends to strike, perhaps I could see some way, but, as it is, I cannot jeopardize my–"

"Ah, but we know both, sir. Precisely when and precisely where Blood lies in wait. With absolute certainty. Please take a look at this chart, most fortuitously stolen from under Cornwallis's prominent nose by my new hero here."

Nick found himself blushing a bright pink as the Marquis spread the chart out on the Admiral's table and used his forefinger to point out important locations.

"Have a look, Admiral. You will see that the pirate armada will be lying in wait here, just to the northeast of New Providence Island in the Bahamas. And here, in heavy red ink, is the course Blood believes your fleet intends to sail. Northeast along the northern coastline of Cuba, steering northward just here to catch the Gulf Stream, up through the straits of Florida just west of New Providence Island, and proceeding up the American coast to the Chesapeake Bay. Is that your intention?"

"It is. It's the only possible route. Of course, Blood would assume that."

"This Black Cross, sir, just to the northeast of Nassau Town on New Providence is exactly where the pirate armada will be on station. He will pounce as soon as you are in the straits, just before you clear New Providence Island."

The plainly shocked Admiral shook his head and looked at Nick. "You swear you saw this fleet? With your own eyes? One hundred armed pirate ships?"

"I did, sir. At Port Royal, Jamaica."

"And this handwriting. You know it to be Blood's?"

"I do, sir."

"How do you come by that knowledge?"

"He sent me a letter once, sir."

"A letter?"

"A ransom note. He'd kidnapped my dog."

"Kidnapped your dog?"

"Yes, sir. His name is Jip."

The admiral put his head in his hands. "So much at stake," he said, "So much to lose. This will be the bitterest of disappointments to our friend, General Washington."

The Marquis de Lafayette put a comforting hand on his shoulder. "Perhaps it need not be, Admiral de Grasse."

"Why ever not?"

"It seems young Master McIver here has conceived of a plan."

"Why am I not surprised?" de Grasse said, a hint of a smile in his eyes.

"If there's but one thing I can say about my young aide-de-camp, it's that he is full of surprises," Lafayette said, laughing.

And so Nick outlined the audacious plan he'd spent many long hours perfecting. He'd spent his whole childhood studying and re-creating all the great naval battles with his little fleets of wooden ships. Now all that knowledge, he dearly hoped, was about to pay off.

Once de Grasse had absorbed the details of the plan and expressed his support for the action, Lafayette stood, clasped hands behind his back. His face had assumed a grave demeanor. "Admiral, there is one other matter I must discuss with you, one of the utmost importance."

"Mais certainement."

"I must insist that our presence aboard your flagship be treated as a matter of utmost secrecy. It is, I would say, a military secret of extraordinary importance to the allies. The entire crew must be sworn to silence upon penalty of death. No one, officers or crew, should ever speak of my involvement in this affair. Nor that of my aide."

"Granted. No one understands the need for secrecy in times of war more than I. But surely General Washington knows of this?"

"He does not, sir. And for reasons I am not at liberty to discuss, he must never learn of it."

"Very well. I give you my word, General Lafayette."

"It is all I require, sir," said Lafayette, bowing from the waist.

"Will you and young Nicholas join me here for dinner this evening? You'll find my officers' company most amusing."

"We should be delighted, Admiral."

42

L
and ho!" cried the maintop watch from his crow's nest high above the decks of the *Ville de Paris* as New Providence Island hove into view. The call from the top of the mainmast was quickly relayed to Admiral de Grasse and the officers standing on the quarterdeck aft of the helm. The Marquis de Lafayette and his young aide stood leaning against the binnacle, discussing the finer points of the plan of battle. Lafayette's suggestions were all good ones and added mightily to Nick's confidence in the proposed strategy.

De Grasse lifted a spyglass to his eye and surveyed the coastline. "No sign of sail," he said calmly. "Chance favors us so far."

They'd been at sea for four days since departing Cap-François. The winds had been favorable as they sailed northwest sometimes hugging the coast of Cuba, sometimes skirting the thousands of cays and islands of the Bahamas archipelago. They'd reached the southern tip of New Providence a full half day ahead of schedule. This boded well.

"Hoist a signal to all ships of the line," de Grasse suddenly called out, "Strike colors!"

"Aye-aye, sir!" Lieutenant Valois said, and ordered the bosun's mate to hoist the appropriate signal flag. Upon seeing it, every captain in the entire fleet of twenty-eight French warships would immediately lower the pure white ensign flag of France.

Nick barely suppressed a smile. His heart was pounding with excitement as he saw the first steps of his plan being executed. It was one of those rare moments he lived and breathed for.

The sun was settling on the western horizon, sending red-gold rays streaking across the white-laced wavetops. The sharp tang of briny sea air filled Nick's lungs with the purest joy. The acres of billowing white sail overhead delighted his eyes, filling them with wonder, and touched his heart with the thrill of a boyhood dream come true. He was aboard a great ship once more, plowing through heaving blue seas, sailing into battle.

He was aboard the *Ville de Paris*, the greatest warship on earth. He could see the green smudge on the horizon that would be New Providence Island. The French fleet was rapidly closing in on the enemy, and the mood aboard the *Ville de Paris* was one of eagerness for battle, the roar of cannon, and the smell of black powder. You could see it in the face of every crewman.

Especially the gun crews and the young "powder monkeys," boys who tirelessly ferried black powder up from below to keep the one hundred or more cannons roaring in the heat of battle. Even a grievous wound or the loss of a limb would not stop these youngest of warriors. They were notoriously fearless. He'd met just such a boy, a boy named Martyn

Hornby, sailing aboard the *Merlin* in the year 1805. Hornby was just his age, and a braver soul he'd never known.

"Hard a'lee!" de Grasse said to his helmsman.

"Hard a'lee, aye!" The man put the great wheel hard over, and the massive warship heeled slightly as she began to carve a turn to port. High in the rigging, the reef-trimmers scrambled to trim their sails for the new course. All were caught by surprise, thinking the ship would set a course nor'west of New Providence to catch the Gulf Stream. They'd done so countless times before. Why go east of the island now?

The French fleet was outnumbered at the very least four to one by Blood's pirate armada. Even the most brilliant naval warrior would be crushed by those overwhelming odds. So, Nick had thought, instead of sailing with the Gulf Stream up the western coast of New Providence, as Blood expected, the French fleet would now sail up the eastern coast of the island.

This strategy of Nick's, as he well knew, was not without problems. Time was of the essence, and this eastern passage would be far slower, wreaking no benefit from the seven knots the northerly flowing Gulf Stream provided. But this new route would give Washington's French allies the one element their very survival depended upon: *Surprise.*

"Hoist the *Jolie Rouge*! De Grasse said. "Signal all ships of the line likewise!"

Nick watched the infamous skull and crossbones, the Jolly Roger, rising swiftly on a halyard to the very top of the mainmast. All hands looked upward and cheered at the pirate flag fluttering high above in the evening breeze This ruse had been the Marquis de Lafayette's idea. Any of Blood's masthead lookouts, upon spying the infamous pirate flag, would think the fleet approaching were merely stragglers, pirate ships sailing at the last minute to join the Brethren of Blood's massive armada.

A few minutes later, as the evening shadows stretched across the quarterdeck, the captain barked, "Hoist the signal 'Douse All Lights.'"

In the waning moments of sunlight, the signal went up. There was no moon and few stars. Providence was with them on this night. The cover of darkness was essential to Nick's plan. In the dusky light of evening, lanterns everywhere in the fleet were being snuffed out.

———

The French fleet, twenty-eight towering silhouettes on the rolling black sea, sailed onward through the gathering darkness, northward into the pitch-black night. Soon, within hours, they would approach the unsuspecting enemy armada. And approach them from precisely where they were least expected. They would steal upon the Brethren of Blood from behind, ghosting toward them with every light aboard every ship, above deck or below, doused. Not a man in the fleet spoke above the faintest whisper.

Nick saw one sailor, standing atop the fo'c'sle, either rum-drunk or stupid, strike a match and put it to his pipe bowl. The pipe was ripped from his mouth by a passing officer, and the slaggard was marched under escort down to the ship's brig, with a sentence of fifty lashes awaiting him.

The French were perhaps two hours away from the enemy position. The small group of officers on the quarterdeck, standing near the helm, had been discussing the last critical elements of the strategy as the battle plan unfolded.

"Precisely how many marines will you need for this delicate operation of yours, sir?" de Grasse asked Lafayette.

"As many as your swiftest jolly-boat can accommodate, Admiral. How many oarsmen does she carry?"

"Eight of my best," de Grasse replied. "Strong, swift, and silent. You will not find better oars in La Royale."

"Then ten stout, well-armed marines and four gun crews would not unduly overburden the craft?"

"*Pas du tout*," the Admiral said. "Not at all."

"It would mean almost thirty men aboard, myself included," Lafayette said. "We can't afford the risk of swamping."

"It will mean exactly thirty, sir," Nick piped up. "That is, if you would allow me to go aboard the enemy vessel with you."

"This is the most dangerous work, Nick," the Marquis said. "There may well be fierce hand-to-hand combat once we board the enemy vessel. I strongly urge you to remain aboard here, out of harm's way. For the time being, at least."

"But I am the only one aboard personally acquainted with William Blood, sir. I would like to face him. He has, over the years, brought much grief upon me and my family. My sister in particular. I assure you, I will be no bother. Besides, he's slippery as an eel, that one is, but I know his ways. I truly believe I can be of help."

"You will need arms."

"I am armed, sir. I have this."

Nick showed Lafayette the double-barreled flintlock pistol, and the Marquis grinned his approval.

"And I give you this," he said, presenting Nick with a beautifully carved dagger. "King Louis XVI gave it to me, but as he now wants my head, I'm no longer fond of it."

"Thank you very much indeed, sir, but I already have such a weapon," the boy said, producing a fearsome-looking bone-handled blade.

"Where did you get that?"

"Why, from Billy Blood himself, sir. Old Bill once nailed my dog's own ransom note to my front door with it. This will not be the first time I've used his own dagger against him. I once plunged it into his leg, 'ere he'd kill my friend Lord Hawke."

"I marvel at this child," de Grasse said, laughing. "He never opens his mouth without something astounding issuing forth. Do not underestimate him, Monsieur le Marquis. Though young, he's obviously experienced. With his knowledge of Blood, I think he might enhance your chances of success."

"I agree. Young Nicholas will join the boarding party."

Nick smiled, greatly relieved. He had not forgotten, nor would he ever, the smirk on Blood's face when he had dropped Kate into the black hole of the oubliette.

"Thank you, sir."

All looked aloft at the sound of snapping canvas. "Bit of a blow building out of the south," de Grasse said, moistening his finger and holding it high. "We should reach the enemy's position destination sooner than I thought. I suggest you all retire to your bunks for an hour's sleep. I'll awaken you in sufficient time to prepare for the preliminary attack."

The French fleet ghosted into Swagman's Bay and silently dropped anchor sometime around three o'clock in the morning. There was severe lightning to the east, but the Admiral was fairly certain they'd not been seen entering.

De Grasse and Valois had searched charts of the whole eastern seaboard of New Providence Island for just such a location as this. Protected by a curving point of high land on its northern extremity, the bay was completely out of sight of the enemy. It required deep water (it was over ten fathoms) and must be within striking distance of the pirate armada. Everything would depend upon surprise. The sudden appearance just before dawn of twenty-eight French warships bearing down. Cannons blazing, shocking, unsuspected, and brutally terrifying to a hopefully confused and disorganized, but far greater, enemy force.

All, in fact, depended upon the genius of Lafayette and this strange and mysteriously wise English boy, Nicholas McIver, de Grasse thought.

De Grasse stood resting his elbows on the starboard rail by the bow. His fleet captains had all reported for a final meeting in the ship's wardroom. The final battle plan had been endorsed by all. The fleet was in full readiness for the pre-dawn attack on the one hundred ships of the pirate armada.

De Grasse was watching the longboat leave the relative safety of the hidden bay. It was carrying the Marquis de Layafette, his young aide, ten highly trained French Marines, and four gun crews, off into the pitch-black darkness. Every man aboard the launch was dressed in black-dyed sail canvas, their faces and hands smeared with burnt cork. A second boat, smaller, with only Valois and only five hand-picked men aboard, also clothed wholly in black canvas, was trailing a few hundred yards behind, in the longboat's wake.

This smaller, secondary gig had been one of Lafayette's last ideas. It was, he'd said, one he'd learned from Washington's Continental artillerymen that cruel winter at Valley Forge. To kill time during the long cold hours, the troops would make small bombs: a small sack, filled with black powder and wrapped into an oil-soaked linen ball, then dipped in boiling pitch and allowed to harden before being plunged into molten wax to waterproof them. They'd been used by saboteurs against enemy vessels large and small to great success.

But now, attached to each bomb was a long-burning fuse cord that would give Valois's men time to get away long before the explosion. The longer the fuse, the more time you had. And, Lafayette and his brave boarding party would need all the time they could get if they were to succeed this night.

Nicholas McIver and the Marquis de Lafayette had together conceived a brilliant but bold and extraordinarily dangerous plan. It was now under way. Only time would tell if victory or death awaited them.

"Gently now, gently," Valois whispered as the smaller of the two advance boats slipped almost soundlessly through the tropic darkness. A thin, wispy fog had rolled in and now lay atop the water, providing additional cover. The two oarsmen shipped oars and let the small craft glide up under the stern overhang of the first pirate ship they'd come to. When they reached the giant ship's rudder, the bowman reached out and grabbed it, stopping all forward motion.

So far, so good.

The narrow little fireboat had not been spotted approaching the enemy fleet. Nor, as far as Valois could tell, had the larger advance boat commanded by the Marquis de Lafayette aroused any untoward suspicion. That vessel had the far more dangerous task. Slipping quietly through the endless maze of the sleeping fleet until they located Captain Blood's infamous flagship *Revenge*. And then boarding her.

"Are you ready, *mon ami*?" Valois asked a crewman standing in the bow. *"Avec le pamplemousse?"*

The man held his grapefruit-sized bomb aloft, and you could see the white teeth of his smile in the midst of his cork-blackened face.

"*C'est bon,*" Valois said. "*Commencez.*"

The crewman stowed the bomb in a burlap sling designed specifically for the purpose. Then he began his rapid climb upward on the rudder, using his hands, knees, and feet, just like a monkey.

Valois held his breath, musket at the ready, watching the man scramble all the way to the very top of the massive stern. There, affixed just aft of the stern rail, he would locate the pintle, a massive rudder bolt inserted into a gudgeon, a large circular iron fitting attached to the transom. The pintle and gudgeon created a hinge so that the rudder might swing freely. It was this gudgeon and pintle arrangement that also held the giant wooden and iron rudder fast to the vessel's stern.

In a sea battle, a ship without a rudder was something akin to a sitting duck—dead in the water. Without benefit of her rudder, any ship was rendered useless, nearly uncontrollable in battle.

The bomber went about his work quickly and deftly. Once his bomb was tightly secured to the gudgeon with tarred rope, the crewman let fall the slow-burning fuse cord. It fell, stopping two feet short of the water. And there all the fuses would remain, unlit.

Until it was time.

The man descended the thirty-foot-high rudder far more quickly than he'd risen. He loosened his grip on the rudder's trailing edge and slid down the wet surface as easily as you would a greased pole. A moment later, he was safely back aboard the gig.

"*Pas de problème?*" Valois asked him softly.

"No problem at all, sir." Again, the white teeth in the middle of the blackened face. Valois was much encourgaged by this first success.

"*Alors*, where away our next victim?" he said.

"Three hundred yards just off our port beam, sir," replied one of the two oarsmen. "A big one, 74 guns, I think. Lanterns fore and aft. All quiet on deck, though."

"*Allons vite*," Lieutenant Valois whispered. "Let us go quickly. So many boats, so many bombs, so little time."

A few hundred yards away, Valois could make out Lafayette's vessel, winding its way through the pirate fleet, searching for *Revenge*.

"There she lies, I believe," Lafayette said to Nick, who sat beside him in the bow. In a low voice, he added, "Blood's *Revenge*." The great ship was lying to under a close-reefed top mainsail, and Nick knew there must have been a great blow earlier in the day, for this was storm-rigging.

"It is indeed," Nick whispered at his side. "I saw her with my own eyes, riding at anchor in Port Royal."

Lafayette looked at him. "Port Royal? I forgot to ask. What the devil were you doing in the most dangerous port in all the Caribbean! *Du monde!*"

"I was only there for a brief time, sir."

"And when might this have been?"

"Some time ago, sir. You see, Blood had kidnapped my young sister, Kate. So I went down there to bring her safe home."

"She is safe now?"

"She is indeed, sir."

"Where?"

"In England, sir. With my parents . . . in the year 1940."

"Where you belong, too, eh?"

Lafayette smiled, tousled the boy's hair, and said, "*Fantas-*

tique, Nicholas! Now listen to me very, very carefully. Once we slip aboard the enemy vessel, I must insist you stay close by my side. No matter what happens. Do you understand?"

"I do, sir."

"*C'est bon.* Tell me something. I've heard tell Blood likes his grog dulcified with cane juice, and he likes it frequent and strong."

"True. Courage in a bottle, my friend Lord Hawke calls it, sir. The demon rum. I once saw Lord Hawke and Old Bill in a swordfight to the death. There was Blood with a sword in one hand and a jug of sugar rum in the other."

"Our cowardly captain is likely now abed in his stern cabin at this hour? Stewed to a turn and dead to the world, perhaps?"

"I'd wager that's correct, sir."

"We shall find out soon enough," Lafayette said, and putting spyglass to eye, he scanned the main deck of the mammoth warship from stem to stern two or three times. They were rapidly closing on the darkened *Revenge*. Being spotted by a lookout now would prove disastrous. They'd be blown out of the water by short-range cannon before they'd crossed another hundred yards.

"Lookouts fore and aft," Lafayette said quietly. "None up in the rigging. No sharpshooters. One fellow with a lantern headed aft, making his graveyard-shift rounds. He is paused on the quarterdeck now, having a smoke at the stern rail. Let's hope he stays there until we heave a grapnel hook up amidships and climb safely aboard."

The men rowed ever so quietly now. Nick could barely hear the whisper of the blades in the water. This would be the most dangerous part. Should one of the watchmen see them, everyone aboard knew, death was certain.

Lafayette, speaking barely above a whisper, turned to face

his oarsmen. "Ship oars. Coast up and lay along her starboard side. Fend us off gently when we have her dead abeam. No noise."

The oarsmen withdrew their oars, and the longboat, gliding silently now, approached the hull of the *Revenge*. Nick could reach out and touch the black hull now, and he did. One of the French Marines in the bow suddenly stood, rocking the little boat slightly. He had an iron grapnel hook, sheathed in hemp, and large coil of line in his hand, while another marine reached for a handhold on the hull and brought them swiftly to a stop.

"Now!" Lafayette hissed.

The marine swung the hook in a great arc and flung the grapnel arrow straight up the side of the *Revenge*. Nick was astounded at the accuracy of the throw. It caught on the rail, with little noise, and Lafayette expelled a sigh of relief.

"Not a word, now, you men," Lafayette whispered. *"Cinq minutes."*

The men sat still as stones for a good five minutes, barely breathing, waiting to see if someone aboard *Revenge* had heard or seen the grapnel hook catch the ship's rail. Nick held his breath. The only sound was the gentle slap of water against the great warship's hull. And the thudding of his heart.

"C'est bien," the Marquis finally said. *"Allons!"*

He stood up nimbly, and grabbed the dangling boarding line with both hands. "I will go first," he whispered, "then the boy, followed by you marines. Oarsmen, when the last man has left the boat, shove off. Lay off about fifty meters. Keep your eyes open and your wits about you. Follow this ship at all costs, wherever the battle takes us. At my signal–this white handkerchief from the larboard rail–return to this boarding line at once. We will need to escape in a great hurry."

And so the twelve began the long climb to the uppermost deck. Lafayette, Nicholas McIver, and ten very professional, battle-tested French marines, muskets slung over their shoulders. Nick could tell by their attitude and ease of movement that boarding an enemy ship in the middle of the night was something they'd done many times before.

Lafayette reached the main deck, grabbed the rail, and hauled himself up and over. He stretched his hand down to Nick and helped him board. They moved away from the rail as the marines appeared one by one, easily mounting the rail and dropping silently to the deck. After them, the gun crews ascended.

"Affix bayonets," Lafayette said, and the ten soldiers quickly attached razor-sharp, dagger-shaped blades to the muzzles of their muskets. In the longboat, Lafayette had ordered that not a single shot was to be fired onboard until they had the captain, Billy Blood, in chains.

The odds were not in their favor. Eleven men and one boy against a ship manned by four hundred some-odd hardened pirates. But Nick was not overly concerned. He had surprise and the Marquis de Lafayette on his side in the coming battle.

Nick shuddered at the thought of marines using bayonets on the two lookouts. It might not be pretty, but it would be effective. At the Marquis's signal, five of the marines headed forward quickly but silently to kill the unsuspecting lookout at the bowsprit.

The other five headed aft to offer the same treatment to the stern lookout. Only one more threat remained above decks, the graveyard shift, and he was still standing at the stern, smoking his pipe.

Lafayette and Nick, moving in a low crouch, quickly made their way aft past the mizzenmast to one of the two sets of steps on either side of the ship. Each led up the quarterdeck and the helm. The doomed man on the graveyard watch was still standing at the rail, smoking and gazing out to sea. Surrounded by the great fleet of the Brethren, he was no doubt dreaming of the untold treasure that would soon be his.

They mounted the portside staircase, taking care to use the leading edge of each step to lessen the chance of creaking wood. When they arrived at the top, Nick saw that the man remained at the rail, his broad back to them, peacefully enjoying his last bowl of tobacco.

Lafayette withdrew his gleaming dagger and held one finger to his lips. "*Attendez ici*," Lafayette whispered. "You must wait here."

Nick waited as told, watching the Marquis steal up behind the daydreaming lookout. As soon as Lafayette was within arm's-length of the man, his left hand shot out and grabbed a fistful of greasy black hair, yanking the lookout's head backward. Then he drew the dagger deeply across his exposed throat. Vocal cords instantly severed, the man made not a sound. The gush of blood spattering the deck was black in the moonlight. Nick shivered, thinking, This is war.

Lafayette carefully lowered the dead man by the hank of hair still clutched in his hand. He plucked the corpse's pipe, still lit, from his clenched teeth and hurled it overboard. After pulling a white silken handkerchief from his sleeve and wiping clean his blade, the Marquis de Lafayette turned to Nick and summoned him with a wave of the hand.

Just as Nick reached his new friend, he heard the ship's bell strike seven bells in the middle watch–half past three in the morning.

There was a tremendous amount of work to be done aboard

Revenge before the burning red sun rose above the eastern horizon.

"Below now, sir?" Nick asked.

"Below."

Nick followed the Marquis, knife in hand, as he dashed across the quarterdeck, descended the starboard staircase into the dark bowels of the ship and the great after-cabin of Captain Blood.

B lood was out cold. He could have passed for a snuffed candle, save for his snoring and snorting like a wounded bull. Mouth agape, unconscious upon the velvet-cushioned banquette that curved under the great stern windows, dead to the world.

Nick could see pale starlight shimmering on the wine dark sea beyond those mullioned windows. The brightness of the sky made him worry for Valois. The young lieutenant's mission was vital. Risky enough on a dark night but extraordinarily dangerous under the glow of a scattering of stars. To slip unseen through the huge fleet, going from ship to ship planting bombs was not work for the unlucky or the faint-hearted.

Valois would need luck indeed, bags of the stuff.

"Nicholas," Lafayette whispered, "I will need something to bind the captain's wrists and ankles to these posts. A bit of line would be ideal, but belts, scarves, anything will do. Look in his wardrobe, quickly."

Nick opened the twin doors of the large piece of mahogany furniture and found it full to overflowing with every kind

of frippery and finery. Blood was famous for his fanciful manner of dress, and there were many silken scarves to choose
from. Nick grabbed a handful.

"Here, sir, I hope these will do."

"Perfect. Bind his ankles tightly to the post. Use two or
three scarves. I'll do the same with his wrists."

Lafayette held his dagger clenched in his teeth as he bound
Blood's hands. Should the madman awaken, he'd find a knife
at his throat before he could summon help.

"Secure at that end, is he?" Lafayette asked.

"He is, sir."

"Fetch that jug of water on his worktable, please. It's time
our fearsome Captain Blood woke up to reality."

Nick did as asked, and the marquis upended the brimming
silver carafe, dousing Blood's face with a torrent of cold water. Sputtering and cursing, he came fast awake. "What?
What? Who–dares–?" he said, slurring his words. Still drunk,
Nick thought, but he'd get over that in a hurry.

"Silence, if you please, Captain," Lafayette ordered, placing
the dagger's tip to Blood's throat and adding, "Do I make my
point, sir?"

"Aarrrgh," mumbled Blood.

Then, to Nick, Lafayette said, "Light a lantern, Nick, so
that the captain might better see his current predicament."

Nick found the lantern match and lit the oil lamp suspended
above Blood's head.

"Allow me to introduce myself, Captain Blood. I am Marie-
Joseph-Paul-Yves-Roch-Gilbert du Motier. Also known as le
Marquis de Lafayette. But you may simply address me by
rank. General Lafayette. But speak softly, I warn you, or you'll
speak no more."

"I'll have yer bloody head, you French dog," Blood said through clenched teeth. You could see murder in the pirate's eyes, but when he went for Lafayette's throat, he encountered the multicolored silk scarves that bound his hands to the post. Next, trying to lash out with his legs, he noticed the same problem with his ankles.

Blood writhed in frustration, twisting, thrashing, and straining against his unforgiving bonds. "*You!*" he hissed. Catching sight of Nick's hated face in the flickering lamplight, his face darkened to a deep, furious scarlet. Just the sight of his eternal nemesis aboard his ship was more than he could take. Nick thought Blood looked like he might have a seizure. Maybe even pop an artery or two.

"You damnable boy! Back again, are ye? You tricked me well in Port Royal, aye. But I'll cut out yer lyin' young tongue and spit on yer bleeding grave afore I'm finished with ye."

"A pleasure to see you again as well, Captain," Nick said, bowing slightly from the waist.

"You're in a pickle, Captain Blood," Lafayette said calmly. "And I'll warrant there's but one way out of it for you."

"Say what yer after and get off my ship or I'll—"

"You'll what, sir?"

"Call my guards and have you both strung by yer scrawny necks from the highest yardarm."

"Your guards, you say? Dead or dead drunk, I'm afraid. Including those two sleepy laggards you'd posted outside your door. They went peacefully enough under the knife, though. Died in their sleep."

Some of the fight went out of him then. He realized his situation was dire and said, "Name your price. What do you want of me, Frenchman?"

"Your ship, sir, the *Revenge*."

"My ship? You're mad."

"Actually, I'm not," Lafayette said, pulling his pistol from his waistband and placing the muzzle between Blood's bloodshot eyes. "You shall do exactly as I tell you to do, and perhaps I'll show you mercy. But hesitate or show duplicity, and it's a lead ball to your pickled brain, Captain Blood. Tell me: Do we understand each other?"

"Aye. Get on with it, then. Speak yer piece."

"In addition to four of my best gun crews, even now preparing your own cannon for firing, a large number of my most seasoned marines now await me on your main deck. Crack shots, all heavily armed, muskets, pistols, pikes. They will accompany you and me on a search from one end of this ship to the other, beginning in the crew quarters.

"Search as you please. Ye'll find no booty aboard *Revenge*."

"It's not your treasure we seek. You will order your entire crew to peacefully throw down their arms lest you be killed where you stand. When this is accomplished, when all your crew's weapons are heaved overboard, you will then order your men to move peaceably into the largest of the for'ard holds. There the entire crew shall remain under guard, lock, and key for the duration of the coming action. Any attempt at resistance will result in instant death for you and them. Is this all quite clear, Captain?"

"Aye," Blood said, and Lafayette studied him carefully. He was no buffoon and would require constant vigilance.

"Cut him loose," Lafayette said to Nick. Nick pulled out his bone-handled knife and sliced through the bonds he'd tied with one swipe. He then moved to free the hands, and Blood saw the knife in Nick's hand.

"Me own knife, you cursed little bugger. Where did you get it?"

"You stuck a ransom note to my door with it once. At the lighthouse on Greybeard Island. I've had it ever since."

"Stuck it in me bloody leg in that melee aboard *Mystère* in 1805, didn't ye?"

"I was obliged to. You were about to kill my friend Lord Hawke."

"Only a matter of time afore I do kill him. Now, cut me loose, damn yer hide, boy, and let's be done with this."

"General," Nick said, "begging your pardon, sir, but you should know that Captain Blood here is in possession of a second Tempus Machina, identical to my own. Now would be an ideal time to relieve him of it."

"Is what the boy says true?"

"Aye, but you'll not get it from me. I'll die afore I give it up. A warning to you both. Should I die, my mate, Snake Eye, will use the orb to track you two to the ends of the earth to avenge my murder."

"It's true, sir," Nick said, "Until we have both orbs, we cannot rest; nor can we—"

Lafayette said, "Nick, listen, there's no time at all for this now. General Washington awaits us, and history's clock is ticking. Perhaps later, when victory over the pirates is ours, we can search for the second orb. But we must hurry now and secure the enemy crew!"

———

Half an hour later, it was done. The entire crew of the *Revenge*, with the exception of her captain and the few absolutely essential mates and sail trimmers needed to sail the vessel, had been force-marched by the marines into the cavernous for'ard hold and locked inside. Two marines, stationed on deck at the open hatch above the hold, had orders to shoot any man who made a sound during their stealthy approach to the waiting fleet.

Lafayette and Nick had captured the great pirate ship without firing a shot. *Revenge* rode at anchor, solitary, near the northern edge of the pirate fleet. The wind was freshening, whitecaps ruffling the sea, and Nick, now on the quarterdeck, saw this as a sign of a benign Providence. Washington, Nick had read in the history books, had often said the Americans would never have been victorious without the helping hand of God. And here perhaps was proof of that statement.

To his left, in the distance, Nick could make out the few lights of a sleeping Nassau Town. Behind him to the south, and well out of sight, Nick knew, were an impatient Admiral de Grasse and his fleet, waiting for a single rocket to be fired across the sky, the signal to race north and engage the enemy. The rocket would also be a signal to Valois to cease his dangerous work and race southward toward de Grasse's oncoming fleet. And reboard the *Ville de Paris*.

Looking southward, Nick could see the thick forest of masts and the darkened hulls of pirate ships beneath them. Nick strained to see Valois, and he finally sighted the silhouette of his small gig racing to and fro amongst the sterns of pirate ships. Having finished planting bombs throughout the sleeping fleet, he and his men were now hurrying about to light as many of the long time-fuses as possible.

On the main deck below him, Nick saw the four gun crews brought over from the *Ville de Paris* feverishly loading the pirate vessel's cannon for the coming battle.

On the quarterdeck of *Revenge* stood Lafayette, Blood, and Nicholas McIver. Blood's pirate helmsman was at the wheel, eyeing the muskets of the marines leveled in his direction lest he attempt something stupid.

"Haul down the Jolly Roger, Blood, and raise this ensign in its place," Lafayette said, handing Blood the pure white flag of France.

Blood murmured angrily but, with a prod from a marine musket, did as he was told.

"Good," Lafayette said, watching with some pride as his beloved flag, fluttering in the stiffening breeze, was hauled aloft. "You have now surrendered your ship. You are now a prisoner aboard my ship, Captain Blood, and you will do exactly as you are told. Order the remaining crew in the rigging to spread all canvas, every yard of sail she'll carry. And have men standing by the for'ard windlass, ready to weigh anchor at my order. Do it now, Captain!"

Blood shouted out orders to his remaining crewmen, and soon the rustle and snap of canvas could be heard as the trimmers high atop the mainmast let fall the mainsail, main topsail, and main topgallant. Trimmers in the foremast and mizzen rigging did the same. Soon *Revenge* was wearing a full suit of sail, from the flying jib on the bowsprit to mizzenmast sails aft. And the wind was still filling in nicely. *Revenge* began to move.

"Weigh anchor and make for the fleet," Lafayette said quietly, and Blood passed the word forward to the windlass crew. Nick soon heard the grinding of the great wooden drum as it wound the heavy anchor line and chain up from the deep. Once the anchor itself was hauled up and secured, Lafayette stepped forward to give orders to the helm. "Helmsman, come right, zero-ten-zero degrees south. On my order, bring her hard right on a course due south. The man looked at him, incredulous. "You heard me. We're going to sail her right through the middle of that bloody pirate fleet."

"Aye," the man said, this bizarre order filling him with dread.

All Blood's shipmates would see that white flag fluttering at the top and they'd open fire. One ship against a hundred? Suicide.

Lafayette put a hand on Nick's shoulder. "Nick, quickly for'ard with you now. Instruct all four of our gun crews to await my signal as planned. They're to hold their fire until we're well inside the main body of the pirate ships. That fleet is a sleeping giant now, but I want *Revenge* at flank speed when we run that gauntlet. The pirate crews will wake soon enough when those time bombs and our cannon start roaring and lead starts flying."

As Nick ran for'ard, he could feel the great ship beneath his feet gradually getting under way. Slowly at first but gathering speed as she caught the wind. She heeled over to starboard, and the trimmers got the sails properly trimmed for the heading. He could hear the rush of water thrown off to either side of her bows.

He heard a loud explosion aft and looked over his shoulder. Lafayette had fired the flaming signal rocket, streaking up into the heavens, trailing a plume of fire. Nick knew that Admiral de Grasse, spotting the fiery rocket against the dark blue sky, would heave into sight behind them at any moment as his French fleet raced northward to join the captured *Revenge* sailing into the jaws of battle.

"Steady, now, steady," Lafayette whispered to the grizzled old helmsman as *Revenge* sailed on toward the ships of the Brethren of Blood. The pirate armada seemed to stretch from one end of the horizon to the other. Still, all was quiet, dark, and peaceful under the starlit tropic sky. The only light coming from the sleeping fleet was the oil lanterns swinging at the bow and stern of every ship. The only sounds Nick heard were the lazy slap of canvas and the creak of rigging. But the wind was freshening; a good breeze for a fight.

Nick had relayed Lafayette's orders to the French gun crews on the main deck and had returned to the quarterdeck. Blood's eyes flared at the very sight of him and he spat, missing Nick's face by inches. Lafayette instantly drew his sword, the flat of its blade at Blood's neck.

"Your life is already hanging by a thread, Captain Blood. Insult the boy again and I cut the thread gladly."

The mood of the small group at the helm of *Revenge* was tense. Every man and boy knew what they were about to attempt was audacious to the point of lunacy. It was one thing for a warship to sail unannounced into an enemy harbor, quickly do as much damage as possible, and then, with any luck, escape with minimum damage and make for the open seas.

But a small fleet, outnumbered at least four to one, sailing straight into the heart of a massive enemy flotilla out at sea? No naval man in his right mind would dare attempt such a suicidal engagement.

Yet it had to be done. All aboard knew it was the only way Admiral de Grasse could ever hope to slip the French fleet safely through the pirate ambush; and surely the only way the French squadron could possibly reach the Chesapeake in time to help eke out a great victory for the allied American and French armies.

Lafayette was well aware that in the entire course of the long and bloody American Revolution, this one single battle at Yorktown and the ultimate defeat of Cornwallis could forever end Britain's hope for victory over her rebellious colonies. But first they had to win the bloody thing.

On *Revenge*'s main deck, Lafayette's gun crews stood at the ready, matches already lit. Two crews on the starboard side, two to port. Despite the shortage of manpower, every cannon was loaded with either ball or grapeshot. When things got spicy, the gun crews would dash from cannon to cannon, fire, and then race to the next. Aloft, high in the rigging, were the marine sharpshooters, each man armed with multiple muskets. When the battle commenced, it would fall to them to pick off the dazed pirates as they emerged from below decks.

Lafayette fervently hoped his sharpshooters would induce fear and panic amongst the pirate crewmen still milling below, awaiting their turn to race topside to their battle stations. Thereby gaining precious minutes for de Grasse to get his ships safely through the trap.

"You seem remarkably calm, Nicholas," Lafayette whispered to the boy beside him. "Lead will fly soon. The air will be thick with it."

"I've seen battle at sea before, sir, and in the air. It's terrifying enough. Still, I am not afraid to die in the course of doing my duty."

"In the air, did you say? Don't tell me you've been up in one of those confounded balloons."

"Actually, no, it was in an aeroplane, sir."

"What the devil is that?"

"A flying machine."

"Ah, of course, a flying machine. I don't suppose I'll live long enough to see that."

"I'm afraid not, sir. 1903."

Lafayette smiled, shaking his head in wonder, and raised the long spyglass to his eye. The Brethren's massive fleet now loomed ever larger. The nearest ship, straining at her anchor rode, lay a scant thousand yards away. Still no warning shot had been fired, and there was no indication that anyone saw the huge *Revenge* racing toward them. Nick judged she must be making a good ten knots, heeled hard over, the vast acres of canvas above him now filled with wind.

For the moment, none of the men gathered at the helm spoke a word. As men will do before battle, they concerned themselves with private thoughts as they bore down on the enemy at great speed. From their vantage point, the pirate fleet looked like a solid wall. It was hard to spot an opening amongst the countless vessels.

"Shall I ease her sheets, sir? Spill a bit of wind?" the pirate helmsman nervously asked Lafayette, hoping to diminish their speed.

There was no reply. Lafayette clearly had no intention of

slowing down as he sailed *Revenge* directly into the midst of the pirates. A moment later he said, "Bring her right ten degrees on my mark...Mark!"

He'd seen his opening. Nick saw it, too, but worried that the width between the stern of one vessel and the anchor line of the next was not nearly sufficient for them to sail through. The pirate helmsman, a weathered and seasoned seaman, examined the narrow entry point with a wary eye but said not a word.

"Helm, what is that nearest vessel?" Lafayette asked. "And how many guns?"

"*Tralee*, sir. Thirty-four guns."

"Leave her be. And the farther vessel, off our starboard bow?"

"*Dragonfire*, sir. Seventy-four guns."

"Pass the word forward," Lafayette said to a marine. "Starboard gun crews open fire when *Dragonfire* comes within range. Rake her with a broadside. Subsequently, all gun crews fire at will. Sharpshooters aloft as well." The battle was joined and *Revenge* sailed deep into the heart of the enemy, firing with everything she had. The sounds of cannon and musket rent the air with a deafening roar.

"The *Ville de Paris* is closing on us quickly, sir," Nick said, "off our starboard bow."

Lafayette turned and saw de Grasse's warship approaching hard on the wind, narrowing the distance between them. He turned to a crewman. "Signal, 'Line ahead,'" Lafayette said. This meant de Grasse's ships were to form up in single file, bow to stern, and follow Lafayette's *Revenge* when she came about to a northerly heading. "Ready about, helm. Put her hard over and come to degrees zero due north."

The crewman quickly ran the appropriate signal flags to the

top of the mizzenmast. As the order was relayed throughout the French fleet, every warship fell into line behind the massive *Ville de Paris*, racing to reach *Revenge* and follow her into battle. Having come about, Lafayette now had de Grasse on his stern.

A marine lookout to port called back to Lafayette, "Small craft approaching port side, sir. No lights. She's headed straight for us."

Lafayette swung his glass round and said, "Valois returns! Good! Ease off, helm, but keep a way on. Prepare to take those men aboard and recover the longboat. Smartly, now."

So, the Marquis thought, Valois's bombs were set, the long fuses lit and burning toward the bombs. If all went well, those small bombs could contribute mightily to the confusion and effectiveness of the pirate fleet's reaction to the surprise predawn attack.

Moments later, Valois, smiling, strode across the quarterdeck and stopped in front of Lafayette, saluting smartly. "It is done, sir," he said.

"It is well done, Lieutenant."

Then, turning to the helmsman, he said, "Flank speed now, come right five degrees, take *Rising Sun* just to starboard, and I don't want to see much water between us, mind. One false move from you and you die where you stand. I can steer this ship if I have to."

The helmsman nodded and put the wheel over.

"Lieutenant Valois, please escort Captain Blood below and lock him up. Post a guard. I don't want–"

At that moment Blood bolted, screaming at the top of his lungs, racing for the steps leading to the main deck, hoping somehow to sound the alarm, awaken his sleeping comrades in nearby ships still unaware of the impending attack.

A marine raised his pistol and took aim at the pirate's back only to have Lafayette firmly grasp his forearm and lower the gun. "No. I want him alive. Round up a small search party, find him, and throw him in the brig. I'll deal with him later."

Suddenly there was a loud explosion and a great flash of fiery orange light shot up from somewhere in the middle of the darkened pirate fleet. The first of Valois's gudgeon bombs, Nick thought. That would wake the drunken pirates up all right, and soon.

"Watch that anchor rode to starboard!" Lafayette shouted at the helmsman. "Left, two degrees!" The helmsman, deliberately or not, had been about to entangle *Revenge* with the *Rising Sun*'s ground tackle. The bowsprits missed by inches, and *Revenge* sailed on toward the *Pearl*, Edward England's vessel.

Admiral de Grasse's flagship remained dead astern, following them at about one hundred yards. Trailing in her wake, the twenty-eight French ships of the line so desperately needed by General Washington at Yorktown.

The die was cast. They were taking the fight right into the very heart of the enemy!

"Sir," Nick said, "might I have your permission to join the search party?"

"I suppose. But why?"

"Because, sir, I know exactly where to find Billy Blood," Nick said over his shoulder, dashing off.

The pirate crew aboard *Rising Sun* awoke to the murderous assault of heavy cannon fire as Lafayette's gunners bombarded the 74-gun pirate ship with equal measures of grapeshot and chain, which shredded her rigging, and solid 34-pound balls, which blasted through her thick wooden hull. Lead and vicious flying splinters found human targets above and below decks. One lucky ball found the base of the mainmast. The towering spar pitched forward, bringing down a ton of rigging as it crashed to the deck, instantly killing two forward lookouts and a number of seamen desperately sheeting in the foresail in an attempt to get under way.

Had *Rising Sun*'s crew been mustered to battle stations, a hundred men might have died. As it was, most crew stumbled sleepily out of their hammocks, headed topside to find out who on earth was shooting at them in the middle of the night.

The great Battle of Nassau Town, as it would later be known, had begun in earnest. The attack on the sleeping Brethren of Blood was led by the captured pirate ship *Revenge*, now under the command of the Marquis de Lafayette and flying a white French ensign at her masthead. She was followed closely into battle by Admiral de Grasse's mammoth flagship, *Ville de Paris*, and twenty-seven more French ships of the line.

Nick saw the three-man search party sprinting down a for'ard staircase in a frantic search for Old Bill. They were starting at the bow, the dead wrong end of the ship, and he instantly decided he was better off on his own anyway. He usually was. He paused and watched in amazement as Lafayette's highly trained gun crews, having commenced fire at the port bow, and fired the forward-most cannon, were racing to the next guns aft. They were swiftly working their way aft, raking *Pearl* with a deadly broadside.

There was no real return fire from the enemy. Not yet, anyway. Nor had he yet heard the stirring sound of drums beating to quarters drifting across the water. Still, Nick knew the worst was to come; there was no way the French fleet would get through this thick maze of heavy warships unscathed.

The portside gunners helped their starboard crewmates, reloading the port guns as quickly as they were fired. As Nick moved aft to begin his search for Blood, he saw the pirate crew emerging from every hatch and opening on *Pearl*'s main deck, scampering to run out her guns. But, aboard *Revenge*, sharpshooters, high above, now began picking off men with startling accuracy. Countless enemy sailors were killed within that first five minutes, either by musketball or flying pieces of jagged wood, as the hull was smashed by the barrage of cannonballs. As Nick had learned in his first sea battle, the most lethal projectiles were not cannonballs but the razor-sharp splinters of flying wood they produced.

The deafening sound of cannon, bucking and roaring as

the flaming matches were held to their touchholes, was punctuated by the sharp, distinctive explosions of the single rudder bombs, the deadly grapefruit planted throughout the enemy fleet by the heroic Valois and his men. They were now exploding every few minutes as the fiery fuses sizzled upward to the gudgeons, blowing the pirate ships' rudders right off their iron hinges. Helmsmen, arriving at their stations, would find their rudderless warships practically useless in the battle to come. So far, so good.

The audacious action seemed to be working, Nick thought with some satisfaction as he ducked into a dimly lit staircase leading below. He took the steps two at a time, knowing time was of the essence now, knowing he'd only a slim chance of success anyway.

The private aft companionway leading to Blood's stern cabin was in semi-darkness. Only a few guttering candles mounted in sconces showed Nick the way. They cast small pools of light every six feet or so, and the corridor appeared to be deserted. Since the entire crew had been rounded up and herded into the forward hold, then locked inside it, he had little fear of sentries or guards leaping from the darkness.

He could see the large door of Billy's cabin at the end of the narrow corridor. He was treading lightly now, scarcely breathing. The door was slightly ajar, and the lantern light inside meant Old Bill was most likely just where Nick thought he'd be. Barely moving his lips, he whispered the prayer that had always provided strength to face his fears: "Nelson the strong, Nelson the brave, Nelson the Lord of the Sea . . ."

Nick McIver pulled the double-barreled pistol from his waistband with his right hand, cocking both triggers. Taking a deep breath and advancing stealthily, he pushed the door open an inch or two and put his eyes to the crack. Blood was in there all right. He was seated at his round table, atop which was a small lockbox, heavily banded with iron and secured by a large padlock. Bill had his hook inserted into it and was trying to open the lock feverishly.

Nick knew exactly what was inside the chest. He had arrived in the nick of time.

Nick stepped inside, his pistol aimed at Blood's heart. "Captain Blood," he said.

Blood looked up and, seeing the brazen boy who'd long bedeviled him, turned red with rage. Nick saw him reaching below the table with his right hand.

"Both hands palm down on the table, sir," Nick said, with a lot more confidence than he was feeling. The pistol in his hand seemed to have a mind of its own, wanting badly to shake, but he was determined to hold it steady and true. His heart was pounding wildly, as if it might burst his ribs.

Blood had no choice but to comply. He placed his hands on the table. "What do you want now?" the captain spat out. "It's always something with you, ain't it now?"

"It's stolen property I'm after this time, sir."

Blood laughed. "And what stolen property might that be?"

"The golden orb inside that chest, sir."

"Golden orb? It's mine, boy. But if you want it so badly, come over here and open the chest. C'mon, come and take it. I'll not stop you."

Nick smiled at the obvious ploy. He knew he could no more unlock and open the iron chest with one hand than fly to the moon. He raised the pistol a few inches, pointing it between Blood's eyes.

"You stole that machine from a distant relative of mine, sir. Captain McIver of the Royal Navy. In the middle of your treasonous mutiny, as I remember it, sir."

"'Twas never McIver's to begin with, boy. It was originally plunder belongin' to Napoleon himself. McIver took it from a French ship he'd captured off the Spanish Main, and I took it from him the night I took my leave of the Royal Navy. Now, leave me be, or I'll have your scrawny gullet slit from ear to ear."

"An unlikely turn of events, sir. You'll recall that General Lafayette holds your entire crew under lock and key. And my pistol has two barrels. One of them is sure to find you."

"Not my *entire* crew, boy, no, not at all. They missed one, you see. And a very dangerous one to overlook, laddie boy." Blood laughed.

Nick then heard an ominous hissing sound behind him, as if someone had poked a sharp stick at a coiled snake hiding in a dark corner. He knew that sound well, and it sent shivers rippling from his spine to his brain.

Snake Eye!

Before Nick could spin and fire, the gruesomely tatooed savage stepped out of the shadows behind him and wrapped two powerful hands round the boy's neck. Nick could feel the cords and blood vessels in his throat beginning to compress and collapse under the pressure of the pirate's cold hard fingers. He could get no air.

"Drop yer pistol," Snake Eye sneered into Nick's ear, "now."

Nick was seconds away from blacking out. He dropped the gun and it clattered to the floor.

"Now, kick 'er away, easy like."

He did, and the painful pressure on his gullet eased somewhat.

Snake Eye's hands were replaced by a serpentine dagger at Nick's throat. Nick knew the knife. He'd once seen Snake Eye use it to slice off a piece of his own tongue and eat it, just to show how fearsome he was.

Blood sat back in his chair and smiled at his victim. "Another unlikely turn of events, ain't it, you young devil? Now what shall I do with you?"

"You'll be wanting this head for yer collection, Cap," Snake Eye said, whipping the knife about, as if preparing to behead the boy.

"Ah, me collection," Blood said. "Pull open that cupboard door and let him have a look, Snake Eye."

Snake Eye reached out with his left hand and flung open the door to a large cupboard. There were four shelves. On each shelf sat human heads in large glass jars, filled with some yellowish liquid to preserve them.

"Space enough for the boy in there. On the bottom shelf reserved for me lowliest foes. And I'll have his head soon enough. But search him first. He's likely to have the other orb about his person."

Snake Eye kept the knife at Nick's throat while he ran one hand roughly over Nick's body from the neck down.

"Raise yer arms, devil!" Blood said.

Nick did, and Snake Eye searched there, too.

"Ain't got it on his person, Cap."

"Where is it, boy? You'll not pull a disappearing act like Port Royal this time, that I'll warrant!"

"I gave it to General Lafayette for safekeeping," Nick lied. In truth, the orb was sewn inside his pillow in the small cabin he now shared with Lafayette aboard the *Ville de Paris*.

Nick could see Blood thinking, he guessed, that the wily old pirate could exchange Nick's life for the orb. But the odds were not in his favor. There were too many marines and sharpshooters protecting the Marquis, and Blood knew it. He used his hook to open the lock, his brow furrowed with thought.

"He can keep his precious head for now," he told Snake Eye. "I'll warrant I made a mistake the first time, throwing him in the oubliette at Fort Blood. I deprived the good citizens of Port Royal of seeing his head on the guillotine block afore it rolled into the basket. They were sore disappointed. Mayhaps they'll get a second chance, eh, boy?"

At that moment there was an enormous crash as a cannonball shattered the stern mullioned windows and then smashed into the far bulkhead of the captain's cabin, splintering it. Cannon fire was nearly continuous now, Nick realized, and the *Revenge* was taking a beating from the Brethren of Blood. He could only hope the surprise appearance of de Grasse and his fleet was giving the pirates a good pounding.

Blood rose to his full height. He was dressed, Nick saw, in a long scarlet silk coat and white satin breeches, which were stuffed into his polished black boots. He'd not lost his ill-deserved vanity.

"I'll be taking me leave now, Snake Eye. You hustle that feisty little bugger for'ard and down to the powder hold. There's a secret hatch down there in the hold, see, kind of hidden-like in the hull."

"Yer secret escape hatch," Snake Eye said, with a nod. "I know it well enough."

"Aye. Give 'er a solid kick and she'll pop right out. I always keep a small rowing gig under tow by that portside hatch, for emergencies such as this one. Take the gig and the boy to Nassau Town. Ain't but a mile distant. Make him row. I'll meet you there later tomorrow at the Greycliff Inn on West Hill Street. Then we'll take him back to Port Royal and give the crowds a proper send-off this time, eh?"

"Aye," Snake Eye said, watching as the padlock was removed. Blood smiled, opened his lockbox, and lifted the gleaming orb out of the chest. The cabin was suddenly filled with fire. He held it up to admire for a moment longer before twisting it open. Using one finger, he deftly entered his time and destination. Then he looked up at Nick.

"Don't look so a'feared, Nicholas McIver. Sooner or later, it was bound to come to this. Crossing William Blood is like jumping into a pool of ravenous sharks. Ye'll soon find yer carcass ripped to bloody pieces!"

"I'm not afraid of you, sir. I never have been."

Blood looked at Snake Eye, and both of them snorted.

"Then you really are the little fool I always took you to be!"

Blood threw his head back and laughed loudly, the silver skulls braided in his black beard tinkling merrily. Then he rejoined the two halves of the Tempus Machina.

Despite his frustration over Blood's escape, Nick never tired of seeing the miracle of the golden orb. He heard the lovely tinkling of tiny bells and saw the captain's shape transformed into countless luminous fireflies. They began winking out, and soon enough Billy Blood was gone. Vanished.

"*Allons*," Snake Eye said, grabbing Nick roughly by the shoulder. "Let's be on our way, and not a peep out of yer smart mouth or I'll take yer head for meself. Stick it on top of a pike and parade it through the streets of Port Royal. Would be my pleasure after what you've caused me."

Nick stepped out of the cabin into the darkened companionway. With the tip of the pirate's dagger in the small of his back, he made his way along the dim corridor, down two sets of steps and forward to the powder hold amidships.

"Open it," Snake Eye said, and Nick pulled the heavy door wide open. The pirate grabbed a burning torch from an iron sconce, and they made their way carefully inside, fire and tons of black powder being a most dangerous combination.

In the light of the flickering torch, Nick plainly saw the small escape hatch cleverly disguised to look like part of the hull. Snake Eye held him tightly by the throat and gave the hatch cover a mighty kick. It splashed into the sea, and all of a sudden Nick saw and heard the ferocity of the battle raging around him: many ships afire or sinking, dead men and debris floating everywhere. Smoke smelling of black powder burned his throat and nostrils, causing his eyes to water. Everywere he looked, in any direction, he saw ships in flames, some of them sailing endlessly in circles, their rudders having been blown off by the bombs.

A small gig was bobbing just outside the hatch, tethered to the hull.

"You board first," Snake Eye hissed, releasing his hold on the boy. "Seat yourself amidships between the oarlocks, facing the stern. I'll be in the bow with a pistol aimed at the back of yer head, in case you get any fancy ideas."

"Aye-aye, sir," Nick said, grabbing the painter and pulling the narrow-beamed little gig close enough that he might board it. He stepped down into it, felt it rock dangerously, got seated, and picked up the oar handles. He tensed his muscles and released them, feeling the tension wash out of him. He was ready. He knew this would be his one and only chance.

Snake Eye emerged from the hatch, his pistol in one hand and the flaming torch in the other. Nick could see him judging the distance to the boat, getting ready to step aboard. Concentrating on that tricky feat alone. In one blinding movement, Nick was on his feet, holding one of the oars over his shoulder like a cricket bat. Just as Snake Eye was stepping down into the boat, Nick shifted his weight, rocking the small gig.

Snake Eye struggled to retain his balance, for the moment

stunned and distracted at the prospect of being pitched into the water. Then he saw what Nick really intended. Before the pirate could make a cry, Nick swung the heavy oak oar with all his might. The flat of the blade struck the left side of Snake Eye's head a mighty blow. The man was staggered but still somehow remained standing. Blood was pouring from a gash just above his ear.

Nick planted his boots against the rider of the gig and pivoted his entire upper body for a second blow, coiling his energy. Now, with barely a pause, he swung the oar in a back-hand direction, far more powerfully, and dealt the stunned pirate yet another fierce blow to the other side of his head.

Snake Eye pitched headfirst into the water and floated there beside the gig, face up, unconscious but still breathing. Nick stuck the blade of his oar in the man's chest and shoved him away. He had considered using the oar to submerge him, hold the murdering pirate under until he drowned, but found himself unable to finish off an incapacitated enemy.

That would make him a murderer, too.

He knew this decision might well come back to haunt him someday, but he quickly reboarded the *Revenge* and raced topside to find Lafayette and inform him of Billy Blood's escape.

Bombshells bursting above Nick's head lit up the whole topside of *Revenge* as he emerged from below. Two motionless marine sharpshooters were hanging upside down in the rigging like dead marionettes. What was left of Lafayette's decimated gun crews were still in action, racing back and forth from port to starboard, reloading and firing the heavy guns as rapidly as they could.

Cannon smoke drifted across the deck as the boy raced aft to find General Lafayette. There were dead and wounded strewn about the deck, but at least the rigging and sails were still mostly intact and, to his great relief, he saw that *Revenge* was still in the fight. Even now, she cut across the bows of a pirate brigantine and raked her with deadly grapeshot.

"Sir!" Nick said, finding the General crouching beside the helm, tending to a gravely wounded man. The man's face was a rictus of pain, and Nick saw that he was biting down hard on a musket ball.

"Find our villainous Captain, did you, Nicholas?" the Marquis said without looking up. He was busy stitching up a gaping wound in an officer's neck with bosun's needle and catgut.

Nick looked closely at the man grimacing in pain. It was Lieutenant Valois.

"Will he make it?" Nick asked anxiously. He'd grown very fond of the brave young lieutenant.

"If God wills it. I've seen my share of battlefield wounds, and this one is survivable. And what of Blood?"

"Blood's escaped, sir!" Nicholas said, still breathing rapidly from his sprint up four decks.

Lafayette looked up, concern darkening his features. "Escaped, for all love? How can that be?"

Nick glanced at the other men round the helm, all pretending not to be eavesdropping on this conversation with Lafayette. Discretion was called for here, and Nick put his lips close to the Marquis's ear. He whispered, "By some extraordinary means, sir. At any rate, you see, he's quite disappeared."

"Ah, *disappeared*, has he?" Lafayette said, and nodded his understanding. "Departed in a blaze of glory, I'd wager."

Nick smiled and nodded "yes."

Lafayette got to his feet after giving Valois a reassuring squeeze on the shoulder. "Corporal, get this man below to sickbay. Hot soup from the galley and a tot of rum. More rum if he needs it."

"And the battle, sir?" Nick asked, as two marines lifted Valois and carried him off to the ship's surgery to rest quietly until they had to leave the *Revenge*.

At that moment, one of the larger nearby pirate ships blew sky high, the explosion rocking the *Revenge* onto her beam ends. The vessel was no more than a pistol shot away. Her masts flew a hundred and fifty feet straight up into the air out of the cloud of fire and smoke that engulfed her. When the smoke cleared, all that remained were floating fragments and corpses, facedown in the sea. The results of a direct hit to the powder hold.

"See for yourself how the battle goes," Lafayette said, smiling as he eyed the trim of the mizzen sail above. "This audacious plan of yours is working beyond my wildest dreams of success. Look there off our port bow. The approaching vessel which just sank that pirate ship is *La Gloire*, Nicholas. The very last of Admiral de Grasse's twenty-eight ships of the line still within the scope of battle. All the others are safely through the pirate gauntlet and running before the wind for the Virginia coast!"

"Well done, sir!" Nick cried.

"Brilliant execution demands a brilliant plan, Nick."

Nick felt his cheeks redden and said, "Sir, when *La Gloire* is safely through, your plan is to abandon this ship?"

"It is indeed. We've no more need of her. Our marines and gun crews will disembark and board the longboat Valois arrived in. They will subsequently rendezvous with *La Gloire* for the voyage to Virginia."

"And you and me, sir? And Lieutenant Valois?"

"Why, Nick, Admiral de Grasse awaits us aboard the *Ville de Paris*, lying not half a mile from here, expecting a rendezvous. Once we are there, we'll see Valois attended to, after which we will retire to our cabin and fetch your wondrous orb from its hiding place."

"Return to Mount Vernon as planned?"

"*Mais oui!* To the little garden house. We shall arrive just before midnight on the night we departed. We'll be snug in our beds and get a good night's sleep before General Washington calls us down for breakfast. General de Rochambeau will be arriving at dawn with five thousand French troops. Then, it's on to Yorktown, where Lord Cornwallis awaits us behind his supposedly impregnable fortifications!"

Lafayette laughed at the notion of any fortifications sufficient to withstand the might and wrath of the combined array of French and American forces.

"I imagine Lord Cornwallis still expects to be rescued by sea at the last moment?" Nick asked.

"Of course. But he'll quickly be disabused of that notion when he sees Admiral de Grasse arrive off Yorktown with twenty-eight ships of the line and fifteen thousand in troops and crew!"

Nick grinned from ear to ear. "We did it after all, didn't we, sir? What General Washington asked of you."

"We well and surely did it, lad. And though no one on this good green earth will ever know about it, or by what outlandish methods we achieved it, you and I shall forever share this sweet victory, this happiest of all military secrets."

"It has been an honor, sir," Nick said.

"Yes. But the honor has been all mine," the Marquis de Lafayette replied, the two of them smiling at each other as bombs burst overhead.

"Helm, put her hard over!" Lafayette said. "Steer due north for a rendezvous with the *Ville de Paris*. My young friend and I have had quite enough of your shipmates' fireworks for one evening."

Nick nestled deep under the covers of his familiar old bed on the second floor at Mount Vernon. The grand estate was beginning to feel like home. Wide-eyed, too excited to sleep, he lay on his side staring through the open window, the dark Potomac sliding by, the countless stars dusting the heavens beyond. The house was quiet, but he thought he heard the soft patter of slippers, most probably Lucy climbing some secret staircase hidden behind his bedroom wall.

He rolled over, clasped his hands beneath his head, and stared at the ceiling. Next morning, General de Rochambeau would arrive from Williamsburg with five thousand more infantry and cavalry to reinforce the American and French troops already besieging Lord Cornwallis at Yorktown.

But, most exciting of all, was the brief conversation he'd had with Lafayette just before they'd wished each other a good-night in the garden house and slipped unseen through the gardens into the darkened mansion. Because of all the sentries lurking about, it was a hurried, whispered conversation, but it had thrilled Nick McIver to the bone.

The Marquis would be commanding one of the American divisions in the coming battle, he said. The Light Infantry. Then he had actually asked Nick to join him and General Washington on the journey to Yorktown next morning! Nick would serve as Lafayette's primary aide-de-camp and thus be an eyewitness to one of the most historic battles ever waged.

He turned over onto his side, closed his eyes, and waited for sleep. Images of home–his father, mother, and sister, Katie–filled his mind. Gunner, too, and his own good dog, Jipper. He'd been so involved in saving Admiral de Grasse's fleet, he'd had precious little time to consider those he loved most. He couldn't help but worry how they were faring under the German occupation, most especially his father now in hospital.

He'd know soon enough, he thought, drifting off. When he'd acquitted himself of his duties to General Lafayette, he would go home to little Greybeard Island. Once there, he and Gunner would no doubt resume the business of making life extremely uncomfortable for the invading Nazis. They'd lost the beautiful old Camel, sure, but there were other ways to . . . to . . .

He drifted off into a dream of glory.

There came a tapping at his door, and Nick wondered if it was part of his dream. Then he heard the door squeak open and saw Mrs. Washington's cheerful face peeking in at him. The whole room was bathed in a rosy glow, and he knew dawn had finally broken over Mount Vernon.

"Awake?"

"Yes, ma'am."

"Hungry, I'll bet," she said, coming across the room to his bed. "May I sit a moment?"

"Yes, ma'am."

She settled herself at the foot of his bed, arranging her voluminous skirts, and regarded him carefully. There was warmth in those beautiful eyes, Nick saw, but worry, too. Her hands were trembling, and she quickly hid them in the folds of her skirts.

"The old man tells me you're going to Yorktown as General Lafayette's aide-de-camp."

"The old man?"

"That's what I call my beloved husband. He calls me Patsy, even though my name is Martha. That's what twenty-two years of a happy marriage does to people. Silly, isn't it?"

"I don't think so. My poor departed mum and dad always used to call each other darling. My friend Gunner always used to say, 'And how are the Darlings this fine morning, Nicholas?'"

Mrs. Washington laughed for a moment and then composed herself. "So, it's true. You'll journey with the army to Yorktown this morning?"

"Yes, ma'am. General Lafayette asked me last evening. I was most honored to accept his kind and generous offer."

"Nick, listen to me. You are a dear boy. Kind and caring, and courageous too. I've grown quite fond of you in the short time you've been here at Mount Vernon. And I'm here to ask just one thing of you. Don't go to Yorktown. Please."

"Well, ma'am, I feel like I have to because–"

"Because nothing. You're a mere boy, not a soldier. Or even a drummer boy anymore. You don't have to do anything. It is going to be a ferocious battle, from what I hear. A fight to the death. Anything can happen. Knowing war as I do, it will happen. Suppose Lafayette's division of Light Infantry is overrun. Don't forget, you're a traitor to your king and country, Nicholas. Do you know what those redcoats will do to you if you're captured? I shudder even to think of it."

"Well, ma'am, I appreciate what you're saying, but I've never been one to run from a fight and—"

"Shh. Let me finish. The good Lord blessed me with four children. Three of them have long passed from this earth. Only my Jacky remains. This morning he asked his stepfather to allow him to go to Yorktown as one of the General's aides. The old man said yes."

"Well, I guess—"

"I've got a bad feeling about my son going, Nicholas. A very bad feeling. And that's partly why I'm here, asking you not to go. You see, I, well, I suppose I have developed something akin to motherly feelings for you, Nicholas. If something should happen to Jacky—well, I just couldn't stand to lose you, too."

For once, Nick found himself at a complete loss for words.

"You don't have to say anything. I just came up here to tell you how I felt. You'll make your own decision, I can see that. Now, you get dressed and hurry downstairs. Mum Bitt has laid out a splendid breakfast in honor of General de Rochambeau's arrival. General Washington wants everyone to have a hearty repast before the long journey south."

She stood up, looking down at him, clasping her hands under her chin as if in prayer. "I'll see you downstairs, I suppose," she said and, her eyes welling with tears, quickly turned away. When the door had closed behind her, Nick leaped out of bed, dressed, and hurried down to breakfast. There were some things about a boy, he supposed, that women just didn't understand.

———

An hour later, Nick found himself mounted on a handsome little paint named Chief, and riding beside General Lafayette. Ahead of them rode General Washington, his staff officers, and his aides, young Jacky among them. All were protected by Washington's personal unit, called the Commander-in-Chief's guard. These troops were responsible for the safety of the General's person and baggage, and they carried a distinctive white flag bearing a pictorial motif and a green scroll with the inscription CONQUER OR DIE.

Behind Washington, stretching for miles, was an army many thousands strong, the combined armies of General de Rochambeau and General Washington. The French troops alone numbered nearly eight thousand men.

The French infantrymen were brilliantly turned out in spotless white uniforms, their legs encased in white gaiters. Nearly all of them wore black three-cornered hats. And the magnificent regimental standards they carried were battle flags divided by white crosses with each quarter sporting a different color, corresponding to the division.

Most of the Continental infantrymen, by contrast, wore dark blue or black coats faced with red, white, or blue satin, corresponding to the regiment. The American cavalrymen wore short coats, buckskin breeches, and high boots called spatterdashes. But many of the Continentals, mostly militia, wore whatever bedraggled clothing they had, and far too many marched without shoes.

Seeing these brave and loyal men, their feet bloodied and

bruised by weeks of marching, Nick remembered something his father had told him long ago when he had complained about not having some silly nothing or other.

"I cried because I had no shoes, until I met a man who had no feet."

Among the militia were several hundred grizzled mountaineers. Sons of the Mountains they were called, a motley assembly of hardened outdoorsmen armed with long hunting rifles and a worthy reputation. These were the sharpshooters, and no one was more effective in a skirmish with the enemy. Despite their shabby attire, they were all soldierly looking, big men who endured privations, fatigue, and long marches without a murmur of discontent.

The army was traveling an ancient Indian path, now called the King's Highway. To Nick's amazement, the size of the army grew with every passing hour. French cavalry racing past them, eager to join their comrades already at the front; farmers and country people, some mounted and some on foot, all carrying the long small-caliber hunting rifles that had proven more accurate than military muskets.

The army spent the first night in Williamsburg, thousands of tents pitched on the green. A huge gala was held at the Governor's mansion in honor of General de Rochambeau, and Nick was thrilled to be invited. He delighted in the many toasts and tributes to Washington and Rochambeau, and the chorus of "Huzzah! Huzzah! Huzzah!" that followed each tribute.

A drenching rain marked the next day's march. It rained all night, and Nick had only his blanket between him and the ground. At the end of a very long march the next day, Nick got a whiff of sea air. Moments later he heard the dull thunder of distant artillery. After a journey of over a hundred miles, they were getting very close now, and couriers bearing dispatch satchels galloped by at breakneck speed, ferrying battlefield messages to Williamsburg and back.

By the time General Washington and the French commander, le Comte de Rochambeau, arrived at Yorktown, Virginia, on September 27, 1781, they were leading a combined force of seventeen thousand French and Colonial soldiers, including militia in rough clothing from all thirteen colonies.

Waiting for them inside the heavily fortified village called Yorktown were eight thousand redcoats. They were part of the finest army the world had ever seen, the elite of George III's expeditionary force to America. The enemy force included two veteran Anspach battalions and a Hessian regiment as well.

The British had built an elaborate system of earthworks and timber around the entire town. When they'd run out of trees, they'd taken to dismantling entire houses in the town of York, taking what wood they could find in an effort to reinforce their battlements.

As Nick rode on, he noticed that the woods on either side of the King's Highway had been decimated for British timber. The road was in awful condition. This was the route over which all of the allied armies behind him and all their wagons and cannon had to pass, along with the cavalry and all the cattle for feeding the troops.

"Nicholas," Lafayette suddenly said, "follow me. I want to show you something." He put spurs to his grey horse and galloped into the woods. Nick spurred his horse on, but having done little riding on his tiny island, he had a hard time keeping up with his new friend. Chief was no match for Lafayette's stallion.

When the path finally topped out at a clearing, Nick was

presented with a panoramic view of the entire battlefield spread out below. The tiny village of Yorktown, situated at the end of a peninsula jutting into the York River, was surrounded by British fortifications. The few houses left, mostly built of wood, were not grand, and the streets were very narrow. Beyond the river and an unbroken emerald green forest, he could see the broad blue Chesapeake Bay.

He reined in his horse. Lafayette was waiting patiently, surveying the scene below with the same spyglass he'd used aboard *Revenge*.

"Have a closer look," Lafayette said, barely able to contain his excitement at what he'd seen. He passed Nick the glass. Cornwallis had taken his stand at the tip of a peninsula. His only hope of escape was now the sea, and those hopes would be dashed with the timely arrival of Admiral de Grasse and the French fleet.

Below them lay the great field of battle itself. In the far distance, a few small British warships anchored in the York River. On the shore, the small town of York, now completely encircled by British fortifications. The earthworks, Nick guessed, were about twenty feet thick and a dozen feet high.

Outside the main fort was a system of redoubts. These were very small defensive emplacements linked by trenches. The trenches and redoubts were meant to protect British soldiers and artillery, forming a defensive perimeter outside the main lines of defense. To Nick, these redoubts looked hastily built, earthworks and timber, although one large star-shaped redoubt on the right flank looked sturdy enough.

Nothing was foreordained. Success hinged upon so many factors: meticulous planning, mistakes, weather, and the commonplace unpredictability of warfare.

The British artillery fire was louder now, followed by tiny

puffs of reddish dirt, explosions that certainly looked harmless enough at this distance. But Nick knew a ball could take off a man's limbs and even his head. And that the mortar shells now bursting above were sending red-hot shards of deadly metal flying through the air, shredding flesh and bone. Thick with shot, ball, and shell, this battlefield was no place for the weakhearted.

In the near distance, he could see the many large tents, or marquees as they were called, of the allied commands, brightly colored regimental flags snapping in the breeze atop their tentpoles. To Nick's left, the solid white flags of France stood out amongst the endless ranks of French troops in their white uniforms, marching in tight formation, precise in their movements.

In the center, between the French and the American positions, stood a large striped marquee, probably Washington's. It stood behind a ten-gun battery of heavy artillery, barrels all trained on the British garrison. Their mission, in addition to enemy bombardment, was to protect the Commander-in-Chief at all costs.

"You see below you the order of battle, Nick," Lafayette said. "The army's left wing, deployed south, southwest, and west of Yorktown, constitutes the entire French Army of seven infantry regiments, plus artillery and cavalry. When our fresh troops arrive today, we will have 8,600 French soldiers under arms. To the right is the Continental Army, 8,280 men, full complement. A fine sight, is it not?"

"Where is your command, sir?" Nick asked.

"With the Continentals, of course. See the three large marquees on the northwest side, to the far right? Those are the division commanders. The forward tent, closest to the enemy lines, belongs to General Benjamin Lincoln, Washington's second-in-command. The middle marquee is my own Light Infantry headquarters, and behind us stands that of Thomas Nelson, former governor of Virginia, who has forsaken the creature comforts of his palace at Williamsburg for the glories of this historic battlefield."

"The army has been digging trenches, too, I see," Nick said. There were scores of blue-coated Continentals in the trenches, firing muskets over the parapet at the British redoubts, then ducking down inside the trenches to reload.

"Yes. Every night, hordes of diggers, miners, and sappers, who plant the explosives, dig new trenches parallel to the British lines, each one closer to the British garrison than the one before. The final trench, when complete, will be only eight hundred yards from the enemy's defenses.

"The men work through the night in absolute silence. And thanks to all the rain, the soil is damp and loamy. Makes for easier digging. The dirt removed is used to create earthworks on the enemy side of the trench. Then reinforced with timber and sharpened protruding stakes of timber called fraising.

"Every trench is four feet deep and ten feet wide. Deep enough to protect the men from enemy fire, and large enough to handle carriages with siege cannon and ammunition. Eventually, parapets will be mounted atop all of the earthworks, made of tight bundles of twigs, to provide additional protection. An elementary component of siege warfare, Nick," Lafayette said, ending his lesson.

"Looks like the French are copying the Continentals' trenches over on their left side of the battlefield," Nick said, pointing out freshly dug trenches full of troops in white uniforms to his left.

Lafayette smiled at the boy's naiveté. "Hardly copying, Nick. The ancient art of the siege is essentially an exercise in engineering, which happens to be one of the Continental army's major weaknesses. Fortunately, the French Army includes the best military engineers in the world. We have been perfecting the art of siege warfare for well over five centuries. And soon both allied armies will be breathing fire down Cornwallis's fat English neck."

First came the rising smoke, then the sound of another fusillade of artillery from inside the British compound, cannonballs flying and eight-inch shells bursting overhead. Nick was surprised to see no answering volley from the allies, and could not help but wonder why the battle was so one-sided.

"They fire their cannon and mortar, but we don't return it, sir. Why?" Nick asked.

"General Washington's orders. We'll not fire a single cannon until every last one of our guns is in place. We are still awaiting the vital siege guns carried aboard Admiral de Grasse's fleet. Should we fire an isolated cannon now, the enemy would simply concentrate on that one and destroy it. No, we shall not fire a shot until every battery is ready to open up at precisely the same moment."

"Makes sense."

"Indeed. He does that quite a lot."

"Look!" Nick cried, "The white steed! The General is arriving at his headquarters."

Nick sensed a great commotion rising up the hill from below. Washington, astride a fresh warhorse, arrived in front of his marquee to the sound of beating drums, flying flags, and the shouts and cheers of his men.

As Nick watched, the long column of allied troops split in half and took diverging roads: the French to join their comrades already encamped on the left side of the battlefield, the Continentals going to the right.

"We should be off, Nick. The General is to hold a briefing for all division commanders in his tent in one half hour."

"After you, sir," Nick said, but Lafayette never heard him. He was already galloping down the hill through the scraggly woods, hellbent for leather, as if he had a date with destiny. Which, after all, Lafayette, as well as every man at Yorktown, truly did.

Nick's first five days as Lafayette's youngest aide-de-camp were notable for two very different reasons.

One, he found himself constantly scurrying back and forth across the battlefield, racing on foot but frequently on horseback, between the headquarters and staff marquee of General George Washington, his own Light Infantry headquarters, and every other divisional headquarters, French or American, behind the allied lines. Nick soon knew why he'd been given Chief. The little paint was resolutely calm under fire.

Every one of the wax-sealed dispatches, he was told, was of "vital importance." Most were marked MOST URGENT. Sleeping little, he soon pushed himself to exhaustion, riding Chief hard day and night through the scrim of haze and smoke rising from the hundreds of smoldering campfires in and around Yorktown.

And, two, scarcely a minute went by when he and his horse weren't dodging whistling British cannonballs. He kept a running count. There were about forty balls an hour during daylight hours, the number dropping to ten or less after darkness fell. But the thunderous roar of artillery never ceased, ever. At night, the British mortar shells would arc overhead, trailing a long tail of fire, and explode in a hailstorm of lethal shrapnel.

And still, to Nick's puzzlement and dismay, the Americans did not return the favor.

One fine morning, Nick was standing outside Washington's headquarters, awaiting the General's reply to yet another disheartening dispatch from Lafayette. These daily updates were regarding the still unknown whereabouts of Admiral de Grasse. As usual on these occasions, the General's noble face gave evidence of the war between hope and despair raging inside him as he tore open the seal.

The hardest part of Nick's job was seeing the pain of disappointment in Washington's eyes each day when he opened yet another disappointing dispatch. If only Nick could tell the General that his worries and fears were unfounded, that the pirate armada had been soundly routed and—but of course he could not.

As Washington handed Nick his hastily scrawled reply, an amazing thing happened. A British cannonball slammed into the earth not three feet from where Nick and the famous General stood. It showered them both with dirt, with Nick taking the brunt of it. Nick was naturally terrified at the near miss, but Washington just laughed it off and said, "Nicholas, you should take that ball home with you and show your friends what a brave boy you are."

Nick opened his mouth to reply and discovered it was full of rich, dark Virginia soil.

Day after day, Nick watched the French and American army engineers raising their artillery batteries. Building earthen walls to surround the guns, they next cut embrasures, or openings, through which the artillery officers pointed the muzzles of their guns at the enemy. They also flattened and firmed the earth, excavating it if necessary, to receive the French-designed *heurtoirs*, which were heavy wooden artillery platforms, where the siege guns would be mounted and carefully aimed.

As for Cornwallis and the British Army, rumors were that they grew increasingly desperate, fearing that none of the much-promised help from Major General Clinton in New York was on the way. No supplies, no powder or ammunition, no food or forage for horses. And, most important, no last-minute escape to the sea, should the battle turn against them.

The noose was tightening, Nick McIver knew, but it would not be secure until de Grasse arrived. And this was the precarious situation that bedeviled them all and haunted General Washington's every waking moment. Even Nick was anxious. After all, who was to say a powerful hurricane had not made a mockery of all their efforts?

The previous afternoon, Nick had overheard a British infantry deserter from inside the enemy garrison give an eyewitness account of their plight. He was telling staff officers at Washington's headquarters that the situation inside was appalling. The men were working day and night strengthening the lines with little time even to eat the wormy biscuits, all that remained of their food. Just that morning, Cornwallis had ordered four hundred horses shot for want of forage. They'd been thrown into the York River, but their bloated corpses had soon washed ashore and the smell was overwhelming.

Sickness, either smallpox or camp fever, was rampant. This was especially true among the Negro soldiers and slaves, and the dead or dying were everywhere throughout the town. Cornwallis was banishing those who could still walk, hoping the deadly infections would spread within the American camp. Fever, he said, was every bit as lethal as a bullet.

Inside Washington's command, the mood was tense. This involved the daily expectation of the arrival of Admiral de Grasse's fleet. Lafayette had assured Washington he had ordered a swift frigate to sail southward from Saint Augustine on the Florida coast in hopes of intercepting de Grasse, and warning him of the pirate armada waiting in ambush.

Despite his overwhelming disbelief that the American swift frigate would reach the French fleet in time, Washington clung to the distant notion of success. He maintained a constant demeanor of confidence around his aides. All of whom well knew that without the arrival of de Grasse, there was always the chance Cornwallis could slip the ever-tightening noose. His troops could yet escape aboard British warships, known even now to be en route southward from the port at New York to effect their rescue.

As the days passed, even Lafayette grew anxious. Where was the great fleet he and Nicholas had so miraculously saved? According to schedules on the charts Nick had stolen, de Grasse should certainly have arrived by now. Had he encountered some great storm at sea that had delayed or even, God forbid, destroyed the fleet? Nick, equally alarmed, attempted to allay Lafayette's fears, but the Marquis said until he saw that fleet sailing up the Chesapeake Bay, he would not rest easy.

———

One morning, after a week of unremitting rain, the day dawned blue and clear. Washington, much invigorated by the climatic change, immediately ordered that the trenches be "enlivened" with colors flying and drums beating. He assigned an entire division to rapidly carry out his orders. The divisional and regimental colors were to be planted atop the parapets, and every division would fly the motto: *Manus haec inimica tyrannis.*

"'This hand an enemy to tyrants,'" Lafayette had told Nick when asked what the Latin expression meant. He then handed the boy a sealed missive marked MOST URGENT and told him to deliver it posthaste to General Washington personally. There was a small smile lurking about the Frenchman's eyes when he handed over the dispatch. Nick, as he leaped into the saddle and charged across the battlefield toward Washington's headquarters, could not help but hope his satchel contained the good news they were all desperately hoping for. Of course, such high hopes had been been dashed before. Always best to assume the worst, he reminded himself.

Arriving at headquarters, Nick was surprised to find that Washington had ordered his battlefield command desk moved outside his marquee. The General clearly wanted the sunshine and fresh air after the suffocating days inside the damp tent. As usual, the boy arrived out of breath and stood before the great man, huffing and puffing for some moments before he could speak.

"Excellency, I bring news from General Lafayette," Nick said, placing the wax-sealed dispatch before Washington. The General's face went dark and glum as if bad weather had entered his mind.

"I scarcely wish to read it," he murmured, hurriedly breaking the seal. "How much longer are we to be left dangling by this infernal French thread?"

He scanned Lafayette's elegant scrawl quickly, moving his

lips as he softly spoke the words written there. At first, his expression was one of disbelief, but it was quickly dispersed as the light of pure joy flooded his eyes. Tears threatened but were immediately vanquished. "It's the hand of Providence," he said quietly to Nick. "A miracle. The only possible explanation for it, I tell you."

"May I ask what has happened?" Nick said, hoping he was not being impertinent.

"De Grasse has arrived!" Washington cried, leaping to his feet and shouting. "The fleet is even now stationed at Lynnhaven Bay in the Chesapeake, guarding the entrance to the York and James Rivers. Twenty-eight ships of the line and four frigates! That will give the Royal Navy's Captains something to think about should they dare approach us."

Rochambeau stepped outside the tent just as Washington flung his hat high into the air.

"Do my ears deceive me?" the French commander asked his friend and ally.

"They do not, sir!" Washington exclaimed. The two men, who had had their differences, now regarded each other for a moment, and then embraced warmly, clapping each other on the back and exchanging words of almost rapturous joy. To Nick, it looked as if the two old soldiers might leap into the air or begin dancing an Irish jig at any moment. He stood transfixed, watching them. The grave importance of this moment in history was not lost on him.

Without Kate's stalwart bravery while kidnapped at Port Royal, without Lafayette's willingness to embrace Nick's improbable tale of the Tempus Machina and act decisively on it, these momentous few seconds of history might never have occurred. And the England he knew and loved would be no more.

As more and more staff officers emerged from the tent and joined in the common revelry, General Washington disengaged himself for a moment and took Nick aside. "Your commanding officer, Nicholas, my dear friend Lafayette, has done our great cause an inestimable service."

"Do you wish me to return with that message, sir?"

"No, Nicholas. Lafayette has informed me that he is heading down to Trebell's Landing, several miles southwest of Yorktown. There, he intends to supervise the unloading of numerous transport vessels from the French fleet. Then he will commence the transport to Yorktown of what he believes and I will concede is a most welcome shipment. Do you know what he means by that, young Master McIver?"

"No, sir."

"It's the siege guns, for all love!" Washington cried. "Do you hear that, *mon Général*?" he said to Rochambeau. "In a matter of hours we shall at long last have the means with which to seal Lord Cornwallis's much-deserved fate! May the Lord bless us all this happy and long-awaited hour."

The possibility of Cornwallis's escape, which had haunted General Washington's every waking moment for months, was finally over. And America's guns would soon answer the British artillery, roaring in anger.

THIS IS A HERO, NICK THOUGHT

W ashington's hour was at hand.

The two opposing armies shivered under an unexpected chill throughout the night of October 8. But things would get very much warmer the next day, of that Nicholas McIver was certain as he finally found sleep beneath his thin woolen blanket. For the first time in recent memory, the British guns had fallen silent. "Conserving their powder for the morrow," one of the young Light Infantry soldiers had told him around the campfire supper.

Nick slept fitfully and awoke at dawn to much warmer temperatures and overcast skies. He could see that the sappers and the miners had been at work throughout the night, ferrying ammunition and powder through the trenches. They continued their dangerous work as the rising sun sent hazy orange rays stretching across the smoky battlefield, even though they were harried by musket fire from the British garrison.

At 9 A.M., Lafayette's Light Infantry struck their tents and repositioned to the right and forward, near the southernmost American battery, a formidable sight now that it was complete. It contained three 24-pounders, three 18-pounders, two 8-inch howitzers, and six 10-inch mortars mounted on carriages capable of throwing shot directly into the enemy's earthworks, where they would burst, destroying the works.

Spirits among the entire army were high to the point of soaring. To Nick, this was something entirely new, and Lafayette confirmed his feelings, saying that the morale of the troops this morning was higher than he'd witnessed at any time during this long and bloody war. Or in any war.

"It's time," he said with a smile. "Mount up!"

"Mount up?" Nick asked.

"Look behind you."

There was Lafayette's horse, curried and combed and splendidly turned out for battle. His own beloved Chief looked nearly as magnificent. Nick smiled and took the reins from the groom. Then, sticking his left foot into the stirrup, he swung himself up into the saddle. He seemed to have gotten much more comfortable riding horses since his arrival at Yorktown. At least he'd grown to like it, thanks to Chief's forgiving nature.

"Where to, sir?" Nick asked.

"Commander in Chief's headquarters. A small ceremony General Washington has arranged. I don't think we'll want to miss it!"

He laughed, put his spurs to his horse, and galloped away at full speed. Nick followed, his heart thudding with excitement. They arrived and dismounted, running toward the vociferous crowd of officers, both French and American, who were gathering outside the General's tent.

There was a massive group gathered round the ten-gun artillery battery that guarded Washington's marquee. All the men seemed to be on tiptoe, peering back at Washington's tent, waiting for him to emerge, anticipation and impatience written on every face. As Nick scanned the huge battlefield, he could see that every allied soldier and cavalryman had his eyes on the General's grand battery.

Where was the heroic figure most of them regarded as father and savior? Wherever was Washington?

Nick shivered with excitement. Another historic moment was about to occur, and once again he was right in the thick of it. A breeze had come up and blown the grey scrim of clouds away. It was now twelve noon on a glorious and sunny autumn day.

When he heard the thunderous roar of thousands upon thousands of troops, Nick knew the great man had at last stepped outside into the sunlight.

Lafayette, overcome with pride and emotion, laughed at the tears that welled up in his eyes and swiped them away with the back of his hand. He looked at Nick, placing a hand on his shoulder and squeezing it. "The hour is upon us," he said, his voice choked with feeling.

"What is happening?" Nick asked.

"Everyone is waiting for the signal that will permit the whole line of our batteries to commence firing."

"Will I recognize the signal?"

"Oh, yes. I don't imagine you need worry about missing it, Nicholas McIver."

Every eye was on a resplendent Washington as he approached the Grand American Battery, flanked by adjutants and aides. Nick had never known another human being who radiated supreme confidence and strength the way Washington did. His men, in fact all Americans, clearly revered him as godlike. Now, in the set of his jaw and the fierce look in his eye, Nick saw why.

Washington's courage and stamina and fortitude had been

tested these last five years, tested in cauldrons of fire and freezing winter storms, tested far beyond the endurance of mere mortals; and he had been found not wanting in any aspect. Because of *him*, the Americans were about to defeat the mightiest empire on earth.

This is a hero.

That was Nick's sole thought as he watched Washington turn to his second-in-command and give him an order.

His words were lost in the tumultuous shouts of thousands, but Nick soon saw what orders the General had given.

It was a single American flag, rising slowly but surely up the flagpole in the center of the grand battery. The colorful flag had red and white stripes and thirteen white stars on a field of blue, representing the thirteen courageous American colonies. As it rose, so, too, did the white banner over the French batteries to Nick's left and the Continental flag over the American batteries on the right. Nick felt a secret pride swell inside his heart as the American flag reached the top, standing out full in the breeze.

Someone nearby shouted, "Happy day! Forty-one mouths of fire are now about to be unmasked!"

Drummers everywhere commenced great rolling tattoos of battle as the artillerymen parted to let General Washington step forward. He paused at the massive cannon at the very center of the battery.

Why, he's going to fire the first shot, Nick thought, and that is just what happened.

Washington strode forward and ignited the fuse of the 24-pounder. These guns could bite hard, sending a ball through two feet of solid oak at seven hundred yards. He

This is a hero.

stood clear, as the piece boomed forth the first American artillery salute to Cornwallis's gunners. The gun spat fire, bucking and bellowing with a thunderous roar. A great cry of "Huzzah! Huzzah! Huzzah!" rose from the battlefield at the sound of it.

A Continental soldier near the front told Nick a few days afterward that he could actually hear the first ball Washington fired strike from house to house inside the enemy garrison. And, he said, he'd been informed that it ultimately went through a house where British officers were having their midday meal, down the length of the table, destroying the dishes and killing the British General at the very end, who had just raised a leg of mutton to his mouth.

The battle was joined.

All the officers attending the ceremony now hurried off to join their men. Lafayette and Nick rejoined their division, now successfully attacking British Redoubt No. 10. The American infantrymen had bayonets affixed to their muzzles, while other soldiers simply had the bayonets attached to the ends of long wooden pikes. The screams of the wounded and dying mingled with war cries from the bluecoats and the redcoats alike.

It was all vicious hand-to-hand fighting, with the clang of metal on metal, pistols fired at point-blank range doing horrific damage to human faces and, above all, the wailing cries of the mortally wounded. Nick had no idea who was getting the best of it until he saw a lone soldier plant a standard atop the British earthworks and unfurl the Continental flag. As it stood, proudly whipping and snapping in the freshening wind, the bluecoats surged forward to the next line of defense.

And now Nick saw and heard every American artillery battery, left and right, open fire in a fierce cannonade. All guns were lobbing their deadly missiles into the confines of Yorktown with steady precision. Seeing the effects of their efforts, the gunners then sought to adjust and correct their pieces so as to cause the utmost damage to Cornwallis's defensive works.

This heavy allied artillery bombardment afforded the troops a desperately needed release from six years of pent-up emotions, past humiliations, and defeats. Now they went on the attack with the utmost fury. No quarter of the British garrison was spared, from the outer perimeter, to the main works, to the interior of the town itself. At every discharge combatants fell before the guns like grass before a mowing machine.

The intense American and French cannon and mortar fire soon took its deadly toll. The guns' first job was to take the enemy artillery out of action. For that, the 24-pounders with a range of nearly 1,400 yards proved especially useful. Second to ruining British guns was destroying their embrasures, those slanted openings in their parapets from which they fired at the oncoming Americans. This and the destruction of the main defensive earthworks caused havoc behind the lines, driving enemy soldiers back from the ramparts.

The brutal pounding of the British Army continued long into that first night, and Nick slept not a wink, the incessant concussion and noise of the nearby cannon was so great.

With dawn's early light, the grand French battery opened fire, bombarding the enemy position with their big 18- and 24-pounders. The French artillerymen had vast experience in siege warfare, and their accuracy was unfailing. It was becoming increasingly clear to the enemy that they could expect to find no refuge either inside or outside of Yorktown.

Finally admitting the inevitable, the remaining civilian residents of the town, mostly British loyalists, fled their homes for the waterfront. There they built what shelters they could on the sandy cliffs. Still, some eighty of the townsfolk were killed, many with arms or legs severed. The survivors could only watch in horror as their houses were destroyed by incessant allied fire.

It was the most extraordinary display of firepower of the entire war. Over the course of that single day, more than thirty-six hundred heavy rounds were fired by Washington's artillery. By that afternoon, the allied cannonade was so intense, British defenders could scarcely fire a gun of their own. The British earthworks, fascines, and stockade platforms with guns and gun carriages were all pounded together into one great unrecognizable mass. Decapitated and dismembered corpses littered the interior of the garrison, the wounded dying, the dead unburied. Cornwallis's troops had a hollow-eyed look that told the British General more than he wanted to know.

It was at this point that Lord Cornwallis decided to personally run for cover. He ordered an underground grotto built in the garden of a house far from the front lines. A good deal dispirited, he still made a great show of having no apprehension of the garrison's falling. Few believed him.

If Cornwallis was apprehensive at the obvious superiority the allies had attained in sheer firepower, he surely wrung his hands in despair upon seeing that the remaining American and French batteries were now complete. A total of fifty-two big guns were now aligned against him, roaring continuously, he said in a desperate dispatch to Sir Henry Clinton, firing in what he called "an awful music."

The allies had launched a thunderous assault that dwarfed anything the British had experienced previously. This new bombardment sent British soldiers careening away from their own battlements in fear and trepidation. But there was nowhere to run.

So incessant was the allied firepower that after a single hour the British guns temporarily failed to respond at all. Their weapons were either too damaged to fire or their gunners' positions along the works had become too hazardous to maintain. The allies had suffered only a handful of casualties. And their guns kept firing.

By October 11, two days after the allies had unleashed their guns, the American parallel directed at Cornwallis's works was within 360 yards of the most advanced enemy post. At dusk that day, the miners and sappers entered the zigzag trench and began digging a second parallel, even closer to the enemy fortifications.

The entire night, Nick observed, there was an immense roar of bursting shell and the diggers were glad of the chance to burrow into the soft earth. Everyone knew this opening of a new parallel was the most hazardous moment of the entire siege, since it was almost certain to draw enemy soldiers out to prevent its completion.

American guards stood watch over the digging for the entire night, muskets at the ready, with strict orders not to sit or lie down. These men were at grave peril, not only from the enemy but from their own gunners in the first parallel. Sometimes American artillerymen accidentally cut their fuses too short. But when morning dawned, miraculously, not a man had been killed.

Bombshells from both besieger and besieged crossed one another's paths in the air. During daylight hours, the bombs were clearly visible in the form of black balls. But at night they appeared to be fiery meteors with long, brilliantly blazing tails, ascending almost majestically from the mortars to a desired altitude and then descending to the precise spot where they would cause the most destruction. The falling shells burrowed into the earth before exploding. Bursting, they hurled fragments of mangled bodies some twenty feet into the air.

And still the battle raged on for four long days.

On the eve of October 15, Lord Cornwallis sat down at his subterranean camp desk and penned the following dispatch, using a cipher, to be delivered to his chief, Clinton, in New York.

My situation now becomes very critical. We dare not show a gun to their old batteries, and I expect that new ones will open fire tomorrow morning. Our fresh earthworks do not resist their powerful artillery, so that we shall soon be exposed to an assault in ruined works, in a bad position, with weakened numbers. The safety of this place is so precarious that I cannot recommend the fleet or army run great risk in endeavoring to save us.

Cornwallis had seen enough.

Under all these circumstances, I thought it would have been wanton and inhuman to the last degree to sacrifice the lives of this small body of gallant soldiers, who have ever behaved with such fidelity and courage, by exposing them to an assault, which from the numbers and precautions of the enemy could not fail to succeed. I therefore propose to capitulate.

Nick was exhausted after another long and sleepless night, but he was up with the dawn, sensing the end was near. Over the rolling battlefield lay a heavy blanket of grey smoke, tinged with red by the rising sun. From the British, only sporadic musket fire. From the Americans, the deafening thunder he had come to think of as nearly a natural part of life. Death, too, had become an almost natural part of life. It was everywhere, and he was sure far, far worse inside the enemy garrison.

He had just taken a tin mug of warm cocoa in his hands from the mess sergeant when one of Lafayette's officers approached him with a message. It would require him to go very close to the enemy fortifications, such as they were now, and the officer warned him to take great care. He was gratified that the men of the Light Infantry seemed to have taken him under their wing. He felt a true spirit of comradeship with them.

Edging his way carefully around Redoubt No. 10, he stopped dead in his tracks, scarcely daring to believe what he saw. A red-coated young British drummer boy, no older than himself, mounted the enemy pararpet and began to beat a parley on his regimental battle drum. This was the sound the allies had been waiting for. It meant the British command wanted to talk.

Almost immediately, a British officer made his appearance outside what remained of the Yorktown works. He was waving a white handkerchief. It was the age-old symbol of truce. The English, Nick knew, wanted to talk. The batteries ceased fire immediately, and an officer from the American lines quickly ran out to meet the British officer. He took the handkerchief and blindfolded the enemy soldier with it. It was only then that Nick saw the enemy officer was also carrying the British flag.

The drummer boy was sent back inside the garrison, and the British officer was quickly conducted across the battle-field to a house at the rear of the American lines.

One of Lafayette's infantrymen sidled up to Nick and said, "Never heard a drum equal to that one–the most delightful music to us all."

"He was very brave to climb up there," Nick said, full of admiration for the boy.

"That drummer was fortunate he was so visible," the man said. "Had we not seen him in his red coat when he first mounted, he might have beat away till doomsday. What with the noise of our cannon, the sound of a single drum didn't stand a chance."

The British officer carrying the flag from Cornwallis bore a message for General Washington. The Commander in Chief, however, was in the midst of serious logistical discussions with his second in command, at his headquarters behind the lines. He was curtly told to await permission to disturb Washington.

Shortly, a mounted Continental officer pulled up outside the marquee, bringing the letter the blindfolded British officer had handed him. Upon receipt of the letter, General Washington broke the seal and opened the single sheet of paper upon which was written the following:

Sir, I propose a cessation of hostilities for twenty-four hours, and that two officers may be appointed by each side, to meet at Mr. Moore's house to settle terms for the surrender of the posts at York and Gloucester. I have the honour to be, etc.

Cornwallis

October 19, 1781. It was a glorious autumn day, the leaves of the trees just beginning to turn shades of red and gold. It was small comfort to the remnants of a great expeditionary army known as the Pride of Britain. This day would find them humbled to a greater degree than they had ever suffered before.

Around noon, to the sound of endless rolling drums, the victorious allied armies marched out and lined up, two ranks deep, on both sides of the Hampton Road from the village of Yorktown. The Americans were on the right, the French on the left. These triple ranks of uniformed men stretched for more than a mile from the British garrison.

Waiting at the farthest end from Yorktown were gathered the American and French commanders of the allied forces and their ranking officers, all mounted on horseback.

At the head of the American line was General George Washingon, his horse, Blueskin, snorting and pawing the ground. He was flanked by his second in command, General Benjamin Lincoln to one side, and General Lafayette on the other. On the French side of the line, Generals de Rochambeau and Barras, splendidly turned out, sat their horses facing the Americans.

This was their finest hour. And they were waiting patiently for this final moment of triumph to commence.

Ordinary country people, from every nook and cranny and bog, sensing history in the making, came from miles around, their numbers swelling beyond count as the day wore on. Even now, the torn and blackened battlefield behind the triple lines of soldiers bulged with wildly cheering citizens.

Boys dangled precariously from every treetop; farmers stood teetering atop fence posts, all hoping for a glimpse of the proud man who had so reviled and disparaged the Continental army over the course of this long and bloody struggle. They'd all come out to see the haughty Lieutenant General Charles Cornwallis, in all his frippery and finery, get his long overdue comeuppance.

It was Nick McIver's great good fortune that his horse was standing directly adjacent to that of his superior officer, the Marquis de Lafayette. Nick felt badly for his fellow aides-de-camp, now standing on tiptoe, but he knew his vaunted position alongside the officers was due only to Lafayette's unspoken acknowledgment of certain secret services he had performed in the course of this battle. Nick inhaled deeply, taking it all in.

The French troops, tall, handsome, and well washed, as was their wont, were splendidly turned out, their pristine white uniforms, various colored lapels, designating their regiments, brilliant in the sun. The colors of France, a pure white banner, fluttered above the heads of each regiment.

Facing them from across the dusty road stood their comrades in arms, the men of the United States Army. They, too, stood proudly at attention, eyes front. But they wore shabby blue uniforms, ragged and soiled. Many stood barefoot but unashamed. The American militiamen among their ranks wore a motley assortment of soiled and irregular uniforms. Some were clothed in the leather hunting shirts and breeches associated with backwoodsmen along the frontier. These were the men of the mountains, the men with the long barrels, the scourge of Cornwallis.

Many of these brave soldiers had endured six long years of punishing and bloody warfare. Among those standing in these lines under the blazing Virginia sun were survivors of the earliest fights at Concord and Bunker Hill. Nick assumed it was these soldiers who took in this moment with more pain and satisfaction than any other soldier present on this final field.

They had suffered every hardship imaginable. Despite hunger, tedium, and no pay, they had managed to survive the killing winters at Valley Forge and Morristown, many of them without blankets or even shoes. Still, few if any of these brave souls now present had any idea of the magnitude of what they had so gloriously accomplished.

They had not only secured the independence of the American colonies but, eventually, changed the history of the world.

Battle-torn American regimental standards, some in tattered ribbons, waved over the Continental lines, while from across the road the stirring music of the French military band, the only such band in America, helped soldiers pass the time until the British appeared.

At two o'clock, it was possible to hear the distant sounds of British fifes and drums coming from Yorktown. It was a signal that the defeated army was assembling behind the garrison walls. The waiting allied armies, the men who had finally shattered the all-powerful British force, went suddenly silent.

At three o'clock, legions of the vanquished army finally appeared, the mounted officers riding through a large hole blasted in their now-demolished fortifications. The officers were followed by the conquered troops in a slow and solemn step. They came with shouldered arms and their colors cased, as Washington had insisted. This was his final retaliation for the many times victorious British generals had refused surrendering Americans the "honors of war."

As the scarlet coats drew nearer, Nick could see the mortification and unfeigned sorrow on the faces of the defeated soldiers. Some cursed, some had tears coursing down their cheeks, and some hid their eyes beneath the great round hats they wore. All the spirit and courage that normally animated the soldiers had slipped from them.

Nick felt a twinge of guilt at the sight of them. But overpowering such feelings was the true belief that he had done what was best for his country. Yes, he had done his duty.

As the group of mounted officers at the forefront of the British Army crested a hill, Nick whispered to Lafayatte, "Which one is Cornwallis?"

"It seems our dear Cornwallis much prefers to lead his army in victory rather than defeat. He pleads illness keeps him confined to his quarters. That redheaded officer riding in the lead is his second in command, General O'Hara. It is he who shall present the sword of surrender to General Washington."

"Isn't that a grave insult to his own troops, for Cornwallis not to lead them at their surrender?" Nick asked. He didn't know much about the finer points of military courtesy, but he knew right from wrong.

"Unforgivable," Lafayette said, "but not surprising. Since Cornwallis has always maintained such an exalted opinion of his own military prowess and viewed the Americans as contemptible, undisciplined rabble, he now finds himself humiliated beyond measure. General Washington is disgusted at this behavior, I will tell you."

"What was his reaction when he learned of this?"

"Washington said a great commander should be above such pettiness and not shrink from the inevitable misfortunes of war. Cornwallis, after all, has often appeared in triumph at the head of his army, and so ought he to participate manfully in their misfortunes as well, no matter how humiliating."

The two watched as General O'Hara rode over to General Washington, explained that Cornwallis was still unfortunately "indisposed," and offered the American leader his sword. This ancient symbolic act acknowledged defeat.

Washington looked at it a moment and waved it away, indicating to O'Hara that he should present the sword to General Benjamin Lincoln, Washington's own second in command. A hush fell over the battlefield as Lincoln took the sword, held it aloft for all to see. Lincoln then pointed the defeated General to the cleared field where he and his army were to "ground arms," or lay down their muskets.

Victory.

Nick could find no words to describe the mighty cry that arose from the victorious soldiers and the vast assembly at the sight of that British sword raised high by the American General. It was the concentrated expression of surprise, joy, pride, and relief that the long and bloody struggle was over. Then the storm burst forth at the highest intensity: a storm of yelling, shouting, stamping the earth, and waving flags, muskets, and swords in the air. The entire battlefield shook with the reverberations of these celebrations.

Once the British had sullenly and angrily grounded all their arms in the designated field, the defeated army turned and retraced their steps, back to a Yorktown now wholly occupied by American and French soldiers. When the last of them had disappeared over the rolling landscape of the battlefield, Nick was surprised to see General Washington put his spurs to Blueskin and head directly toward Lafayette.

He reined in his great warhorse and smiled with sheer delight at Nick and Lafayette.

"My dear comrade," he said to the Marquis, "the Continental Congress has ordered a special medal be struck in recognition of bravery, gallantry, and great achievement. It is my very great honor and privilege to bestow the very first one struck upon you, my dear friend, Marie-Joseph-Paul-Yves-Roch-Gilbert du Motier, Marquis de Lafayette."

Nick smiled at the use of Lafayette's full name, but his eyes were on his new friend. No one deserved this more than the gallant Frenchman who had risked all for a country not his own.

As Washington pinned the shining medal on the Marquis's uniform, the sun caught it and the glint lit up Lafayette's eyes. They were brimming with tears. He reached toward Washington and after a quick embrace, the American general, perhaps the greatest leader of men the world had ever seen, galloped away at full tilt, his great cause now finally secure.

———

Lafayette watched in silence as his friend and hero rode off to join in the chaos of celebration already forming in front of

Washington's marquee and wherever men gathered on the battlefield. After a few moments he turned to Nick.

"Have you the golden orb on your person, Nicholas?" he asked.

"Always, sir," Nick said, patting the pouch slung under his left arm.

"Follow me, then, lad!" he cried and galloped away.

Nick put spurs to Chief and tried valiantly to catch up. Within a few minutes, he knew exactly where Lafayette was headed.

The General was waiting for him when he arrived at the clearing atop the hill overlooking the battlefield. It seemed like months since they'd first seen this vista together, and it was much altered from that first time. Thousands had died on this pockmarked and hallowed ground. Only the camp-fires sending their smoke skyward remained unchanged. Something was missing and Nick realized it was the thunder of guns. The mortars were muzzled and the heads of the cannon hung low. The battlefield was as still as death.

"Time for you to go home, I suppose," Lafayette said.

"I suppose so, sir."

"My heart is so full of things I wish to tell you that I cannot summon a single one. I can only thank you from the bottom of my heart, Nicholas McIver."

"I am deeply grateful for your trust, sir. And—so much more. So terribly much that I don't know how to—"

"Say no more, Nicholas. But, listen, I want you to have this. It rightly belongs to you, and I would have given my right arm to tell General Washington so. But of course I could not. Without your help and bravery in coming here to America, we should have lost this battle and, with it, this war. It's a pity Washington will never know."

Lafayette began to unfasten the medal from his breast.

"No, sir! It belongs to you! General Washington awarded it to you! You have fought at his side for six long years."

Lafayette smiled. "I'm still a young man, Nick, a military man to the bone. There will be plenty of battles and more medals perhaps. This one is most deservedly yours."

"But–"

"But me no buts! Come closer so I can pin this where it rightfully belongs."

Nick looked down at the medal gleaming on his chest. Emotion threatened to overtake him. He knew it was time to say good-bye to this great man who had befriended him.

"If you don't mind," Lafayette said, "I'd be more than interested to watch your departure with the orb."

"Not at all," Nick said, dismounting and giving Chief a farewell hug. Pulling the gleaming machine from his pouch and twisting the two halves apart, he inserted the coordinates for the Greybeard Inn, Greybeard Island, on the afternoon of the day he'd left his home. He'd be home for supper, he thought, with Katie and his dear mother and, he hoped, perhaps his father.

"Sir," Nick said, about to rejoin the two halves, "it occurred to me that there was a certain sadness in General Washington's eyes when he saw us at the surrender. Is everything all right?"

"Not really, Nicholas. His last child, the boy, Jacky, whom you met, died in his arms last night. He was taken by the fever."

A lump formed in Nick's throat as he thought of General Washington telling his wife Martha the terrible news. She'd "had a bad feeling" about her son going to Yorktown. And she had begged Nick not to go.

"Will you do me a great favor, sir?" Nick asked. "It's most important to me."

"Anything on this earth."

"Would you kindly inform Mrs. Washington that Nicholas McIver sends her his deepest sympathies and condolences for her loss and that . . . and that someday he shall return to Mount Vernon under happier circumstances and spend long summer days with her, walking in her beautiful gardens."

"I will do it as soon as I see her, Nicholas."

"Good-bye, sir."

"Good-bye, Nicholas. I hope we meet again."

"All things are possible," Nick said and, rejoining the two halves of the Tempus Machina, he disappeared in a tinkling of a thousand bells and the flickering countless golden fireflies.

EPILOGUE
HOME AT LAST!

· Greybeard Island, 1940 ·

Nick reluctantly closed the wonderful book he was reading, *Treasure Island*, and laid his head back against his pillow. His mind was so flooded with vivid memories of his own latest adventure he could scarcely keep up with the doings of young Jim Hawkins and the evil pirate Long John Silver.

It had been, naturally enough, a happy homecoming. His parents, thanks to the Baroness de Villiers, were safely home. Neither his sister nor his parents had the slightest idea that he'd ever been away. However, during dinner, he'd felt enormous guilt over not telling his father about the loss of the Sopwith Camel and had told his father of ditching her in the sea. He'd left out the part about the aeroplane being on fire in order to save his poor mother undue concern.

They were all so grateful that he was safe and alive that the loss of the Camel was soon forgotten in the latest news about the Nazis and the plight of the islanders in the face of the ongoing occupation. As long as we stay together as a family, his father had said at dinner, and take good care of each other, we'll surely survive to see better days.

Nick sighed, wondering what new schemes he and Gunner could concoct to make the Germans sorry they'd picked these particular English islands, and reached up to turn off the light above his bed.

A soft tapping at his door was followed by his father's face appearing in the flickering light. "All tucked in?" he asked.

"Yes, father."

"I've good news that should make you sleep better tonight."

"What is it?"

"Your mum and I were just listening to the BBC from London. Prime Minister Churchill has just announced that the Yanks are coming to our aid after all. They are going to give us battleships, tankers, and destroyers in something called the Lend-Lease Program. It's the beginning of the end for Hitler and his Nazis, the Prime Minister says. Isn't it wonderful, Nick? Isn't that great news? The Yanks are coming after all!"

"Wonderful news, Father," Nick said, smiling as Angus McIver softly closed the door.

Nick pulled Lafayette's medal from beneath his pillow and pinned it to his pajama-top pocket.

Then he reached up, switched off his light, rolled over, and, with a most contented smile on his face, fell fast asleep.

He had done his duty.